BRYAN FARRELL

How To Contact The Living

First published by Seven Bells Books 2024

This novel is entirely a work of fiction. The names, characters, and incidents portrayed in it are the work of the author's imagination. Any resemblance to actual persons, living or dead, events, or localities is entirely coincidental.

7BB-001

www.bryanfarrellauthor.com

First edition

ISBN: 978-1-0687222-1-9

This book was professionally typeset on Reedsy.
Find out more at reedsy.com

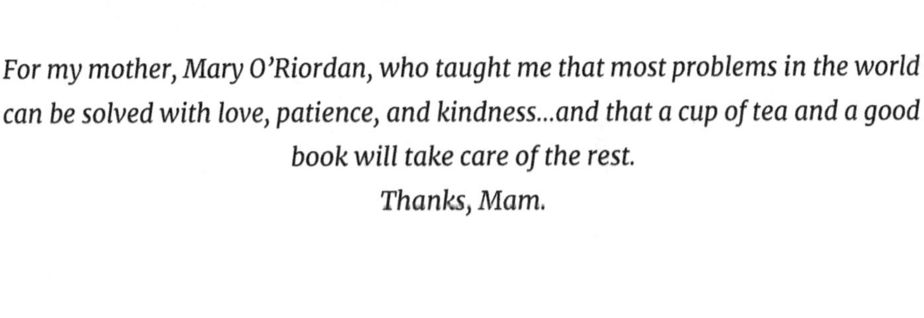

For my mother, Mary O'Riordan, who taught me that most problems in the world can be solved with love, patience, and kindness...and that a cup of tea and a good book will take care of the rest.

Thanks, Mam.

"Death or glory becomes just another story"

The Clash

Prologue

Forrest Avenue was a nothing street slicing like a thin blade through the middle of a nowhere suburb. Not rich, not poor, just nowhere.

Tree-lined and barely wide enough for two cars to squeeze past each other, it was the start of a shortcut imparted to him by an in-the-know traffic cop from his station some months prior which shaved close to ten minutes off his journey home compared to the expressway, even though said shortcut was made up of a number of these narrow streets which forced him to stay well under the speed limit to allow for pets, kids and old folks popping out from behind trees and parked cars, an especially hazardous phenomenon in the evening twilight. On the radio, Elvis belted out "Suspicious Minds" and Owen Hoath thrummed his fingers along on the steering wheel to the last song of his life.

When sudden movement snagged at the corner of his eye, he slowed his car to a crawl. He turned to look but there was only a house like any of the others around it and nothing seemed amiss. He wondered why something that had likely been a pulled curtain or a closing door had caught his eye so forcefully, was about to drive on and put it down to "over-copping", what his sister called his professional paranoia, when it happened again.

A single window was set into the house's redbrick base, next to steps leading to the front door. Something had been placed inside this basement window to block the glass but a corner had been pulled back and light shone out in the dusk. By the time his eyes confirmed that what at first appeared to be a trapped bird was in fact a hand slapping against the glass, it had disappeared.

He brought the car to a complete stop as he stared at the large triangle of exposed light and waited, catching renewed movement just before the glass broke outwards.

The hand reappeared immediately, fingers now jutting out through the newly made hole. Even in the half-light and with a sizeable front lawn between him and the house, he could see that the hand was small and was ripping itself bloody on the jagged glass.

A part of him was still on his way home, looking forward to seeing his wife and to the small pleasures of a weekday evening; dinner, TV and maybe sex if one of them didn't fall asleep first. That part of him was still hoping that the mints and soap he had used liberally before leaving the station would be enough to cover any traces of his illicit lunch time cigarette. That part of him had put down whatever he was seeing to an unsupervised child in their parents' basement, one who would soon be dripping tears and blood onto the kitchen floor while a grown-up grabbed antiseptic ointment and bandages. So, he was almost surprised to find he was already pulling over to the curb, already picking up his radio handset, turning off Elvis who was trying to warn him that they were caught in a trap, can't walk out.

He radioed in and established who and where he was before requesting an additional unit to assist with a possible domestic disturbance. When the dispatcher told him a patrol car was on its way, ETA ten minutes, he responded that he would hold position in his car and keep eyes on the house. Even though he'd identified himself as a detective, he still mentioned that he was in plain clothes and driving an unmarked car because he didn't need some itchy-fingered rookie yelling threats while he tried to calm them down and pull out his badge without getting shot for his troubles.

The hand had disappeared while he was on the radio, the window now a small and unremarkable black rectangle, so someone had either turned off the basement light or replaced the covering. The other windows had the curtains or blinds drawn and he didn't detect light escaping anywhere, not even a crack around the front door. He wanted very badly to look stupid when he and his back-up knocked and bothered an already harried parent, busily bandaging their adventurous child's hand, but something inside him gnawed at that prospect with increasing ferocity.

He sat and waited for his back-up because smart, well trained law enforcement professionals didn't enter unknown situations alone. When a hoarse scream issued from the house and was cut off just as abruptly, he transferred his standard issue revolver from the glove compartment back to his belt holster. As a smart, well trained law enforcement professional, he knew he should stay put or failing that, at least call in that he couldn't wait for back-up, but he was already out of his car and running across the street while telling himself all this.

He crossed the yard and ran up the front steps, hammering with his fist on the door and yelling "*Police*" before backing as far to the side as the little porch allowed, crouching against the wall.

No response.

He beat on the door again, commanding anyone inside to open up.

Despite the adrenalin, he could still feel the potential for embarrassment bubbling, could foresee the hell he'd catch when the innocent homeowners went on TV to complain about crazed wannabe heroes who should go and bother the real criminals and use their taxes for something worthwhile etc. etc. But if he was wrong, he'd take his licks and it would be fixed. If he was right, and he waited for his back-up, maybe it couldn't.

Besides, innocent homeowners would be opening up by now or at least twitching curtains. Even less than innocent ones would usually be yelling belligerently through their door to ask what he wanted.

This house stayed still and sullen.

The handle didn't budge when he tried it. The door was sturdy and the steps offered too limited a run-up for him to get it open with his shoulder or foot. In the movies, the hero cop takes down the door with one kick and then each of the bad guys a bullet a piece without losing stride. In reality, one man without a battering ram or back-up is more likely to give himself a fractured ankle or a dislocated shoulder while giving the person on the other side of the door plenty of time to line up their shot.

Moving around the side, going low and quick past the darkened windows in case someone threw one open and started blasting, he heard a door slam somewhere inside the house.

The back door was older and less substantial than the front, a diamond-shaped glass panel set at head-height which, like the neighbouring window, gave a view of floral curtain and nothing else.

The knob moved freely but the door wouldn't open. He pushed harder and found that the resistance was located at the top alone. He pulled out his gun, took a breath, and drove the handle through the glass.

He reached in with his free hand, avoiding the shards of glass sticking from the frame, and grabbed at the material covering the little opening, pulling out a tangled mess of curtain, black plastic and electrical tape, an inexplicable decorative arrangement that upgraded his alarm bells from ringing to screaming. He threw it aside and reached back in, all too aware of how vulnerable his groping hand was to a knife or a meat skewer or biting teeth. He finally found the bolt at the top of the door and fumbled it open.

Now there was no resistance when he turned the knob. Allowing the door to swing open gently, he stepped aside, using the wall for cover.

When no shots came flying at him from inside, he stood before the doorway, peering into a space so untouched by the last throes of evening twilight that as he held his gun before him, it disappeared into a blackness so absolute, he might have been facing a room full of unseen attackers.

He stepped inside and felt along the wall until he found the light switch which revealed that for now, all he was facing was an empty kitchen.

Small with worn but clean linoleum flooring, cream-coloured cabinets and no place for someone to hide. The large window over the sink was covered with black material thicker than the plastic used to cover the door panel and which was nailed instead of taped to the window frame. The garish floral curtains on show from the outside were just set dressing, no-one would ever look through these windows.

He moved across the kitchen to the single open doorway that must lead to the rest of the house. He strained his eyes, but the kitchen light only went far enough to create an army of shapes and shadows in the adjoining room. He registered a chemical smell and a stronger organic one beneath it but instead of dwelling on the implications he laid a finger on his gun's safety and flicked it off, marvelling at how his eyes and weapon seemed to move in perfect unison, as if attached on a pulley system. Considering how little he'd had occasion to handle his gun, he took this as a comforting sign that somewhere in his lizard brain, his academy training was doing its work.

Stepping into the darkness, he felt for another switch on the wall but this time wasn't so lucky. He swore under his breath and gripped his weapon in both hands, squinting at the murk in front of him; trying to catch any movement but seeing none.

Moving forward cautiously, he willed his eyes to adjust but they were being slow and stubborn and he cursed himself for the flashlight left in his car. He bumped into something and after a moment's panic felt the back of a couch which he used as guide, brushing his hip against it as he crossed the room, finding the front door and a set of switches next to it. He flicked them all and whirled around as the room lit up.

Someone was on the couch, the top of their head just showing above the back he had walked alongside; pale, hairless and gleaming under the light.

He pointed the gun and hesitated, wanting to say loudly and forcefully, *"Police, don't move"* as much to steady himself as to warn them, but this house was deathly still, the head wasn't moving, and he knew it would be worse than yelling in a graveyard. He moved around the couch until he had a full view, the mingled smells of cleaning products and spoiling meat growing stronger.

His team had been briefed on The Cherry Tree Killer, every cop in the city had been. It was well over a year now of missing children, pleading parents, finger-pointing, and no end in sight. The Cherry Tree Killer or just Cherry Tree, so called by some journalistic genius because the first two known victims were from opposite ends of Cherry Tree Road. The second child was really from around the corner on Donnito Street and subsequent victims hailed from all over the city but why let the facts get in the way of tabloid expressionism. He tried to remember the pictures of the missing children flagged as possible victims, but it was impossible to reconcile the figure before him with the few photos he could remember in any detail.

He had seen dead bodies before, part of the job, but never one that filled him with such sorrow or such pity. The hair on the boy's head had been shaved off, the eyebrows too. The eyes were mercifully shut but he was sadly sure it wasn't a figment of his imagination that the eyelashes were also gone. The child was naked, small hands resting in his lap, the nails cut painfully short, showing purple crescents of exposed skin that would have been red and sore had the blood been flowing.

The last three victims had been found similarly shaved and preened, profilers calling it a new development in the killer's progression. Owen thought progression was a dirty word for this sort of thing. He didn't entertain the notion that this had been the child at the basement window for the same reason he didn't reach out and shake a shoulder or put his head against the narrow little chest to listen for a heartbeat. The yellow sheen of the skin and the odour of putrefaction that defied whatever chemicals had been applied to the body meant the boy had been dead a few days.

He knew that by the time police discovered the body of Virginia Holcomb, the first child identified as a victim of Cherry Tree, she had spent a month in the killer's company. Signs of sexual assault but no DNA. Signs of beating but not enough to cause death. Signs the body had been gouged and invaded with foreign objects but not so viciously as to kill. As if he wanted to see how far he could stretch his new toy before it broke. The multiple stab wounds covering the little girl's face, throat and torso had done it. The official line was that the shock had killed Virginia Holcomb before the blood-loss could. He had been with the department long enough to wonder if this hadn't been a soft untruth offered for the family's sake.

He could see no wounds on the child before him, but they'd be there somewhere. Maybe Cherry had poured the same bleach used to clean the body down the little boy's throat first. How long had he been here before he was allowed to close his eyes for the last time? How many torments and mortifications to earn a look of nobility on his features that a hundred years of living wouldn't buy? A look that suggested death had in the end been accepted as the nearest thing to the warm embrace of his mother he could hope for.

If he had a final moment where his mind screamed at him to fall back, this was it.

His instincts told him to get out, his reason told him to listen to his instincts, and his training shouted at him to take his instincts and his reason outside and wait for back-up. His eyes took in the ruined, discarded thing left sitting in front of him, transfixed on the slightly puffy face that should have looked tragic and ridiculous but instead looked dignified, almost regal, and he thought of the hand in the basement window, of the child still alive somewhere in this haunted house, and the moment for last doubts passed.

Now, the gun shook in his hands, but it didn't feel wrong. It felt like an engine, humming and vibrating.

He headed into a hallway where the light from the living room showed doors on either side and stairs at the end climbing up into darkness. Like the kitchen and the living room, the walls were bare, no pictures, no photos of anyone, smiling or otherwise.

The first door opened to a small guest bathroom, just a toilet and sink. He turned on the light before moving on because if he couldn't have daylight, he'd take all the help he could get. If it had still been bright out, he would have ripped the coverings from every window he found, regardless of the danger of showing himself, just to get rid of the mess of shadows and black he was pushing through like thick, threatening undergrowth.

Before he had a chance to try another of the hallway's doors, he heard movement upstairs.

He eyed the unopened doors before him, thought again about the basement and the bird-like hand in the window but when more noise came from overhead, the choice was taken from him.

He kept his back against the wall as he climbed the stairs in case one of the doors he hadn't tried burst open behind him. Upstairs, he was grateful to find a light switch straight away but much less so to find himself presented with even more closed doors. Five terrifying, frustrating possibilities that represented more time than he felt he had. Was the child in the basement still down there, bleeding out on the floor, or were they up here, behind one of these doors with a desperate and cornered Cherry Tree, a monster deciding how best to finish his own horror story?

The first door on his right led to an empty bedroom where he quickly established there was nobody behind the door, under the bed or in the closet.

An unloved guest room; plain bedclothes, utilitarian furnishings.

The bedroom directly opposite was just that. Posters on the wall yelled loudly about kids' movies and TV shows while cartoon characters frolicked on the neatly made bedspread. A small mountain of stuffed animals occupied one corner of the room. Too much colour, too busy. As if an alien had made a shrine to what they thought human children might enjoy but had unknowingly constructed something to give even the most ADHD-afflicted kid a migraine.

A latch and open padlock hung off the door. The window was covered like the others but also had a series of long metal bars crossing it horizontally, set into the wall on either side. Other than the bed there was no furniture, even the door of the built-in closet had been removed.

He looked again at the stuffed toys. Nothing sharp, no hard plastic, nothing that a desperate child could use as a tool or a weapon. He didn't start to cry, didn't scream or fire his weapon into the ceiling, but he began moving much faster, sick of the dreamlike pace at which he seemed to be wading through the house. He moved faster than he knew was wise but the movement felt liberating, an action against the oppressive surroundings.

He marched across the hall and wrenched open the next door and, with a clock ticking in his head, launched in feet before eyes; never good.

The floor shot out from beneath him and he scrambled for balance on wet tiles but over-corrected and fell forwards instead, his chest colliding painfully with the edge of a bathtub while his knees cracked to the floor. One flailing hand bent backwards against the side of the tub while the other arm ended up submerged to the shoulder in the startlingly cold liquid within, the shock causing him to lose his grip on his gun.

He fished for his weapon frantically, causing the contents of the bath to slosh onto his face, into his eyes and mouth, and the harsh burn of chemicals was much worse than the cold of the water they were mixed with.

Crawling away from the tub, coughing and retching, he used the sink to pull himself to his feet. He wiped at his eyes with his jacket collar, but it was soaked and didn't help. He smacked at the light switch before turning back to the tub.

Through bleary, stinging eyes, he saw that it was full of a dark, reddish-brown liquid that was completely opaque. A small leg attached to an even smaller foot and nothing else moved obscenely on its disturbed surface.

He didn't allow himself time to be disgusted before he rushed over and thrust his arm back in. When the sound of breaking glass came from the top of the hall, he didn't waste time looking around, just registered where he needed to go next.

The fumes made his head spin, his throat want to close, but adrenalin did its best to cancel out these effects. He grabbed something that wasn't a gun and pushed it away, doing his best not to dwell on the flesh he had felt disintegrating under his grasp. He finally found what he was looking for and dragged it out of the mess, liquid pouring from its barrel.

As he ran out of the room, he slid involuntarily so he gripped the door frame and swung himself in the direction he needed to go, momentum speeding him toward the room at the top of the hall. Eyes swimming, blood booming in his ears.

He flung himself shoulder-first at the door, not caring that he knew better. When it didn't give, he hit it again with no more luck. When he grabbed the handle, he realised it wasn't locked.

In the second that hung in the space between turning the handle and throwing open the door, he had just enough time to wish goodbye and good luck to the part of him still heading home to Anna, and to hope that the dripping gun in his hand would still fire. He did not have time to think about the choices taken from him or to regret ever having learned about a shortcut through a nowhere street.

That would come later.

Chapter 1

Sitting on the cold cement floor was giving me a sore ass and cramped legs but these were a small price to pay in pursuit of pseudoscience. My mother said once, "Wil, I don't know where this morbid fascination with ghosts and dead things is going to lead you" and my father said way more than once, "Wil, if you don't learn to buck up and apply yourself, I don't like to think about where you'll end up". I looked around at the crumbling, rusting interior of the prison and couldn't help but smile.

I never considered myself a true believer so much as someone who truly wanted to believe. I had no personal experience of the paranormal, no inexplicable night-time childhood incident to set me on my course. Instead, the supernatural crept into my youth through books and films, becoming a fantasy that made more sense to me than knights and dragons or small Japanese creatures that needed to be captured and collected. The fantasy became a preoccupation and the preoccupation became habit, a permanent part of my personality. My investigatory experience was a history of confirming that none of the lights or smells or noises I came across were the least bit otherworldly in nature. So it goes when you're chasing ghosts, most of your time is spent proving that what you want to believe in doesn't exist.

The east wing of the prison stretched out before me, tall and narrow, lit only by the moon peeping in through the skylight windows. Most of these were missing their glass and I wondered whether a window with no glass was really a window anymore and not just a hole. There were rows of cells on both sides of the corridor and above these, another floor of the same. The upper cells were reached by stairs and a metal walkway that ran along the four walls. The vast space between the opposing sides of this walkway was fitted with an iron mesh to deny the dubious luxuries of suicide or a hospital stay to the prisoners housed in the upper cells.

By the time the place was shut down, it was known as Parkhurst Correctional Facility but when it opened (and then locked) its doors over a hundred years earlier, it was simply Winter Prison, named after its commissioning governor, Terrence Winter. The prison eventually took the less ominous name of Parkhurst from the township that grew around it to accommodate the guards, bakers, butchers, and other merchants, along with their families, that made their living off the backs of the inmates. As the city expanded, the township became a suburb with the prison lurking on its outermost edge, hidden behind artificial hills to save the free Parkhurst residents a constant reminder of why they were able to take advantage of such low property prices. These hills were reputed to be filled with city waste and the bodies of careless or recalcitrant convict labourers. Whether this was true or not, plenty of death had been recorded within these walls, some doled out by the inmates, some by the guards, but most by the government. Hangings which eventually gave way to electrocutions as science caught up to society's desire to punish.

Given this history it had, as per Doug's classification, a "promise of high yield". After a year or so with Douglas J. Allan Paranormal Investigations, this was my eleventh investigation but despite Doug's occasional promises of high yield and my own brilliant methods, we had not yet managed to crack the case of life after death or solve the mystery of the paranormal in general.

Regardless, I knew in a few weeks' time we'd be poking around some other building, all of us stuck like our peers, from the enthusiastic amateurs to the televised "professionals", between dreams of personal glory and the nobler fantasy of lifting the curtain and proving that life isn't as boring as ninety years of breathing or as obvious as crumbling walls and rusting iron.

There was also the desperation to recapture childhood thrills, for some the first time they saw a bedtime shadow move out of sync, for most of us a memory of the time our parents sat us in front of a TV in the hopes of a few moments of peace without paying attention to what was on. I'm sure if an honest poll was conducted of the world's leading paranormal experts, more would credit their career choice to movies like *Ghostbusters* and *Poltergeist* that brought the supernatural to the masses than to parapsychologists like John Beloff and Harvey Irwin who brought it to the textbooks.

Something stirred along the corridor.

I watched as one of the cell-doors opened slowly, the torturous sound of squealing metal echoing toward me as a rich, red glow crept into the corridor.

With as little movement as possible I brought up my camera and clicked off two shots while quietly saying, "Flash, flash" for the benefit of the recording equipment. It took a while to get used to vocalising every action and sound for posterity but by now it was a firmly ingrained habit.

Familiar hopeful butterflies in my stomach touched down again as a living, breathing head attached to a disappointingly corporeal body came into sight. The miner's lamp crowning the head was filtered red just like my camera flash, the purpose being to preserve an investigator's night-vision, though it doesn't hurt that it looks cool.

"Time is zero-four-fifty. Have exited Cell Twelve-B, north end of east wing. Closing door." The door closed with another metallic scream. "Approaching Wil Tagg. End recording."

Liam walked toward me, one hand moving to his homemade utility belt, turning off his audio recorder with a soft click. Even in the half-light, I could see his blue overalls were coated in some kind of white dust.

"Zero-four-fifty. Still seated at south end of east wing. Liam Andriano has exited Cell Twelve-B and is approaching. End recording."

He turned off his headlamp, switching to his similarly red-filtered flashlight. I stood, switched mine on too, and saw that his face was covered in the same chalky substance as his overalls. Now that he was up close, the smell told me it was soot.

Liam happily spent most of his time during investigations in air-conditioning shafts, wall cavities and other hidden crevices. I once suggested that his fixation with small spaces was fuelled by a subconscious urge to crawl back inside his mother's womb. He had countered that the same could be said of any man during sex. I swiftly ended the conversation at that point, unable to match his gambit.

"How did you get in there? I've been here since we set up."

He wiped his brow, uncovering a swath of pink skin amidst his powder-coated face. It was of constant amazement to me that he didn't suffer from serious respiratory or skin conditions.

"Started off in an oven, there was a hole and…" he paused to check his watch, "two hours and eleven minutes later I'm in Twelve-B."

He sounded neither mystified nor surprised by this series of events.

"Anything interesting?"

"Architecturally yes, otherwise no," he replied. "Took some temps and EMF's."

Common speak for temperature readings (I had an infra-red thermometer in my backpack) and Electromagnetic Field readings (I favoured a Trifield meter, also in my backpack). There's no proof that temperature changes or disruptions in the EM field are proof of ghostly activity but until someone proves otherwise or invents working proton packs and ghost traps for us to play with, we have to make do.

"You get anything out here?" Liam asked in return.

"Not that I noticed but maybe something will turn up later," I said. "Just about to do question time if you want to join?"

He nodded and I placed my recorder on the ground between us.

"This is Wil and Liam, located at south end of east wing," I began awkwardly. "Time is zero-four-fifty-four. If there is anyone here that would like to talk to us, please feel free to do so."

After a suitable pause to allow the recorder to pick up any EVP's (think electronically captured ghost-talk) I continued.

"Can you see us? Can you hear us?"

I was glad that the low light prevented us from having to look each other in the eye because I always felt stupid conducting question time, like a kid playing celebrity interviewer.

After another pause, Liam chipped in, and I felt less self-conscious.

"What is your name?" He spoke loudly, with no trace of discomfort. "How can we help you?"

"Where are you?" I added after another pause.

"Are you dead? Do you know you're dead?"

We went on like this for fifteen minutes, questions followed by silence rather than answers.

"Do you know that I love you?" I always finished with this one, figured it had to be a button-pusher.

"What happens to our pets when they die? Are you a dog?" Liam's standard sign-off ended with a series of barks and growls.

We lingered for a couple of minutes, letting the recorder run in case anyone wanted to leave a parting message. After this, we took apart the tripod and wireless camera that had been feeding back to Central Control and started making our own way back there.

As we moved through the prison, I did my best not to drop Doug's expensive camera while Liam swung the tripod around like a baton, giving me his critique of a Supernatural rerun he watched lately. We crossed an open courtyard and entered the main building where we stopped talking, wary of fouling up someone else's recording.

Turning a corner in a service corridor at the back of the building, we stopped short, shielding our eyes from the overpowering white glow flooding from an open doorway up ahead. We looked at one another, shrugged, and went into the light.

Chapter 2

Once my eyes adjusted to the glow, they took in a large space that once served as the prison kitchen. Long departed fridges, exhaust hoods and other appliances had left their phantom, grease-brown imprints on the grubby walls.

In the middle of the room, a spotlight and video camera stood side by side, looking down at a set of old-fashioned keys on the floor. Between the light and the camera, a middle-aged woman sat on a folding chair, also looking at the brass keys.

Across the room, a matching spotlight and camera took in this scene and an almost matching woman, her hair a little darker, half-moon glasses perched on her nose, sat on an identical folding chair, observing.

Marian and Eloise Davis were sisters whose sole areas of interest in the field were psychometry and the use of trigger objects. Psychometry refers to the ability to make associations such as memories or feelings from touching a person or object. Trigger objects, such as the set of old prison keys the sisters were using, are items believed to hold a special significance to a place or person, used in the hope that a spirit will concentrate its energy on acting upon said item. They once caught on camera an antique fire-fighter's helmet wobbling slightly without being touched. I had seen the clip, it was pretty good. Better yet, the group they were part of at the time was called IN-SPECTRES. Much better than DAPI which, when spoken (*dappy*), sounded like Swedish baby food.

Marian kept her focus on the keys while Eloise looked away from her sister just long enough to give us a distracted smile. Not the most exciting pair but give them an inanimate object to play with and just watch them light up.

We continued on, eventually passing through a tall archway into the mess hall, a cavernous space in the middle of the prison, lit up with several of Doug's spotlights. It housed Central Control which referred to two separate yet mutually inclusive components. It was the nest of computers, monitors and other tech that co-ordinated and recorded our activity and it was also Douglas J. Allan, who sat amidst the glowing screens and tidily spread cords, collating, compiling, commanding. With his sensible haircut and starched short-sleeve shirts, he looked as if he had been assembled in the same factory as his gear.

One of the laptops by his side displayed thermal imagery from a camera mounted somewhere inside the prison while another acted as a computerised ghost-box, randomly generating sequences of numbers and letters as part of a program that Doug and his son Cal had developed based on the idea that an entity would be able to interact with the program and create words or number sequences out of the chaos. I wasn't sure how the ghosts of illiterate convicts would wrap themselves around this but it definitely looked impressive.

Doug had a tablet in his hand and was flipping through the feeds from various cameras we had set up around the complex. When he looked over his shoulder and saw us standing patiently, awaiting instruction, he made a series of quick movements with his finger and popped the tablet back into its dock, now displaying four different feeds, each taking up a quarter of its screen.

On the bottom left tile, the view was dark-green, night-vision, showing a seated figure and a large square object in an otherwise empty space. My heart gave a little kick.

We waited while he typed some figures into a spreadsheet on the widescreen monitor before him. We didn't expect a "won't be a second" or a "sorry, be right with you" and weren't disappointed. Liam busied himself scraping some black stuff from under his right thumbnail with his left thumbnail but only succeeded in transferring it across. I watched, hypnotised, as he began the process again in reverse while I ran through names that shat all over DAPI. Dark Ops, Night Watch, P.A.R.A Troopers or just P.A.R.A. (Paranormal and Anomalous Research Agency). Liam once came up with I.N.D.A.R.K. but we were never able to come up with the component words to justify the acronym.

"Anything?" Doug asked without bothering to turn around.

We both answered in the negative.

"It's zero-five-fourteen, I want us out before zero-six-hundred. Wil, help Samantha pack up. Liam, collect Stuart."

We about-faced and marched off like good henchmen. The group had done a walkthrough on arrival so we knew where to find the others. If anyone felt the need to move from their area during an investigation, they first needed to report back to Doug. The only exception was Liam, due to his almost constant motion through pipes, crawlspaces and other womb surrogates.

As we mounted the metal staircase that led from the mess hall to the upper floors of the main building, a thought occurred to me.

"I didn't see any oven in that kitchen."

"Huh?"

"The oven you said you went through earlier?"

"It was down in the basement, in the crematorium."

When we reached the top of the stairs, I turned my flashlight on him. He smiled, cream-coloured teeth showing from a death mask apparently made up of the ashen remains of at least a few inmates. I could tell he wasn't joking, just serenely happy, a man living his best life, one who attended paranormal and psychic conventions to converse with likeminded people, went to hiking and camping expos to see if the latest climbing or spelunking gear could aid his endeavours. He did this without shame or self-consciousness, and I envied him.

The only person I had ever spoken to outside of the group about what we did was my brother Jo, short for Johan just as mine is short for Wilhelm, which are the kind of names you end up with when both parents have German heritage but neither has a sense of humour. Even then, it was delivered with some inward cringing and a warning not to tell said parents, who I didn't want to give yet another reason to bemoan the fate of their single, late-twenties, non-college-educated son who drank too much and earned too little. At least they had Jo, the younger, college-educated, engaged to be married, and all-round better child who made in a month what I made in three. He had been living in Bangkok the past few years, working as head of something for a company that wasn't an airline but issued airline tickets or maybe made systems that issued airline tickets. I could never remember and had asked too many times to ask again. He was engaged to a woman he'd met at his company where she held a job as important and indecipherable as his.

We walked together for a bit before Liam stopped and gently knocked at a closed door. He waited a moment before entering.

"Stuart, wake up, it's home time," I heard him say.

I kept going as what first sounded like a gentle buzzing grew louder and louder until it was the roar of a thousand pissed-off bees. I mounted a small set of concrete steps to the room housing this noise, shone my flashlight on the closed iron door, and saw a familiar piece of red tape with the simple identifier "SAM" inscribed in thick marker. To most people, the sound coming from behind that door would be enough to get their fillings vibrating and their feet moving in the opposite direction but as soon as I heard this blank, static sound, I only saw Samantha, her face and other body parts.

Sam had chosen one of the solitary-cells as her base. In the early days of Winter Prison, a stay in one of these tiny rooms could last as little as one day or as long, in one case, as eleven years. In the museum section of the prison there was a glass-encased relic dubbed the "Holy Helper" which looked like a vicious cross between a chastity belt, muzzle and bear trap. It had been fitted to any particularly self-enamoured inmates in these cells to ensure they had no time for diversion from prayer and reflection. I entered the room, pointing my flashlight at myself to show who was there, in a romantic frame of mind despite the setting.

She sat on the floor beside a bulky instrument that looked like the lovechild of a boombox and a small spacecraft. She reached over and pressed a button on its side and silence filled the tiny room. Parts of me I hadn't known were clenched loosened themselves now that Sam's white noise generator was shut off.

"Zero-five-twenty, cell door opened by Wil Tagg in the last thirty seconds. End track."

She clicked off the recorder that hung from a cord around her neck and turned on her own flashlight, thoughtfully pointing it at the wall rather than my face.

She wore no ear protection during her white noise sessions but assured me that once you got used to it, the sound was as soothing as the ocean lapping against the shore. She would spend further hours listening back to her recordings at home to check if a talkative spirit had piggy-backed on the thick, senseless soundwaves. Searching for EVP through hours of audio was a drawn-out process for which I had neither the patience nor fortitude. I took the briefest audio recordings possible and by the end of dissecting those I had usually begun to tab between my audio analysis program, Goodreads and porn.

"Time to saddle up and ride out," I said, and then groaned inwardly.

I was never great with the ladies, but I was hopeless around the ones I really liked. The first time I met Sam, she was wearing skinny jeans which emphasised the sparse but perfectly proportioned curves of her slim body, and her glossy black hair was brushed over one shoulder, leaving the other side of her long, pale neck on display. All this and a *Kolchak – The Night Stalker* t-shirt. I hadn't even been able to say hello or introduce myself properly, had instead cough-laughed a noise that sounded like my name.

After our first meeting, I spent three months and four investigations trying to work up the courage to ask her out. Then she had shown up with an engagement ring on her finger. Now, I was stuck admiring her from afar, sneaking glances both affectionate and yearning, which sucked but at least meant I didn't need to do anything about it.

She rose to her feet in a way that couldn't have been as graceful as it looked to me and then stretched, arching her back and exposing her navel. I did my best to avert my eyes without missing anything.

"Any excitement tonight?"

"Nope," I replied, playing it safe.

"Maybe next time...we *live* for next time," she said playfully.

I smiled because I couldn't think of anything charming or relevant to say and busied myself dismantling one of Doug's camera/tripod combos. When she bent over to grab her gear, I told myself to stop looking, but I was barely listening.

As we left the room, she closed the door behind us and tore off the piece of red tape bearing her name before smacking it lovingly onto the side of her generator.

By the time we arrived at the top of the stairs, Liam and Stuart had just reached the bottom and were stepping into the light emerging from the mess hall. Stuart had his clipboard tucked under one arm, a pillow under the other. He was adamant the pillow was required because the canvas of the folding chairs didn't agree with his bulk, but I had yet to take part in an investigation that didn't end with our resident medium fast asleep, head resting on pillow, snoring gently.

"Liam and I have a theory that Doug keeps Stuart around because he hopes a spirit will possess him while he's sleeping," I whispered, as we took the stairs.

It certainly wasn't because of an overwhelming success rate in contacting the beyond. He occasionally suffered headaches he interpreted as anxious ghosts trying to communicate, other times found himself unable to breathe as a vengeful spirit clamped his chest. It sounded a lot like migraines and asthma to me.

"I think Doug's happy to have anyone around who'll follow his orders," she replied under her breath. "Stuart's van probably doesn't hurt either."

While I composed a perfect response that would serve as an expansion of her statement and an act of complicity between us, we made it downstairs, through the hallway, and back to the mess hall in silence at which point I realised my latest chance to shine so brightly that she broke apart her engagement just to have me had been missed.

Liam, Stuart and the Davis sisters were gathered around Doug who was issuing instructions. I looked over at Liam who flicked his head at Stuart and rolled his eyes with exasperation rather than malice.

In truth, the main reason that Stuart Westing was part of DAPI was because he wanted to be. If you are willing to show up on a semi-regular basis with the required gear then you will find a place in the paranormal community, which is inclusive above all else, even if this inclusiveness has allowed for the cynical shysters and disturbed minds that many consider a general representation of our community.

While Doug, the legally responsible party, made his way around the compound to ensure all doors and windows were locked, the rest of us hustled the gear out to Stuart's van.

Stuart carried out a single bag and then stood, holding the van's back door open, as if without him martyring himself in the cold dawn air, it might swing shut and kill one of us. Soon after we had retrieved the last of the equipment, Doug appeared to confirm that we were done and then retreated into the prison to fetch our remaining member.

Doug's son Cal, who was somewhere between his late teens and early twenties – it was hard to tell with all the black eyeliner – was also part of DAPI but whether by choice or due to his father's insistence, I didn't know because Cal never actually spoke to any of us. Other things he didn't do included smiling, taking photos, recording audio, or helping with the gear. His contribution involved placing himself far away from the rest of us and attempting to commune with the dead in the old-fashioned "I invoke the spirits" style, surrounded by thick black candles and ominous looking books which I hoped didn't contain any spells or incantations that worked because if ever an individual looked like he'd happily put up his hand for Slytherin, it was Cal. I could just see us all writhing on the floor as he cruciated us one by one.

When father and son appeared at the prison doors, Cal favoured us with a dour look before heading to Doug's immaculate SUV with his army surplus duffel full of candles and malice. He climbed into the passenger seat and slammed the door and as Doug locked the jail doors, I was sure I saw his shoulders twitch. I was sure they twitched again as Cannibal Corpse's classic ballad "Meat Hook Sodomy" erupted from his vehicle. Death metal is a bit melodramatic for my tastes, I'm punk through and through, at least in terms of musical taste, not so much politics, ideals or standing for anything, but I could appreciate Cal's dedication to his image.

"Zero-five-fifty-eight. We are out and locked," Doug intoned, shoving the keys he had used to lock the door and the antique set the Davis sisters had used through the mail slot. "Team instructed to meet at usual location, one week from tomorrow, nineteen-hundred hours. All members instructed to have their reports completed and uploaded prior to meeting." This was Doug's way of saying "*Bye guys, it's been such fun. See you at my place next Monday, 7pm, bring your homework!*"

He pocketed his recorder and walked away without another word. Soon his car was leaving the lot, trailing death metal as it passed by the sign that read "Thank you for visiting Parkhurst Correctional Facility Visitor Centre and Museum – Tell your friends that prison *can* be fun!"

No-one saluted ironically at his taillights or voiced any opinions. It takes a certain type of person to unify and direct people, to source leads and convince right-minded individuals and institutions to allow a group of strange strangers into their house, heritage-listed building, disused church, or active cemetery. DAPI was Doug's baby and if you didn't like it, then you could go play spooks by yourself.

After saying our goodbyes to Sam and the sisters, who were carpooling in the sisters' mint-green hatchback, Stuart, Liam and I piled into Stuart's van. Having to white-knuckle through haphazard driving and directionless stories wasn't great but neither of us possessed transport and throwing Stuart an occasional twenty to keep fuel in his tank was cheaper and easier than trying to get an Uber at odd hours in odd places. As we left the prison grounds, he narrowly avoided hitting their carefully crafted sign while once again telling us about the time he heard a disembodied voice tell him to stop eating white bread.

When Stuart dropped me outside my apartment building, I stayed at the curb just long enough to savour the usual squealing brakes and angry honks as he pulled back into traffic without signalling. Satisfied, I hurried inside and pounded up the two flights of stairs to my one-bedroom mansion.

My apartment was small but the rent wasn't bad for a place just outside the city centre and the big plus was the private laundry room which led on to the bathroom. Due to some complex system of vents and fans running throughout the building, my little laundry always smelled of cigarette smoke and fried onions but otherwise I had no complaints. I took a quick shower then dressed for work.

While I was trying to find a clean shirt, I heard yelling coming from somewhere but was in too much of a rush to pay attention. Still buttoning and tucking my shirt, I raced out of my apartment, slamming the door behind me on my way out.

Another shout.

This time it sounded like someone calling my name. Sounded like it was coming from the other side of the door I had just closed.

I checked the time on my phone, swore and went back inside for a quick evaluation but there was no yelling person in my home, and my TV and stereo were both off.

The yelling started again from somewhere else, and I shook my head. Probably coming through the vent in my laundry room. It still sounded like someone calling my name, but it was probably some irritable spouse or roommate yelling something like "*I WILL take the fucking garbage out*".

I cursed their garbage and ran.

Chapter 3

My computer's clock ticked over to one, so I removed my headset and pressed the lunch button on my phone. If I was five minutes late getting back or died choking on a sandwich, it made no difference, in exactly sixty minutes my phone would return to ready mode and if I wasn't there, the little robotic voice would still say "*Incoming Call*". Our phones didn't ring any more, even the illusion of choice had been taken from us, and now the calls just pumped into our ears, leaving us helpless to do anything except say "Thank you for calling Alliance Worldwide Insurance, how may I help you?".

Before working for Alliance as a customer service agent, also known as a phone monkey, I had worked as a bartender, aka drink monkey, and apart from the insurance industry allowing me the luxury of sitting rather than standing, it didn't make much difference if I was handing out pale ales or health cover. Either way, I sold my time and service to a corporation and when I had done this for enough hours in a row, I was allowed to go home before starting over again the next day.

I grew up believing in the Minutemen's D. Boon when he sang about promises that don't mean shit, and about reading the lies between the lines, and I still agreed with Fugazi's strident warnings to pay attention to what you're buying, to know when to say no, so I wasn't unaware of the delicious club sandwich-like layers of moral compromise and modified principles that needed to be swallowed for a punk kid like me to graduate from selling a fatly-taxed, highly-profitable opiate to spending my days instilling fear in people about their money and possessions, but if I didn't wake each morning as proud and purposeful as my teenage self would have liked, I at least went to sleep each night with roof overhead.

Rising from my desk, I inadvertently made eye contact with Mandy who was stuck on a call that sounded like it was going around in circles. She smiled at me and rolled her eyes. I pulled something between a grimace and a grin and quickly looked away as I gathered my stuff.

Mandy's first week at Alliance coincided with a mandatory-attendance office party at which, due to a combination of social discomfort and free booze, I got drunk and then drunker and then either asked her out or propositioned her, I could never remember which. I also couldn't remember her exact response, but I woke up alone the next morning so had to assume the worst. Shortly after this, with her training finished, she was moved to the desk opposite mine. Since then, we spent our days on either side of the same thin partition and I did my utmost to avoid talking to her, or being alone with her, because she was way too nice to me and I couldn't tell if this niceness was due to guilt-fuelled sympathy for the rejection she'd given me, her way of dealing with my awkwardness, or of hiding her own, but I couldn't be party to any of it.

Several times, I had been on the verge of simply apologising to her, telling her I wasn't normally a lecherous creep, but the words wouldn't come out. Plus, if all I had done was ask her out, I didn't want to make things worse by dredging it up again, as if I'd decided to come at it from another angle.

"Hey, apropos of nothing, I'm not a rapist so it is totally safe to go for a drink with me."

So, I kept my distance, kept making accidental eye contact and offering apologetic half-smiles when I did. I'd seriously considered closing my eyes and feeling my way to and from my desk but that was likely to lead to an even worse moment of impropriety. Based on the normal interactions I heard Mandy have with others, she was whip smart and funny. Once again, as I headed for the elevators, I tried not to think of what might have been.

I joined a handful of others waiting in complicit quiet by the elevators. The only two things most of us had in common were that we wanted to get downstairs, and we all worked for the same multinational insurance provider, often referred to in the media and our minds as All Liars, due to current business methods and a past shrouded in suspiciously high profits made in some otherwise distracted European countries during the early nineteen-forties.

As usual, despite this dearth of common interest, somebody cracked under the pressure and broke the silence which had been working perfectly well. Soon, a chain of unnecessary pleasantries began to coil through the group.

"How are you?"

"Good, you?"

"Can't complain...who'd listen! Busy?"

"Oh, you know it! You?"

"Oh yeah!"

As we stepped into the elevator, an older guy with a decent moustache asked me how my day was going without managing to sound the least bit curious. I wanted to say, "*Not great, I had to kill my giraffe this morning, I think he was cheating on me*", but instead, I gave an oddly pitched laugh and said something about Mondays. When we reached the ground, we poured out like escaping prisoners.

I bought a deli sandwich and headed to my usual lunch spot in front of the city library, where perfectly maintained gardens attracted their usual afternoon collection of college kids, office workers and old folks. Peaceful but central enough to escape the fate of the parklands on the outskirts of the city that had been given over to drug dealers, homeless people, unsuspecting tourists, and old folks. You can't keep retirees away from a nice bit of greenery.

I grabbed an unoccupied bench and soon I was chewing automatically on my overpriced sandwich while lost in my second-hand copy of Peter Underwood's *No Common Task – Autobiography of a Ghost Hunter*. Underwood was describing the beginnings of the Ghost Club and I imagined myself in their London chambers, nestled in an overstuffed leather chair by a roaring fire, a huge brandy balloon in one hand and a cigar in the other while Arthur Conan Doyle and I discussed our latest adventures in spiritualism. Between the fire and the brandy, good old C.D. and I were getting nicely toasted, sharing ever more hair-raising tales, while the London fog pressed against the windows to eavesdrop. I was so caught up in my Boy's Own fantasy that I was almost late back to work, where there was sadly neither brandy nor cigars.

The day dragged on and my lack of sleep caught up with me, making every call more of a chore than usual. Not for the first time, I wished I had the skills to escape this infinite phone loop, to produce something tangible and helpful to the world for which the world in turn would pay me. Where would I and all the other phone monkeys find ourselves when the zombie apocalypse hit? Where would the office chimps and retail baboons end up when law and order was a memory? We'd be herded into cages by the carpenters and the mechanics. Lumberjacks would eat us for energy, doctors would strip us for parts, and farmers would use us as fertiliser.

Cheerful disposition intact, I survived the workday and made it back to my apartment that evening where I gratefully shut the door behind me, locking out the world.

I fired up my laptop and four hours, three beers, one packet of jerky, and half a cup of coffee later I had loaded, tagged, and analysed about half of my photos, videos, and audio clips from the previous night's investigation, finding no sign of anything even faintly supernatural in the mix.

By the time I got to bed, my body was begging for rest but my brain was still rattling. I'd never been interested in counting sheep, so I stared at the insides of my eyelids and listed great TV shows cancelled after one season. *Brimstone...Kolchak...Dead Last...Eerie, Indiana...*did that qualify since they had made a spin-off titled *Eerie, Indiana: The Other Dimension*? Did *The 13 Ghosts of Scooby-Doo* count as a stand-alone show?

Eventually, my mind drifted and these weighty questions gave way to a deep, exhausted sleep.

Chapter 4

A week passed and after work the following Monday, I caught a bus to Doug's neighbourhood, a mostly middle-class suburb on the southern outskirts. Not wanting to be the first arrival, I walked around the neighbourhood for a while, killing time. Doug and I had only been alone in each other's company once, at a café in the city after I submitted a membership query on DAPI's website, and once was enough. I assumed then that his brusque manner was his way of sizing up new members, but I soon learned it was his way of sizing up the world.

By the time I approached the house, it was five minutes before the meeting was due to start and I was pleased to see Sam's car and Stuart's van outside.

When Doug answered the door, neither of us spoke but I at least offered a smile which was not returned. Doug closed the door behind me as I walked down the hall to his study. The only rooms I had seen in his house were this hallway, the study and the guest bathroom and there were no photos in any of them. Not of Doug or Cal or the Mrs Allan that the wedding band on Doug's left hand suggested was, or had been, in the unseen picture. Did he gather up the photos before each meeting, unwilling to have us peeking into his private life? Where was his wife? Liam and I had theorised death by natural causes, death by Cal, or that maybe Monday was gym night.

Some mismatched chairs and a couch were arranged in a semi-circle before the desk in the utilitarian study which contained no fragments of Doug's personality, if indeed he had one, and held nothing on the walls apart from a large TV mounted above the desk.

Stuart was parked in his usual spot on the couch, fiddling with his infrared thermometer. Sam, Marian, and Eloise stood by the window, huddled over Sam's phone. From their various gasps and exclamations – *"You can totally see a wire pulling that book"* – I guessed they were poking holes in the latest paranormal viral sensation, purported footage of "genuine poltergeist activity" in a Tokyo classroom. Liam leaned against the wall by Stuart's couch, playing with his tablet. Cal was nowhere to be seen but he rarely attended these meetings and since his main contributions were sitting and seething, he wasn't missed.

I offered a hello to the room in general and stood next to Liam.

Even after a year of being around these people, some of my teenaged-to-perfection anxiety came back when I walked into our meetings, as if the cool kids would all just stop talking and dead stare me back out the door. I knew I wasn't a teenager anymore, and I knew classifying these people as the cool kids was a wild swing, but I still found comfort in Liam and I having a little subset of our own, in having a sorta-kinda friend, one I could engage in conversation while easing my introverted ass into the group dynamic.

Liam tilted his tablet's screen toward me. He had taken a snap of Stuart on the couch but messed with it so that Stuart had a blood-covered alien bursting out of his chest. I nodded in appreciation before pulling out my phone and covertly capturing a quick video. After a few swipes, I presented Liam with a clip of Stuart fiddling with an over-sized cartoon dildo instead of his thermometer, gaining a return nod of recognition.

"Did you come with Stuart?" I asked.

"No, got the train," Liam replied. "A bag-lady asked me why the spaceship was so full tonight."

"Some guy behind me on the bus coughed the whole way, kept spraying my neck."

"Public transport at its finest," he said, shaking his head. "Can't wait to get my licence. A few more lessons and I can re-take the test."

"Did you get anything the other night?" I asked, eager to change the subject. Driving was a sore point.

"No, you?"

"A bunch of shots of nothing with the usual mix of dust and bugs thrown in."

"Might not be dust or bugs," Stuart chimed in from the couch, not looking up from whatever he was doing to his thermometer. "Could be spirit orbs."

Liam nodded in agreement.

I groaned.

"Spirit orbs" refer to the circular blobs of light that pop up in photos and occasionally video footage. If you've ever taken a flash photograph in a dark room, you've probably seen one. Bugs, dust, or other random particles captured in the light, nothing supernatural about them. Yet, for an embarrassingly high number of paranormal investigators, these "spirit orbs" are potential manifestations. The theory being that ghosts choose to appear as these balls of light because less energy is needed to make a concentrated sphere than a complex human form. Orbs which on closer analysis have a brick-like texture are said to be especially indicative of a metaphysical source. Because everybody knows souls are made of bricks. Certain paranormal researchers have wasted decades squinting at blown up images of mosquitoes and airborne dirt and holding them up to the world as proof of afterlife. The popular opinion, which I shared, was that this was exactly the kind of thing that landed us in the same corner of the public consciousness as people who saw Hitler's face in their scrambled eggs.

"You guys are orbs."

Before they could respond to my witty, well-thought-out rejoinder, Doug entered the room and as he sat behind his desk, the rest of us took our own seats. Sam ended up on the opposite end of the semi-circle which was nice because I could cast longing looks at her every so often and make it seem like I was staring into space.

Liam hit the lights and on the large screen over his desk, Doug guided us through images of the previous week's investigation put together from the individual contributions we had uploaded to the group's cloud.

If I went on the cloud tomorrow, I'd find the meeting minutes, as well as Doug's preliminary case-report. Over the following days, I'd find new files as well as excerpts and modified copies of my own, which meant he'd been working through our uploads. At first, I'd taken this process as a judgement on my abilities to analyse my own footage but when I mentioned it during one of my first van rides, Liam said he found it comforting to have a second pair of eyes look over his stuff, in case he missed something. Stuart had agreed, shrugging and briefly putting the van in the way of oncoming traffic in the process, and I had to admit their logic was sound.

I sat quietly as we flipped through a few dozen orb photos. The rest of the group engaged in animated debate and when Sam joined in, I silently forgave her. Other than orb photos, no-one had captured anything on camera worth checking twice, not even a blurry light-rod to break things up.

Sam played some audio, pointing out various instances where she heard something of note but the rest of us heard only flat, drilling static. I tried to look encouraging yet non-committal.

Stuart presented a report which included the moon phase, solar activity, external temperature, and humidity reading from that night. Being the world's most dormant medium, he had a lot of time to devote to his weatherman duties. Whenever I glanced at Doug during Stuart's lengthy reports, it was hard to tell if he was apathetic or riveted behind his usual expression of mild indigestion.

After Doug and Cal, Stuart was DAPI's longest serving member while I was the newest. Others had drifted in and out. It's just how it is. People spend hundreds on "guaranteed" ghost hunting gear then get fed up sitting in the dark doing nothing. Of those who had moved on from DAPI, some had started their own groups, entered their own niches. One ex-member went on to become an online features editor for *The Anomalist*, another committed suicide by jumping off a rail bridge. I supposed both had continued researching the afterlife in their own way.

The Davis sisters played fifteen minutes of footage. Between both cameras they had run, there would have been twenty plus total hours of footage from that night. Ten of a set of keys, ten of Marian having a staring competition with a set of keys. The fifteen minutes felt long.

Liam and I played some audio and video and gave a summary of our movements during the investigation. I used my most optimistic phrasing but it still sounded an awful lot like "*I sat in the dark and did nothing*".

We left as a group, no hanging around for coffee and small talk. Everyone had homes to go to and our host never seemed eager to keep us in his. Stuart was taking Liam and offered me a lift, but his route didn't take him past my place, and I didn't want to take advantage. I thanked him anyway, feeling a twinge of guilt for my low opinion of him, implacable even in the face of such off-handed kindness.

After exchanging quick goodbyes, I started out for the nearby stop where I faced a fifteen or maybe twenty-five-minute wait or had maybe already missed the bus. The later the hour the less the metro bus schedules meant. It was cold so I zipped up my jacket, burrowed my face into the collar. I stuck my earphones in, letting the fast and loud sound of Minor Threat warm my ears, and shoved my hands deep into my pockets.

The stop, the same one I'd arrived at, was nestled at the edge of Doug's suburb on a leafy residential street which, while still painfully middle class, was less well-maintained and noticeably busier than Doug's since it acted as a thoroughfare from the city to the suburbs further out. Low brick walls afforded no security function whatsoever but did provide a clear barrier between the residents' front yards and the sidewalk which had been cracked and lifted in spots by the trees running the length of the street.

When I made it to the bus shelter, I sat on the metal bench but quickly leapt up again, feeling like I'd just been paddled with an ice block. I stepped out of the shelter toward the curb and with strong gusts of wind cutting through me, fixed my gaze up the street, to the corner where hopefully my bus would appear any minute.

Minutes passed and even nestled in my pockets, my hands became numb with cold, while my vision grew blurred from staring into oncoming headlights. I was contemplating my wait and the cold and the music in my ears when suddenly all these things were pushed aside by a roar from behind me.

With my entire body tensed, I looked over my shoulder at the shelter before immediately snapping my head forward again, hoping I hadn't caught the attention of the person standing there, my quick glance only sketching the vaguest outline of a male in dark clothing.

I stepped forward, edging as close to the curb as I could, and bopped my head to music I wasn't really hearing any more, hoping to signal that I was too enslaved to the rhythm to engage in conversation, roared or otherwise. I stared even harder at the nearby street corner, willing a bus to materialise, placing a thousand curses on the head of every bus driver in the city.

After a couple of minutes, I started to calm down, sure I was being stupid.

Scolding myself for an over-active imagination, reasoning that the roar I'd heard was probably a sneeze, I resolved to start watching some romantic comedies to break up my steady gruesome diet.

When a voice started to creep into my ears between Threat's buzzsaw guitars and machine gun drumbeats, I reassured myself that the guy was probably on his phone.

Then I felt fingertips brushing my spine and all my self-affirmations collapsed as the drooling homicidal maniac behind me grabbed my neck and shoved a handful of razor blades and broken glass into my mouth.

Of course, it had just been the wind blustering against my back, and this vision had come and gone in a flash, but it left me shaken, and certain that I couldn't go any longer without quelling my fears by getting a better look at him.

I would casually turn my head.

I would see a regular citizen talking on his phone, wishing he was home.

If we made eye contact, I would offer a polite smile and a comradely *"that darn bus"* eyeroll. Then, I would relax and pass the time calling myself names and enjoying my hypothermia until that darn bus showed up. I surreptitiously turned off the music but kept bopping along to the silence as I prepared to make my observations.

Unfortunately, without the music, he didn't sound like a bored guy on the phone, complaining to someone on the other end about his late bus. The inarticulate sounds coming from behind me were more like the grunts and groans of a man in pain, or close to orgasm.

What if someone I knew drove by and saw me casually hanging around a bus shelter while another guy masturbated? This scared me more than the mouthful of metal and glass because it seemed more likely.

Furious with myself, my shelter buddy, the bus driver, the bus, public transport, and life in general, I hurried away from the stop and didn't turn back to look until I was a couple of houses away.

An empty bus shelter, fluorescent light hammering down on a scuffed bench and nothing else. No sign of anyone, not even a car approaching.

I spun around in a full circle but couldn't see the guy anywhere. I would have preferred to see him on the bench with his pants down, tugging away and following me with his eyes, because at least I would have known where he was.

I decided it was time to splash out on an Uber but first, I wanted to put some distance between me and the shelter. As I turned to continue my escape, I was struck across both shins and almost knocked over, staying upright only by stumbling back a step and throwing my arms out for balance.

A security light activated at the front of a house, and I felt a warm rush of relief that rather than being tackled by my shelter buddy, in my disorientation I had walked into the decorative wall bordering the house's yard.

When I held a hand up to shield my eyes against the blinding light, my warm relief turned freezing cold as my vision recovered enough to see the figure standing directly before me on the other side of the wall. Almost as if they had been politely waiting for me to see them, they spoke.

"*Funt.*"

I didn't know if this was a grunt or a swearword but either way, I had no response. With the light behind them, they were a featureless silhouette but while I couldn't see their face, I could see their outreached hands snatching at me.

I jumped back, away from the front yard and the grasping hands, and backed into something solid, prompting a high-pitched scream that I recognised as my own.

Whirling around, I found I'd backed into a telephone pole but then, realising how vulnerable I'd left myself to my attacker, I spun back around, both wanting and not wanting to face them, and as I did, headlights cut across my already fuzzy vision.

The bus had passed the empty shelter by the time I started running towards it, waving my arms above my head, but the driver saw me sprinting along the curb and was charitable enough to hit the brakes. The door hissed open, and I leapt aboard, certain I was only inches ahead of my shelter buddy's clawing hands.

In a panicked voice that didn't sound like mine, I told the driver that I was being chased, that there was a psycho out there, and we needed to get out of there fast. I looked behind me, expecting to see my tormentor sprinting for the bus, but there was no-one there. The doors clattered shut and we pulled away.

I looked out at the front yard as we passed, but the sensor light had switched off and I couldn't see anyone amongst the darkened shapes of trees and bushes swaying in the wind.

As the blessed motion of the bus carried me away from whatever the hell had almost happened, I got my breathing under control. When I could talk, I started to explain my situation to the driver.

"You need to pay the fare, sir," he said, cutting me off.

I continued, aware that I probably wasn't conveying to him the gravity of the situation he had saved me from but hadn't even made it past explaining about the masturbatory grunts when he interrupted again.

"The fare," he said, more firmly, and finally I recognised the outright disinterest on his face, his eyes alternating between me and the road ahead. He was a city bus driver working a nightshift, he had seen it all and probably never gave a fuck in the first place. He had already marked me down as drunk, high or crazy and none of those mattered to him, as long as I paid the fare.

I stood dumbly for another moment, gawping at my saviour, then fumbled my pass card from my wallet and validated it on the little machine. As I made my way to an empty seat, the few other passengers onboard were kind enough to pretend they weren't watching me.

More and more miles stretched out between me and Doug's neighbourhood and the driver's lack of concern, the brightly lit normality of the bus, and the image of myself reflected in the wary faces of my fellow commuters all helped to rationalise what had happened. Teenagers pulling a prank. A drunk or a junkie wandering around the 'burbs, probably more scared of me than I was of them. I should have faced whoever it was instead of pretending both he and I weren't there and getting all worked up in the process.

When I made it home, I quickly locked the door behind me and despite my rationalisations, I checked the locks on every window and turned on every light in the place. I stank of sweat and sour, spent adrenalin and when I got in the shower, I didn't draw the curtain, didn't close my eyes even when they stung from shampoo. I'd locked the bathroom door, but my stinging eyes kept returning to the handle, half expecting to see it turn.

I hadn't been mugged or beaten but no matter what names I called myself, no matter what harmless scenarios I put forward, I couldn't help feeling frightened and ashamed and couldn't have said which felt worse.

After my shower, I grabbed a six-pack from the fridge, set it on the coffee table and downed it so quickly that the last beer was almost as cold as the first. I drank some more beers from the fridge after that. I vaguely recall checking the time and knowing I should go to bed because I had work in the morning, but don't know if this was before or after I pulled out the whiskey.

I put on Abbott and Costello's *Hold That Ghost*, a movie that never failed to cheer me up, but only made it as far as the nightclub scene with Ted Lewis singing "Me and My Shadow" before I had to turn it off, wholly unnerved by the funny, flimsy little song.

Still, even after shutting it off, the words played over and over in my head, like a threat.

When it's twelve o clock we climb the stairs, we never knock, because no-one's there.

I put on the loudest, stupidest thing I could find on my TV and between it and the whiskey, did my best to obliterate myself, the night's memories, and the song spinning through my head as I huddled in my apartment in the small hours of the morning.

Me and my shadow, all alone and feeling blue.

Chapter 5

A phone was ringing.

I tried to open my mouth, but my lips were glued together. I tried to open my eyes, but it was too bright, and my lids were too heavy anyway. The thick smell of cigarette-smoke and fried-onion signalled that, not for the first time, I'd passed out on the tiled floor of my laundry room. Based on how nauseous that smell was making me, I knew that when I stopped being drunk, I'd be massively hungover.

My phone was still ringing, and it was the most insistent, most truly terrible thing I ever heard. It penetrated my ears, pierced my brain, and drilled through every tooth cavity I never knew I had. Without the benefit of eyesight or full body sensation, I retrieved the phone from my pocket and pressed it to my head.

"Wil? Hello?"

Once I recognised the voice, I held the phone away from me, clearing my throat and tearing my lips open in the process. Forcing my eyes open, I squinted at the time on the screen.

Dammit.

"Hi Heather, sorry I haven't called."

"Wil, are you coming in today? You were meant to start two hours ago."

"Sorry, I've been a bit sick."

I didn't have to try hard to sound unwell.

"I wish you called me earlier to say so, I was worried."

She did her best to cover her frustration with concern but wasn't fooling anyone. Heather Bryant wasn't a terrible human being, but she was still my boss, which meant to her I was a unit of productivity, a piece of office equipment. If she could have turned me off and on again to get me working, she would have.

Heather spent her days veering between overly enthused or overly stressed or both simultaneously, all while rocking a fashion style best described as substitute-art-teacher-meets-hotel-receptionist, always topped off with a brightly patterned silk neck scarf from a seemingly endless collection, an apparent attempt to inject some pizazz into her personality, her wardrobe, and possibly her life.

"Sorry, Heather, I've got food poisoning, I think. I was going to call but it's been coming out both ends, and I didn't want to call you from the toilet."

There was silence on the other end. It was a dirty trick on my part but she had me backed into a corner. I felt sorry for her, really I did. She was middle management, earning a few grand extra in her salary for the pleasure of being crushed to death between us bottom branch phone monkeys and the marginally higher branch of management above her that wasn't senior enough to be self-assured or self-determined and as such could only offer vague demands and unrealistic expectations instead of guidance or assistance in her efforts to keep us primates in order.

"Well, I'm sorry to hear that," she said eventually. "I just wanted to check up on you."

I said nothing, letting her play on.

"Hopefully you'll be in tomorrow, Wil. Call me in the morning if you won't be. If you can call, if you're not..."

She trailed off awkwardly and I knew we were done.

"Thanks, I should be in, but I'll be sure to let you know if not."

Formalities completed, we hung up on each other and I fell back into my induced coma, my forehead pressed against the cool tiles.

I dreamt I was outside the house I grew up in, in the backyard, and my older cousin Nathan was playing the game he always played when his family visited, once he grew tired of dismantling my toys or telling me all the reasons why I was a baby and why he was so popular in his school and why I should wish I was him instead of a baby. He stood before me, poking my forehead over and over with his index finger. "*Poke*" he said each time, tonelessly, waiting for me to crack and start crying or, even worse when one is facing accusations of babyhood, running to my parents.

Poke.

I stood, arms by my sides, wanting to run away, to yell at him to stop, but although I was a grown man, I was also nine and desperate for the approval of my worldly twelve-year-old cousin. So instead, I stayed put and as I often did during this game, pretended I was a porcupine covered in sharp quills, imagined Nathan's finger was being torn apart each time he touched me, and I didn't even feel him because I was curled up in a prickly little ball in my mind, feeling nothing.

Poke.

This time though, Nathan screamed and pulled his hand away, spikes jutting from it like splinters, and I looked down to see that I had become the porcupine, with thick, bristling armour glowing a warm brown in the sunlight. When I looked up, Nathan's face had changed to that of a man, a stranger, anger showing in his dark eyes, but then he was just Nathan again, nursing his injured hand, and I let out a rebel porcupine yell before chasing him around the garden with glee.

Some time later, my bladder woke me and sent me scrambling to my feet, practically leaping the short distance to the toilet where I urinated long and hard before flushing away a foamy head that any drink monkey would have been proud of pouring.

I brushed my teeth, tongue, lips, and throat then stood in the shower, futilely trying to scrub away the raw alcohol my pores were pumping out. I got dressed then cleaned up my empties in the living room. When I opened the curtains, I saw the sun setting outside and my disorientation segued into regret. I had wasted most of a day off unconscious on the floor.

Thinking over the previous night's events, it all seemed so unremarkable. I had sauntered through a dozen supposedly haunted buildings but let some idiot at a suburban bus stop scare me out of my wits. I laughed at last night's fear as only a perfect combination of time, distance and alcohol will allow while I went from room to room, turning off the lights I had left on and opening windows to air the place out.

I forced soup and a sandwich on my stomach which begrudgingly kept both down. Not long after eating, despite only being awake a short while, I began to nod off in front of the TV.

Drunk sleep only counts for a third of regular sleep, so my mammoth blackout still amounted to just five or so hours of rest. With a *Scrubs* rerun playing on the TV, I struggled to keep my eyes open while formulating a plan to turn off the TV, find my phone, set an alarm for the morning, brush my teeth, and go to bed. It all sounded so exhausting that I only made it as far as turning off the TV before I fell asleep just thinking about everything left to do, the remote still in my hand.

When I opened my eyes, it was full dark outside and with the TV off, the only light in the room was the residual amber glow of the streetlights coming through the window. Normally, my apartment felt like my fortress of solitude but now, it felt unsafe, unknown, as if I had blinked and that had been enough time for tricksy, sneaking hands to move things around so that everything was just slightly out of place and off-kilter. Shadows and shapes that should have been familiar felt odd and alien, crowding toward me at oppressive angles.

It took me a moment to put my finger on the cold feeling creeping up my spine.

It was the feeling of being watched.

No sooner had this occurred to me, than the noise started.

Fuzzy and staticky, it sounded like it was coming from the TV, but the screen was blank, and I was sure I had a hazy memory of shutting it off as I went to sleep.

I was dreaming, I decided. This would explain the inexplicable sound and the sense of disorientation I was experiencing inside my own home. It was a relief, because it also explained away the stubborn chill that had lodged itself in my spine, but it was also annoying because it meant I was asleep but not in bed and not with an alarm set and I needed to wake up and right these wrongs immediately.

The noise swelled, jumbled and crackling, and this annoyed me further.

My thoughts were as jumbled as the sound. I wanted to find the remote and hit the mute button but I also knew the TV was off so that wouldn't do any good. I glanced down and saw the remote still in my hand but when I tried to tighten my grip on it, to press the mute button that I knew would do nothing, I couldn't move my hand.

This began a chain reaction of attempts at movement that confirmed that not only were both hands frozen in place, so was the rest of me. I couldn't turn my head or move my arms, never mind use my legs to stand.

The sound grew even louder, somehow muffled yet resounding at the same time, and finally I realised it was not coming from the TV.

It was coming from right beside me.

Panicked, I tried to look, but my frozen head refused the order, leaving me unable to do anything except stare ahead at my dead television while the buzzing feedback began to break up into all-too-human grunts and groans, very much like those heard near a bus shelter in my not-too-distant past.

As if by listening more carefully I was giving shape to the sounds, like tuning in a radio, they formed into words.

"Wil, I know you can hear me."

The sound that had been a voice all along was coming closer, becoming louder and clearer with every syllable, and I knew if it came any nearer, lips would brush my ear and if that happened, dream or no, it would be too much for me.

"I know...know you...hear."

I told myself this was ridiculous and that in waking reality, in my real apartment, next to my real couch, there was nobody crouching, watching me in my numb helpless state.

Suddenly, my legs jerked, my fingers twitched, and I knew I had control over my body again. As this happened, the voice started to fade again, the words becoming less clear.

"Wil, listen...me...Wil."

Now, if I wanted to move, I could have.

But if I turned my head, I would see something I did not want to see, and if I stood, the hand now creeping into my peripheral vision, about to land on my shoulder, would grab it and push me back down. The scratched silver watch I could just make out on its wrist was the worst part, far too detailed and weighty for this cheesily-lit B-movie of a nightmare.

Safer to pretend I heard nothing, saw nothing. Just a happy porcupine, nothing to see here, move along.

Safer still to pretend *Scrubs* was still playing on the black screen before me.

When hysterical laughter burst out of me, it scared me, too loud and too sudden in the knife-sharp tension of the room but I kept it up, imagining J.D.'s anxious, puppy dog expression on the screen, worming his way out of another escapade that would leave him embarrassed yet enlightened. As long as I kept laughing, I didn't have to acknowledge the hand now clutching my shoulder, its grip tight and testing, or its owner, moving as if about to step between me and the TV, robbing me of my ability to pretend myself away.

"Wil...stop...you...hear...me."

I laughed louder and harder and told myself I didn't feel the grip on my shoulder squeeze like a vice, didn't hear the voice yelling for me to –

"LOOK AT ME!"

I woke on the couch, laughing maniacally and spluttering for breath, and for the first time since I was a kid, whipped my head around to make sure nothing had followed me out of my nightmare.

I was alone in my apartment.

Leaning over, I kissed my coffee table, grateful for its solidity, getting dust on my lips. I stood, staggering a little, but anxious to get up before my body betrayed me again. It was still dark in the apartment but it was silent now and the shapes and silhouettes of my possessions, of the little life I had surrounded myself with, looked like home again.

It was two in the morning by the time I got to bed, angry at myself for being awake, for the tired tomorrow I felt shuffling toward me. It was bad enough getting to sleep this late on a worknight but it was made all the worse by the fact that hungover sleep, while better than drunk sleep, still only counts for half of the regular kind.

Exhausted but unable to settle after a day of bad dreams, or to shake the feeling that I was not alone, I lay in bed, doing my best not to think about my dream or that voice, restraining myself from checking the closet or under the bed for its owner for the umpteenth time.

I began to mentally list Ramones albums in chronological order, then in order of preference, and finally put myself under, hoping only for a dreamless sleep.

Chapter 6

Too few hours later, I woke to the same headache that greeted me the day before and took it onto a full bus where I inserted myself like a Tetris-block into the heaving mass of sad-eyed people as we lurched away. I was tired, the bus was stuffy, and I had a long day of work to get through before I could return home where I planned to give my apartment an overdue clean followed by a proper dinner and an early bedtime.

I clutched a hand strap overhead with one hand while my other was pinned by my side in the crush. My music had somehow put itself on track-repeat but I had no way to reach into my pocket to correct it without molesting my fellow commuters. "Die, Die My Darling" by The Misfits is a stone-cold classic but by the fourth time around it was doing nothing for my headache. I tuned it out as best I could until the horror-punk blended with the bus's labouring engine and it was all background noise. I breathed in sweat, perfume, and aftershave instead of air and tried to avoid falling asleep on my feet.

It took two more "Die, Die My Darlings" for me to register that whatever was digging into my lower back was too persistent for a stray elbow or bag.

I looked back, turning my head as much as I could, given I was unable to move my upper body.

The woman behind me was too short to reach any handhold and too old in an era when age has no cachet. The seats were filled with younger men and women, earphones in and heads down, while someone's grandmother stood, fighting an epic battle against gravity and sharp corners.

I looked away, deciding an occasional bony hand in my back while she steadied herself would be my part-payment of our societal debt.

Throughout my journey, this altruism was sorely tested as the jabs came quicker and harder. At one stage I was hit between the shoulder blades so hard, I couldn't help but jerk away. The hand retreated and I worried I had sent her rolling around on the floor like an abandoned Coke bottle, but when I looked back she was still there, fighting the good fight, and not long after, the barrage resumed.

Three "Die, Dies..." later, on the edge of the city centre, the bus finally emptied enough for me to make some space between me and granny. I reached into my pocket and turned off the music, a blessed relief.

The bus got moving again and just as I started to relax, I was hit so hard across the backs of my knees that I would have gone down if I hadn't been holding the hand strap.

I whipped around to find only empty space behind me. Through the window, I saw the elderly lady on the curb, rooting through her oversized handbag which she had rested on a bench.

Feeling like a fool, I looked away, thinking of how much fun the real culprit must have had, watching me twisting, jerking and casting accusatory glances at the blameless granny. Approaching the next stop, bodies shifted as more people readied to get off and the sound of hushed laughter carried through the din.

I glanced around as casually as possible and for the first time, saw the two uniformed schoolgirls occupying a seat just across the aisle, a little behind me. They were in hysterics, cupped hands covering their mouths. I glared at them but they were too preoccupied, or too smart, to acknowledge me.

I turned away, tensing against their next attack. Under better circumstances, I would have been quite content to be felt up by a pair of Catholic schoolgirls, but these were not better circumstances. I thought of the other people on the bus watching me getting beaten up by two teenage girls, wondering why I was just taking it.

He must like it!

My armpits dampened with nervous sweat.

I saw myself whirl around just before their next jab made contact.

"Don't do that again, girls, it would be a mistake," I'd say, all adult authority.

"*We didn't do anything,*" they'd reply, all teenage outrage, rolling their eyes at one another.

My only recourse would then be to make my way to the driver and explain that I was being picked on by the two schoolgirls back there but rather than allowing this tragic sequence of events to occur, I got off two stops early.

The city air was full of exhaust fumes and anonymous undercurrents, but it was sweet after the stifling bus which I walked away from with head held high, surreptitiously sticking out my elbows to dry the pits of my shirt. It was only Wednesday, and I already wanted to beat this week to death.

By the time I jabbed the lunch button on my phone, my frustrations had channelled into a broad and unfocused anger at my customers, computer systems and coworkers.

I sat on a bench outside the library and ate my lunch quickly, keeping a wary eye on my surroundings, not daring to put my earphones in for fear of being ambushed by whatever fresh bit of madness the world had in store for me.

Scattered about the gardens, friends and couples ate together, laughing and chatting. I envied them their support and company and thought that maybe I should call my brother. I couldn't think when I had last spoken to Jo. He'd listen. He'd say something funny and make me forget about my problems. But this stirred a memory of promising to call him months ago and it all became too murky and guilt-ridden, and since I was in bad enough shape as it was, I'd just have to get over this stupidity by myself.

Inhaling my food without incident, I went inside the library to use the toilets, after which I planned on stopping at a nearby record store on my way back to work. For some time, I had been ogling a used (Very Good Plus condition) vinyl of Dead Boys' first LP but had dismissed it as overly expensive. Now, some indiscriminate expenditure might give me the strength I needed to see the rest of this day through.

I made my way across the library's large foyer, savouring the eternal sameness of the air-conditioned interior and the faint but ever-present smell of books both old and new. I turned a corner, walked down the corridor to the men's room, and pushed open the door with my elbow. The rusted mechanism atop the door had been getting increasingly overenthusiastic for some time now and after forcing my way in against it, I quickly stepped out of the way as it slammed the door shut with a bang that reverberated against the tiled walls.

The bathroom was empty, even the stalls, and it was a relief to be alone. I unzipped in front of a urinal and let out an involuntary sigh as the gentle sound of piss hitting porcelain came to my ears. I preferred using the facilities here to the office where co-workers insisted on chatting with me while we held our bare penises in our hands.

Despite the numerous empty urinals, someone stepped up to the one directly beside me, interrupting my day's first moment of serenity.

With my recent luck, I wasn't taking any chances so I tried to speed things up before he could offer to hold mine or ask if I wanted to cross streams. As I urged on my annoyingly full bladder, it occurred to me that I couldn't hear my neighbour's business taking place and that I hadn't heard the door crash shut as he entered.

Curiosity getting the better of me, I allowed myself a sidelong glance.

The man beside me wasn't facing his urinal, he was facing me, and before I had time to concoct an exit-strategy or consider the ramifications, we locked eyes, which was when he shouted my name and punched me in the face.

Chapter 7

I'd taken two real punches in my life before this, not including the brotherly displays of affection Jo and I inflicted on each other over the years.

Ten years old, the first punch. With the sun in the sky and a juice box in my belly, I hurried to the school sports field to kick a ball around with my friend Robert Surname-I-Don't-Remember. Robert was lagging, wasting precious lunch time, so I punched his shoulder, said something motivational like "Hurry up, fagbot!" and jogged ahead. Before I knew what was happening, I was tackled from behind and wrestled to the ground. The fall winded me, leaving me helpless as I was straddled by Robert, furious and crying. His flailing slaps didn't inflict any great damage but just as I recovered enough to push him off, he landed one sweet, stinging fist to my ear. I leapt to my feet, prepared to defend myself, but Robert just lay on the ground, sobbing. I was never vicious, a fatal flaw for a child, so I stood, unsure whether I should comfort or kick him. As I put one hand on his shaking shoulder and massaged my hot, swollen ear with the other, the kids that had magically appeared around us when the smell of blood drifted into the air dispersed in disgust. Once he gathered himself enough to talk, I learned that the boy I thought of as a friend saw himself as my victim, a constant sufferer of my flippant moods and loose fists. He was almost certainly overly sensitive, he was an only child, but at the time I was horrified to think of myself as an abuser. We made up two minutes later and I vowed to never bully again, which was for the best as I really didn't have the physicality for it.

Twenty-three years old, the second punch. Her name had been Tara and I guess it still is. We had been together for eight months, my longest relationship and about four months past when I had decided to end it. Unfortunately, I didn't know how to deliver the parting words because I had always been the remainder, never the divider. I figured if I could get her to break up with me then I wouldn't have to be the bad guy, could instead give a little speech about not holding on to what wasn't meant to be however much it hurt me to let it go. But no matter how many unanswered calls, forgotten dates and deteriorating personal habits I threw her way, she wouldn't budge. Perhaps my apologies were too sincere, it's not like I wanted to be mean to her, she was good to me, much better than I deserved, but she wasn't leaving me with any option. We both knew she would eventually want me to do or be something I couldn't, no point dragging it out until then.

The night came, in a dive bar with too many adult juice boxes inside me, when I accidentally let slip my nefarious plan, in a short lull while the covers band took a smoke break. Once the drunken cat had torn its way out of the bag, I attempted to segue into my "*letting you go for your own good*" speech but, tongue-tied thanks to cheap jugs of house beer and having to shout over the returned band as they murdered Iggy Pop's "The Passenger", it all came out so wrong that even I was offended. She cried, called me an emotional zombie, and socked me one in the eye, but I didn't sense conviction in the tears, the words, or the violence, just irritation that I was first to the button we both knew needed to be pushed. I never saw Tara again but she left me with a black eye that lasted two weeks.

Twenty-eight years old, the third punch. The men's room of the city library. An iron-knuckled blow to the point of my chin that made the two before it feel like caresses. If I was in a movie, I would have been knocked out, but this was something more like real life so instead I yelped and stumbled backwards, clutching my jaw with one hand while holding the other protectively in front of me, all too aware that my exposed member was finishing the job I had asked of it on the floor, my shoes and my trousers.

My attacker's face split into a grin, and he spoke slowly, carefully enunciating each syllable.

"Hel...lo...Wil."

Whatever rusted survival mechanism existed inside me whirred to life as I backed toward the door, still holding one hand in front of me while hurriedly tucking myself back into my pants with the other. He didn't take his eyes from mine and didn't stop smiling. Sweat or tears stung my eyes and the stranger flickered as if he was a dying light bulb. I blinked and he came back into focus.

He started to say something, but I got there first.

"WHAT THE FUCK?"

He tried to speak again but I was too busy escaping to listen.

I turned my back to him, threw myself at the door and wrenched it open. I heard him shout my name once more, followed be the crash of the door closing, but didn't look back until I made it to the end of the corridor and then only for an instant before running across the foyer to the security desk.

"A crazy guy just punched me in the face…in the toilets…he's crazy!"

I didn't add that he knew my name or that he hadn't tried to steal my money or touch me inappropriately, that he had just grinned at me. Those were matters to be considered after he had been safely tasered to the ground and handcuffed.

The security guard seated behind the desk studied me and I had a horrible sense of *déjà vu but t*his time I really had been attacked, my aching jaw pulsed in agreement, and I wasn't going to allow him to dismiss me like the bus driver had. Thankfully, after taking a moment to take me in, he stood as quickly as his immense bulk would allow and pulled a radio from his belt.

"You hurt?"

I shook my head. I wanted to hug him.

He spoke into the walkie and told someone called Jace to come to the foyer *now.* There was a muffled burst of words and static in return and he slotted it back into his belt where there was no gun or taser, but I could see pepper spray, a flashlight large enough to do some damage and a bunch of plastic–cuffs.

He asked me again if I was hurt and I said no and when he asked me to give a description of my assailant, I told him he was tall and white with dark eyes, dark hair and dark clothes. So, I was pretty sketchy on details, but I figured there wouldn't be too many psychopaths for them to choose from lurking in the men's room.

A kid with greased-back hair that emphasised the improbable right-angles his ears formed with his head appeared by my side. Jace did not have pepper spray or cuffs on his belt which I took to mean that the big guy was his superior. His uniform shirt was a couple of sizes too big for his scrawny frame and his face was aglow with excitement.

Having briefed Jace, Big Guy came around the desk and led the charge to the toilet corridor.

"Come with us but stay at the top of the hall, tell us if you see him," he said over his shoulder, hitching up his pants as he walked.

I stopped at the top of the corridor as instructed and watched them disappear into the men's room. I didn't want anyone to get hurt but I hoped my attacker would put up a good enough fight to make my breathless flight seem reasonable because my ego was in worse shape than my jaw after the beating it had taken the last few days. If he got past the guards and came running out, should I clothesline him? It looked easy enough on TV. The door banged shut behind them on its faulty mechanism and I jumped.

Half a minute went by before the door opened again. I bit my lip in anticipation.

An elderly gentleman stepped into the hallway, scowling and tucking his shirt into his pants. Big Guy and Jace followed him out and waved me over. Big Guy held out my backpack questioningly in one hand and I took it from him, surprised that it wasn't on my back. The door slammed shut and we all jumped this time except for the older man who continued adjusting himself. He was wearing black hearing-aids in both ears.

"Sir, is this the man who hit you?" Big Guy asked me, gesturing at the man.

"No, definitely not."

Big Guy stepped across the corridor and knocked hard on the ladies' room door.

"Security, anyone in there?"

When there was no response, he threw open the door and entered. Jace quickly took a back-up position by the door, holding it open, and I had no doubt I was witnessing hours, maybe even days, of training at work. The old guy looked at me, then at Jace in the doorway and beyond him to Big Guy pushing open stall-doors and his scowl intensified.

Big Guy returned, shaking his head, and gave Jace a meaningful look.

I knew what they were thinking. The corridor was a dead-end which meant if anyone left the toilets after me, we would have seen them from the security desk. By now, they had no doubt noticed the wet patches on my pants and the faint smell of piss that went with them, because I certainly had, even in my near hysteria.

"Sir, did you see anything?" Big Guy asked the other man, speaking loudly and slowly.

"Not a thing," the old guy yelled back, probably thinking he was whispering.

Without a word, I pushed open the men's room door and went in by myself, less afraid of facing the weirdo who'd punched me than the indignity I could sense rushing toward me out in the corridor.

The place was empty, all the stalls were open and there were no vents or other escape routes. If I could have flushed myself away, I would have but since that wasn't a possibility, I returned to the guards and the old man who fixed me with the same reproachful look, as if they had choreographed it while I was away. The door banged shut behind me but this time we were all ready for it.

"Sir, would you like to make a complaint or have us contact the police?"

I was immensely grateful that Big Guy was nice enough to play this out.

"No, that's fine. I'm not hurt, just got a shock."

My jaw did in fact hurt like hell but I needed to get out of there before matters got worse. I felt six eyes burning into me. Jace looked particularly aggrieved. He had been ready to make his first library-bust and my lies had taken that from him.

I thanked the guards for their time and in a loud, clear voice apologised to the other man for wasting his.

"I'm not deaf, youngster. But that's fine, forget about it."

He waved me away with a liver-spotted hand.

I hesitated for a moment, on the verge of pleading my case and my sanity, then turned and walked away, leaving them in conference outside the toilets.

"Sorry about that, sir," I heard Jace say, as I turned the corner and pointed myself towards the exit.

"Kid's crazy, you know!"

My curiosity overriding my desire for escape, I knelt and played with my shoelace in case they came around the corner to find the crazy kid eavesdropping.

"Probably high. My son was on the drugs in the seventies and he's still crazy."

"Well, I don't know about that, sir," Big Guy said, sounding as if he wanted only to return to his chair.

"I saw him!"

"The attacker?" Jace asked hopefully.

"No, I saw *him*, the kid. I was in there on the toilet, straining in vain and I heard him shouting. I'm not deaf." A brief pause, as if he was challenging either of the younger men to say differently. "You can see through the gaps between the doors and the frames in there, shitty workmanship, so I lean over to take a look. Curiosity never gets old, they say. Kid's jumping around with his pee-pee out, acting like a maniac. I thought he was going to come over and attack me. Didn't want to say so in front of him in case he did. Up to you but I'd be making sure he's not running around the kiddie section with his pee-pee back out."

Any thoughts of stepping back into the corridor to defend myself fled and I followed them out of the building before the guards could come looking for me and my pee-pee.

I didn't slow until I was back on the sidewalk and out of sight of the library. When I was sure I wasn't being chased, I stopped, stared ahead of me at nothing in particular and suppressed the urge to scream.

After a while, I gave up hoping a passer-by would stop and explain the joke. I looked at my phone and saw I still had five minutes of lunch left. It was inconceivable that less than fifteen minutes had passed since I'd entered the library. It was equally inconceivable that I had to return to work and spend the rest of my day acting like nothing had happened.

Except, for all intents and purposes, nothing had. I had seen the stranger and felt the blow to my head, but I had also seen the empty men's room and heard the old man's version of events.

I got walking again, my head hanging low, watching the ground pass beneath my feet, my shadow mimicking me in a long diagonal. From somewhere in my addled mind "Me and My Shadow" started playing again and I started humming, the song less threatening in the daylight.

I kept moving and humming while I concentrated on my shadow, pretending he was the solid reality going about his day and I was the trick of light. As a trick of light, I did not need to worry about pain, humiliation or fear, I just needed to keep pace with my owner as he went on his way.

Freed of earthly concerns, my thoughts wandered back to the stranger in the toilets and to those dark eyes that had bored into me, intent and serious, untouched by his smile, and further back still to the man at the bus shelter the other night and I told myself I was being silly, that to imagine they were one and the same was a desperate attempt to give shape and purpose to a series of shitty events that had neither.

I watched my shadow and I watched my feet, while I walked and hummed and thought about all the things that couldn't be possible.

I thought of yesterday's dreams, of the scratched silver watch I had seen from the corner of my mind's eye, and dismissed as revisionist fantasy my sudden recollection that an uncannily similar timepiece had been attached to the wrist attached to the fist that had been briefly attached to my face minutes ago.

Me and my shadow, strolling down that...

A hand grabbed my shoulder as a car blew past with its horn blaring, missing me by inches. One of my feet still hovered over the curb in mid-step. I looked at the hand that had stopped me from walking into traffic and it felt like waking from a daydream. My eyes travelled from the hand to the grave eyes of its owner.

"Hi," I said. "I like your watch."

Chapter 8

He applied a little pressure to my shoulder until I took the hint and moved back from the curb. He withdrew his hand slowly, never breaking eye contact.

"Can you hear me?"

He enunciated each word loudly and carefully, and I suppressed a rogue urge to tell him 'I'm not deaf, youngster'. Youngster didn't fit anyway because he had maybe ten years on me.

I nodded.

"Can you see me?"

"Yes."

He touched the back of my hand with his index finger. Neither hot nor cold, none of the usual sensations of human touch. It felt more like being poked with an inanimate object, like a pencil or a carrot.

"Can you feel me?"

"I felt that."

"Do you know who I am?"

My head tried to nod *yes* and shake *no* at the same time, resulting in a spasmodic motion indicative of neither and both. I didn't know his name, but I knew who he was to me. He was a stranger at a bus stop, a half-glimpsed figure in my dreams, a violent offender in a public bathroom.

"I need some of your time," he said, gesturing back in the direction I, or rather we, had just come from.

We walked side by side and even though I kept my eyes front, worried that if I stared at him too hard I might lose the last little piece of my mind I had left, I could feel the ghost watching me. As soon as my thoughts offered up that word – *ghost* – a hostile chorus of dissenting voices shouted it down.

He's not a ghost, he's a dangerous stalker who you're strolling around the city with like a moron...

and...

He's the mental breakdown you're having as a result of too much alcohol and ghostbusting combined with too little sleep and human company...

and...

He's your neurons firing off random bursts because you were hit by that car and are now lying in a puddle of your own shit and blood, waiting for an ambulance.

In the corner of my eye, I had the same sense of him sputtering and growing dim that I had in the library, except now my eyes felt clear and the same bright midday sun was bearing down on both of us.

"You know what I am, don't try to convince yourself you don't."

As if by magic, he was solid again. He came to a stop and so did I.

"Wil, look at me."

I did as I was told and without missing a beat, he ran at a middle-aged suit walking towards us. I tensed for impact, but they went right through one another. Mr Business continued on without so much as a sneeze or a twitch while my guy was bent double and shaking, a pained growl pouring from his agonised O of a mouth. When somebody else passed me and walked through him before I could give a warning, he jerked upright as if electrocuted, face contorted in pain. I would have asked if he was alright but I was busy concentrating on not running away.

He gathered himself in time to sidestep the next passer-by and we moved on without comment, as if we had only stopped for him to tie his shoelace.

We ended up back outside the library, the park quieter now that most of the lunchtime crowd had dispersed. I flicked my eyes around, hoping the guards hadn't set up a watch for me.

He headed for an empty bench and gestured for me to sit. I collapsed onto it while he stood over me. I wondered if this was a dominance tactic.

"Call Heather Bryant, I don't want you to lose your job."

It took me a few moments to understand who Heather Bryant was, why I should call her, and where my phone was. I held the phone to my ear and stared at his midsection, studying the empty holster attached to his belt.

"Heather speaking."

"Hi Heather, it's Wil. This is embarrassing but I've been sick on myself."

"Jesus, Wil...that's not good. Are you ok?"

"A little better now but I'm gonna go to my doctor just in case. Sorry, I would have come back in but I'm a bit of a mess, with the vomit and all."

"Do you want me to pick you up and drive you there? You don't drive, do you?"

If this was a gambit intended to call my bluff rather than an offer born of genuine concern, then she had underestimated me. Under normal circumstances, had I been faking, I would have accepted her offer before dashing off to buy some yoghurt, muesli and grated parmesan to smear on my front.

"No, that's ok, thanks. I'm waiting at my stop already. The stain isn't too bad but I'd prefer no-one I know sees me like this. I'll go home and get cleaned up before going to the doctor."

"Well, alright then. Maybe you came back in too soon," she said. "Think you'll make it tomorrow?"

"For sure I will, just needed a little more rest, I guess. Thanks, Heather and sorry again."

We said our goodbyes before I hung up and put my phone away.

"Can you still see and hear me?"

"Yes."

"We should go back to your place. It will be easier to talk there."

I nodded dumbly.

"There's something we need to do first."

He pointed at two young women on a nearby bench, eating salads from plastic containers and talking between mouthfuls.

"Walk over and ask if they want to see you do something amazing."

"That sounds kinda creepy."

"Trust me," he said, as he walked towards them, cutting off any further discussion.

This was a day for some suspension of disbelief so I followed even though my inability to soberly initiate contact with members of the opposite sex was why, on the rare occasions I woke up next to one of them, it was usually without knowledge of their name or their likes and dislikes, and with the taste of the drinks that had transformed me into a slurred, amnesiac love machine still coating my tongue.

I stood before them, painfully aware of my still-drying pants, and waited while their conversation faltered as they progressed from not noticing me to determinedly ignoring me to falling silent and eyeing me with unveiled suspicion.

"Hi, would you like to see something?"

"No, thanks," the one on the left replied promptly.

She had been carrying most of the conversation before I had interrupted. Apparently, someone called Janna was a lazy bitch and everybody in the office knew she was only getting ahead because she was dating Morrison who was a dick anyway.

"Tell them it will only take a minute and they won't regret it."

"It will only take a minute, you'll be glad." I reached for the jokey, confiding tone of a street magician but sounded like I was coaxing them into an unmarked van with promises of puppies and candy.

They looked at each other uncomfortably and the talkative girl pointed out to the other, but for my benefit, that they needed to get going or they'd be late getting back. They began to gather their purses, phones, and salads but before they could stand, he moved behind me and grabbed me around my midsection.

He lifted me into the air and swung me from side to side like a ragdoll. Again, there was that same lack of sensation and I felt blankness rather than warmth in his embrace, felt it on my skin as if I was shirtless, as if he could touch me but not my clothing.

When he put me down there was a moment of silence before the talkative girl started saying "*Oh my god!*" and her friend began clapping excitedly. No fear and no panic because nothing's shocking anymore. I however was a little shocked, not to mention winded.

"How did you *do* that?"

"Tell them it's a secret but you'll do it one more time if they film it for you on your phone. Has to be yours."

I relayed the message.

"Can she use hers as well?" The spokes-girl pouted while gesturing at her friend who looked at me beseechingly, holding up her massive phone.

"No," he said. "You don't want this getting around, you need a low profile for the foreseeable. Just tell –"

"Sorry," I said, cutting him off. "It's for a YouTube channel we're putting together. Gonna make it hard to go viral if all our clips are already online before we even launch."

I didn't know why he didn't want them having a copy, or why I needed a low profile, but after years in insurance, I could lie with the best of them.

There was some back and forth while they tried to pump me for information. No, the channel didn't have a name yet because it was still in development. Yes, I'd take their details so that our people could contact them for their info and tag and thank them when the video dropped.

Finally, my phone was in the quieter one's hand. They sat forward, determined this time to see the wires or the hidden rig that eluded them before.

"Ready?" he asked.

"Ready?" I asked in turn.

"Ready!" the girls chorused.

He picked me up again and this time, after shaking me from side to side, spun me around a few times. The movement made me nauseous but I smiled throughout as if it was all part of the act. He planted me back on the ground and I held an unsteady hand out for my phone, which was returned with some reluctance.

After I dutifully took their names and numbers, the quiet one, Brigitte, looked at her chunky diamante-encrusted watch and hissed before showing it to her friend, Ginger. They rose, once again gathering their belongings.

Brigitte hurried off but Ginger hung back.

"How do you do it?" She asked, her voice sugary sweet. "Come on, I won't tell."

I shook my head and tried to look sympathetic but firm.

"Ginger, we're *super* late!"

Ginger, a pretty enough girl to be accustomed to men telling her what she wanted to hear, looked *super* annoyed and like she'd have a lot more to say if she had the time to say it. Instead, she made a high, impatient sound with her throat and brushed past me to catch up with Brigitte. They scurried away in skinny jeans and heels not built for speed.

I sat down heavily on their vacated bench.

"Watch the video."

I had to hold my phone in both hands to keep it steady.

I heard the girls' squeals of delight as I leapt into mid-air without moving my legs, watched myself shake about before spinning wildly, an inane grin plastered on my face. When the clip ended, I played it again. There were no arm shaped furrows around my stomach where he held me, no second shadow with my own and no indication there was anyone assisting me as I flew around on the spot like Superman's idiot cousin.

"Keep that clip," he said. "If you start to think you're imagining any of this, watch it."

I nodded.

"What time is it?"

"Two-fifteen," I answered automatically.

"It takes me ninety minutes to walk from the city to your place," he said. "Have a window open for me by three-forty-five. If you don't see me around then, watch that clip, and remind yourself I'm real and that I'm probably already in your apartment with you."

What does that mean? Why don't you just take the bus with me? Why can't you check the time on your watch? How can you touch me when the rest of the world walks through you? Who are you? What are you? How long have you been watching me? Why me?

"Ok," was all I said aloud.

He scrutinised me for a moment and I squinted up at him with the sun in my eyes.

"You're dealing with this well, Wil. I'll explain everything later."

"Ok," I repeated.

He took a few steps in the same direction as the girls before disappearing entirely. He didn't fade or become translucent, he didn't wink out with a flash of light. He was there and then he wasn't.

I felt held together by string that was quickly unravelling and I needed to sit for a minute, catch my breath and ravel.

I watched the video again.

The bench I was sitting on was real, so were the girls that sat on it before me. I was pretty sure that I was real, as was my phone, as were the cars and people passing by now and the ones captured in the background of the clip. Given everything I knew was real, it made little sense to think that he wasn't.

Chapter 9

After making it home with fifteen minutes to spare, I headed straight for the living room window which was tall, narrow and swung to the side on old hinges the paint had long since flaked from. I opened it up as promised.

Since I was expecting him to appear on the street below, I was startled, to put it mildly, when he appeared right in front of me. His feet were level with the sill as he stood on thin air, two stories above the street, waiting for me to move out of his way.

"What happens if I don't invite you in or revoke any invitation you think you have?"

He may have been a life-changing, universe-altering being but I'd decided precautions were needed.

"Lack of an invitation hasn't stopped me before," he said. "It would just be easier on me if I didn't have to pass through you or your window."

"Well, I do not invite you in and I revoke all previous invitations, inferred or otherwise," I said as commandingly as possible before stepping aside to see what would happen.

He stepped over the sill with minimum fuss, ducking his head. Staring at the floor, he descended until his feet were on it, or just above it, I couldn't tell.

"I'm not a vampire," he said, walking past me, while I reached into my pocket for one of the items I'd purchased on my way home.

I passed the Christian Soldier Warehouse every workday but unlike Liam, who bought some of his gear there, I never had reason to set foot inside since, unlike the bulk of the clientele, I believed in neither the coming Rapture nor the need to meet it fully stocked and armed. Below a faded banner on their window which read 'Onward Christian Soldier…to Savings!!' an array of camping gear, military surplus and religious paraphernalia sat behind smeary glass; one-fifth scale Jesus-statuettes amongst samurai swords and water canteens. Today, the place had loomed large in my mind as soon as I started home and I had ducked in and out again quickly enough to catch the next bus passing.

I held the little Virgin Mary-shaped squirt-bottle high, aimed it at his back and squeezed hard.

The jet of holy water went through him and hit the ground with an unceremonious slap. Other than a slight hitch in his shoulders, he didn't react.

"Again, not a vampire."

"Just being careful," I said, putting the bottle down.

"Do you want to finish?"

I hesitated for a moment, politeness getting the best of me, but then reached into my back pocket and pulled out another CSW special, a silver-plated crucifix which I held up for him to see. He signalled his assent, and I held the cross before his face. Seeing no reaction, I pushed it through his forehead. He grimaced but didn't melt into bloody goo or explode into cinders.

Based on his lack of response to the cross or the holy water, I was hoping it was safe to write-off vampire or demon as possibilities, but that all depended on the lore being correct.

Next, I surrounded him with a circle of salt which he stepped out of with no problem, putting paid to the theory of ghosts not being able to pass over salt lines or circles. I told him this test was for purely scientific purposes but in truth, with my jaw still aching from the hit I'd taken in the library, I was keen to find a way of putting an obstacle between us if he ever decided to go for me again.

For good measure, I threw a couple of handfuls of the salt at him but, other than mixing with the holy puddle on my floor, its only effect was to make him shudder as it passed through him.

"You really feel it all, don't you?"

He nodded.

"Is it painful or is it more like...?"

I wasn't sure what it might be more like.

"Electro-nausea is as close as I can get to a description. Even though I can pass through things and things can pass through me, I think a part of me still knows it's not natural and reacts badly."

"Like your brain or your nervous system?"

"My brain and my nervous system are buried with the rest of me. Rotting. But some part of me."

I had no response to that, so I took a seat on the couch, offering him the same, but he shook his head and remained standing.

"Right now, I'm concentrating on your floor. If I try to sit, I'll probably get it on the third try but I'll end up in your downstairs neighbours on my first and with my head sticking out of the cushions on my second."

"But if you can touch me and stand on the floor, shouldn't you be able to sit on a couch or open a window?"

"I'm not standing on the floor," he said. "I'm just staying level with it. Believe me, you're the only thing, living or otherwise, I've been able to physically interact with since I came back, and I think the important word there is *living*."

I wished my notebook and pen were next to me, this was gold.

"Turn on your laptop."

I did as instructed, resting it next to me on the couch while it blinked and whirred to life.

"This isn't some vicarious thing where you watch me pleasure myself while I watch porn?"

What seemed funny in my head sounded plausible and upsetting when spoken aloud.

"No," he said, the shadow of a grin tugging at his stubbly cheeks. "If that was my thing then I've already spent countless ecstatic nights in your company."

I pretended to need all my focus to type my password as the blood rushed to my face. I could see him eyeing me, waiting for a reaction, so I hid my discomfort with indignation while staring determinedly at the screen.

"If you've been here so long, maybe you should have spoken up before today."

"I've been with you for the last four months, Wil. Here, at your office, at your ghost club, in your bedroom while you fall asleep and when you wake up. I've screamed at you, jumped through you, whispered to you, begged you. You're a hard man to get a hold of."

I didn't need to look at him to tell he was angry.

"Four months is a long time to keep trying," I said, hoping to defuse things as I moved the cursor about on the screen.

I supposed any man killed in his prime would have some rage issues if he was left around to feel them. He emanated an air of permanent pissed-offness that would have seemed cool in a movie character but up close felt unnerving. Even when his lips made the shape of a smile, which they didn't seem to take to naturally anyway, those dark eyes burned on.

"Sorry," I added as a general statement.

"I tried thousands of people without so much as a sneeze in return," he said, waving away my apology. "Then I come across your friend Liam outside a café, talking about DAPI and where and when the next investigation/séance thing would be. Figured it was worth a try, so I made sure I was at the old bank in Westbay when you guys were. I never believed in this stuff but..." He held his hands out, palms facing upwards to signify that what he had believed in didn't matter much now. "I tried Liam, the fat guy, your crush, the sisters, tried Doug and Cal and got nothing from anyone. Then I walked up to you and said hello. Remember that?"

"No, I don't," I replied, irked that he knew to refer to Sam as my crush.

"You stopped what you were doing and looked straight at me. Not through me, you looked at me dead on. Wasn't even a second, but it was there. Then you looked away and went back to what you were doing and no matter what I did I couldn't get your attention again. I wasn't able to get through to you until the last couple of weeks and even then, it still seemed like you weren't interested. Like you didn't want to see me, which is pretty fucking strange for a ghost hunter."

I looked up from the computer, feeling he was owed something for my ignorance, however unintentional I knew it to be. "I'm sorry, I really don't remember seeing anything. If I did then..."

"You did."

"Then I don't know, I'm just sorry. If I'd known or registered it or whatever, I wouldn't have ignored you. I wanted, I *do* want, to see a ghost."

"Well, whatever the case, you're the only person who's reacted to me since I've been like this. That's why I couldn't give up on you."

I felt guilty for his failed attempts at communicating with me but also special, which was not a sense of myself I was used to. Out of the thousands of people he had tried to reach, only I was able to reach back across the gap.

"I always left the room."

"Sorry?"

"I always left the room when..."

He jutted his chin in the general direction of my crotch then my laptop.

"Uh, thanks. Anyway, what am I doing on my computer?"

"Proving something to yourself so I don't have to. I need you to search something. Tell me when you're ready, I know how slow your Wi-Fi is."

I clicked on my browser and waited while my aging laptop and crappy internet provider made awkward advances on each other. When it was ready to go, I looked up to ask for his guidance.

He was gone.

Chapter 10

I squeezed my eyes shut, held them like that for a minute before popping them back open.

He was still gone.

I opened my mouth to call his name but called out hello instead because I had no clue what it was. I walked around my apartment, doing my best to mentally summon his voice, his face, those eyes, while still calling out, getting only silence in return.

Standing in the hallway, with two laps of my place completed and unable to summon the effort for another, the truth came at me hard and fast, as if it had been waiting impatiently for me to quiet down and stop pushing it away.

There was no ghost and never had been. A misspent life of loneliness, silly ideas, and bad movies had rotted my mind. Maybe the next visitor, instead of the surly stranger, would be Genghis Khan or Joe Strummer or Marilyn Monroe or all three of them, and I'd never let them leave or wouldn't be able to make them and I'd give myself wholly to the depressive, regressive tendencies that were a part of me as long as there had been a me to remember. My family could visit me in a place where I wouldn't be allowed shoelaces or a belt, patting my hand and dabbing at my chin drool while I told Genghy to calm down, or asked Joe to sing "Death or Glory" for our guests, after I'd introduced them to the blonde bombshell I planned on making my wife. Take *that*, JFK!

I felt tears prick the corners of my eyes and just then it occurred to me to reach into my pocket for my phone so I could check the video, if there was a video. Before I could get hand in pocket, I was tackled and bounced from the wall to the floor.

Winded, shocked, and delighted, I looked up at the ghost standing over me.

"Can you see and hear me?"

I wanted to say yes but I was still trying to catch my breath and not sob with relief at his reappearance. Minutes earlier, I had been trying to figure out a way to prevent any future attacks from him but now, I felt only gratitude for my cracked elbows and deflated lungs because these were better, more temporary hurts, than a busted-up brain.

"Wil, can you see and hear me?"

"Yes, I can."

He reached out a hand but seemed to think better of it, let it fall to his side.

"Sorry about that, but I lost you," he said.

"Totally understandable," I wheezed.

After I got to my feet and dusted myself off, we resumed our positions in the living room, me on the couch with my laptop, him standing by the coffee table.

"Search for Owen Hoath."

"That you?"

He nodded but before I could say "nice to meet you", he had started spelling his name.

I searched and came up with plenty of results, mostly from news archives. A few images appeared at the top of my search and in one I saw a young, determined-looking man in police dress-uniform in front of the kind of swirly grey-blue background favoured by school photographers. The face was younger, less-lined, and shaved to a pink-sheen instead of coated with a five-o-clock shadow but the mouth made the same hard line and the eyes were unchanged, looking back at me from beneath the peak of his smart navy-blue cap, giving the impression they had left me weighed, measured and found wanting before we ever met.

I skimmed the results and quickly realised that even though his name meant nothing to me, I knew who Owen Hoath was, or at least how he died, because it had been news, big news, at the time. I clicked into the top result and as it loaded, he moved to the side of the couch and leaned in to watch my screen. I felt uncomfortable, as though he was seeing me read his diary, but he just flicked his eyes to me and back to the screen.

"Go ahead, read."

Police have released an official statement regarding the tragic events which occurred yesterday evening, Tuesday August 7th, in a private residence in the inner-east suburb of Elmsview, resulting in the deaths of three people, including the man police have now identified as The Cherry Tree Killer.

The deceased are confirmed as Police Detective Owen Hoath, 36, Esther Peridou, 10, and Stephen Hill, 54, in whose Forrest Avenue home the fatalities occurred. An additional body discovered in the house has been identified as James Wray, 9, who is believed to have died some days prior.

The statement verifies initial leaked reports that Stephen Hill has been named as the person behind the series of child abductions and murders committed by The Cherry Tree Killer. Police advise that while their investigation is ongoing, the discovery of additional and as of yet unspecified evidence on the premises has left them confident that "the Cherry Tree Killer's reign of terror has ended" after a fifteen-month period in which the kidnapping and murders of at least six children were attributed to the vicious serial killer. A number of other missing children have been investigated as potential victims, including James Wray, declared missing eight weeks ago and Esther Peridou, abducted from her home less than two weeks ago.

A press conference will be held today at 11.00am during which further details will be released. Law enforcement officials have expressed their sympathies to the families of the deceased children and to the family of Detective Owen Hoath.

I went back to the search results to look for a later article and found one from a true crime site, part of a larger entry on the Cherry Tree killings, written a few years after the news article.

Detective Hoath radioed into Central Comm. at 6.36PM to advise of a possible domestic disturbance at 7 Forrest Avenue and to request back-up

to respond to same. He advised he would continue to monitor the premises and wait for additional officers before approaching the house. However, he subsequently entered the house alone.

The body of James Wray, killed within the preceding seventy-two hours, was in the downstairs living room which Detective Hoath would have passed through before continuing upstairs.

In the master bathroom, the bathtub contained the dismembered and partially decayed remains of another missing child, Alex Sai, placed in a solution of water and chemicals in an apparent attempt to dissolve them, though sources have theorised that Hill was in fact cleaning rather than disposing of them [citation needed]. An unnamed police source referred to the sight of the bath and its contents as the most sickening sight he had seen in a career spanning thirty years.

Marks leading from the bathroom floor to the master bedroom, as well as substances found on Det. Hoath's clothing, indicate the bathroom was the last room he entered before returning to the hall and proceeding to the master bedroom to confront Stephen Hill.

In his book The Cherry Tree Killer – A Monster Felled, psychologist and author Stephen Pewtie writes "the sights Owen Hoath witnessed in that house of horrors would have been enough to terrify and disgust even such an experienced police officer and I have little doubt that had the brave detective survived his encounter, he would have suffered such severe distress that even with the gratitude of a city of children and parents, the resources provided by his department, and the support of his loving family, he would still have struggled to recover mentally and emotionally".

Pewtie goes on to opine that "these scenes of torture and perversion disorientated but also drove Hoath, filling him with a righteous fury, leaving him in no state of mind to wait for back-up even when he must have known he had cornered a dangerous man, one the entire city had been hunting for and haunted by for so long.

He entered the bedroom and engaged in an altercation with Stephen Hill that left Hill dead on the floor with multiple gunshot wounds and Det. Hoath lying next to him, his life's blood escaping from the savage

scalpel-wound Hill inflicted on his throat".

The article stated that the body of Esther Peridou was found in the basement, where she had bled to death from wounds inflicted by the same weapon that killed the man in front of me. Defensive wounds on her hands and arms, coupled with the broken basement window, led to the conclusion that Esther's struggles and efforts at escape had attracted the attention of the off-duty detective and most likely been the cause of Hoath breaking protocol by going in alone ahead of any backup arriving.

The still-locked basement door meant he had likely never made it to her and that around the same time he lay dying next to Cherry Tree, Esther died alone on the basement floor.

There were quotes from other sources, some referring to Owen as a hero, others as something less.

"If Hoath had not possessed a John Wayne complex far too rampant in modern law enforcement, he would still be alive and would have been able, with the support of his fellow officers, to take Hill into custody to assist authorities with investigations into children still listed as missing. How many families will never be able to turn the final page on the story of their grief because Detective Hoath wanted the glory for himself?"

This rhetorical question was courtesy of "well-known crime-journalist and author" Richard Dees, who I had never heard of, in an excerpt from his book *Cherry Red – No Child Safe*.

The outcome didn't change, no matter how many opinions they threw at it.

Two dead men in an upstairs bedroom, three dead children scattered around the house, and the remains of two more discovered in the following days, buried in the backyard in various containers and states of decay. Police discovered mementos from two more children in the house, both presumed dead and classified as victims, though their remains were never found. They still had him pegged for another four missing kids but never found sufficient evidence to make them official. Taking into account the bodies found dumped throughout the city during this "reign of terror", the final documented tally for Stephen Hill aka The Cherry Tree Killer, or just Cherry

Tree, stood at thirteen children and one off-duty police detective.

I put the laptop aside, hoping I had read enough for now. Gruesome shit was all good fun when it was make believe, reading about the real-life version made me feel unclean.

"Horrific stuff, right?"

I nodded.

"You need to hear what really happened."

Chapter 11

"Love you, see you later."

The last words he spoke to his wife. Not poetry, but a better sign off than many get.

He had called this out as he left the house. Anna was in the kitchen, chopping carrots and celery as part of her latest healthy lunch plan, trying to shed unwanted pounds that Owen could never detect but according to her, the bathroom scales could. Some mornings they would have walked out together and shared a quick kiss before heading to their cars. Other days, if he left himself more time, he'd stop in the kitchen to embrace her from behind, kissing her neck and hair while she continued her chopping. He'd tell her she should eat what she liked, that she looked perfect, and she'd tell him he had to say that.

He couldn't remember if she had called back to him that morning, to say "I love you too", couldn't remember if he had waited to hear it before closing the front door and heading to his car. He hoped she heard him and, if she had responded, believed he had heard her.

The last day of his life went by like many before it. He visited with bad guys and good guys, went to the courthouse to give evidence against one of the sloppiest armed robbers he had ever come across, then headed back to his building where he spent a couple of hours doing the kind of paperwork TV cops were always pushing aside for something more exciting.

He took a late lunch at a café with some colleagues after which they all ordered coffees to go. While the others headed back to work, he took a seat at one of the café's outdoor tables. He took out a plastic lighter he wasn't meant to have and a half-empty pack of cigarettes he definitely wasn't meant to have and lit one up. He officially quit years earlier but every so often his hungry lungs took over his body and drove him to the nearest convenience store. Sometimes he'd finish the whole pack, sometimes he'd throw the lighter and unopened pack away before he did something he'd regret, and sometimes he'd make it through half a pack before the guilt got too much for him and then he would dump the remaining smokes, chastising himself in the mild way you do when you know you'll commit the same crime again.

He could remember the taste of his last coffee and his last smoke and with hindsight regretted neither the two and a half sugars in the coffee nor the nicotine, ammonia, hydrogen cyanide and countless other goodies in the cigarette. He was however grateful that the shame had crept up on him that day, prompting him to discard the lighter and smokes on his walk back to work. If not, they would have been in his desk drawer and, knowing no better, someone might have put them in the box of his personal possessions for Anna. She had never asked him to quit but no-one had been prouder of him when he had and that was reason enough to be ashamed.

Also, as a cop and a man, he knew how a woman's mind could lead her, under the worst circumstances, to wonder what other hidden sins had been committed. Having too often seen the messy results of unfeeling honesty, he quietly believed that white lies were the scaffolding of a good marriage, but he was glad there was no stray lighter or cigarettes around to make her think where there were smokes, there must be fire.

He went to the men's room with rationalisations about white lies and scaffolding rolling around in his mind the same way the guilty but beautiful taste of coffee and smoke rolled around in his mouth. Popping in the first of several breath mints he'd go through that afternoon, he washed his hands with soap and hot water until the stink of tar had gone.

He headed home, took the shortcut that would kill him. Listened to Elvis but didn't hear the warning in the King's words. Saw the small hand that would bring him to the house. Entered that house and saw its horrors. Lost his gun in a bathtub full of too many bad things. Heard the breaking glass, found the gun, ran to the room at the top of the hall. Eyes swimming, blood booming.

"Do you ever...?"

I stopped myself, literally biting my tongue to do so. He was on a roll, words pouring out in a steady stream, and while he had no choice but to tell me some of this, the finer details, like his last words to his wife or his sneaky smoking habit, felt like little gestures of trust, or at least openness, and I regretted interrupting this free flow.

"Do I ever...? Go on."

"Do you ever think about Esther, the girl in the basement...that maybe...?"

"That maybe I could have saved her if I had gone down there first? That maybe if I did things differently, I could have got myself and that poor girl out alive?"

I nodded, annoyed that the niggling opinions of "well-known crime-journalist and author" Richard Dees had wormed into my brain and out my mouth.

"The noises were coming from upstairs," he said, offering a weary shrug. "I did what I thought was right."

He looked at me as if inviting reproach, or at least an argument, but I had none to give. He did what he thought was right. If this was wrong and there was a price to pay, he had paid it.

But still, you had to wonder.

After crashing through the bedroom door, Owen didn't take time to gaze into eyes one reporter described as "light placid green, sparkling with innocence" or to appreciate the neatly combed hair and immaculately pressed clothes Stephen Hill's coworkers all agreed were a constant of the man. The blue baggies over his shoes and matching Sani-gloves on his hands were the only features that caught Owen's eye. In those Sani-gloved hands, he held a heavy-based lamp with which he had evidently been trying to smash his way out through the window behind him, one he had nailed shut in the past.

Owen looked upon the dreaded Cherry Tree Killer, nothing more remark-able than a man-shaped absence, and he did not see him. Instead, he saw the thing downstairs that more resembled a broken toy than a young boy.

Instead, he saw a doll-sized leg left to wallow in the grizzly slop that was still burning and stinging him inside and out. Instead, he saw a bird-like hand, forced to impale itself on a spear of glass.

He admitted that while his decision to kill the man was based on emotion rather than reason, he couldn't say it was done with no forethought. He allowed a second to go by in which he entertained a future where Cherry Tree surrendered and was whisked away in a screaming cop car to a long life of media interest, multiple appeals, and perverted, awe-filled fan mail.

He took two quick steps towards Cherry, knowing he couldn't claim self-defence if the shot came from too far, couldn't stop that future from happening if he didn't move before he had a chance to doubt himself. Cherry didn't cringe, didn't make a move towards him, just stood frozen, cradling his lamp.

Owen fired a bullet into his chest and another through his throat. Critical enough to kill without stinking of assassination. Cherry dropped to the floor, blood spurting through the new holes Owen had put him in. No last villainous words, no pleas for forgiveness, just a dented lamp rolling awkwardly away.

He looked at Cherry's spasming body but still didn't really see him. He had never fired his weapon outside of a target range before, had always been staunchly anti-death penalty, but in that moment, he had no room for regret. He was busy thinking, not about what he had done, but what still needed to be done.

He would go to the basement to help the child who had brought him to the house and then he would get a knife from the kitchen and start making this look like self-defence before back-up arrived. A couple of slashes to his forearm, his blood on the floor seeping into Cherry's, the knife in the dead man's hand.

But this was another future that would never happen.

As he stood, seeing and not seeing the dead man at his feet, a fine line of pain raced across his throat. Immediately, the front of his body was engulfed in warmth, and he looked down to see a wave of blood splashing down his shirt.

From a million miles away, he heard the sound of his gun clattering to the floor as he clutched with both hands at the widening slit above his clavicle, trying to stop the preposterously hot flow from escaping through his fingers.

He spun around unthinkingly and fell to the floor, slick with both his and Cherry's blood.

She was on him straight away.

He could only catch glimpses of her face, tight lips and thin cheeks, as her hair fell into his eyes and he thought, of all things, of Anna on top of him in their bed, their bodies straining together as her beautiful chestnut brown hair brushed his face and filled his senses. The vision disappeared as quickly as it had come and the coarse, black hair hanging down over him and the sinewy body pinning and clawing him were an indecent mockery of it.

He held one hand against his wound and tried to fend her off with the other, but she pinned it beneath her knee. She wrenched the hand from his throat and when he tried to use it to push her off, he found it had grown too weak to do anything but flap uselessly against her thigh.

The scalpel she used to open his throat was still in her hand and she jammed it back into the gaping hole, tearing and twisting. He saw his blood soak the blue Sani-gloves she was wearing, just as the man had worn, until they were a wet purple. He couldn't fight or ask her to stop, could only try to breathe as he choked and writhed beneath her.

At some point, when she knew he was finished, she got off him and stood over Cherry's body, her back to Owen.

"You don't deserve to die in the same room as my Stephen, in the same house. You are filth, you are dirt in this home."

He saw himself springing into motion, subduing her before making his way to the basement, to the owner of the helpless little hand. He saw the concerned faces of the paramedics looming over him as he was whisked away in a screaming ambulance to a long life of media interest, multiple surgeries, and perverted, awe-filled fan mail. He saw himself in a hospital bed, Anna chastising him for almost getting himself killed until the nurses gave him a temporary reprieve by telling her that he needed his rest.

But when he tried to begin the chain of actions that would lead to all of this, he found he no longer possessed any limbs or muscles that would do as he asked.

The woman was still talking but his eyes were closing, her voice fading, and he didn't try to get it back. Blood washed over his face, pumped from his nose and his mouth and back down again and every part of him that should have been filled with air was filled with hot, thick liquid until he was drowning in it.

In some distant way, he felt his body convulsing and banging on the floor, begging for breath he couldn't give, but then it was winding down, giving in to the safety of the numbness that was spreading from the hole she had made in him like an infection.

He thought of the children he and Anna would never have, wishing with everything left of him that they hadn't let their plans and careers stop them from trying until earlier that year, until it was too late, so that she could have had someone with her, to give her love and receive hers when he was gone. For her to have some part of him with her always.

At the last, he tried to picture Anna's face because it seemed the most important thing he could possibly do but hard as he tried, he couldn't summon it, which was a failure terrifying in and of itself. He could see her nose and her lips, her cheeks and her eyes but they wouldn't come together, they floated on a dark red surface, all separate and sundered.

He told me again that he didn't regret killing Cherry Tree.

What he did regret was spending his final minutes in that house, a place of filth and squalor no matter how clean it looked. A hungry mouth full of sharp teeth that stank of evil no matter how much bleach was poured down its throat.

Chapter 12

I sat quietly, turning everything over in my head, staring at a point just past his shoulder which kept him in sight but didn't necessitate eye contact.

I spent my childhood fantasising about finding a dusty Necronomicon on the back-shelves of my school library, full of wonderful, terrible knowledge meant only for me. I spent my adulthood researching forgotten gods and mysterious murders, poking about in graveyards and ruins, all in search of something hidden but waiting to be found. Despite this, nobody had ever given me a magic ring to keep secret and safe, no owl had shown up with an invitation to the life I was meant to be living. A life spent thirsting for something rare and precious and now, with the words of the dead poured into me, I just felt nauseous.

Finally, I met his gaze.

"What then?"

Nauseous maybe, but not yet full.

"Not a good enough ending for you?"

I met his stony stare with a smile, refusing to offer the apology he seemed to expect.

"It's not exactly the ending, is it?" I said, gesturing at him to illustrate my point.

At first, when I realised who he was, I had envisaged helping him say goodbye to his wife or unearthing a stash of dirty money earned from years on the take to provide for future of same. She'd give it to charity, absolving his tainted soul in the process. He'd go into the light, leaving me with some crucial life lesson or, at the very least, a lucrative publishing deal. Paranormal

"How To" books were a booming market, the likes of Joshua P. Warren's *How To Hunt Ghosts* had been shifting units for decades, and there was no reason my firsthand experiences couldn't do the same once they were edited, packaged and marketed.

The book deal and subsequent lucrative multimedia opportunities were still possible, but it seemed high-emotion low-risk hijinks were not. There was a killer out there, this mystery woman, who had done things nobody alive knew about, not the cops and not the journalists.

Only me.

So, if he hated having to share his whole story then too bad, better to tell it all now and get it over with, because I knew eventually, whether either of us liked or not, he would have to.

The disgruntled look he gave me made my interior bravado and self-assuredness fall over each other as they ran for cover. However reasonably we were conversing, I was still alone in my apartment with an angry dead man and my lower brain functions easily defaulted to...

HOLY.

SHIT.

GHOST.

RUN.

Then, his face softened to a more passive scowl, and I was ok again, treating my moment of pure terror as a passing chill.

"I was in an ambulance. The EMT was leaning over me, and I figured if I was back enough to know where I was, to notice that the guy's nose hair needed a trim, then I was going to make it. But then, I realised he wasn't working on me, he was working on some old lady that I was laying half in and half out of. Where my body and hers were...overlapping, I was in fucking agony, like I was being burnt alive except – "

"You weren't alive."

"Bingo."

"You must have died in that ambulance, not in the house itself, if that's where you came back, don't you think?" I sounded way too excited and made a mental note to dial it down.

"Maybe," he said, as if this was the least important question in his world. "I put my hands up to my throat. Couldn't feel any wound or stitches which was good, but also couldn't feel my throat or my hands which wasn't so good. Then the EMT reached right through my face to get something from his box of tricks and I freaked out and jerked away and the next thing I know I'm stuck in the middle of the street, literally. I was in it up to my chest, couldn't get myself out while cars were driving through me. I'm screaming for help, but you can guess what that got me."

"Nothing," I said helpfully.

"Nothing," he confirmed. "Just more cars zooming through my head. Hey, you drive?"

I never liked getting broadsided by this question, one I could only respond to by admitting that I was only a pretend adult, one with no idea how to make a vroom-vroom go-go.

I had one lesson with my father when I was seventeen. I wasn't ready but Jo was begging to learn and the more he pushed the more my parents pushed me, never saying aloud what was tacitly understood; the eldest should do these things first. I sat behind the wheel, teeth clenched and legs shaking. Following my father's steady voice, I turned the key, switched on a turn signal (and accidentally the wipers at the same time) and in the ensuing chaos of checking mirrors and mashing pedals, shot down our driveway, across the street and onto our neighbour's yard. My father yanked the handbrake up and we didn't hit the neighbour's house, we didn't even upset their grass, but while my father chuckled with our neighbour, who'd come out to see who was driving around his front door, I slunk back to my bedroom, mortified. Jo had his first lesson later that year and I watched from my window as he successfully manoeuvred down our driveway, up the street and out of sight. I resisted any attempts to get me back on the horse, despite my father's repeated protests that not learning to drive was yet another way I'd found to shoot myself in the foot. According to the same man, I shot myself in the foot so often, it was a wonder I could walk.

"No," I replied, settling for simplicity.

"Doesn't matter," he said. "Might just have been useful."

"Useful for what?"

"We'll come back to that," he said, giving me a pain in the pit of my stomach.

"So, I'm stuck in the street but eventually manage to pull myself out and get to the pavement. Where I start sinking again. That's when I knew I'd go nuts if I didn't get the hang of this shit quickly."

"How did you?"

"Like I said, concentration. Stay aware, keep my surroundings in my mind. Hurts like a bitch any time I go through anything or anything goes through me, which is a good incentive to stay focused. That first night, before I tried to figure out anything else, I learned how to focus on the ground, how to keep level."

"So, theoretically, if you wanted to, you could sink right into the earth, through the core and come out the other side?"

"Maybe, but I'd probably be in too much agonising pain to get a kick out of it."

Registering his lack of interest in the subject, I didn't push on, but my mind disregarded his objection completely and imagined his ghostly descent through the planet, passing through vast caverns full of Morlocks and dinosaurs on his way, science be damned.

"When I was able to stand, I walked, like a baby at first, better after a while. Found myself downtown. The digital banner on the First National Bank building said it was four-thirty in the morning, weather was mild with a chance of showers, and a year had passed since I walked into that house."

I did some quick mental arithmetic.

"So, you've been back over two years now? Jesus, all that time..."

No wonder he was pissed off, it was a miracle he wasn't batshit crazy after a couple of years as the invisible man.

"Yeah, all that time. And then there was you."

As I fired more questions at him, he had the good grace not to pretend he had any choice but to answer. He didn't remember anything between Cherry Tree's house and the ambulance. No white light or angelic choirs, no brimstone and sulphur either. No, he couldn't fly but he could float with a reasonable degree of control. He hadn't seen any other ghosts walking around but pointed out that if they were wandering around minding their own business, they'd look like regular living people to him. He needed to concentrate on me even harder than he did on his surroundings in order to make and sustain contact and, as we had learned, I needed to concentrate on him in return to properly bridge that gap.

He let me take photos of him using different settings on my camera. Of course, they didn't turn out to be of him at all, just shots of my living room. Next, I recorded some audio of him speaking but when I played it back, I heard only my own voice, as if I had just done another pointless round of question time. Still, all of this was ammunition for the various analysis programs on my laptop I was just itching to start playing with. I could see he was becoming impatient and when I pushed our newfound friendship by suggesting we take some readings with my infrared thermometer, he stopped me from scurrying off to retrieve it.

"Wil, it's getting late," he said, pointing at his watch which we had established was very much stopped. "And there's something else I need to tell you. I was going to hold off but it's better you hear it now, save yourself some grief."

I nodded as casually as I could, my stomach sinking as I sat down on the couch again. Could the dead see those about to join them? Was there a black cloud of cancer floating around me or the words *"To be hit by truck"* carved into my forehead by the tip of a scythe?

Typical.

Finally, something interesting was happening to me and I'd be dead before I could even enjoy it.

"It's about Doug and Cal."

"What about them?" I asked, my otherworldly fear bustled aside by a tragically human hunger for gossip.

"They've been running an experiment on you DAPI guys."

"We run lots of experiments, that's kind of the point."

"Not like this. They've been offering the rest of you up. Telling anything that might be out there that you guys are open season, so feel free to possess at will."

I opened my mouth to disagree, to tell him he had misunderstood something, but he spoke first, eyes directed upward like a child reciting a party piece.

"Subject fell asleep in the cafeteria area. I monitored on camera while Cal read entirety of the Herald Daemon, Latin edition, from rear of building, citing the subject's name and location in the appropriate places. This was repeated three times. No noticeable effect on subject, will continue to monitor. This was the fourth attempt at induced possession of Stuart Westing."

He lowered his eyes back to me.

"That's one of Doug's recordings, as best I can remember it anyway," he said. "I guess they pick on Stuart since he's usually asleep, but they've tried it on all of you."

I thought of Cal lurking in the background of our investigations, all of us oblivious to the fact that his half-assed incantations weren't just summoning spirits but actually offering up our bodies and souls to any stranded entities looking for a ride, ignoring his whole black mass shtick because we expected nothing less from the kid with the blackened fingernails, self-harmer soundtrack, and entire Yankee Candle Spooky Season range. Meanwhile, Doug sat in plain sight, recording us all in the manner we were used to.

"Those. Fucking. Dicks."

"Thought you should know what your friends are up to. Obviously, nothing will come of it, but still."

"How do you know nothing will come of it?" I demanded. "You're here. That opens the floor to other possibilities."

"I tried possessing you, nothing happened," he said, waving an annoyingly casual hand at me. "And that was after you'd seen me that first night *and* while they were doing their summoning thing. I tried the rest of the group as well. No go."

"*They* don't know it's not working," I protested, feeling like he could sound at least a little ashamed of himself. "They have no clue who or what might be circling around looking for landing lights."

Maybe there aren't unseen hordes of demonic entities looking to Airbnb our bodies, but maybe there are. I thought Owen's dismissive attitude was a bit rich considering his circumstances but took some solace in the thought that if he hadn't possessed us, hopefully nothing else had either. Still, how could he be sure he hadn't been pushed toward his encounter with Liam by unseen forces? How could he be sure Doug and Cal's misguided antics didn't have the malevolent spirit of Cherry Tree whispering in Stuart's ear while he dozed?

"Hey, I'm not defending them," he said, realising I wasn't rolling around with laughter. "It's a shitty thing to do. Doug seems less enthusiastic than Cal but agrees it's an 'ideal scenario for long-term experimentation on a controlled test group' and that if all they accomplish is turning you guys into a bunch of walking, talking, supernaturally charged trigger objects, it might add a 'promise of high yield' to future investigations. He likes that phrase."

"Yeah, he does," I grumbled.

"The other thing you should know –"

"There cannot be another thing."

" – is that Doug doesn't have a son."

"So, Cal's adopted?"

Tame news compared to finding out they were evil soul pimps.

He shook his head.

"Not adopted, not his son. They're lovers."

This was harder to swallow than the evil soul pimp thing. I could picture Doug and Cal coldly experimenting with my very being, but my imagination refused any attempts to visualise them spooning.

Still, there was the house with no photos, no hint of a woman's touch. Was the wedding band on Doug's finger a souvenir from a Mrs Doug who left, maybe after finding him spooning Cal, or another way to divert suspicion away from the truth?

"Lovers," I repeated to myself. "Cal's just a kid though." I felt a healing revenge taking shape. "I'm going to call the cops and get Doug thrown into prison and Cal sent back to whatever poster-covered, dirty sock-filled bedroom he ran away from."

"Hate to disappoint but Cal's nineteen. He wasn't when they got together, but you won't get them to admit that."

With my immediate means of vengeance taken from me, I sat quietly, thinking over every moment I had spent in their company, trying to dredge up missed signs. I could almost hear the secret laughter they shared at our expense. Was Cal's emo-kid look just a façade? Did he and Doug spend their evenings by the fireside, toasting their experiment's continued success, the flames throwing a warm glow over Cal's scrubbed, ruddy cheeks and the pastel-coloured sweater draped across his shoulders?

"Listen, Wil, you need to get some sleep. You've got work in a few hours. We'll pick this up again."

Pulled from my bitter reverie, I checked the time on my phone. It was nearly three in the morning. As if a spell had been broken, my parched throat, full bladder, and drooping eyes all suddenly made themselves known.

When he moved to the window, I stood on pins and needles numbed legs and opened it for him.

He stared downward and a moment later started to rise from the floor, flicking his eyes between his floating feet and the sill like he was judging a pool shot.

I watched as he went out the window, a tall, well-built man in sensible slacks and slightly wrinkled jacket, stepping through thin air. He turned back, looking down on me, which seemed to be a recurring theme.

"What's next?" I asked. "You need me to find the woman, right? I don't know how I –"

"One step at a time, Wil, it's late," he said, making a halting gesture. "All I need you to do right now is make me a promise."

"A promise?"

"I know I'm the Holy Grail for you guys, but you have to keep me to yourself. We've got work to do and it'll only get complicated if there's too many people in the mix."

"I guess that's OK, for now, but in the future..."

I didn't want to perjure myself by promising an eternal vow of silence that would scupper my future as a New York Times best-selling ghost whisperer, or any subsequent Netflix deals.

"We'll burn that bridge when we come to it," he said. "For now, it's just you and me. Deal?"

"Deal," I said, trying not to let on how cool it felt to part of a "you and me" with Ghost Cop™.

He turned away and slowly descended to street level, raising a hand in parting as he did. I wanted to shout down after him and ask when I would see him next, ask again what exactly he wanted me to do, but I was afraid he might tell me, so I shut the window instead.

After cleaning up the sacred, salty puddle on my floor, I took my excitement and dread to bed with me and we all tried to get some sleep. When they refused to settle down, we all rewatched the clip on my phone since my dread had pointed out the whole thing might still just be a bad bout of food poisoning, more salmonella than shamanism, but the video hadn't changed.

By four, I was back on the couch, staring at my computer screen, the cursor twitching in time with my bleary eyes. I began to type.

"Love you, see you later."

The last words he spoke to his wife.

That didn't seem quite right, not for a start, so I shook out my hands and tried again.

Forrest Avenue was a nothing street slicing like a thin blade through the middle of a nowhere suburb. Not rich, not poor, just nowhere.

Chapter 13

"Joke or no?"

"No joke," I replied, not changing my answer from the first time he asked me.

"The motherfuckers." Liam, who usually kept his emotions tucked within the crawlspaces of his Zen-like interior, was pissed.

"Yep."

"And we used to kid around about them, you know?"

"I know. Cal and his candles and..."

"Slytherin-ing around the place," he said, finishing my sentiment. "And Doug only hanging onto Stuart so he could..."

"Slip a spirit into him while he was sleeping," I said, finishing his.

"But I never actually thought..."

"Me neither, man."

A pause.

"Definitely not a joke?"

"Definitely not a joke."

"The motherfuckers."

"Yep," I agreed once more.

Another pause while Liam contemplated asking me if it was a joke again and I used my plastic chopsticks to push around the cold, shallow remnants of my Phở , as if I might divine meaning from its scraps.

The first half of my workday had blurred by while I autopiloted through call after call, assuring people how much Alliance cared about their health, car, home and contents, while my new mantra cycled around in my sleepy head.

Ghosts are real, Owen Hoath is real.

I strived to keep his face clear in my mind's eye, spurred on by the fear of him trailing behind me, screaming my name while I reverted to blissful ignorance. When I lost the line of his nose or the angle of his jaw, I looked up his photo online. I watched my lift-off video a half dozen times, at my desk, in the toilets, whenever the doubt started creeping in because I knew when it came to Owen, believing was seeing. When I made it to one pm and stood, inevitably locking eyes with Mandy before joining the crowd waiting for the elevator, my silent refrain went around and around.

Ghosts are real, Owen Hoath is real.

After yesterday's revelations and the late night that followed, I was tired and craving some comfort food. My building wasn't far from Chinatown and my stomach led the charge to the Asian food hall that sprawled through the hollowed-out interior of a redbrick behemoth, once upon a time the city's grain storage depot, with open archways on either end leading out to the bustling streets. It wasn't the quietest place to conduct a phone conversation but it was raining heavily outside and my corner table, obscured by steam, rushing bodies, and mostly good-natured shouting between vendors and patrons afforded even more privacy than a secluded bench by the library and besides, I was giving that part of town a wide berth.

As soon as Owen told me about Doug and Cal, I knew I couldn't stay in DAPI. The anger from the night before had been joined by a deepening sadness that caught me by surprise, which was saying something just now. In a city that didn't know me, working for a company that didn't see me, I hadn't realised how much DAPI had done to keep me from feeling completely adrift. I knew I enjoyed it, enjoyed being a part of something, but I never knew how much I'd grieve its loss. This sadness threw more fuel on the resentment I felt at Doug and Cal because on top of everything else, they'd gone and cut away my anchor, the fucking pirates.

While I sat waiting for my food, I considered phoning Doug to yell things like "hypocritical Satanist" but couldn't make myself press the call button. What if, after finding out what I knew, he and Cal kidnapped me and sacrificed me to some ancient Kandarian demon they'd stumbled across on Wikipedia? I started to have worrying thoughts about the DAPI member who supposedly committed suicide but stopped these before they spiralled into panic. Depressed, lonely young men throw themselves off bridges, sad but true, though I couldn't help wondering if they'd already started their experiments by then, if he'd died with a black mark on his soul those sneaking fucks had put there. Fears of abduction, death and eternal damnation aside, I was as good at speaking with Doug as I was at dealing with conflict and a two-for-one didn't appeal.

There was also Stuart, but if I used him as a conduit to spread the word, he was sure to report back to good ol' Central Control first and give him a chance to explain. Doug wasn't stupid and given a head start, could easily come up with a lie disgraceful enough to have me excommunicated from DAPI before I had a chance to warn anyone about what he was up to and make any subsequent tall tales I might spin about him and his "son" sound like vengeful nonsense.

That left Liam, the obvious candidate, but I found it no easier to call him, even though, since we were sorta-kinda friends, there was at least a chance he wouldn't think I was a lunatic or a liar. Partly, my hesitation was down to knowing I couldn't tell him how I knew what I knew. I made Owen a promise and even if I hadn't, I knew from my shallow surface to deep in my selfish depths that I wasn't prepared to share my Ghost Cop.

Once my Phở arrived, I took a few strengthening mouthfuls, steeled my spine, and readied for an uncomfortable conversation full of feelings, explanations, and other irritations. I called Liam who, after hearing my news about Doug and Cal, was by now uncharacteristically, if understandably, irate.

"How did you actually find this out?"

It was my turn to pause.

"Heard some things I wasn't meant to," I said. "Did some snooping, watched them while they were watching us."

"You should have told me, Wil. I could have helped."

"I didn't want to talk shit about them and break up DAPI without making sure I was right." Sometimes when I'm lying, I convince even myself.

"I guess," he said. "You know, this means when I joined, Cal was only like sixteen. I was in that house with them, in abandoned buildings with them." I could almost hear him shiver. "If Cal's parents had sent the cops...you know what normals think about people like us."

"It definitely wouldn't have looked good."

"Imagine trying to convince them we weren't some paedophilic death cult. I mean, he's always looked young but not young-young."

"I know," I assured him. "Hard to tell with all that make-up."

"I bet this is why Cal doesn't come to the meetings at Doug's. He's probably upstairs, drawing pentagrams over our heads in cat's blood."

"I mean, that's not *not* a possibility," I agreed.

"What did Doug say when you called him out on all of this?"

"Uh, well, I haven't told him that I know."

"So, you quit but didn't say why?"

"I haven't spoken to him at all," I said, wishing I didn't sound exactly as defensive as I felt. "But I'm out. I thought you all deserved to know everything so you could decide what you want to do."

"Have you told any of the others yet?"

"I only have a couple of DAPI numbers in my phone and the only email address I have besides yours is Doug's." I dropped my chopsticks onto my tray next to the plastic Chinese spoon I'd used for the broth, pushing it all away from me.

A pigeon swooped down from the exposed steel beams above and landed on a nearby table, lured by the siren song of a half-eaten, congealing pad Thai left by the previous occupant. It took a couple of cautious looks to either side then went to work, its head jackhammering into its inherited lunch. It looked so happy, at one with its world, and as its wings did a little flutter of contentment, I envied it.

"You want me to pass on the others' details to you? I think I have them all," Liam said, leaving me to wonder why he did when I most certainly didn't. Maybe he was closer to the others than I was, than I'd assumed he was.

"Do you have Sam's number?" I asked distractedly. The pigeon was so engrossed in its gorging that it had stepped onto the plate, standing amongst the noodles and shrimp it was devouring.

"Pretty sure I have everyone's," he said, emphasising the indefinite pronoun.

"Maybe it's better if you tell them then, since you have *everyone's* numbers already," I replied, still smarting at the idea that the little subset I had imagined Liam and I formed, a part but apart, might have been fifty percent smaller than I'd realised all along.

"It's your story, Wil, it should come from you."

"Yeah, but they know you better, obviously. They'll trust you."

"You want me to arrange a meeting so we can tell them together?" He sounded confused. I was confused too. The conversation was heading in the wrong direction and I was the one sending it there. I should have sent an email, I was better by email.

A young guy wearing an apron and pushing a cleaning cart approached the table where my pigeon friend was eating. Neither saw the other until the last minute and there was an equal amount of startled flapping on both sides before the bird retreated to a spot on the floor, looking on in outrage as the remainder of its meal was scooped away.

"To be honest, Liam, I just wanted to tell you so you could pass it on. Like I said, the group doesn't know me very well and you've got all their contact info so..."

My "so" died a slow death.

"I like you, Wil, but I guess you're right, I don't know you very well," he said, which stung because I had assumed he would know to exclude himself from the generalisation. "You say this is the truth, not a joke or some weird lie, but you're not willing to help me tell the others."

"I'm quitting because I know what's happening. You're grownups, you can decide for yourselves," I said, an edge to my voice that surprised even me. "I've done my best."

How could he expect me to stand before everyone, being cross-examined, when he didn't even trust me? He probably wanted to get me there so they could tear strips off me for telling fibs about their fearless leader before telling me I couldn't quit because I was fired.

Hungry for distraction, my eyes followed the pigeon as it gave up on its lunch and hopped over to the open archway leading out to the rain spattered street. It looked left then right, as if considering its options and the rain in equal measure.

Maybe I wasn't telling the entire truth and maybe I hadn't really done my best, so what? Let them deal with it and then, if they got back in touch, I'd know they believed me, actually wanted me around. If not, then let them stay with Doug. I'd keep going with Owen and someday they could say they used to be in a group with *the* Wil Tagg, paranormal expert extraordinaire, online sensation (@spiritinfluencer) and host of such hit shows as *Paranormal People* and *The Ghost Guide* (working titles).

"Ok," he said.

"You'll tell the others for me?"

"Yep."

"Good," I said, not knowing what else to say. I'd gone into this call hoping to salvage exactly what Liam was offering, the chance of keeping the group together without Doug and Cal or failing that, me and him joining a new one together, maybe even forming our own. Now, we felt so far from any of those possibilities, they seemed laughable.

"I really hope you're telling me the truth, Wil. Otherwise, people are going to get hurt for no reason."

"I told you, I'm not a liar," I said, getting even angrier despite not being sure how I ended up angry in the first place and despite the fact I was lying a little, for the greater good. After what Owen told me, I could have just dropped out and said nothing to anyone but instead of being appreciative for my help, my warning, he was making me feel like shit.

Having finally made its decision, the pigeon flew directly across the street, only making it halfway before a delivery van smacked into it and carried it away, trapped in its grill. I winced, feeling genuine sorrow for my feathered friend and their poor decision-making, but as it raced away faster than it had ever moved in life, plastered to the front of the speeding van, I couldn't help but think of Owen, just as dead as that pigeon but not letting it slow him down either.

"Well, thanks for telling me all this, I guess," Liam said. "Bye, Wil."

He didn't hang up and I still had a chance to apologise, to say I considered him a friend and regretted never showing this, to ask for his help and explain I wasn't sure if I could handle what was happening or what might happen, that I didn't know where Owen Hoath would take me. That I was scared. and this, above all, was what was making me so angry.

Whether it was anger or intellectual greed or fear of intimacy that stopped me from translating any of this into words, it didn't make a difference because whatever it was, I didn't fight back that hard. They could all have each other. I would have Owen.

I said a brisk goodbye and swiped the call away, dropping the phone on the table as if it might bite. I hoped Liam wouldn't call back to try and make me see sense. I desperately wanted him to call back and make me see sense.

My phone lay silent and unmoving until I picked it up and got ready to head back to work. Standing at the exit, where my pigeon buddy made its last decision, I looked out at the rain and hoped I was making a better one.

Chapter 14

Friday evening removed even the small distraction of work and I was left with nothing to do but wait. I made cups of coffee that went cold, tried to watch TV but eventually just turned it off and sat in silence, medicating myself with huge doses of chocolate and Sour Patch Kids.

After a restless, sugar-shaky sleep, I woke on Saturday and spent the day wandering my apartment, occasionally stopping to sit still and meditate on Owen Hoath in case he was standing right next to me, desperate for my attention. I considered heading out for fresh air and new pacing grounds but was too worried I'd miss his arrival, so I settled for opening all the windows to let in the air and any other interested parties. I added more forgotten coffee cups and candy wrappers to the growing collection.

By that evening, I had devoted myself entirely to constant circuits of my place. As it grew dark outside, one of my laps took me near my bookshelf and I picked up a copy of Joe Nickell's *Investigating the Paranormal*. One of the most intelligent and professional paranormal investigators ever to publish but his book, like all the others, was full of questions and now I had at least some of the answers. This lifted my spirits a little.

I took it with me on my travels around my apartment, idly flipping through the pages. I skipped the section on *"Spirit Painting"* since Owen didn't seem like the artistic type and moved on to *"Communicating with the Dead"* but Joe had nothing to tell me I didn't already know. "A waiting game", he called it. Thanks Joe, no shit.

"Wil!"

I dropped the book but managed not to jump or scream. I made a show of casually picking it up and returning it to its shelf, as if throwing literature on the floor was a weekend pastime of mine.

"You like to keep a boy waiting," I said to Owen, who was standing in my apartment.

"Wanted to give you a few days to process everything and I didn't want you to miss any more work," he said, studying the sea of candy wrappers and half-empty receptacles on my coffee table. "I don't know what your savings are like but if you end up unemployed and homeless it's going to make it harder for you to help me."

"Your concern is touching."

He didn't respond and I couldn't tell if he was gathering his thoughts or making me wait, just like I couldn't tell if his failure to announce his arrival from outside the window rather than in my living room had been thoughtlessness or a deliberate bit of mischief.

His lack of apology for the nervous wait he had abandoned me to did not help my mood, just as him scaring the book out of me hadn't helped my bleak ex-DAPI, post-Liam-break-up state of mind. I tried my best to set my frustration aside but, as he got back to telling me what I needed to know, couldn't help considering the logistics of kicking him in his ghost balls.

"When I came back, I needed to find out what happened after I was gone, if the kid in the basement had survived, if the woman was locked up or dead. But it had been a year, Cherry and I weren't frontpage primetime news and I couldn't turn a page, open a drawer, use a computer or a TV remote. I went to my station but after hanging around there for a week, I didn't hear anything. The guys kept my desk empty, with a little plaque on it which I thought was a classy touch but still, not helpful. I didn't know where else to go so I went to my parents' house, spent my time attempting to get through to them and trying to learn something."

We were in what had become our usual positions, me on the couch, him standing by my coffee table, hands hanging loosely by his sides, kind of awkwardly. I guessed his pockets were just for show now.

"Sometimes my father talked about what happened to me over the phone with my uncle Timmy but only when he was the right kind of drunk and even then, you'd be surprised how much people can talk about something without talking about it. My mother keeps a shoebox of newspaper clippings in her closet that she pulls out sometimes and cries over. It took some time but between my dad shouting down the phone and my mother's ritual, I learned the waving hand belonged to a little girl called Esther Peridou and that she died. That I hadn't saved her. Nobody had."

"You tried though." Sure, he could be annoying, but facts were facts. "You died trying."

"Thanks, I guess."

I offered a "you're welcome" shrug.

"I found out as far as the world was concerned, Cherry Tree acted alone and he and I had killed each other. No-one had caught or killed the woman because no-one was looking for her."

"What about your wife?"

"What?"

"Sorry to backtrack, but you went and saw your parents? You didn't go home to your wife?"

"No," he said, hands twitching by his sides.

"How come?" He caught me staring at his hands, so I cleverly shifted my gaze to his shoes.

"I couldn't...I *can't* face being with her but not being with her."

"There's a chance though, you got through to me."

"Not to anybody else, not then, not now. And even if I could get through to her, what difference would it make?" He stilled his twitching hands by squeezing them into fists. "Eventually I'd have to leave her again only it would be even worse because I'd have to *make* myself leave. Anna thinks I killed the person that killed me, that I'm at peace now. It'd be fucking cruel to let her find out otherwise."

"But –"

"Wil, I'm not here for your emotional support, I'm here to make sure this woman is caught and stopped before she can do any of it again. My wife can't help with that, nobody can, except you."

"Understood. I was just –"

"One day," he said deliberately, bringing me to a halt, "my mother is on the phone to my sister Jen, and I hear my nephew Justin is doing a school project, some video montage thing, on his Uncle Owen, the hero. Her words, not mine. At this point, I'll take what I can get so I head over to their place in case he's got something worth seeing. Since I last saw Justin, who's always been a good kid but a little on the oddball side, he's grown about a foot and sprouted some shit on his chin that you'd call hair if you were feeling charitable."

"I rocked a patchy chin strap for a hot minute when I was sixteen," I said, stroking my jaw nostalgically.

"For me, it was a moustache. Thought it would make me look like Magnum PI or Apollo Creed but this brainy girl I had a thing for told me I looked like Frida Kahlo so I got rid, after I went to the school library to find out who that was." He stroked where his own facial *faux pas* had been but instead of tracing its outline, his thumb and index finger sank into his face. He yanked them out, frowned and sighed deeply from his breathless, long-gone lungs.

"Who's Apollo Creed?"

"Are you being serious?"

I nodded.

"From *Rocky*," he said, caught between outrage and offence.

"Oh gotcha, I think I saw it like once when I was kid, not really my scene."

"It's the greatest movie ever made," he said flatly, his eyes widening at my dubious expression.

"Pretty sure that's *Evil Dead 2*," I said, really enjoying myself now.

He took a moment to gather himself, looking like he was either about to launch into impassioned defence of *Rocky* or simply give me the old one-two, and then continued.

"Anyway...for this project, which he was calling a 'multimedia collage', he chopped up news articles along with photos and videos of Cherry and his victims, of me all the way back to when I was a kid, and random crime scenes, roadkill, abattoirs, logged-out forests, all sorts of stuff."

"What was the theme?"

"Fuck knows. If I'd gone vegan, I'd still be alive? But in one article from some supermarket tabloid, there was a throwaway mention that Stephen Hill was survived by his eighty-two-year-old mother who was rotting in an unnamed old folks' home somewhere in the western suburbs. This was the first I heard about it, and it felt like a thread worth pulling."

I got up to stretch my legs, cramping after their day's pacing, and carefully stepped around Owen.

"That's a shit-ton of persistence," I said, leaning back against the kitchen counter. "I can see why you made a good cop."

"Who said I was good?"

"A lot of the articles I read these last few days had the words "highly decorated" before your name," I said, moving over to the fridge.

"I got a couple of pats on the back over the years but if I'm proof of anything now, it's that medals don't mean much. Besides, I can't take any credit for keeping after this one, what the fuck else could I do?"

Leaning into the fridge, I tore a bottle of beer from its six pack and held it up as an offering before I could stop myself. "Shit, sorry," I said, hurriedly putting it back. "Think I'll just have a water."

"Have a beer, Wil, I was more of a wine guy anyway."

I retrieved my beer, still feeling foolish, and returned to the counter.

"You don't look like a wine guy." I twisted off the cap and threw it over my shoulder. It landed in the sink with a satisfying clang that gave my self-esteem a little boost.

"Anna got me into it. Adds less pounds than beer," he said, casting an appraising grin at my midsection which I was now casually sucking in.

"So, I start doing the rounds of retirement places in that part of town and eventually I find one Veronica Hill in a home over in Morningside. I hang around and listen in and after a few days, I know I've got my woman. She keeps asking the nurses when Stephen is coming, and they always answer 'I'm sure he'll visit tomorrow' like it's in the manual. I guess that's easier than telling her over and over that she's lost her son and her mind."

"Do you think she or the other old folks sensed you at all? There's a theory that age strips away layers, gets you close to the other side."

"Most of them didn't seem close to anything except shitting themselves."

"Do you think if you die old or with Alzheimer's then that's how you are in the afterlife or do you think you get to come back as the best version of yourself or do you think most people stay non-corporeal once they're gone, like don't come back in any real shape, not like you?" I took a swig of beer, my brain foaming with the possibilities. "I wonder if you could be non-corporeal but still have dementia."

"You done?"

"For now," I said, taking a breath.

"I'm there for days except it feels like Groundhog Day, the same routine, same meals, same questions, and I'm thinking this might be Hell, that I should leave before I get stuck in her loop, but then Bill Hanover comes to visit."

"Who's Bill Hanover?" I asked, worried that I'd missed something.

"Turns out he's Veronica's nephew, Cherry's first cousin. Visits his aunt every second Tuesday, always arrives an hour before dinner and tells her how disappointed he is to cut the visit short when the attendant comes for her. He spends that hour sitting with her and holding her hand while she calls him Stephen or George, who was Stephen's father, or Daniel, who I think was Bill's. She asks after assorted family members and he tells her they're all fine, even if half the people she's asking about are probably dead. One time, in a moment of clarity, she calls him by his correct name and asks when Stephen's coming to visit. He's straight out with 'I'm sure he'll visit tomorrow' like he's been to the staff meeting.

"That first evening, I got his name from the visitor's book and when he was leaving, I followed him out and got his make, model and registration and even if it meant nothing, it felt like I was finally doing something. He was Cherry's age, he was a relative, and close enough to the family to keep visiting Veronica Hill so it felt like a reasonable assumption that he'd kept at least a passing acquaintance with Cherry before he died. I stuck around, hoping he'd visit again and once I caught on to the fortnightly routine, I only had to hang around the home on his visiting evenings, since nobody else ever called on her. It was a relief to be able to get away from that place."

"What did you do the rest of the time?" I asked, returning to the couch with my beer.

"Wandered around the city, screamed in people's faces," he replied.

"Everyone needs their hobbies, I guess."

I was pretty sure he almost laughed at this but when it came to poker faces, he had a whole deck.

"Every second Tuesday, I'd sit in on their visits and each time a little something more would come out. The name of another family member, a mention of some old vacation. Nothing helpful but I was long on time and short on leads, so I kept hoping. I also figured it would be good to get a look around Bill Hanover's house but had no way of knowing where he lived. So, I started tracing his route from the home back to his place. Every time he left, I'd run after his car for as long as I could keep up with it and when his next visit was due, I'd wait around where I lost him and see where he came from."

"Sounds like slow going," I said.

"It was, especially since being whatever the hell I am doesn't come with superpowers like teleporting or superspeed. If anything, it makes running harder because I gotta concentrate on every single step so I don't run right into the ground."

"You did get the ability to walk through walls and the power of flight, or at least levitation," I said, helpful as ever. "Plus, invisibility."

"Yeah, well, on the subject of invisibility, it was around this time I came across Liam and then you," he said. "Invisibility sure didn't feel like a superpower while I was screaming in your face, hobby or no."

I sipped my drink and kept quiet.

"So, there I am, trying to work out the way to Hanover's place one block, one street corner per fucking fortnight and all the time, I'm thinking about the woman, about what she's doing while I'm spinning my wheels. Because people like her don't stop. At best, they pause, and I don't know if she's even done that. If she's being careful, taking it slow, she could be continuing her and Cherry's line of business this entire time without anyone knowing."

I put down my beer, suddenly it didn't seem so appealing.

"It felt like I was never going to get through to you, was never going to make it to Hanover's place which was most likely a dead end anyway and all the time there's this clock ticking that nobody else knows about and maybe another kid has hours or minutes or seconds left and there's me, standing at a set of lights, rain falling through me like a swarm of bees, squinting at headlights in the hope I spot Hanover's car in enough time to figure out yet another scrap of my bass-ackwards map. By now, I'd marked his drive so far from the home that I wasn't even going to have time to run after him and listen in on his visit but that was just another dead end so what the fuck did it matter? I'm so caught up in these happy wonderings that I don't see Hanover until he's right in front of me, waiting on a red light, and I have no clue what direction he's just come from."

"Shit," I said softly.

"Shit is exactly what I think to myself." He allowed himself a grin. "Until I look in the passenger window and see a torn, brown, letter-sized envelope sitting on the empty seat."

"No?" I groaned.

"William Hanover, 13 West Street, Elmsview," he said, the grin turning rueful. "Same neighbourhood as his cousin, just a couple of streets back. I was still on the other side of the city. If it wasn't for that envelope, I'd probably still be piecemealing my way to his place. The light turns green, Hanover takes off for his visit with his aunt and I start walking to his place. That was last month."

I didn't think he'd appreciate a high five so instead I offered a slow clap, needing to let the tension out somehow. He waved me off but I kept it up a little longer, even added a couple of whistles.

"Alright, alright," he said, but didn't sound annoyed.

"You start at your parents' house and end up at the home of Hill's cousin, a guy who grew up with him and lived two streets away. That's some Sherlock work right there."

"No, just boring old police work. One foot in front of the other, one thing at a time."

"Whatever, Joe Friday, you go on being modest, and I'll go on being impressed." And I was impressed. For all the baggage he brought with him, for all the impending trouble I could sense he represented, he truly was a miracle. A dead man who made contact with the living and a cop through and through, in life and the afterlife.

"What do you think," he said, serious again, "the chances are that Hanover and his cousin, who grew up together, lived their lives in the same neighbourhood, had nothing to do with each other as grown men?"

"Pretty slim," I said. "But that doesn't mean Hanover knew what his cousin was up to."

"No, but there's a possibility. Just like there's a possibility he knows the woman, even if he has no clue she was involved, or knows something of no significance to him that's crucial to us."

While once again, I found the "us" flattering, it was tainted somewhat by an unappealing vision of Bill Hanover tied to a chair, me beating answers out of him while Owen cheered me on. "You've looked in his house? Followed him around?"

He nodded.

"Anything suspicious?"

"Not that I've seen but remember he's living in a house full of drawers I can't open and pages I can't turn."

"So, you've been waiting for..." I cocked a thumb back at myself at the same instant he shot an index finger at me. "You need me to break into his house."

"I can make sure he won't be there. I'll watch your back and –"

It was my turn to wave him off.

"I'll do it."

It wasn't bravery or a sense of duty that made me cut him off mid-sales pitch. It was disgust. He'd studied me in intimate detail over the past months and what he found was someone who couldn't be expected to do the right thing for its own sake. Like he said, he hadn't come back for emotional support, nor had he come back to make friends, least all with me. The details of his death and his return, his patience with my questions and experiments, the dramatic reveal of his efforts to track down Hanover, all were offered to soften me up, to make me feel involved, invested, a part of the story, a part of "us". I wasn't disgusted that he thought so little of me, I was disgusted that he was probably right.

"When?" I asked.

"He's night porter at a motel downtown. He leaves home around nine-thirty pm, gets back in the morning by seven-fifteen. His working nights change week-to-week but the roster for the week ahead goes up in their staffroom on Saturdays. I checked when it went up earlier today and he's working tonight."

"So, did you leave me hanging for the last couple of days, with no word, because you were worried about my job and my mental health or because you were waiting on Hanover's roster?"

"One thing doesn't necessarily exclude the other."

"For a miracle, you can be a real prick."

When he repeated Hanover's address and asked if I could find my way, I nodded. When he told me he'd start running and meet me there, I nodded some more. Nodding meant I didn't have to open my mouth to gulp for air or to tell him to slow down and give me a minute.

Chapter 15

The city flickered past, shadowy outlines and shapeless lights. My cab driver had quickly given up her attempts at conversation and the only sounds were the rattle and hum of the engine, the background chatter on her radio, and my screaming nerves. I had hailed the taxi well away from my building, giving the cabbie an address a block away from Hanover's. Before that, in my apartment, I was halfway through using my personal account to book an Uber straight from my place to the one I was going to break into before common sense kicked in and I started smashing the cancel button.

I was wearing black sneakers, black jeans, and a black beanie, but the ensemble was let down by my dark blue hoodie. Typically, apart from my strategically-inappropriate *Ghostbusters* hoodie with large white lettering on the back (*Dial 555 2368 – We're Ready To Believe You*), all my black hoodies were so badly in need of a wash that any visual camouflage they provided would have been undone by the giveaway smell.

In one pocket, I had my small Maglite and in the other a pair of thick, woollen gloves that weren't ideal but were the only pair I had. I considered bringing my backpack but had a superstitious fear that I'd leave it behind in Hanover's house like I had in the library toilets. The same reasoning led me to leave my wallet and phone at home too. I brought enough cash for taxis and took the keys for my apartment, one for the building and one for my door, and placed them in my sneakers, the discomfort offset by the reassurance there was little risk of them falling into enemy hands.

We turned onto a side street and took a couple of turns that matched the online map directions I'd done my best to memorise.

"This you?" she said, bringing the car to a stop.

"Yep," I said as confidently as I could.

I paid and told her to keep the change but since I'd handed her a twenty for an eighteen-fifty fare, she didn't get too emotional about it. I took a last look at her dash clock, five to midnight, and stepped into the kind of still suburban street that instantly makes you feel like an intruder.

While the cabbie turned around, I took a few slow steps toward the house she'd dropped me at but once she was out of sight, I returned to the street, once more mentally overlaying the blue line I'd studied so intensely on my phone at home onto my surroundings, and headed in what I hoped was the right direction.

There was a strong wind, every banging door and unidentified crash making me jump, certain that a Neighbourhood Watch's worth of suspicious residents was about to pour out their front doors to lynch me first and ask questions later about what I was doing lurking around, dressed like a ninja on casual day, mere feet from where their precious children and automobiles were sleeping. Every time a sensor light lit up someone's lawn, I resisted the urge to raise my hands over my head.

When I found West Street and what I was eighty percent sure was the right house, I picked a spot further along on the opposite side of the street and waited. No cars or people passed and most of the houses, including the one I thought was Hanover's, were in darkness. The only sound was the wind and the loose bits of suburbia it was knocking around. The moon was hidden behind cloud but the orange streetlights were keeping the street brighter than I would have liked.

Jo and I had grown up on a street like this, in a cookie-cutter house just like the ones surrounding me. I could picture the little bedroom that had been the centre of my universe, where I'd hidden from my parents, school, girls who I couldn't talk to and boys who wouldn't talk to me. I remembered the marks on the walls where countless posters had been replaced or rearranged and the dent in the ceiling I made by throwing my TV remote for no reason. When I tried to remember the rest of the house though, the geography fell apart. I could recall every square inch of my bedroom but not the colour of the kitchen walls or what kind of furniture we had in the living room.

Jo, despite being three years younger, had predictably achieved launch first, leaving the house for higher learning a year before I left for minimum wage. He returned home most weekends with dirty laundry and breathless tales of college life. He'd ask what I was up to, I'd say 'nothing' or near enough to it, and he'd try to hide the pity in his eyes, after which I'd retreat to my room, leaving him to be fawned over by our parents. Years later, once he graduated and went travelling, and with me out on my own, our parents were left with no dependants, so our father retired from the cutthroat world of real estate and as his last hoorah sold our house, downsizing at an undisclosed profit to a two-bedroom bungalow, near enough to smell if not quite see the ocean. It was beach-adjacent rather than beachfront, but they loved it, speaking about the ocean breeze the way some people talk about crystal meth.

"WIL!"

He ran toward me from the end of the street, one foot occasionally disappearing into the asphalt and making him hop. I bit my tongue and hoped that the damp I felt in my crotch was just part of the full-bodied sweat I'd been enjoying since we parted ways.

"WIL, I'M HERE! CAN YOU SEE ME?"

"*I see you, stop shouting,*" I hissed.

"Nobody else can hear me," he said, stopping a ways off. "Doesn't matter *HOW LOUD I YELL.*"

"I don't care, just keep it down."

"Alright, alright," he said, not turning away quickly enough for me to miss his smirk. "Hanover should be at work but let me double-check his place in case he's called in sick or some shit."

He walked toward the house that I had correctly picked as Hanover's. On one side, there was a garage with roller door, down and no doubt locked. On the other side, between Hanover's and the fence separating it from the neighbouring property, there was a gap leading into darkness. Owen walked through a front window and I was alone again, making a mental note to ask later if he could feel the wind rushing through him.

I wondered what it felt like to be a couple of blocks away from the house he was murdered in but then of course, it was hardly his first time back. Hill's house had surely been one of his first stops when he went looking for the woman.

"WIL, COME OVER, ALL CLEAR!"

I flipped my middle finger at Owen, who had reappeared outside the house, but he was already heading around the side, into the darkness. I followed, grateful to be stepping into the shadows and out of the light. With the house looming on one side and the fence on the other, the narrow path was so dark that I walked straight into the wooden gate that Owen must have gone through.

"Thanks for the warning," I said, rubbing my nose.

"Pull yourself up and get an arm over, there's a latch halfway up on this side," he said, clearly distraught on my behalf. "You just need to get your fingers around it and pull up."

He was all business now, volume as low as requested.

"Wil?"

"I'm just putting my gloves on."

"Why?"

"Fingerprints, DNA, et cetera. Weren't you a cop?"

"I was, and unless your prints are already on file, you don't have anything to worry about."

"Easy for the dead guy to say," I said, then thought about it. "Sorry."

With gloves on, I grabbed the top of the gate and hoisted myself up, pushing with my feet against the fence and wall on either side for purchase. When I got on top, the edge dug into my stomach and made it hard to breathe while I strained for the latch, eventually fumbling it open. The gate swung inward with me on top before I scrambled down and locked it behind me.

The backyard may as well have been a swimming pool full of ink for all I could see. I took out my flashlight and turned it on.

"Put that away."

I played the beam over the back fence, wondering if a run and a jump would get me over it in an emergency.

"Put it away."

"*Why?*" I asked, still smarting over his dismissal of my gloves.

"Because if anyone looks out their window, they might guess it's not Hanover prowling outside his place with a flashlight."

I shoved it back in my pocket. This was becoming even less enjoyable than I'd anticipated and my expectations hadn't been that high. Owen guided me toward a pair of glass sliding doors at the back of the house. I tried pulling them open but they didn't budge.

"I hope you remembered I can't pass through solid objects when you were coming up with this plan."

"Keep going, there's a window at shoulder height a little further along."

I started to feel along the wall.

"Hey, who lives in Stephen Hill's house now?"

"Huh?"

"You've been back there, right?" I whacked my hand off a downpipe, smugly grateful for my thick gloves. "Looking for the woman."

"Yeah, of course," he said, sounding a little off. I wondered if I'd said something to offend him, or if the house he was murdered in just wasn't his favourite topic. "Nobody lives there, I doubt there was any interested buyers. Hopefully they'll put a bulldozer through it."

"Aha!" I found the window but feeling along its edges, my satisfaction turned to uncertainty. "It's small."

"You'll fit," he said. It was too dark to see anything more than each other's outline, so I didn't bother to shrug. "It opens out, so you need to pull. There's no handle on this side but it's the downstairs bathroom and he always leaves the window open a crack. Work your fingers in and heave on it, you'll be able to force the lock."

I felt again and discovered the crack he was talking about. It wasn't wide enough for a child to fit a finger in and I told him as much.

"Try without the gloves."

"Owen, it's too narrow."

He didn't respond and I could feel his impatience. I wished I was defiant enough to turn my light on him to see what kind of face he was pulling.

"Head back out front."

As instructed, I retreated to the side of the house, an optimistic butterfly fluttering its wings in my stomach, thoughts of escape on its tiny mind.

"Go down the street, find a car that looks new enough to have a decent alarm system, and set it off."

The butterfly clutched at its chest and fell to the pit of my stomach, dead.

"Noise is bad. Isn't that the point of sneaking?" If my assault on the gate had proven anything, it was that I would not present enthusiastic police dogs with a challenge.

"You *have* to break that window," he said, as if there was an open door somewhere I refused to use. "People pay less attention to a car alarm than the sound of breaking glass."

Faced with the blunt momentum of his logic, and forgetting the whole "being dead" thing, I envied him. He was able to think up useful shit on the spot while in times of crisis, my brain spewed up obscure paranormal trivia and punk lyrics. In this instance, the immortal words of New Found Glory came to mind.

I've figured out my situation, I am an endless source of useless information.

Thanks, brain.

I opened the gate and stood to one side to let him take the lead.

"Wait, if I'm breaking glass anyway, shouldn't I go for those doors instead of that tiny window?"

"Those doors are thicker, probably some kind of safety glass. That bathroom window is regular old frosted glass, easier and quieter to break," he said, passing by.

He stopped in the middle of the street, illuminated by the nearest street-light but casting no shadow. "All clear. Walk slow, but not weird slow. If someone comes along just keep walking. There's a BMW over there that should work."

I emerged from the safety of the shadows to look where he was pointing. A few houses down on the other side of the street, the back of a silver car protruded from the driveway. I walked toward it, slow, but not weird slow.

"Their upstairs lights are on," I whispered as I passed him.

"Once the alarm goes, run back, and break that window. Lock the gate behind you, but don't slam it. You'll be out of sight before anyone's looking." Once again, he made everything sound so simple and safe that I felt stupid for wasting his time with objections. "I'll hang back to make sure."

I moved down the street, considered whistling nonchalantly and thought better of it. I reached the driveway and stepped over the threshold, shifting from pedestrian to trespasser. I took one more glance at the upstairs windows before slamming myself against the car.

I had bolted across the street, past Owen and into the darkness beside Hanover's house before I realised the roar of blood in my ears and the rattle of my breath were unaccompanied by a car alarm. Owen stayed in the middle of the street, staring into the sky as if he could wish himself away.

"Go again, Wil. Didn't quite get it."

I trudged back down the street, took another look around and pushed against the car.

Nothing.

I tugged at the door handles, at the mirrors.

Still nothing.

I aimed a frustrated kick at the front wheel, lost my footing and hit the concrete on my back, staring up in astonishment at the same black, cloud-weighted sky Owen had been gazing into.

Dazed, it took a while for my success to sink in. The car, the one I was now lying beside, was screaming.

I got to my feet and fled once more to Hanover's, latching the gate on my way around back.

I managed to feel my way back to the bathroom window but then realised I had no idea what to break it with.

Picturing Owen's reaction if he returned to find me in front of the wholly intact window jogged something loose. I pulled off my hoodie and wrapped it around my arm. When I drove my elbow against the window, my only reward was a nauseating twang that ran from my elbow to my wrist but I elbowed it again and this time, the glass gave way. I used my hoodie to knock out the remaining shards still in the frame, reassured that even from where I was standing, the car alarm was the only thing I could hear.

By the time the alarm stopped, I had my hoodie back on and an empty window frame in front of me. I entertained a flash of memory, of thoughts of glassless holes some night a lifetime ago.

When Owen reappeared, I broke his rule just long enough to shine my flashlight on my handiwork before I reached in, undid the latch, and pulled open the frame. While I was doing this, he went through the wall beside me.

"Toilet's right below the window," he said from inside, voice shaking. "Lid's up, seat's down. Let's go."

Chapter 16

Two scraped knees and one soaked foot later, I was picking myself off the tiled floor, brushing away glass that I had failed to cut myself on by luck rather than design. Joining Owen in the hall, I followed him to Hanover's kitchen.

"Light switch is over here."

"Isn't it better if I use my flashlight now?"

"Same sentiment as outside," he said. "A few ceiling lights look less suspicious than a flashlight moving around in the dark."

Deferring to his wisdom, I said nothing and turned on the kitchen light.

While he headed back outside to make sure nobody was stirring, I gulped some water straight from the faucet to wash away the cotton in my mouth and the deceased butterfly in my stomach. He came back with the all-clear and since neither of us knew what I was looking for, I looked everywhere.

At first, I was careful, putting things back as they were, until Owen instructed me to do the opposite. "If Hanover doesn't have anything worth finding here, then our next best hope is that his house getting tossed makes him reach out to someone who does, so let's make fucking sure he knows about it."

He didn't need to tell me twice. Not having to worry about tidiness would make things a lot faster for me. I worked my way through the modern kitchen, all trying-too-hard black and red laminate surfaces, poking through cabinets and drawers, cereal boxes, and a family-sized jar of peanut butter.

Next, I moved on to the garage where I stirred through a dozen half-empty paint cans in case they were hiding anything while a dusty elliptical trainer watched from the corner like a neglected pet.

By the time we made it to the living room, my nerves had all but disappeared, becalmed by the familiarity of my circumstances. I was in a strange building in the middle of the night, searching for what was probably not there at all, a situation I found myself in at least once a month with DAPI.

They hadn't extended the kitchen's Euro-futurism vibe to the living room which had a more relaxing mix of beiges and creams. The couch, probably sold as Tuscan Ecru, just about melted into Crème Latte carpet and New England Bisque walls.

I picked up a laptop from an end-table but it was password protected which was disappointing yet predictable. Spotting some framed photos on the fireplace mantle, I put down the unhelpful laptop and went for a better look.

One showed a smiling couple with lapels and flares competing for vastness, squinting into the sun with their arms around one another, the little boy in front of them doing that grimace-through-your-teeth thing kids do when grown-ups tell them to "*Say Cheese*". The trio stood in front of the house I was now in which I guessed made the little boy Bill Hanover and the grown-ups his parents.

Another photo showed the same backdrop with a different couple. The grown Bill Hanover looked somewhere between the little boy he had been and the man his father was in the earlier photo. He was lanky yet soft looking, like a piece of slightly melted string cheese. I couldn't see any family resemblance to Stephen Hill but then me and my first-cousin Nathan, he of the Almighty Poke, looked about as alike as chalk and a completely different brand of chalk. Hanover had his arm around a blonde, too good looking for him. There was no kid.

"Hanover and his ex-wife."

"How do you know?" I asked.

"I know that's Bill and I know he was married so, as a cop, I tend to make crazy connections."

"She's pretty hot, too hot for him anyway." I picked up the photo for a better look. "How do you know he was married?"

"I've heard him mention her. Karen The Bitch. His words, not mine."

I pulled apart the frame, dropping pieces on the mantle, but there was no document secreted in the frame, no cryptic clue scrawled on the reverse of the photo, and the same went for the older one of him and his parents. I picked up the photo of Bill and Karen again.

"There's no chance she's...?"

I looked from the photo to Owen but he shook his head.

"No. But maybe she knows her, maybe *he* knows her. We'll see."

I lowered the photo and looked Owen in the eye for a long moment before I found the courage to ask the question I'd been avoiding.

"If we find the woman –"

"*When* we find the woman..."

"Yeah, *when*, sure," I said impatiently. "What then? Citizen's arrest? That's not a real thing, right?"

"We find out where she lives," he said. "Then I find out when she won't be there. We get you into her empty house and do what we're doing here. We'll find something, they're never as smart as they think. They keep things they should throw away, collect what they should burn. We send whatever you find to the cops, or send the cops to it, and they take it from there."

It sounded so clean, so simple, so impossible.

"But what if we don't find anything to prove to them who she is?"

"Worst case scenario, we'll have to wait for her to make an attempt on somebody and set the cops on her before she sees it through."

I stared at him until I was sure he was being serious.

"Just to clarify, if I can't dig up enough dirt on her, I'll need to watch her until she's about to murder someone, most likely a child, and get the cops there in the finite space between her starting that act and completing it? All while not getting myself murdered by her for interfering or shot by the cops for just being there?"

"If she keeps to previous M.O., she'll abduct and hold her victim for some time before she kills them," he said. Any idea he had that this would be reassuring to me was disavowed by the look of outright dread that must have been writ large on my face. "For now, think of it as extra incentive to really dig into the evidence side of things, OK?"

Rather than answer, I resumed tossing the room with added vigour.

When I found something of note, I'd hold it up for Owen to inspect. He'd move in for a better look and when he did there was no warm breath, no brush of cloth, no smell of deodorant or sweat or today's lunch or any of the other exhaust fumes of humanity we take for granted.

Eventually, I settled back into the search, my heartbeat settling along with me. We'd take it one step at a time, like the dead man said. Work the angles, dig the dirt, and my years of searching for ghosts would turn out to have been the perfect practice for searching for this ghoul, like it was always meant to be, my long-delayed destiny delivered neither by owl nor wizard but a surly, existentially challenged, forcibly retired police detective. Rather than a waste of time, my tenure with DAPI would prove to be my making.

"Hey, what did you think of DAPI when you saw us doing our thing at the bank that first night?" I was flicking through a paperback Grisham, having already emptied most of the bookcase searching for anything hidden amongst Hanover's book collection, mainly legal thrillers and police procedurals.

"Same as always; let them notice me, let me get through to them. I guess after that, I thought it was funny how you all talk to each other like you're soldiers or scientists not..."

"A bunch of losers?"

"I didn't say that."

"You didn't not say that."

"Everyone has their own thing," he said in a way that implied not everyone should be allowed to have their own thing. "Any time I've been around DAPI since then, my main thought, other than please let this motherfucker stop ignoring me –"

"Wasn't ignoring you," I interjected for posterity, turning *The Lincoln Lawyer* upside down.

"– has been that if you guys worried less about your cameras and thermometers and YouTube uploads and more about paying attention to your surroundings, you might actually find what you're after."

"A lot of people agree with you," I said, stepping away from the bookcase to work on the couch. "Some of the big paranormal guys like Troy Taylor think there are too many people in it just to play around with gadgets."

"You don't agree?" he asked.

"I agree to a point. But I like gadgets." I found a few coins down the back of the couch and pocketed them, because every little helps. "Plus, it's too depressing to accept there isn't a way for one person to make contact and record it somehow, to show the world it happened."

"You can't record me."

"Not yet, but maybe I'll figure something out." I unzipped a cushion and felt around inside. "Be pretty amazing if I could, wouldn't it?"

I waited for a response and when none came, I looked up just in time to see him passing through the curtains and out the front window.

"Great chatting with you too."

Chapter 17

Upstairs, in the master bedroom, the only item of interest was a vintage Polaroid camera. When Owen returned, I clicked off a shot at him and was pleasantly surprised when it flashed and whirred since I thought it might just be a paperweight by now. When the photo came out, I couldn't resist shaking it, despite knowing you're not meant to. When the image cleared, I held it up for Owen to see.

"Too bad," he said, a little dismissively, studying the contents of the bedside table which I'd dumped onto the bed before getting distracted by the camera.

I picked up a pen from the mess and, somewhat clumsily with my gloved hand, wrote the date and Owen's name on the photo, which showed only an empty doorway, before pocketing it.

In the main bathroom, I checked the cabinets and toilet cistern, squeezing out bottles of shampoo and shower gel to make sure they contained only shampoo and shower gel. On the windowsill, there was an abstract metal statuette that might have been two androgynous figures locked in either sex or combat, or might have been an exploded flower, but the ornament concealed nothing other than its meaning.

I had to fight off the lazy relief seeping in as it became increasingly likely Hanover was a dead end. I tried instead to share Owen's disappointment, to remind myself that people like me weren't meant to be needed by people like him, that this was an honour, not a burden. People like me were meant to sit in cinemas watching people like him do great, dramatic things while we slurped on drinks and sucked popcorn kernels from our teeth before returning, bleary-eyed, to our real world.

In a spare room, half guest room and half storage space, I found a bulging document organiser and fumbled as far as "D" before finally accepting that it was either my sanity or my gloves, so I took them off. Warranties, receipts, bank statements, a photocopy of Hanover's passport reconfirming he was close in age to Stephen Hill. Owen stood over me, not-breathing down my neck, dismissing each new document with a frustrated grunt. A copy of divorce paperwork showed William and Karen Hanover nee Taylor were still in the process, had only begun it the past few months in fact.

Nothing stood out but then, if I were Hanover, innocent or guilty, I'd have destroyed anything linking me to Hill the moment the news broke and hope I didn't wake up to a front yard full of cops and reporters.

I opened the room's built-in closet, crammed with black garbage sacks full of women's clothing that I guessed Karen The Bitch had yet to take, or maybe Hanover was holding hostage. Pulling them out one by one, I emptied the bags onto the carpet until the closet was empty, exposing grubby walls, bare floorboards and a single shelf that ran along the bottom of the closet, presumably intended for shoes. A single lightbulb hung from a cord overhead and I tugged this on the off chance it opened a secret door at the back of closet.

Instead of a hidden passage, I was rewarded with an electric shock.

I backed away, muttering obscenities and cradling my hand.

"Did that shelf just move when you were fucking around in there?"

"By fucking around, do you mean getting electrocuted?"

"Well, it looked to me like it dropped a little on one side while you were fucking around getting electrocuted."

Shaking out my hand to get some feeling back, I scowled at the shelf in question. It spanned the width of the back of the closet, high enough from the floor to accommodate a row of shoes on the floor below it and another on the shelf itself.

"It looks the same to me."

"You sure?"

I scowled at it harder.

"I mean, maybe it's dropped a tiny bit on the left but I don't know."

I was just being polite but figured he wasn't going to let it go until I checked it out, so I stepped back into the closet, ducking away from the hanging cord of death, and kicked the shelf.

It really was loose.

I knelt down for a closer look.

Compared to the shelf itself, which was dusty and slightly battered, the screwheads attaching it to the back of the closet were worn and shiny, as if they'd only recently been driven in.

I pulled and the shelf came away from the wall a little before the screws caught. There was now a narrow gap between the shelf and the wall and when I leaned in closer to inspect this, I was rewarded with a strong oily smell that I was sure hadn't been there before.

I hurriedly backed out of the closet on all fours and once I was clear of any electrically based danger, jumped to my feet.

"Screwdriver," I said by way of explanation as I exited the room, caught up once more in the thrill of the hunt.

I found one in the garage and returned, taking the stairs two at a time in my excitement.

The screws came out easily enough. I lifted the shelf away and where it had been, where the back of the closet met the floor, there was a hole in the drywall the size of my fist.

The odour of oil grew stronger and now I could also detect a metallic undertone.

"Anything?"

I realised not only could Owen not smell what I could, but I was also blocking his view. I leaned to one side long enough for him to take in the jagged, flaky-edged hole I'd exposed in the wall.

I reached in and almost instantly, my fingers brushed against something hard and cold.

Oily and metallic.

I closed my hand around the object and pulled it out. When I saw what it was, I panicked and flung it away, sending it through Owen.

In perfect harmony, for once, we looked at the handgun resting on a pile of women's clothing and then back to the hole I'd pulled it from.

I reached inside again, more cautious this time, but couldn't feel anything else. I laid flat on the ground to get my arm in further, jamming my shoulder right up against the wall, and was rewarded for my efforts.

This time I retrieved a squarish object wrapped in a similar black plastic to the trash bags I'd just emptied. I unwrapped the plastic and found within it a stack of Polaroid photos. I took a look at the one on top, then the next one, and then let them all fall from my hands.

Somehow, I got to my feet, all motivations noble or selfish evaporating and leaving me a scared man in a strange house in the deepest hours of the night with only the ghost of a murder victim for company.

"I have to go home now."

I scurried past Owen and managed to take the stairs three at a time on my way down.

It was dark in the downstairs hall, but I could still see a pair of legs descending from the ceiling as I headed for the guest bathroom. I sped up but Owen was down and blocking the door before I could get to it. His trip through the floor left him shaking in pain even as he held up a hand to stop me.

"I'm sorry but I'm not a cop. The only badge I have is for being a Certified Paranormal Investigator and I had to print and laminate it myself. This is way too much." The words came out in a breathless tumble, wheedling and pathetic and I didn't care as long as I got through the door and out of that house. "I'm alive. You're dead. I can still get hurt...or worse."

He couldn't speak but I knew he'd be fully recovered in a moment and able to stop me.

I stepped forward and thrust my hand out. Since our focus was elsewhere, Owen's on his pain and mine on escape, our connection was weak enough for me to reach through him and grab the door handle.

As I barrelled through, he yelled in anguish just as our heads occupied the same space and I had the unnerving sensation that the awful sound was coming from me, that I was the one in pain, but then I was through the door and scrambling out the window to freedom.

Running along the side of the house, I had the gate in my sights but just before I reached it, a shadowy figure burst from the wall and blocked my path.

"Stop," Owen growled.

A moment's hesitation and I took off again, ready to pass through him once more.

This time, he was ready.

He shoved me hard in the chest with both hands. His strength and my forward momentum conspired against me and for a disorientating moment I was horizontal in mid-air and then I was hitting the concrete path with a full-bodied thud, cracking the back of my head.

For the second time that night, I found myself unexpectedly cloud-gazing but then a rounded shape full of shadows and shades that might have been Owen's face obscured my view and two inky, shining circles that might have been his eyes looked down on me. Inadvertently, reluctantly, I made eye contact and this made me think of Mandy from work which in turn made me laugh but it sounded more like a moan and then I fell silent while everything blurred in and out of focus, the wind-blown night sounds fading away until only one remained.

A door somewhere, slamming in the wind.

Creak.

Bang.

Creak.

Bang.

The night became a series of disconnected moments spinning through my possibly concussed head, the rhythm of creaking and banging punctuating each like a shotgun blast.

Owen is yelling at me but sounds like he's underwater. I touch the back of my head and the pain is so bad I almost fall down even though I don't remember getting up. I wave him away and turn back from the gate without further objection.

There's me throwing up in Hanover's backyard and so much for my precious DNA.

Back on the bathroom floor but this time I've cut my hands on the shards of broken glass and here, have some more DNA.

I'm back upstairs, feeling around inside the closet hidey-hole but there's nothing else in there.

Owen directs me as I put the shelf back over the hole, just leaning it against the wall now rather than screwing it in. Then he has me refill all the trash bags and throw them back in the closet. He has a reason for this but I don't understand, I'm just a clothing-transferral machine.

I'm downstairs, clutching a shopping bag. I look inside, wondering what I've bought. A handgun, a laptop, and a collection of Polaroids of...

I'm on the street. I look behind me and see Owen standing out front of that house, watching me leave. I'm wearing my gloves again.

I'm in the back of a taxi that I am sure will crash and then I will die and the paramedics will find the contents of the bag I'm squeezing against my chest and everybody will think I was one sneaky monster.

An angry cab driver face is saying something.

I'm holding out money at the angry cab driver face.

I'm outside my apartment building, still holding the bag, but I'm locked out, creaking and banging against the door. I am possibly crying. I touch the back of my head again. I am definitely crying.

I'm sitting on the curb outside my apartment building. My shoes are on the ground before me, a silver key shining from each one.

Chapter 18

My parents always spoke of the one-hundred-and-ten-minute flight that took them from their ocean-based life back to the urban sprawl they raised me in like it was a transpolar feat of endurance. The first day of any visit would be given over to them complaining about this and telling me I'd have to come to them next time. I'd keep saying 'sure thing' and eventually they'd fall back on their favourite subject; Jo and How Well He's Doing.

This included how happy he was with his lovely fiancé, a brief summary of his position within his company, which they had no more luck than me in describing, and an impassioned address on his importance to the Thailand office, though both pronounced it Thighland despite having visited him three times over there and mustn't that have felt like exploratory space travel.

Implications would be made that if I focused on a career, any career, dressed better, got my driver's license, and generally pulled myself together, I too could have a life filled with purpose, financial gain, and the love of a good woman. Of all my failings, my father was most bothered by my lack of a driver's license, given his opinion that public transport was for miscreants. An opinion not to be swayed by my arguments that *everybody* used public transport, that having a car in the city was an unnecessary expense. He'd scoff, I'd swear under my breath, my mother would throw her hands in the air. It was a lot of fun.

I loved them, but in the distant, forgiving way I loved TV shows from my childhood. Great to remember, nice to catch a glimpse of, but they struggled to stand up to close scrutiny or repeat viewings.

It was a couple of years since I had seen my brother, the King of Thighland, in person. He stopped by on his way to visit our parents, said that his frequent flyer miles would get me there and back if I cared to join, but I firmly yet politely refused and when my refusals grew more firm and less polite, he let it go and we spent a couple of days watching movies and drinking beer before he continued on his way. Jo had always been my best friend but I knew his interest in seeing me was due to present pity and past loyalty and I didn't need to prolong the time I spent seeing myself through his eyes, someone he could remember looking up to if not quite why, an older brother who no longer stood up to close scrutiny or repeat viewings.

I had no social media presence and when people asked how I survived without it, I'd say my real friends didn't need to know what I ate for breakfast or receive updates on Current Mood. Of course, the greatest ROFL of all was the pretence I had real friends. I was a gatherer of acquaintances, like co-workers or people I met some other way such as DAPI, with whom I'd share a drink or a conversation about a particular TV show. One of us would move on to a different job, a new neighbourhood or watch the final season, and that was that.

All of which meant there was no reason for me to expect any visitors when I awoke that Sunday afternoon. No reason to keep mistaking the throbbing in the back of my skull for a fist banging on my door while I carefully showered, mindful of the soft spot on my head and my various cuts and scrapes. No reason at all to think someone was going to show up and, with pleasantries exchanged, make straight for the bag of horrors hidden in my bedroom closet. I convinced myself I could smell its contents, that the mingled stink of gun-oil and pure evil would permeate my apartment and then the building until questions were asked about its source.

Without even the strength to pace, I lay facedown on the couch, a bag of frozen peas melting on the back of my head while I pieced together the final fragments of the night before, which was hard because it involved starting from the point at which I'd tried to flee in hysterics and dwelling on that wasn't as fun as you'd think.

I had gone back into the house.

Why?

Because the blow to my head had knocked the sense out of or back into me, depending on how you looked at it. Owen had sent me back to the hiding place to see if there was anything else and when there wasn't, he told me to return the shelf, and the bags of clothes once I'd refilled them. We had never been trying to conceal our search, quite the opposite, so why?

I could see him talking at me in Hanover's living room, my world creaking and banging in and out of focus, the bag full of items he'd had me gather closed tightly in my hands, the same bag now doing a great Tell-Tale Heart impression in my closet. The plan had always been for him to stay behind and watch Hanover, see who he reached out to in case it gave us a fresh lead, but he'd never expected anything like what we came across. He'd had me cover up the hole because...

I grabbed the half-defrosted bag of peas and pushed hard against the back of my swollen skull in an attempt to jolt my memory. It hurt, but it worked.

...because there was a chance Stephen Hill had access to his cousin's house and might have stored his sickening souvenirs and emergency weapon there without Hanover knowing, and they were still there only because Hill was too dead to retrieve them, and the woman didn't have access to Hanover's house. Maybe she had no clue what Hill hid there, or wasn't worried about anybody finding them, let alone tracing them to her.

If Hanover knew nothing, then he'd act like any other citizen finding their home turned inside out, would either go from room to room in a stupor before calling the cops, paying no undue attention to the closet in his spare room, or immediately retreat to his car and make the call from there in case someone was still in the house.

But, if Hanover ignored the rest of his topsy turvy home and made a beeline for the messy but otherwise innocent looking closet, it meant he was a part of it all and the Cherry Tree Killer was three people, not two.

Owen said Bill Hanover got home around seven-fifteen in the morning which meant hours had passed since he would have walked into his house and seen my handiwork.

If he wasn't an innocent, if he headed straight for that closet and knew what had been taken, then he might have decided his time was up and ended it all while I was still sleeping. Owen would have looked on as Hanover shoved his head into an oven or opened his wrists, helpless to stop the man who might be his last lead take himself out of the equation. If Hanover had killed himself, I wondered if he passed Owen on the way out, perhaps mistaking him for Death.

Was I just meant to wait for word to come from Owen about our next move, or was there something I was supposed to be doing in the meantime?

I remembered getting halfway down Hanover's street and looking back at Owen, outside the house, calling something out to me.

Groaning in frustration, I once again reached back for the bag of peas sitting on my head. Bracing myself, I pressed hard but this time, instead of jolting my memory, I managed to knock myself out which, all things considered, was a relief.

When I came to, it was dark outside, I was half on the couch and half on the floor and my face was resting on something soft and wet that turned out to be the bag of peas, now split. I found my phone and saw that I'd fast-forwarded to seven pm.

No missed calls or messages, which was par for the course, but there was an email from Doug with the time and place of DAPI's next investigation. In two weeks' time, they would be visiting the Apollo Playhouse, one of the city's oldest theatres. This was a little sooner than I would have expected but you couldn't be too rigid in your scheduling when someone went out of their right mind long enough to offer up their premises. I would have loved to poke around inside the Apollo, alleged home of a whole troupe of long dead thespians who refused to take their final bow, including the ghost known as Bloody Banquo, victim of a prop mishap during an energetic production of the Scottish play in the 1930's.

Given there was still a DAPI for which to plan such an undertaking and Doug, not a man to forget to edit an email distribution list, still considered me part of it, I guessed he hadn't yet learned what I told Liam. I wondered if he was simply the last to know, or if Liam had held off telling the others yet, maybe giving himself the weekend before passing on the poisoned gift I had dumped in his lap.

I tried not to think of the other option, that he had already told everyone and Doug's email was his sly way of letting me know that he and Cal had gotten away with it, that nobody trusted anything I had to say and had all shared a laugh at my expense and moved on, my already fading memory invoking nothing more than headshakes and relief that I had my psychotic break over the phone rather than in person.

I deleted the email.

Whatever happened in my absence, DAPI was the past, no matter how much it stung not to go chasing after Bloody Banquo and assorted supporting players.

I retrieved the bag from my bedroom closet, gingerly placing it on the floor by the couch. I took out the gun first and laid it between my feet, the barrel pointing away. Fifteen minutes later, it was in much the same position but with the slide racked back, safety on, and magazine ejected. Turning off the YouTube handgun safety How-To video playing on my phone, I pulled out Hanover's laptop and spent twenty minutes getting nowhere with his password before giving up and moving onto the bag's remaining contents with great reluctance and suddenly shaking hands.

I withdrew the Polaroids and fanned them out on the coffee table.

The first photo was of a red-haired boy, surely not yet in double-digits. He was naked and looked almost translucent in the camera flash. He wore a more desperate version of the grimace-like smile young Bill Hanover had held in the photo on his mantle, tears visible on his freckled cheeks. None of the children in the other photos looked any older, a few looked much younger. Some were also naked while others were in underwear that was often stained, some of these stains were red.

I closed my eyes and waited for the room to stop spinning.

When I was able, I opened my own laptop and looked up photos of known and suspected victims of Cherry Tree but none matched the children in the Polaroids. I didn't know if that meant Stephen Hill and the mystery woman had a longer list of victims than anyone suspected or if Hanover had a list all his own.

Were the kids in these photos alive or dead?

The backgrounds in the Polaroids were blank walls, anonymous wooded areas, or too dark to identify. They could have been taken anywhere, by anyone. I used my phone to take photos of the individual Polaroids and did a reverse online image search for each but came up with no matches.

No answers, not online and not in my silent, spinning apartment.

I deleted the pictures from my phone, its recycle bin, and closed down the private browsing session and VPN I'd used for the searches. I wiped down the photos, the laptop and finally the gun and stashed them back in my bedroom closet. I might have erased important fingerprints but my own were the most important of all and I had no intention of leaving them.

Back on my laptop, after scrubbing my hands under scalding hot water, I started a new folder into which I moved the document I started the other night, updating it with recent events including last night's break-in. I also added articles related to the lives and deaths of Owen Hoath and Stephen Hill, poring over each one as I downloaded them. Most likely a useless endeavour but starting a case file in the same way I would have for one of my paranormal investigations was something to do.

One article included a photo of Owen's widow, taken at his memorial service. Anna Hoath was pictured wearing black, her chestnut brown hair tied back in a severe bun, face set as if well aware of the cameras circling her like sharks, waiting for her to break down in messy, mascara-black tears so they could take a nice, juicy bite. She was staring blankly at something out of shot and no amount of make-up could hide the bags under her eyes, her only visible concession to weakness. I tried to imagine what it must feel like for Owen to have lost this woman, how it might feel to love someone so much you were completely incapable of being near them, but I couldn't manage it.

I called it a night and headed to bed, was just starting to drift off when my phone rang.

An incoming video call from Jo.

I hovered my thumb over the green button for a moment before taking it away. I couldn't face a chat right now, trying to pretend everything was fine and normal and there wasn't a horror show hiding in my closet and I wasn't tensed like a clenched fist waiting for word from Owen. Jo let it ring out and then immediately began typing a message.

Hey bro, sorry I missed you, guess you're having an early one for a change. Hope all's good. Call me some time, it's been forever! Love you. PS Lawan says hi.

Forever was a slight exaggeration but it had definitely been a while since our last talk. Jo had called on my birthday but I made some excuse to cut it short and return to my celebratory *Ghost Adventures*-marathon, full of promises to call him back for a "proper chat" in the near future. I began to wonder when I had last been the one to reach out but my head hurt enough without making things worse. He was probably just calling out of politeness anyway, ticking "Check on Wil" off his To Do list. I'd seen pictures of his fiancé, pretty with high cheekbones and long jet-black hair, but we'd never met, and I doubted she had said hi or anything else to me.

I couldn't think of a reply so I put the phone down, promising myself I'd write back tomorrow.

In the darkness, my eyelids growing heavy again, I made one last concentrated effort to reach out to Owen. For an instant, I saw eyes glinting in the far corner of my room but then a pair of headlights washed through my curtains, bringing sleep, and carrying away wishful thinking.

Chapter 19

It was a busy morning at work. Heather had us pushing a new package which meant redirecting each caller from whatever they'd actually called about to a heart-to-heart about consolidating their car and home insurance with Alliance, taking extra time, specifically an additional two and a half minutes allocated per call, to share scripted statistics which obscured the truth that the only advantage of this exciting offer was the free toaster that came with it. Given the inadequate and loophole-riddled coverage offered under our home insurance, it wouldn't even cover them when the cheaply manufactured two-slice blew up their kitchen.

I still hadn't heard from Owen and spent my morning bus-ride on my phone, searching in vain for news out of Elmsview, though I wasn't sure if break-ins or suicides were considered newsworthy in a city full of both. Finally, as a test, I looked up the only non-celebrity suicide that came to mind. Chris Collins was the DAPI member who had thrown himself from a bridge, specifically a rail overpass that carried the Northern Line across a network of slummy side-streets and backroads in that part of the city. This represented everything I knew about him and the online results neither added to this nor assured me that if Hanover killed himself, I'd find anything about it online. The only article I found on Collins was an op-ed piece raging about the lack of security personnel on the city's public transport network which treated his death more as a useful example than a tragedy.

By lunchtime, my unsettled stomach wasn't begging for greasy beef and hot chilis but on Mondays the Mexican food truck near All Liars was looked after by the owner's daughter, a spectacularly attractive young woman whose full lips and bright smile were ample compensation for burritos that were never as evenly proportioned or tightly wrapped as those her father made every other day of the week. Our brief interactions usually brightened up my worst day but today this exchange provided neither distraction nor comfort and I ended up tossing the half-eaten burrito in the trash, indigestion welling up in my throat, before heading back to my desk early, simply because I could think of nothing else to do.

I wasn't one to pine for companionship but just now, thoughts of a warm embrace, a soft touch or a smile that came for free rather than at the cost of a poorly constructed burrito were almost overwhelming in their attractiveness. It had been almost a year since I'd last slept with someone and there'd been little warm or soft about it anyway. She made her escape from my place the morning after and I had the decency to pretend I was asleep while she did. My last real relationship had been Tara, giver of the black eye that lasted a fortnight, and that had ended five years ago. It began at an after-work drinks thing that Amir, an ex-co-worker, had dragged me to. Tara's friend Megan from Complaints, thankfully since departed from All Liars, had dragged her along. We got drunk, woke up together, and neither of us had the sense to let the other exit gracefully.

I finished my working day unembraced, untouched, and un-Owened.

When I left the office, it was already getting dark, the days getting shorter and shorter now. Even in my bleak frame of mind, I couldn't help but be buoyed by the cold, grey twilight that said summer was well and truly gone. Hang me for an emo, but I've always found it too hard to see the mysterious possibilities in bright days and summer nights, have always preferred the wolfhowl wind and the sheltering rain, the darkness full of promise.

Scores of likewise emancipated workers swarmed around me, milling about coffee stands, queueing at bus stops long on lines and short on buses. It was Monday evening, not Friday or even Thursday, so most of my fellow escapees didn't look happy, just mildly relieved. A mass of people so large and solid they should have been waving signs and singing protest songs in response to military aggression made their way to the train station because all they wanted was home and they wanted it now. The Stranglers growled and throbbed in my ears as I weaved my way through the crowds, still unsure if I was heading for my own stop or the one that would take me to Elmsview where I could get a look at Hanover's house and see if there was anything to be seen.

On the sidewalk, bodies pushed and shoved and after working my way through one particularly dense knot of slow movers, I stopped just short of walking into someone who was faced in my direction, standing stock still amongst the throng.

I looked up, an impatient glare ready for the idiot taking up valuable walking space, only to see a face I recognised all too well.

Doug stood, heedless of the crowd flowing around him, arms crossed and face puckered as if I was late for an appointment I'd never made.

My budding frown wilted into my best deer-in-the-headlights while I quickly side-stepped, only to find my new path blocked by Cal.

He leaned against Doug's car, even though I was pretty sure we were in a no parking zone, eyeing me with his custom blend of boredom and vague recognition. On his t-shirt, Hellboy was nailed to a cross, blood pooling at his feet to form the inspirational words "*Kill Your Heroes*".

I attempted something like a pirouette to go around Doug's other side but was boxed in by the steady stream of passers-by. When I tried instead to squeeze between the two of them, Doug shuffled over and Cal pushed himself from the car, somehow languidly yet swiftly, narrowing the gap. It felt like we were stuck in one of those classic "you go right, I'll go left, no, my left" loops which usually take place before two people walk right into one another. In fact, that's probably exactly how we looked to anyone who might have noticed us over their phone or their will to go home.

Doug and Cal did some more fancy footwork and suddenly my back was against the car, and they were closing in around me.

Doug jabbed his finger at me and said something I couldn't hear. When I shook my head, he rolled his eyes and pointed at his ears. I reluctantly pulled out my earphones, removing the last barrier between us.

"Need you to come with us, Wil," he said, probably repeating himself, which he hated.

"I'm not in the group anymore," I replied stonily, if stones can sound terrified.

"That doesn't matter," Doug replied, a man who knew how to sound stony.

I couldn't think of a response other than "No" and didn't think they'd accept that. I couldn't believe they were standing over me, intimidating me like this, and I couldn't believe how well it was working. I needed to take some control before this got any more ridiculous.

Making a split decision based on his age and build, I decided Doug was my best bet. I thrust out my hand to push him out of the way.

Having sent my hand out to remove the obstacle before us, my brain then issued instructions for my legs to move through what would now be a clear path. There followed quite a bit of confusion as it reconciled these reasonable expectations with the reality that my legs had nowhere to go because Doug was standing exactly where he'd been and my hand, which had never touched him, was in agony.

Cal held my hand in both of his and to my tear-filled eyes, it looked like he had removed it and put it back on the wrong way around.

I blinked to clear my vision but my hand looked the same, fingers wiggling back at me as if waving for help. I reached out my free hand to help its partner but Cal did something imperceptible to my trapped hand that made that seem like a terrible idea.

He stepped closer to me, our joined hands now hidden between us, and I smelled cigarettes, coffee and hair gel along with the salty tang of my own tears.

"Help," I said, not exactly a shout but not a whisper either.

The foot traffic had eased off slightly, allowing a few people to slow down and eye us without fear of being trampled. Just then, Doug burst out in spontaneous laughter, probably the most chilling moment of the whole ordeal.

"That's what she said last night, am I right?" This from Cal, sounding like an 80's movie meathead. He did something to my wrist with one of his thumbs that made me nostalgic for the pain that had gone before it. He favoured me with a leering grin while Doug chuckled on.

The handful of concerned citizens who slowed now picked up their pace again, one woman pointedly rolling her eyes and wrinkling her nose in disgust at my entire gender.

"Don't forget his bag," Cal said through his smile, eyes locked on me while Doug scooped up my backpack, which had once again jumped ship at the first sign of trouble, opened the car's back door and tossed it in. Cal pushed me in after it.

I scrambled across to the opposite door and tried to open it with my newly freed hand which did nothing but flop uselessly against the handle. By the time I tried with the other, Cal was already sitting next to me, shutting his door. It didn't matter anyway, my door was locked. With escape currently off the cards, I focused my attention on my hand which was screaming in pain as I clutched it in my lap like a broken bird. Specifically, to my mind's eye, a broken pigeon.

"It's not broken." Cal might be able to read my mind but I knew from experience he was a liar.

Doug got into the driver seat, and again I reached out with my functioning hand to try the doorhandle and when that didn't work, the window. Neither of them bothered to say "resistance is futile" or "escape is impossible" because the locked door and motionless window did it for them. Doug started the car and scanned his mirrors while Cal side-eyed me, seeming to find me slightly more of interest now that I was in agony and afraid for my life.

"Belts," Doug said.

Cal reached across me, securing mine and then his own, silencing the beeping that I'd barely registered amidst the chaos.

I was stunned by how rapidly events had overtaken me but not too stunned to foresee my impending torture and death, to picture the monitoring devices and recording equipment surrounding me, capturing every slash and scream during Doug and Cal's latest experiment, some Dennis Wheatley-inspired Black Mass that would be more veins wide open than *Eyes Wide Shut*. I found myself wishing for Owen even though he wouldn't be able to do anything. He couldn't even pick me up and run away with me unless he used me as a battering ram against the window first.

Doug pulled out but it was still rush hour and we came to a stop about three car lengths from where we started. I could still see my office building and even in my fear and pain I marvelled that something interesting was happening within its vicinity.

I looked to the other side, out my locked window, and saw a car stopped directly beside us, travelling in the same direction. In the back, a little girl of about ten wearing a pink tiara appeared to be singing, bouncing up and down in her seat. If Doug edged a little more forward, I would be parallel to the two adults in the front, but I decided now wasn't the time for hesitation or choosiness.

Shouting as loudly as I should have when we were still on the street, I began a plea that might have grown up to be "HELP, THESE MEN ARE KIDNAPPING ME! PLEASE ALERT THE AUTHORITIES AND WHILE WE AWAIT THEIR ARRIVAL, HAVE YOUR PARENTS OR CAREGIVERS INTERCEDE ON MY BEHALF" but only lived long enough to be become "HEL –" before its life was cut tragically short by Cal jabbing his hand into my throat.

My cry became a thin wheeze as my windpipe closed in on itself. Through my gasping panic, I saw the little girl staring at me wide-eyed. I waved at her desperately and she stared for a moment longer before a smile spread across her face. She held up a hand and flopped it about and I realised she was mimicking the useless hand I was unthinkingly flailing in her direction.

Traffic moved again and by the time I saw the adult passenger turn around to see what all the commotion was in the backseat, they were gone.

I clawed at my throat with both hands, good and bad, unable to breathe. I thrashed around, sure I was about to suffocate to death, but then Cal grabbed me by the shoulder, took a second to gaze into my bulging eyes, and shot his hand into my throat again.

Having opened whatever it was he'd shut, Cal sat back and looked out his window while I took huge, greedy breaths that felt amazing even though they hurt.

We got moving again, more quickly now as we left the city centre, and with my breathing under control and the pain in my hand easing off, I tried to gather myself. I needed to get out of this farcical situation before Doug got us out of the city, away from other people, and it became a serious one.

When we stopped at a red light, I looked out my window and straight into the eyes of the same little girl. She giggled and flopped one of her hands at me in our secret club sign.

I took a deep breath then slammed a pre-emptive elbow into Cal's midsection before throwing myself against the window.

"HELP ME! PLEASE, TELL YOUR PARENTS, CALL THE POLICE! I –"

Something happened to where the back of my neck met my spine that I assumed I had Cal to thank for. My entire body went limp, my face pressing against the window while my world became a tunnel with the kid at the other end, giggling and waving.

The front passenger turned around again, eyeing first the little girl and then me. She gave an embarrassed look and mouthed an apology before turning to have stern words with the child about making fun of differently abled people. I tried to scream but my face was sliding uselessly down the glass, they were already moving on, and the tunnel was closing in around me.

Determined to fight, to live, I struggled for consciousness, willed myself away from the light at the other end. It was only when everything went dark that I realised my mistake but by then, I was already gone.

Chapter 20

When I came to, I was being carried along, supported by a body on either side of me while my feet trailed on thick carpet. I recognised Doug's hallway, the narrowness of which meant we were moving almost sideways in an awkward diagonal line of three. I tried to pull away but Doug and Cal tightened their grips and kept going, past Doug's study where we held our meetings, past the small guest bathroom we were given begrudging use of, and deeper into the house than I'd ever been.

Stopping at a closed door, Cal shifted my weight long enough to open it and then I was being dumped into a swivel chair. Immediately, I tried to stand, to run, but none of me was working right and I fell straight to the floor. I heard the chair fall and one of them swear and a smile tugged at my lips even as I blacked out again.

"What are you going to do?" Doug's voice, cutting through the darkness.

"Have a sandwich, maybe a nap. He needs time to come around before we can get started." Cal's voice in response.

I was seated once again, presumably back in the office chair. After my brief return to consciousness on arrival, I had been out for who knows how long, maybe minutes, maybe hours. My hands were bound behind the chair with what felt like tape. My head had lolled back and I left it there, keeping my eyes shut in case opening them cost me what little time I had left.

"I hope you didn't damage him."

Cal said something unintelligible in response.

"What does that mean?" Doug asked.

"My Wing Chun master used to say it. It's Foshan–Cantonese for 'do not strike when you should not but do not be afraid to strike when you should'. If I hadn't put him down in the car then someone would have seen or heard him and called the cops. You want a sandwich?"

"I'll eat when it's over."

"Want me to give him a couple of wake-up slaps?"

"No," Doug said, after some deliberation. "We'll wait, it's better if he's wide awake."

Beginning to feel like I might drown in the blackness behind my eyelids, I opened them a crack, hoping my abductors weren't looking right at me. They stood in the middle of the room, equidistant between me and the open doorway, Doug with his back to me, blocking my view of Cal and his of me. I opened my eyes a little more, letting them adjust, and experimentally tensed my wrists but it did nothing to loosen my bonds. I shifted my feet the slightest fraction, they moved freely.

My instincts told me that if I had a slim hope left of escaping with my life, it was now or never. I flexed my leg muscles to make sure they were more prepared for this attempt than the last. Satisfied, I jumped to my feet and launched myself across the room.

The ergonomic chair kept me bent at a forty-five-degree angle but this suited my purposes fine. Doug only had time to turn and take a stumbling step back, leaving him and Cal next to each other and facing me, before I threw myself at them, turning my body to hit them side-on. My lowered head smashed into Doug's chest while Cal got the brunt of the chair's metal base.

We all went down together, the two of them softening my impact. Doug was pinned beneath me and in headbutting distance, so I gave him plenty of them even though, having never headbutted someone before, I wasn't sure if I was doing it right. Cal was tangled up in my legs and the chair base, but I could feel him starting to untangle himself so I kicked out viciously and repeatedly, could feel these kicks connecting even if I couldn't see to aim them. While they were both grunting and swearing, I was silent and determined.

Eventually, Cal managed to grab my jack-hammering legs long enough to flip me and suddenly I was looking up at the ceiling, the chair's backrest now separating me and Doug. I heaved up and down, using my weight combined with the chair's to pummel Doug.

Somewhat inevitably, my glory was short-lived.

Once he was free and clear, Cal got to his feet and went behind me, grabbing the back of my chair and dragging me off Doug. I managed to slam a parting kick into Doug's groin before Cal tossed me to the floor, safely away from both of them, and hurried back to kneel by his partner.

"Jesus, Doug, are you OK?"

He lay on the ground, folded in two, hands cupping his crotch. He didn't move or respond to Cal. Meanwhile, I was doing my best to get to my feet and make a run for it but on my back, still tied to the chair, I was as helpless as an upended turtle.

"Doug?"

He moaned and moved one of his hands to his head. Cal leant closer, his hands cupping Doug's face, both of them speaking in murmurs too low for me to hear. Cal gave Doug a kiss on the forehead that was as tender as it was discomforting and then turned, eyes burning into mine. He had a large welt on his forehead that looked very much like a shoe imprint, a stream of blood ran freely from one nostril, dropping onto the beige carpet and it served them right for murdering someone in a room with beige carpet.

"HELP! ANYONE! SOMEONE! HELP ME! POLICE!" Between Cal's death stare and my complete inability to move beyond rocking back and forth, I decided that in lieu of escape, rescue was my final hope. "I'M IN DOUG ALLAN'S HOUSE! THEY'RE TRYING TO KILL ME! HELP!"

Cal walked over to the desk by the window, which was unfortunately closed, and picked up a roll of duct tape. He tore off a piece and smacked it across my mouth hard enough to make my teeth crack together. I kept making noise, more out of desperation than hope because between the shut window and shut mouth, nobody was going to hear me.

Cal helped Doug to his feet and walked him out of the room, closing the door behind them and leaving me on the floor where I eventually gave up my muffled shouting.

Between my exertions and the fresh panic taking hold now that all avenues of escape were blocked, I felt dizzy, unable to catch my breath. My chest was heaving, vision blurring, and though I'd never hyper-ventilated, I suspected I was dancing on the edge of it now.

What brought me under control was the realisation that I'd be making things easier for them by passing out. I steadied my breath, taking even measures in and out through my nose, until my heart slowed, and the dizziness faded. Able to think clearly once again and unsure how long I had left, I decided to make my final moments count by having my life flash before my eyes.

Nothing happened.

I tried again.

Still nothing.

Was it too much to ask for some sort of meaningful narrative to comfort me at the end, a sense-making montage of the events that led me to this point?

While I willed and waited, my eyes wandered the room, from the plush reddish-brown leather couch to a framed photo of Doug and Cal with the Eiffel Tower behind them and, even more of an architectural wonder, a shared smile lifting their faces. On the wall nearest to me, tastefully surrounding a large TV, glass-doored shelving held a mixture of knick-knacks and books including a few leather-bound titles that might feasibly have been covered in human skin. On the desk, a statuette of Iron Maiden's Eddie stood victorious atop a mountain of skulls, incongruous next to an expensive-looking crystal lamp that cast a soft, warm glow on Eddie's snarling face and the bloody stains on the carpet nearby.

Hoping to kickstart something so as not to waste any more of my last breaths contemplating the decor, even if this room was at least a warmer, more interesting space than the one out front which I suspected was not Doug's study but rather a holding cell for us cattle and our grubby monthly visits, I tried to think of who would miss me when I was gone. When this didn't trigger anything, I thought instead of who I would miss.

I considered the women on the peripheries of my life like Tara or Sam or Mandy or even the Mexican food truck girl but found too little to miss because I had made them all into dreams or fantasies and you can only miss imaginary beings so much. I thought of Liam and DAPI and felt a twinge, thought of my parents and felt a stronger one. Then I thought of my brother and his stupid, smiling face that I'd never see again and tears stung my eyes and ran down my cheeks.

Finally, my thoughts went to Owen.

I should have felt sad that I would no longer be around to help him and even more sad that this might lead to more death, but my grief for myself loomed larger. I was leaving Owen alone, possibly for eternity if he couldn't fulfil what he was here to do, but what cut me deeper was knowing somebody would find the bag hidden in my bedroom closet and I'd go from being a murder victim or a missing person to a horror story, one the police and the media would tell my family and the world. My boss Heather would get interviewed by TV news, awkwardly fixing her hair and neck scarf while telling them I was a quiet guy, kept myself to myself, maybe a little off but she had no idea, just your classic serial killer eulogy.

I called out to Owen in my mind, begging him to appear and pick me up, man and chair, and use me to bludgeon Doug and Cal to death. I called out to Jo as well but even if I managed to activate some psychic sibling Bluetooth, he'd never make it back from Thigh-land in time to save me or hear me apologise for being such a terrible excuse for a big brother.

I squirmed and writhed with renewed effort, straining my wrists against the tape, kicking my legs.

The door flew open and Cal stormed in.

Once again, he snatched up the roll of duct tape and then seized my flailing legs, running loop after loop of tape around them until they were stuck fast to the chair. Grabbing me under my arms, he hefted me up until the chair was upright on its wheels.

He had washed up and changed his clothes, still all black everything, and other than a few scrapes on his face and arms, didn't look near as damaged as I would have liked. Even the shoe-shaped welt on his forehead was fading away.

"All clear."

Doug's reappearance was much more satisfying. He had also changed, seemed to actually have showered. One of his eyes was swollen and purpling and a plaster was stuck across his nose, a crimson-stained tissue blooming from one nostril. His lower lip hung low and raw, giving him a vaguely surprised appearance.

He walked in with his legs far apart, as if headed for a showdown after a long day spent riding the range but instead of a six shooter, he was armed with a frozen steak held against his inner thigh. I would have recommended a bag of peas instead, more manoeuvrability.

Watching Doug lower himself gingerly onto the leather couch, I couldn't help wishing Owen was there to see my handiwork. For a man without a history of violence, more experienced in taking punches than giving them, I fought the good fight at the finish, had not gone as gentle as expected.

Cal took hold of my shoulders. I bucked in the chair, trying to turn my head to see what he was up to. I waited to feel something cold and sharp insert itself somewhere unwanted, recalling vividly Owen describing the sensation of drowning in his own blood.

"Ready?" Doug asked hoarsely, looking past me at Cal, who must have signalled his assent.

"Alexa, lights out."

The room went dark at the exact same moment Cal spun me around.

Behind my gag, I screamed.

Chapter 21

Massive, windowless walls, covered in peeling grey paint that glistened with dampness, loomed from a floor so pocked and spongey it might have been natural rather than man-made to a ceiling thick with dust-sodden lengths of cobweb that hung like seaweed suspended from an upside-down sea. Cold white beams coming from the spotlights that stood in the corners of the cavernous space provided just enough light to take it all in.

I stopped screaming, not because I was any less frightened, but because something popped in my throat and made it hurt too much to keep going.

A figure, small with distance, crouched by the far wall. There was something about the way they held themself, how they moved, the casualness with which they rifled through their duffle bag in this bleak cave most people would have been rushing to escape from. Impossibly, and despite my unfamiliarity with this place, I felt a strange certainty it was me over there, that I was somehow looking at myself.

They straightened and began to walk through the hall, coming closer, holding something in their outstretched hand. I bit down hard on my lip, bracing for the sight of my own face and wondering what that might mean.

As the figure drew nearer still, it was bathed in one of the criss-crossing beams of light. Even from a distance, I recognised Chris Collins from DAPI's archives, all slouch and unfashionably tousled hair.

His lips were moving as he approached and though I couldn't hear him, I could see the recorder in his hand, could guess what he was saying.

"Are you there? Do you want to talk to me? You can talk into this box."

He stopped suddenly, midstride and midsentence, looking from side to side before doing a full three-sixty, the recorder still held out. When he turned back to me, his brow was furrowed, head cocked. He stayed this way for maybe half a minute before giving a visible shrug and continuing on.

Everything went dark again.

I didn't think I could be more terrified than I already was but Doug and Cal showing me video footage of Chris Collins, presumably at some investigation, certainly did the trick.

Would the next clip show them murdering him? Would there be a post-credits sting featuring his corpse being thrown from a certain overpass?

I had told myself I was being silly when I entertained the notion that Doug and Cal were involved in the death of Chris Collins. Now, there didn't seem anything silly about the idea that the last thing Chris saw, the last thing I would see, was their passive faces from the other side of a camera while they performed their last tests or experiments or whatever they called killing people for kicks. I imagined them playing back the moment of my expiry over and over, trying to see any visible sign of something leaving or entering my body.

The screen came back to life and I began to shake uncontrollably, wished I was brave enough to shut my eyes.

Chris was back in his original position by the far wall, but the footage had been altered.

The playback was slowed to about half-speed and the colours were inverted and strange; the grey walls were now a bleached, headache-inducing red, the muddy-coloured floor and ceiling a harsh yellow while the thick cobweb waves floating from the ceiling had taken on the clotted texture of sour milk. The spotlights were black circles sending out beams that started as inky purple but, as they stretched to their furthest points, faded to a sickly hue that brought to mind a bad case of pink eye.

Chris Collins had become a human-shaped figure of uneven whites and greys, like he was made of static. Once again but slower now, he stood and walked toward the camera. Despite whatever they'd done to the footage, I could still make out his face once he reached the first beam of violet light, even if his features were now almost pixelated, could still make out his lips moving as he asked his questions, even if they looked like lead slugs.

The clip paused.

Cal's hand reached out and tapped the screen, at a point toward the rear of the hall, close to where Chris had started. When he took his finger away, it left a white smudge.

The clip resumed, Chris once again advancing toward the camera.

The smudge began moving too, which meant it was something recorded on the footage itself rather than smeared on the screen by Cal, though I couldn't have said for sure whether or not it had been there before.

The round shape, bobbing in mid-air, was easy to spot as it went after Chris, a brilliant white standing out amongst the washed out, degraded colours around it.

Despite my terror, despite everything, I rolled my eyes.

Here, at the end of my days, a fucking orb video.

The smudge, which I refused to think of as an orb even if it was vaguely spherical, overtook Chris and then stopped directly before him a split-second before he halted, once again acting out the pantomime of a man who had seen or heard something inexplicable.

After offering a slow-motion shrug, he continued forward, the smudge moving aside as he did so before circling him like a fat, frenetic firefly.

Darkness again.

I barely had time to catch my breath before Chris Collins was staring me right in the eye, causing me to jump as much as the layers of tape attaching me to the chair allowed.

The location had changed, the speed and colour were back to normal, and Chris's face filled the screen.

Up close, I could see the same shock of hair I'd seen in every image of him, short but unruly, like he had tried brushing, gelling, or flattening it but had given up on everything halfway through. He had the same indoorsman pallor as me, a couple of shades above translucent, with large greyish-blue eyes that gave off a vulnerability verging on wounded.

"Investigator Christopher Collins is participating in this interview to follow up on our most recent investigation, conducted at the Acheron River

Customs House."

That made sense, the huge space I had seen, glistening with moisture, would have housed whatever goods people transported on the river before the road, rail, and air became more efficient means of moving freight inland. The city's seaport was a bustling hub but the tumbled down remains of the Acheron River docks were something I'd only ever glimpsed from afar, sitting forlorn and forgotten on the other side of a high fence that surrounded the place.

Chris looked awkward, like he was posing for an ID photo and wasn't sure whether to smile or look serious. It was hard to tell at such a close angle, but I was pretty sure he was in the front room where we normally held our meetings.

"Describe your role in the investigation," Doug prompted, in a tone that encouraged Chris to go with serious.

"Um...general investigator with special responsibility for the main goods depot hall," he replied, sounding both proud and embarrassed.

They went back and forth for a while but it was less an interview and more Chris reconfirming statements Doug made about his activities and movements during the investigation. It felt redundant and Chris seemed to know it but probably put it down to Doug being Doug, as I would have.

When he stood briefly to retrieve a bottle of water, I saw he was wearing a *Changeling* t-shirt featuring the cobweb-covered wheelchair from the movie and given my situation, I was unsure if the twinge of jealousy I felt over the dead man's tee was proof of a nervous breakdown or my general lack of common sense.

"So, to summarise, nothing noteworthy or unusual became apparent during your investigation of the customs house, either in any general areas of the site or in your special area of responsibility, the depot hall."

Before answering, or rather echoing Doug, Chris's gaze flicked to one side, and when he responded an instant later, he was doing a poor job of stifling a grin.

"No, nothing to report."

The next clip followed without any pause this time.

The colours were all wrong and the speed was halved, just like the doctored clip from the customs house.

Because of the distortion, it took me a moment to understand that I was seeing the same interview I had just watched but from further away, the angle high and wide. Two grey, static-blurred figures sat in what was definitely Doug's front room. I knew one was Chris and the other, sitting opposite him, beside a tripod mounted camera aimed at his subject, was Doug.

"So, to summarise…"

Doug's voice was now a deep, languid drone that turned his "so" into "sooooo".

Cal's hand emerged from the darkness to tap the screen again, in case I had missed the white smudge hovering by the window. I hadn't.

Doug finished speaking.

This time, Chris's slight hesitation before responding, his sideways glance and suppressed grin, became a drawn-out silence in which the smudge moved from the window to just by Doug's shoulder, lining up pretty perfectly to where Chris's eyes had flicked in the close shot.

If my gag were removed just then, it's likely that instead of making another attempt to scream for help, I would have started asking questions. I was under no illusion video footage could be implicitly trusted, especially footage that had clearly been altered, but it certainly looked like Chris was interacting with the smudge, seemed to have shared a joke with it when not so long before, in the customs house, he had barely sensed it.

Another clip.

An unaltered view of a studio apartment's interior and judging by the Casper sticker on the closed laptop and the huge black and white poster on the door of famed paranormal investigator Loyd Auerbach, his sunglasses and scalp gleaming, I could guess whose.

I had read Auerbach's *ESP, Hauntings, And Poltergeists: A Parapsychologist's Handbook*, I don't think anyone with a digital recorder, an EMF reader and a dream hasn't, and recognised the quote that ran across the top and bottom of the poster.

"Faith is belief without proof. Faith is fine, but don't call it science."

The door opened and Chris entered alone, in mid-conversation.

The steep angle of the shot meant the camera must have been placed high and, much like the one used for the wide shot of Chris's interview, I suspected its subject was unaware of its presence. This suspicion was reinforced by the fact that the lens was partially obscured, as if hidden behind something on a high shelf.

"And then he sets fire to the mummy, looks up at the stars, and dies. It's amazing." He went to a beaten-up fridge that sat between the bed and open bathroom door in the cramped studio. He grabbed a Coke and took a large swig before throwing himself down on a two-seater couch pushed against the foot of the bed. "Yeah, I think he's definitely meant to be the real Elvis but I think black JFK isn't really JFK."

The sinking feeling I'd had since he shared the sly little aside in Doug's front room sped up and crashed to rock bottom. I knew he wasn't on a call or talking to himself because I knew he wasn't really alone, knew the empty space between him and his apartment door, to which he was addressing his cinematic critique of *Bubba Ho-Tep*, was not really empty.

"Just because you think it's stupid doesn't make it so."

Silence.

"Well, what's your favourite movie then?"

Another moment's silence and then Chris issued a standard geek-issue snort of derision.

"Adrian! Adrian!" He exclaimed in slurred Stallonean, pumping a fist in the air. "Each to their own, I guess, but I gotta say, that's a real middle-aged-hetero-white guy pick."

A new clip.

The camera angle didn't change, the lighting was the same, and the transition was so quick it looked like a bit of video-edited magic that Chris was no longer on the couch but was instead walking through the door again. This time though, his clothing had changed, and he wasn't talking.

He slammed the door and perched on the edge of the couch for an instant before jumping up again. He took his phone out of his pocket and held it to his ear, lowered it, put it back to his ear, lowered it again. If he wasn't so clearly distressed, it would have been funny.

The next time he brought up the phone, he threw it against the wall. It rebounded harmlessly so he threw it again and harder before stamping on it for good measure.

When he sat on the couch this time he stayed there, holding his head in his hands and I heard his muffled sobs, saw dark stains forming on his t-shirt where tears were landing. After a while, he took his hands away, wiping his face with the front of his shirt.

"Owen? Owen, are you here? Please, I need you!"

Back to the start and Chris's static-blur alter-ego walked in, slowly now, and when the door finally slammed home, it sounded like an explosion.

The Auerbach poster was yellow and purple instead of black and white, the computer Casper now crimson, as if he had been mistaken for a rag and used to mop up blood. As Chris moved toward the couch, the smudge came through the closed door behind him. Compared to poor Casper, the smudge glowed an irreproachable white.

I needed this procession of clips to stop so I could think, so I could speak and be understood and made to understand. My thoughts felt like the colours on the screen in front of me, over-saturated and inside out. I yelled as best I could with my lips taped together.

"It's almost over," Doug said from behind me.

When Chris threw his phone at the wall, the smudge dodged it, but I knew he hadn't been aiming at it. He thought he was alone because the smudge that was an orb that was Owen *fucking* Hoath wanted him to think that.

As Chris cried into his hands, his tears steadily and inexorably spreading in a pool of not-quite-white on his chest, I looked at bloody Casper, the friendliest ghost we know, and recalled a line from the 90's movie, less clever than Auerbach's quote but more fitting just now. *"All I want's a friend".*

"Owen? Owen, are you here? Please, I need you!"

What had been painful to hear before was heartbreaking now; every pleading syllable dragged out to breaking point while the thing that I could now only think of as Owen looked on and did nothing.

The scene changed and we were outside, at night.

I tried to refocus but I felt punch-drunk, as if each clip was doing me damage, and I was remotely aware I was crying again. My tears weren't for me this time, they were for Chris, who stood alone on a train platform, hugging himself against a strong but blustery wind that would stop entirely only to kick up again fiercer each time, sending everything movable in the frame leaning, flapping, or swinging to the left.

"Last one," Doug said, with a hint of apology.

The camera was right across the tracks from Chris but the dark, swaying shapes crowding the edges of the shot were a giveaway that the people behind it had got this close to their subject unseen thanks to some camouflaging bush or tree.

"I'm so scared, I don't think –"

The wind picked up and snatched away the last of Chris's sentence.

The audio was patchy, full of background noise, which meant they had a directional microphone aimed at him, a device which never worked as well in real life as it did elsewhere, especially not on a night like this with wind swirling around its parabolic bowl.

"But what if it's *not* right, just because you think it is doesn't make it so. Being dead doesn't make you all-knowing."

Chris's voice was weak and ragged and it wasn't all down to the microphone or the weather. He stared at where I was sure Owen's infuriatingly implacable face was throwing his infuriatingly implacable morals at him. Owen, who told me he'd failed to contact anyone before me. Owen, who told me he'd been missing for the year between his death and return but had instead been with Chris Collins in that time, including the night I was seeing now, one I was sadly sure was Chris's last.

"I'm sorry, I *can't*," Chris said, between heaving breaths. "I need to go home. I need more time to –"

The clip switched to the altered version of itself that I couldn't help but think of as "*Filmed in Illusion-O*" like the cheesy William Castle gimmick from the original 13 *Ghosts* movie which allowed the audience to see the ghosts when they put on the "*Special Ghost Viewers*" except instead of cardboard and blue and red cellophane, Doug and Cal had made theirs from a mixture of playback speed, contrast and colouration.

Rather than go back to the beginning, this clip simply played on.

Owen, in his white, spherical form was a few feet away but as Chris spoke, he closed the distance so quickly that even at half-speed, it was fast. He got so close that a glowing edge of white bled into Chris's chest and then Chris's head snapped back in slow-motion, giving me unpleasant shades of *Rocky*.

"It doesn't matter," Chris said as he staggered back, his voice deep and distorted. "Hit me all you want. Doesn't make you less dead or more right."

Owen closed the distance once more but did not hit him again after all. Chris laughed but even if it had been at normal speed, there would have been no humour in it.

"No, you won't. I'm going to talk to the rest of the guys in DAPI like I should have all along. I'll tell the cops. I don't care what they think about me."

A roar came from the TV's speakers, ferocious enough to swallow the keening wind and the scraping branches and Chris's defiance like they were nothing. For a second, I thought I was hearing the manifestation of Owen's fury but then the train pulled in, blocking the view.

When it rolled away, the platform was empty of man and ghost.

The picture and playback speed returned to normal while the camera and the men with it broke cover and raced across the tracks. For the first time in my life, even if it was recorded rather than live, I heard Douglas J. Allan utter the word "*fuck*" and then the audio cut out completely, leaving the footage to play on in silence.

The Doug that once was appeared on camera, climbing awkwardly onto the platform before turning to offer his hand. His eyes were wide and a pair of headphones rested haphazardly on his ears, the cord hanging uselessly, the mike presumably abandoned in the rush.

Cal got himself and the camera onto the platform in one clean movement without taking Doug's hand and ran down the exit ramp, the camera swinging about wildly. Parked cars, sparse moving headlights, a few pedestrians but no Chris.

Back up the ramp and onto the platform to join Doug, who was watching the train recede from view, the last of its light shrinking to something as small as an orb before vanishing completely.

Doug turned to the camera, his face contorted in panic, a question on his lips.

The screen went dark and the lights snapped back on but neither of these things made me jump because I didn't have enough surprise left in me.

I had believed all along that I was the one in the know, about Owen Hoath, about everything, but it turned out that the truth wasn't just beyond my reach, it was out of sight.

Chapter 22

I cradled the mug in my hands, enjoying the warmth, enjoying anything that involved being alive considering it wasn't that long since I thought all my lasts (beer, sandwich, kiss, coffee) had passed me by, dim and unremarked upon. If I had less to think about, I might have promised myself that from now on I would live, laugh, and love and do whatever else aspirational home décor instructed but as it was, with my thoughts grinding and clanking, the best I could do was savour the coffee that a part of me still worried might be poisoned.

Other than a few tender spots, some chafing, and a blood-ruined shirt, I'd escaped unscathed compared to Doug who, on the couch opposite me, drank his coffee in methodical sips while massaging his throat and running his fingers over his various cuts and contusions. One of his eyes was bruised and swollen and he paid particular attention to this, experimentally parting the lids with his fingers. Beside him, Cal stared past me, having drained his mug in a few swallows. Apart from the barely perceptible bruise on his forehead, he didn't look much worse for wear.

I had been to the guest bathroom to clean myself up. No-one had followed me to stand guard and I had returned willingly to sit on the seat I was previously taped to which meant that technically, the kidnapping portion of our evening was over.

I took another drink and cleared my throat.

"Have you been following me? Are there cameras in my apartment?"

"Yes, we have been following you," Doug replied. "And no, there are no cameras in your apartment."

I stared, waiting for him to elaborate but he just kept taking his injured bird sips, eyeing me reproachfully when his self-examination touched on a particularly sore spot.

"I thought you were about to murder me," I snapped, feeling pretty reproachful myself.

Cal groaned and shook his head, still hundred-yard staring over my shoulder.

"Hey, I was beaten up and kidnapped and bound and gagged. What the fuck was I supposed to think?"

"We tried to speak to you outside your office, but you were making a scene and we couldn't risk you getting away," Doug said, sounding more upset about me making a scene than almost getting away.

"You have my email, my phone number."

This time they both shook their heads, Doug wincing when he remembered he shouldn't have.

"We had to get you alone, really alone and we didn't think we'd get more than one chance to do it without Owen finding out," Doug said. "Maybe our haste made us heavy-handed –"

"Maybe?"

"...but we're trying to help you."

"Like you two helped Chris?"

Cal's hands were on his knees and now the knuckles whitened as he gripped tighter. Amongst the shades of yellow and purple on his face, Doug blushed.

"Wil, you don't know everything, neither do we. Listen to our side of it. Then, if you're willing, tell us yours."

I let the moment drag out, indecision rather than an attempt to build suspense.

"Did you know anything about what you just saw in those clips?" Doug asked, more insistently. "About your supposed friend and Chris Collins?"

"No, Owen said..." I stopped myself from saying "*Owen said I was his first*" because that was just too tragic. "Owen said he hadn't been able to make contact with anyone else."

"Well then, if you're worried that speaking with us means breaking his trust, know he's already broken yours. If you're worried about betraying him, know that's exactly how he wants you to feel." Doug's voice strained from injury rather than emotion. "He's done everything he can to isolate and control you and whatever the 'why' is behind that, it can't be good. I don't know what or who this Owen really is but he's not your friend, any more than he was Chris's."

Another moment passed before I made the decision that really wasn't my decision at all. I needed to know everything they knew; it was too dangerous not to.

"I'll listen. But first, just for curiosity's sake, what age are you, Cal?"

His brow knitted and then smoothed again before he answered.

"Twenty-seven."

I laughed, which felt weird but good. Fucking Owen. Cal glared in confusion which was all the reason I needed not to explain myself.

"Hey, before you start, can I grab my phone to record this?"

"This isn't your pet project or some bullshit investigation. Lives are at stake," Cal said, as flatly and undramatically as it's possible to say, 'lives are at stake'.

Reeling from being in the presence of two consecutive sentences from him, I held up my free hand in surrender and used the other to tip my mug towards Doug who cleared his throat, straightened the pleats in his jeans, and began.

"Chris Collins joined DAPI a month after Cal and I started it, before Stuart or anyone else. He was about your age and his role was much the same, general investigator, and like you, he was very capable."

I held back from asking him to repeat what had sounded suspiciously like a compliment.

"That first clip, from the customs house, was recorded three months before Chris died. None of us noticed anything during the investigation but as you saw, Chris in fact did, if only for a moment. Maybe he thought it was a fly or gust of wind, we don't know, and he never mentioned it.

"As part of our post-investigation process, Cal selects image, video, and sound files from team member uploads and subjects them to various distortions, enhancements and filters. The original raw data is always saved and clearly labelled," he added hurriedly, lest I condemn them as reckless corruptors of data.

"In the days following the customs house, Cal began his usual process and while trialling the set of modifications you just saw, he found the orb."

I winced but what could I say, an orb was an orb, chalk one up for the other guys.

"It only shows up on recordings if those very specific modifications are applied. If we change the speed by half a second, shift the white balance, even adjust the contrast, it disappears. It's a fluke Cal came across it all."

Cal started to pick at his armrest, which I guessed was his equivalent of saying "gee whiz".

"Once Cal found it in the footage from the depot hall, we went back through the rest of that night, using Cal's filter. It was with Chris from when we started recording until we stopped and in between, despite other investigators being nearby, it never ventured far from him. Next, we looked at footage from the prior month's investigation at Buxley Hall –"

"The old military academy out near the airport? That place looks crazy, what did –"

I cut myself off before they had to. Not the time to geek out. I took a breath and gestured for Doug to continue.

"The orb showed up in the Buxley Hall footage too. For most of the night, it moved back and forth amongst the team but at the end of the footage, not long before we left, it began to focus on Chris."

"He must have reacted to it," I said. "Something too small for you to catch on a recording."

"That's what we assumed."

A sharp intake of breath, a widening of the eyes. Some small sign telling Owen that Chris was his guy.

"We looked back over earlier investigations but there was no orb, so it seems Buxley Hall was where it began."

"While you were digging through all this footage, which I'm assuming would have taken days, did you bother to fill Chris in?" I already knew the answer, knew I was meant to be letting them have their say, but Chris Collins wasn't around to be angry on his own behalf.

"Cal insisted we should but I felt that if we did, if we disturbed the course of things, the phenomena might stop."

"The phenomena for which you at least had a second-row seat."

Another barb for Chris's sake but even as I spoke, I questioned what I'd do in the same circumstances.

"Correct," Doug said plainly. "As the footage from the customs house showed, in the month since Buxley Hall, Chris was reacting to the anomaly more strongly and I felt it was only a matter of time before he became fully aware. I was worried that when that happened, if he knew that we knew, he might leave DAPI in order to keep it to himself rather than share it with us. Of course, we should have told him. Even if he tried to exclude us at first, the chances of him duplicating Cal's footage were almost nil so he would have come back to us eventually, he would have wanted to be able to record what was happening. I was stubborn and impatient."

"You were a dick." Cal said, managing to sound a little human himself. "We both were."

"We arranged the one-on-one with him here because I wanted close up footage and you can see that in the week between the customs house and that interview, he had already become completely aware of the presence. If he, or it for that matter, had known what we knew I'm sure they would have been more discreet, or not come at all.

"I know the curator at the Treasury building and was able to arrange an investigation there at short notice so we could keep studying Chris but when I sent out the usual group email, he replied to say he was leaving DAPI, for personal reasons. I was angry but also relieved because his quitting made it even easier for me to see him as a stubborn research subject instead of a person. That's when I suggested following him with our cameras and that's when Cal took it upon himself to contact Chris, since he could see I had no intention of doing so."

We both looked at Cal who took a deep, aggravated breath before making his contribution in staccato bursts, as if prolonged verbalisation caused him pain.

"Tried calling Chris, he wouldn't answer. Emailed him, told him we knew he was experiencing something, had footage he'd be interested in. Waited two days. No reply. Convinced myself I tried to do the right thing, which was bullshit. I could have pushed it, doorstepped him, gone to his work. I didn't. We were as bad as each other, no matter what he says," he concluded, jerking his head sideways at Doug who waited a moment to make sure he was done before picking up the story again.

"We agreed to treat Chris as the subject of our investigation and to approach him again with an offer to collaborate once we had enough material gathered to publish our findings."

To Doug's credit, he didn't try to make it sound like anything other than the excuse it had been. Cal muttered something darkly that might have been "co-authors".

"We started following him but we both work full-time so couldn't devote ourselves to it as much as we would have liked. We spent evenings in my car, watching his apartment building but he didn't venture out much. His place was ground floor and after a week of seeing very little, we decided to break in and plant a miked camera so we could get clean, close-up AV." Doug mentioned their decision to commit this crime without any noticeable change in tone. "One night, we filmed him leaving his apartment and once we checked the footage and saw that the orb had left with him, we took our chance. I kept watch while Cal broke in through a back window, leaving a ball amongst the broken glass to make it look like an accident. I stole that from an episode of *Father Dowling Mysteries*," he added, a little bashfully.

Once that was set up, they stopped following him and concentrated on the feed from his apartment.

"Did you ever manage to get audio of Owen?"

"No, we could never get anything, no matter what we tried on the audio we captured, even when it was clear Chris was in conversation with him."

"Pitch shift? High-pass filter?"

"Obviously," Cal said, eyeballing me.

"'It seemed like they had a friendly relationship," Doug said, moving us swiftly on. "Unfortunately, by the time we monitored the apartment –"

"Bugged," Cal interjected. "We bugged his apartment."

"By then, there wasn't much left in the way of introduction or exposition, not on Chris's side of the conversation anyway. The most we learned was that the entity calling itself Owen claimed to be the spirit of a deceased person, one who had apparently lived in relatively modern times and probably been military or law enforcement. Chris had agreed to do something for this Owen that worried him greatly but whenever this worry broke into outright panic, Owen seemed able to calm him down and keep him on track."

"He's good at that," I said, but when Doug raised an eyebrow, I shooed him on.

"Once Owen had reassured him, Chris was always eager to move on to other topics rather than dwell on whatever it was he was so scared of, which was frustrating, but we still experienced some interesting interactions. Chris conducted quite a few interviews with Owen about the afterlife and the nature of his non-corporeal state. At one point he even ran through Moody's identifiers with him. Apart from a few comments Chris made, we couldn't hear the answers, but it was fascinating just the same."

Raymond Moody's 1975 book *Life After Life* collected individual accounts of Near-Death Experiences from across North America and listed a startling number of common elements, referred to as identifiers, including white light, review of your life, and out of body travel. Moody argued these commonalities showed that what had been dismissed as stress-induced hallucinations were something much more, perhaps even proof of an afterlife that these NDE-survivors had all shared a peek at. Doug and Cal watched Chris run through these identifiers with someone with full death experience, forget *near*, the answers just out of their reach.

"Did you see Chris taking any recordings of his own?"

"Some but he'd all but given up by the time we were watching his apartment. He did write everything down though, every interview, every conversation. He was always taking notes."

"What happened to them?"

"His parents cleared out his apartment. They might have thrown them away, we don't know."

"You never tried to get them?"

Doug's gaze drifted down to the floor while Cal's fell on me.

"I said I'd leave him if he went after Chris's notes," Cal said. "We'd already stood back and watched him die, we didn't deserve to benefit."

"You were right," Doug said. "Once some time had passed, I saw that." He was still studying the carpet but was now frowning at the blood stains on it, no doubt running through a mental checklist of his cleaning supplies. Having put together some kind of housekeeping plan of attack, he refocused.

"Eventually those interviews tapered off and their discussions became shorter, less frequent, and more sullen on Chris's part. All of which made it even harder for us to follow what was going on. Whatever Chris had agreed to was obviously dangerous, for himself and maybe others and if he was caught, he expected to be arrested. As their plans progressed, it got to the stage where Owen was clearly having difficulty calming him and as you saw in the last footage from his apartment, Chris was on the verge of a breakdown. We –"

He started coughing, went to take a drink of his coffee but found his mug empty. He stood and limped for the door, getting out the word "water" between hoarse splutters, leaving Cal and I behind in a silence so uncomfortable that I flailed at the first bit of conversation that floated to mind.

"So, what do you do for a living?"

I'd always assumed Cal was in high school or college or had been kicked out of one or the other so when Doug said they both worked full-time, my curiosity was peaked.

"Travel agent," he answered, after scowling at me for so long I assumed I wasn't getting an answer.

I let this sink in. My first guess had been S&M club DJ, so this was unexpected.

"Any good deals for Thailand?"

Before Cal could provide travel advice, or tell me to go fuck myself, Doug returned with glass of water.

"Given Chris's increasingly erratic state, we discussed intervening before he hurt himself or anyone else..."

"Before he did some stupid shit he couldn't take back," Cal clarified.

"...and we did consider it very seriously," Doug said wistfully, clearly wishing they had done more than just consider. "Now the connection had been made between them, it seemed Owen could choose to hide his presence from Chris at will and was spending more and more time watching him instead of interacting, except when he really got out of control and needed talking down. That was cause for concern but..."

And that "but" was so heavy I almost heard it drop to the floor.

"...we were still getting footage, were hopeful of more, hopeful of finally cracking the audio side of things if we had enough time and material to work with. Also, knowing Chris, it was hard to believe he'd ever harm anyone. He was the definition of a gentle soul."

"All the more reason he could have used your help," I said, not meaning it spitefully, only wishing they had heeded their better angels instead of leaving Chris with his worst one.

"Instead of helping, we escalated our efforts. Chris had been leaving the apartment more frequently, most likely scouting for whatever it was he was building up to. The camera in his apartment died not long after the footage you saw of him destroying his phone but regardless, by then we'd decided to start following him again, had both booked time off work to do so. We finished our workweek that Friday evening and drove to Chris's street. It was just after midnight when he walked outside and even under the streetlights you could see he was as pale as a...he was very pale. We followed him to the train and..."

"You saw what happened next," Cal said, briefly squeezing Doug's hand in his own, a signal I took to mean he would carry the load the last little way. Doug obviously read it the same because he cast Cal a grateful look before sitting back to sip on his water.

"By the time we got back to the car, the train was long gone. We had no idea which stop he was headed for," Cal said. "Drove back to his street and parked, nothing else we could think to do. He didn't come back that night, or the next morning. Didn't have a phone to try calling. Kept watch through the weekend. Still no Chris. Then it was Monday morning. News comes on the radio. Roadwork crew has shown up at the closed off underpass beneath the train stop at Stanway and found a body. Stanway is two stops from where we lost Chris. Neither of us said anything, knew it had to be him. He'd been lying there all weekend."

"What did you do next?"

"Drove home, caught up on a weekend's worth of sleep."

"You didn't tell anyone? You were the only ones who knew why he killed himself. If he did kill himself."

Maybe Chris *had* jumped, unable to cope with what Owen demanded of him.

But, what if Owen's inability to stay on a moving vehicle was another deception, one designed to fool me into thinking I could get away from him anytime I wanted? Then he could have been with Chris on that train platform. Worse again, if his need to hoof it everywhere was an outright lie and he could ghost-port anywhere he wanted at the speed of thought, then he might have got there first, been waiting for Chris.

Maybe he had hit him again in anger, they had struggled, and there had been an accident.

Maybe it had been no accident, not if Owen decided Chris was about to become an unmanageable problem, an obstacle instead of the way.

My head churned with the mix of too much information and none at all.

"What we knew didn't change anything."

I was too worked up to reply to Cal, too sad to argue, too angry to cry.

Amidst the churn, the only truth solid enough to hang on to was that Chris Collins, a young man with wounded eyes and a gentle soul, who loved the same movies I loved, who dreamed the same ghostly dreams I dreamed, had ended his twenty odd years surrounded by dead machinery and red lights on a shutdown street as broken and abandoned as him.

Chapter 23

"What about Owen" I asked, after giving myself a moment. "Did you try contacting him yourselves?"

"Whatever happened to Chris, this Owen played some part in it and frankly, we didn't want the same happening to us. We didn't attempt to contact him, if anything, we were terrified of him coming after us, whether to recruit us or punish us for spying on him."

"But surely if Owen knew you were watching them, he would have told Chris, had him take steps?"

"When more and more of their conversations began taking place out of the apartment, we suspected Owen had found us out," Doug replied. "Recent events, by which I mean how hard he worked to isolate you and hide his return from us, seem to confirm this. But we don't think he ever told Chris, perhaps because Chris was already on the verge of a nervous breakdown and Owen thought finding out that we were watching him would break him completely or possibly he was worried that if Chris knew we were still involved somehow, he might change his mind about speaking with us, reach out for support, and this might lead to us convincing him not to go along with Owen."

The three of us shared a look that said 'if only'.

"We kept cameras running here in the house for months after Chris died, but never found a trace of Owen, or had any sense of him trying to get through to us. Of course, even if he had, it likely wouldn't have worked since we don't seem to have the same wiring as you and Chris," he said, sounding somehow both jealous and grateful. "We kept on running Cal's filter on DAPI footage, in case Owen tried to pick off another team member, but despite him doing just that with you, we've never caught him on camera again."

"What about the old Community First bank in Westbay a few months back? That was when he first tried getting through to me."

Doug shook his battered head as gingerly as he could while Cal contented himself with eyeing me like I was the slowest kid on the special bus. Neither said anything, they didn't have to.

Despite everything I had learned, I was still sticking to Owen's story.

He never would have gone anywhere near their cameras. He would have watched DAPI from a safe distance and worked on each of us at home, at work, anywhere Doug and Cal weren't, until he got the reaction he wanted and found his newest partner.

"When did Liam call you guys to tell you what I'd told him...about you two?"

Here, I felt my cheeks warm with well-earned shame.

"Friday morning."

I called Liam on Thursday. Which meant he'd taken a day to consider what I dumped in his lap before doing something I was too cowardly to do and calling Doug to give him a chance to explain. My cheeks felt another surge of heat at the realisation that Owen had bet on my unwillingness to do this, had counted on my cowardice.

After answering Liam's call, it had taken Doug five minutes to understand what they were being accused of and another five to find out where the accusations came from. He didn't bother to explain himself after this, had simply hung up, so there was a good chance Liam had taken this as an admission of guilt and gone on to tell the rest of the group what he thought he knew.

"I'll call the others," I said. "I'll tell them I was wrong or I'm a liar or whatever, otherwise there's no more DAPI."

I had already accepted this loss for myself, even if I had essentially been fooled into quitting, but whatever Doug and Cal had done in the past, they didn't deserve to lose DAPI because of me parroting Owen's lies.

"Wil, we'll worry about DAPI down the line," Doug said. "There's more important things to worry about right now."

His tone was serious and pragmatic and still couldn't mask his disappointment.

After Doug told Cal about Liam's phone call, they discussed visiting my apartment and demanding an explanation, then they discussed it further and Cal suggested skipping the explanation and proceeding directly to a beating.

Thankfully for me, they kept discussing, asking each other how I had discovered the real nature of their relationship, why I would twist it to make it seem criminal, and how I could know about the experiments Liam accused them of conducting with the group.

"You really have been pimping us out to the other side?"

"We did try something like that, long before you joined," Doug replied, without a hint of regret. "Nothing came of it, so we gave up on the idea."

Once they decided there was no reasonable explanation for how I knew what I knew, they landed on the unreasonable one.

They rechecked footage of me from past investigations but still finding no trace of Owen, they allowed themselves the hope that their fears were unfounded.

"...that you were just a fucking prick and I could beat the shit out of you," Cal chipped in.

But if past experience had taught them anything, it was caution.

They found a cheap and cheerless apartment being Airbnb'd in one of the buildings across from mine. On Saturday, they checked in, set up their equipment, and spent hours watching me pace around my apartment while I waited for Owen's return, my open windows and blinds allowing them a good view.

Hours passed, night fell, and their soaring sense of relief was punctured as they watched me move to my window to talk to nobody.

Cal had been playing back samples of footage throughout their stakeout using his filter. When he did it this time, I was no longer talking to nobody and the familiar white ball of light buzzing back at them from their computer screen confirmed the worst.

By the time they realised I had left my apartment, off on my journey to Bill Hanover's, it was too late to follow. They witnessed my return hours later with a mixture of gratitude that I had lived to return and concern at my condition which included my *almost* all black I've-been-up-to-something ensemble, a plastic sack I was clutching like a baby, and my general shambling, footwear-removing disorientation.

They extended their Airbnb stay to continue their vigil, but only caught glimpses of me on Sunday while I barricaded myself in my apartment, melting peas on my face. They couldn't risk popping over for coffee and a chat in case Owen saw them. They still didn't know what to do but shared a mutual understanding that getting to me without Owen finding out seemed like an eminently sensible course of action. If indeed this latest ball of trouble to bounce into their lives was in fact Owen, Chris's Owen, and not some new player.

Their decision to stay away from my apartment was validated late last night when they caught the orb entering my apartment through my bedroom window.

"Last night? As in Sunday night...like today *is* Monday, right?"

I wasn't being rhetorical, I was genuinely all over the map, or calendar, or whatever.

Cal did the nodding for them both and I tried to compute that today was only Monday and yesterday was Sunday and it had been less than forty-eight hours since I'd broken into Hanover's house and not even a week since I came face to face with Owen in the library toilets.

"Wait, that doesn't make sense," I objected, having run these staggering calculations through my mind a second time for good measure. "I never saw Owen last night, I waited all day for him but he didn't show."

This time it was Doug who looked at me with the kind of pity usually reserved for a three-legged stray on a rainy day. Cal held up one hand and started counting backwards from five, lowering fingers as he went.

"Five...four...three...two..."

"The eyes in my bedroom," I just about shouted, getting up to speed just as Cal made it to his final finger. I remembered falling asleep, the brief glimpse of something in the corner I'd put down to wishful thinking, and a shudder ran through me from toes to shoulders.

After what happened to Chris, what they "allowed to happen to Chris" to use Doug's words, they were not keen on inaction or hesitation but they clung to their knowledge of what Owen was capable of and to their belief that it was in everyone's best interest to get to me without his knowledge.

This meant letting me go to work this morning in case Owen was waiting at my bus stop or my office and it meant holding off while I ducked out to eat half a disappointing burrito.

When I left work, they hung back just long enough for Cal to play back a snippet of footage through his filter and finding nothing otherworldly staring back at them, they launched into action.

They kept a camera running on their dash throughout the intervention that had so quickly escalated into an abduction. They found no sign of Owen on this footage, having gone over it while I was in here, sleeping. I corrected Doug by saying "knocked out" but he ignored me.

"Maybe this Owen knows we've been interfering again, maybe despite every precaution we've taken, he's still one step ahead of us. We've been as careful as we could, but we couldn't stand back and let another day pass, not when anything could happen to you."

Doug said this apologetically, one hand out in a halting gesture, as if I was about to curse them for so fecklessly trying to save my life.

Instead of cursing them, I honoured our agreement and told my story.

Chapter 24

At first, a small, mean instinct encouraged me to hold back but the telling was addictive in its comfort and soon my words were tumbling over one another to get out.

I told them about bad dreams and library toilets and the break-in and Bill Hanover and what had been in his closet and ended up in mine and exactly who Owen was and had been, about what happened to him and what was happening to me because our stories had intertwined so his was a part of mine and mine a part of his.

I told them about the woman we were searching for.

"What happens when you find her?" Doug asked.

I thought about this for a moment.

"I kill her," I said. "At least, that's what Owen wants me to do, what he wanted Chris to do." I couldn't think of a better explanation for Chris's behaviour, how terrified he'd been. "I think he was upfront with Chris about it and that didn't go too well. This time around, he's soft-selling me a nice line about catching her and finding evidence and whatnot but that's not what he wants. He wants her dead."

"Will you do it?"

"I prefer the evidence and arrest idea, even if that's only smoke Owen's been blowing. A full signed confession would be ideal."

"But if you can't find any evidence, or somehow appeal to a better nature that a serial killer surely doesn't have, then you'll kill her with the gun he helped you get?"

"Doug, right now, I don't know what the fuck I'm going to do."

"He's told you enough to get you where he wants you and no more," he said, adamant now. "Chris died and that wasn't enough to stop him doing it all over again. At worst, he'll get you killed, at best he'll make you a killer."

"What would you have me do?"

"Pack up the gun, the photos, the laptop and send them to the police, let them do their job. Tell Owen you'll have no part in what he's doing. Stay here with us, we've got a spare room. We can keep an eye on you, stop you from doing anything you don't want to do."

"Don't get me wrong, that all sounds great," I said. "But what then?"

"What do you mean?"

"If I don't help him get this woman, it means she's still out there, free to do whatever she wants to whoever she wants. Owen is the only one who can find her and fuck my luck, but I'm the only one who can stop her." I felt a great weight press down on me at the realisation that I actually meant what I was saying, that I would see this through now, no matter what. "Meanwhile, if I step back, he'll eventually give up on me and then, however long it takes, he'll get through to someone else and put them in the same position I'm in right now, except he'll make sure the next poor idiot won't have the benefit of your help or mine."

"Stay here, Wil," Doug said once more. "Please."

"No," I said, not without regret.

Cal's gaze returned to the floor, away from me, as if already writing me off.

"If it's not me it will be someone else. It's as simple as that," I insisted. "I need to find out what happened at Hanover's and I need his help to find this woman, but once he points me in the right direction, I'll cut his lying, life-endangering ass out of the picture, and use my own judgement as to what happens next."

I chose to ignore the sceptical glances thrown my way.

Sure, I had never *consciously* chosen to cut off contact with Owen but I was sure I could force the same results my ignorance and lack of concentration had maintained for however long he had been trying to get through to me. If I had a capacity for anything, it was wilful ignorance.

"But he's still the one doing the pointing Wil, don't you see how dangerous that is?" Doug demanded, a statement rather than a question. "Just stay here tonight at least, it will give us all some time to think. You have to let us help." Also not a question, maybe a plea.

"I'm grateful, honestly, but if Owen is wondering where I am and finds out I've been here, he might just save himself an argument and start trying to recruit elsewhere right away," I said. "Listen, I'm not refusing your help. you've already given it, a lot of it, but I need to go now and unless you're planning on tying me up again, you have to let me."

I was barely on my feet when Cal sprang to his, making me regret my bravado.

"You think you're doing the right thing, stepping up and taking responsibility, finally becoming a man or some such shit," he said, jaw squared, his glowering face thrust into mine, like he was considering a headbutt. "This isn't that time. There's too much we still don't know about what this fucker Owen is up to. Listen to Doug, stay."

I couldn't argue with anything he'd said, not without lying, so I didn't try.

"No," I said. "I'm sorry, but no."

He glared at me a moment longer and then as abruptly as he'd stood, he turned on his heels and left, heavy boots stomping up the stairs.

Doug watched him leave and then turned back to me. He studied me for a long moment during which I did my best to look resolute, or at least not to cry, and then he rose shakily to his feet, emitting various groans and hisses.

"Wait here, I'll get your things."

He plucked the empty mug from my hand and left the room.

Minutes later, I was in the passenger seat of Doug's car as he backed out of his garage. The dashboard clock read one-twenty am, about eight hours since I'd left work rather than the eight lifetimes it felt like.

"You make a nice couple."

He gave me a wary side-eye, as if waiting for a punchline.

"Sorry, I just meant...I don't know what I meant."

His features relaxed as he signalled for a left turn that would take us off his street.

"We have some mutual friends, occasionally throw dinner parties, we even go out on dates," he said, adjusting his rearview mirror. "I tell you this because between the lies Owen told you and the ones we've told, it's probably hard to think of us as a normal couple."

"A little, I guess," I said. "But just from the last few hours, I can see you're good together, at least as a snatch and grab squad anyway."

The faintest of smiles tugged at his cheeks.

"At first, when we started to see each other, I thought people would laugh. A desperate old man with a troubled young one. Then we started DAPI and when our first members assumed we were father and son...it was easier to go along with it, as if we were sharing our own private joke instead of being the butt of everyone else's. Of course, Cal never cared but I..." Doug trailed off, offering a dismissive shrug.

"What about the ring?" I asked, gesturing to the wedding band on prominent display on his hand resting atop the steering wheel.

"An old story and not one you need to hear."

I looked over but he kept his focus locked on the road ahead, making it impossible to read his expression. I stayed quiet for a while but once he'd taken the ramp on to the expressway, sparsely dotted with other vehicles at this late hour, I asked him something else that had been bothering me.

"After what happened with Chris, you guys kept DAPI going, kept investigating even though you were scared of coming into contact with Owen. Why?"

He drove on in silence a little longer, changing lanes to overtake a lumbering fuel truck, his eyes on the road but his mind obviously elsewhere. I envied this skill.

In the years since that failed driving lesson with my father, I'd looked up instructors, had even gone as far as making a couple of bookings, but always ended up cancelling. Whenever I tried to visualise myself behind the wheel, casual yet focused and in control like Doug was now, it seemed absurd.

"We felt a responsibility," he said eventually, giving each syllable careful consideration. "If Owen or any others like him were out there, the least we could do was keep watch, keep an eye on people like our members who would be prime candidates for contact. For my part, I hoped we might meet a better representative from the other side, one that would prove that passing on to a different plane of existence doesn't mean we need to lose our humanity."

"If it makes you feel any better, I think Owen was probably a dick when he was alive too."

He really smiled this time.

"Also, truthfully, I love it," he said. "Cal loves it too, even if he acts a little too cool for school." Doug proved his own tragic lack of cool by throwing air quotes around the phrase.

"I'm sorry about DAPI, about what I told Liam," I said. "Even if you won't let me call them, I bet it's not too late for you to call and tell him and the others the truth about you two."

"We'll see."

"But you just said how much you love it. Won't you miss DAPI?"

"I told you, that's not important," he said, a reply but not an answer.

I guiltily remembered how little I had wanted to stand in front of them all, sharing my accusations against Doug and Cal, and could only imagine how little Doug and Cal would want to stand there, defending themselves against those same accusations.

"Well, I'm still sorry."

"Remember that feeling, whatever happens next," he said. "Maybe it will stop you from doing some stupid shit you can't take back."

Mercifully, there were no air quotes this time.

I nodded but stopped short of making a promise I wasn't sure I could keep. I laid my head back against the headrest and watched headlights and taillights and streetlights blur together.

"Wil."

I jerked awake.

We were parked and the clock on the dash now showed eight minutes past two. I wiped drool from my chin.

"You know where we are?"

"Yeah," I said, looking around. "Couple of blocks from my place."

"Didn't want to get too close," he said, scanning the street ahead which was empty, as far as either of us could see. "Cal changed my entry in your phone's contacts and added his too. We're under the names Ben and Bert, in case someone is looking over your shoulder. I'm Bert, I believe, but it doesn't matter. Call one of those numbers and we'll come."

My phone had Face ID, which didn't work with my eyes shut. Reflecting on how they went about unlocking this while I was passed out would, at a more innocent time in my life, have been cause for cross-examination, or at least curiosity.

"Great," I said, at a time in my life when I appreciated expediency.

Doug shifted in his seat to face me, inviting eye contact and an intimacy that made me feel about as uncomfortable as I could see it made him.

"Owen would never have come near DAPI again if he had a choice," he said. "My guess is that after Chris, he did exactly what he told you, tried every person he came across, and when that didn't work, I bet he tried other paranormal groups thinking that if it worked once, it would work again. But it didn't, so he had to come back to us, and then he found you."

"That all sounds pretty likely," I said, as if my muddled brain had even begun to process anything about anything.

"My point is, the specialness isn't all in Owen, it's in you too, don't forget that. Whatever happens, remember that he'd be nothing without you, don't let yourself believe it's the other way around."

"Thanks, Doug, I –"

I was saved from awkwardly dissecting his appraisal of my qualities when Doug's phone rang and he held up a prim finger to quieten me. He said "yes" twice and "no" once before hanging up. He sat back in his seat and the intensity of the previous moments dissipated.

"Cal checked the footage from the cameras we had running while you were in the house," he said, pocketing his phone. "It doesn't look like Owen was there with us, for all that means if he watched where we hid the cameras in the first place. If he knows where you've been then..."

"Then I'll deal with it as best I can."

I pulled up my backpack from the floor, rested my hand on the door handle.

"Thanks again Doug, to both of you."

He just nodded, checking his wing mirror as if getting ready to take off, except the engine wasn't running. His hands were still on the wheel, and as calm as he seemed, his knuckles were as white as Cal's had been earlier. I could even hear the soft squeak of leather beneath his grip.

"You could still come back with me," he said.

"No, I can't."

He brought his gaze back to me with apparent effort. His eyes were red-rimmed and moist but there were no tears.

"Then be careful and be smart."

"I will, I mean...I'll try," I said, climbing out of the car into a strong yet surprisingly warm wind.

With the door still open, I leaned back in, wanting to say that I was sure if Chris were here to see what they had done for me, he'd be...proud? Happy?

But I couldn't speak for Chris Collins any more than I could forgive them on his behalf. That was the past and Stateless put it best in "Yesterdaydreamer", the final song on their final EP before they broke up the band and my heart in the process, when Kat Hart screamed that the past is always beyond repair.

Instead, I thanked him for the ride.

He made a face that looked very much like he was considering whether one more abduction might do the trick but then said goodnight and started the engine.

I closed the door, watched him drive up the street a little before making a U-turn.

He slowed on his way past me, watching me, and I almost gave him what he wanted, a wave, a yell, a "yes" to his invitation to go back with him, because a large part of me wanted that too. But the better, braver, infinitely smaller part of me won out and I held myself together as he drove away, his taillights disappearing from view.

Reluctantly, I turned for home which if I was lucky, was cold, dark, and empty, and if I wasn't, held a waiting presence who may have already decided that he'd rather throw me off the nearest overpass than have me interfere with his plans.

As I walked, the garbage-scented wind blew hard against me, throwing street grit into my eyes, as if trying to tell me I should be running in the opposite direction, chasing after Doug and all the help I could get.

Chapter 25

My exhaustion trumped my fear, allowing me a few hours' sleep before my alarm went off and I snapped awake, groggy and frightened but otherwise unharmed.

The day passed and the next and then impossibly another one with no word from Owen.

I went to work and came home and went back to work in a fugue state of worry and nerve-shredding jumpiness, somehow getting enough food and sleep to perform my functions at All Liars, even if I had trouble concentrating on what callers wanted, more than once realising I'd hung up on someone who was still talking.

At home, I perched on the edge of the couch, lay in a tight ball in bed, twitching at every noise, waiting and watching for Owen, unsure whether or not I wanted him to appear and feeling truly haunted for the first time since meeting my ghost.

My sleep was plagued with recurring nightmares in which I was chased down maze-like streets that were strewn with Polaroids that I dared not look at too closely, eventually ending up in my little laundry room, slamming the door behind me so that it echoed like a gunshot against the tiles. Each time, I pressed myself against the door, trying to hold off my pursuer. Each time, Owen appeared inside anyway because of course, he was the one chasing me. When I opened my mouth to tell him to fuck off, it was his voice that came out, telling him I would do whatever he wanted.

I would have channelled some of my nervous energy into adding recent developments to my manuscript but couldn't risk the chance that Owen was there with me all along. If he was, and if he had no idea of my visit with Doug and Cal, he had to believe I was still clueless and on mission.

Instead, I settled for opening the document and adding only two blank pages to the beginning. One, I left blank, a placeholder for a title I had yet to come up with. On the second, I typed "For Jo, my brother and my friend" before closing it again and leaning back on the couch like a man in the electric chair, waiting for them to throw the switch.

I spent that weekend in my apartment, going out of my mind, while I waited for Owen with a mixture of impatience and dread, reminded of a long afternoon once spent in my dentist's waiting room ahead of a root canal. The waiting sucked but the end of the waiting would suck too.

On Monday, I woke to my alarm feeling sore and tired and though I hadn't planned on it, I called in sick. For once, I would actually have preferred to be at work, but I was well aware how poor my performance had been on the phones over the past week. I hoped the extra day would be enough to get my head a little straighter or failing that, at least mean eight less hours in which I was at risk of saying something so fundamentally stupid and/or offensive that it got me fired, seeing as Owen wasn't the zany ghost of a seventeenth century buccaneer leading me to buried treasure and early retirement.

I went to the movies, not caring what I saw as long as it was loud and distracting. I watched the latest Pixar sequel and then a raucous workplace comedy set amidst a hotel's annual staff party. The Pixar movie was forgettable, which was fine by me, but the comedy was actually pretty good, even if I felt it was a cheat not to feature a single zombie in a movie called *Staff Infection*.

After leaving the theatre, I loitered around a nearby book shop until it started to close. Then I sat in a café drinking a coffee that was worth neither the price nor the sullen service from a bored barista too old for his skinny jeans.

I wished I had a friend to hang out with and not tell what was happening. It's always easier to pretend everything is ok when you have someone to pretend it to.

When the aging hipster started putting chairs up on tables and giving me increasingly dirty looks through his ironically huge glasses, I got up and left. I didn't bother to say thanks and he didn't bother to say goodnight.

I went to a pizza place, got a booth, and nursed a Coke and two slices of Pepperoni Passion for the best part of an hour before leaving, my unsettled stomach roiling from either the pepperoni or the passion, and heading home, having run out of ways to put it off.

I entered my darkened apartment, closed the laundry room door on an especially potent fug of nicotine-flavoured onion, and walked into the living room.

"Wil."

My hand paused halfway to the light switch.

Owen stood by the window, silhouetted against the glow of streetlights, his features impossible to make out.

I flicked the switch but even with the light on, I still couldn't read him. I hoped the blood pounding in my ears wasn't as loud to him as it was to me.

"Hey," I said.

"Where you been?"

I almost lied about being kept late at work, but it wouldn't help to complicate things unnecessarily.

"Didn't feel like going to work today so I called in sick and took myself on a date instead. The movies, a romantic café, a slap-up meal, the works."

"No wonder you agreed to come home with yourself," he said, and I realised he was cracking a joke. "I went looking for you at work. I was there this morning when the place opened but there was no sign of you, so I came here but still no you."

"Shame you didn't come looking for me sooner, I was at work a whole five days last week without hearing anything from you."

"You alright, Wil? You seem a little worked up."

"I haven't seen you since we broke into somebody's house where I found a firearm and photos of you-know-fucking-what and I've been waiting for the cops or Hanover or the woman to break down my door and I've been waiting for you to show up and tell me a single goddamn thing and I've been squeezing my brain every minute you haven't in case it's my fault so yeah, fair to say I'm worked up."

All of this was true and even if these words were poor substitutes for the ones I couldn't say to him, they helped vent some of the anger and terror I felt in his presence.

I stomped over to the kitchenette, making a show of slamming together the makings of a coffee so that I could turn my face from him and settle into my role as the clueless but frustrated patsy.

"Wil."

I opened the fridge and retrieved the milk, giving it a safety sniff before slamming the fridge door shut.

"Wil?"

I opened and closed cabinet doors with no specific purpose, rattled cutlery around in the drawer while retrieving one lonely spoon.

"WIL!"

I flinched so hard I felt a muscle twinge in my back.

"CAN YOU SEE AND –"

"Jesus Christ, yes, I can see you, I can hear you," I said, throwing the spoon into the sink. "You don't need to scream in my ear."

"Well, you weren't answering so I figured you'd tuned out again," he said.

"I'm pissed off with you so I was ignoring you while I made myself a coffee," I said, promising myself that when the time came, I'd be more successful at actually ignoring him than I had just been at pretending to ignore him. "Is that allowed?"

"Listen to me, will you?"

"I'm listening, I'm listening," I said, leaning back against the sink, my arms crossed protectively over my chest.

"We've got her."

I took a second to process this.

Then I took a few more.

"How?" I asked finally, though I could just as easily have said who, what, where or when. I almost said bullshit, because it surely had to be.

Chapter 26

When Bill Hanover came home and found his place tossed, he paid no special attention to the closet in his spare room, made no attempt to move the bags of clothing aside to check the hidden space in the wall.

He did not rage and rave like a cornered animal, nor did he climb into his oven, or take his toaster for a bath.

Instead, he called the police.

While he waited for them, he wandered from room to room in a somewhat dazed fashion, not ever seeming to Owen to even consider the risk that whoever broke in might still be there.

By the time two uniforms showed, Hanover had familiarised himself with his changed surroundings well enough to give them a comprehensive tour, his bemusement giving him the air of a slightly stoned real estate agent as he pointed out such features as the broken bathroom window, the torn apart kitchen, the space where his laptop had once been.

When they asked if anything else had been taken, he told them it didn't look like it. The cops left with his contact details and a description of his laptop, in turn leaving Hanover with a case number and advice not to hold out much hope for said laptop.

Owen followed the cops out of the house and accompanied them as they went door-to-door around the neighbourhood. Of the residents who were home, nobody had seen or heard anything the previous night, which was a relief to my ears.

The owner of the BMW with which I'd scuffled mentioned his car alarm going off but explained it had been windy and it wasn't unknown for it to go off under such conditions. One cop made a joke about getting what you pay for and the guy replied, straight faced, that 'quality always comes with a price'. Once they were back on the street and out of earshot, they'd taken turns repeating this to each other while trying to maintain the dignity appropriate of public servants.

"So, he knows nothing?" I asked.

"Who? The BMW guy?"

"No," I said impatiently. "Hanover."

I'd given up on the coffee, deciding I was too worked up to add more caffeine to the mix, and was sipping on a glass of water instead as I leaned over the kitchen counter, which acted as a barrier between me and Owen, even if it was only a psychological one.

"I would say Bill Hanover knows less than nothing."

"You couldn't have come and told me that sooner?"

"I couldn't risk leaving him alone so soon after we shook up his place," he said. "Maybe we'd missed something else in the house. Maybe, despite how calm he was acting, he was about to break any second. Maybe he had a split personality and the other part of him was the cross-dressing serial killer who slit my throat."

So, with his own collection of maybes, he stayed glued to Hanover. He'd run to the retirement home in Morningside ahead of Hanover's usual visit with Veronica Hill only to sit in on a conversation heavy on weather and the quality of food at the home and disappointingly light on the break-in or anything at all to do with her son, other than Hanover's reassurance that Stephen would visit tomorrow.

In Hanover's house, he listened intently to every phone call, leaning in as close as he could, trying to hear the other person, even though it meant taking the contact-pain every time Hanover flung out an arm or launched into jumping jacks or any of the other aerobic peculiarities people do without thinking when they're on the phone. Hanover was already laughing it off, using the same lines over and over. "Could have been worse, at least I wasn't home...I needed to upgrade my laptop anyway so now my insurance can do it for me." That kind of thing. While Owen recounted this, I absently wondered if Hanover's home and contents were insured by All Liars, in which case the amount they'd give him towards a new laptop and window would be cancelled out by the lack of a no claims discount on his next renewal. The house always wins.

All useless, all normal, until this morning.

"I was hanging out at the shithole where Hanover works and it was getting near the end of his shift, after a busy night of sitting behind reception, listening to podcasts, and occasionally helping drunks get into their rooms. The morning shift was about to come on, so I left and started hoofing it back to his house, to be there when he got back. I waited for him to pull up and then I slipped in the door behind him to save myself the fun of going through it."

He spotted it before Hanover, a simple brass Yale key attached to a faded auto-dealership keyring lay just inside the front door, as if it had been pushed in through the mail slot.

Hanover's eyes might not have been as sharp but he still possessed a sense of smell, which was one up on Owen. He started sniffing, something clearly hooking his nostrils, and as he looked around, finally spotted the key.

He picked it up, gave it a once over, and immediately headed out to the garage, trailed by Owen.

The elliptical trainer that had resided in the corner of the garage was gone, a fact Hanover seemed to have expected, seeing as his only reaction was to utter three words.

"Karen. The. Bitch."

He turned on his heels, walking through a less than enthused Owen, and made a call that finally sent Owen looking for me.

"But you said Karen Hanover looks nothing like the woman who killed you, remember?"

He held up a finger to quieten me in a manner eerily reminiscent of Doug and I gripped the edge of the kitchen counter to stop myself from losing it. He could have told me what he knew straight out but this slow drip of revelation was all part of keeping me intrigued and involved and now that I had seen behind the curtain, it made me furious.

Karen Hanover, the once and future Karen Taylor, had come home one last time but it had not been her idea. It had been her sister's.

Alice, younger sibling of Karen Taylor, referred to by her brother-in-law Bill Hanover with the less than loving nickname Malice.

"Don't call her that," Karen said to Bill, her voice over the phone sounding more tired than outraged, unwilling to hold up her end of an argument they'd had too many times.

"How is baby sis?" Hanover asked. "Bite the heads off any infants lately?"

"Bill."

"She ever give you any of that rent she always promised us? I guess you can keep it now if she does." To Owen's ear, even Hanover hadn't sounded overly invested in this diatribe, was just working from muscle memory. Karen asked him if he was done and after a couple more shots, he said he was.

Karen had heard about the break-in through the family grapevine. When she told her sister about it, Alice had immediately asked if her stuff was OK. Unable to answer this question, Karen had, after some pressing, admitted she still had her key, had been putting off giving it to Bill until she'd had a chance to pick up her elliptical trainer, and could bring Alice to check on her stuff and collect it if it was still there.

"You should be thanking me anyway," Karen said. "We came in Alice's station wagon so I could fit the machine and now that she's taken her stuff too, we're both out of your house and your life."

"I don't love that your mental cunt of a sibling was back in here, but I'm glad I wasn't around for it," Hanover admitted. "I hope you stopped her from stealing any of my shit, or pissing in my milk carton."

His tone gave Owen the impression that rather than hypotheticals, these were actual events that at least Hanover considered to have previously occurred. Karen hurried past this conversational roadblock by assuring him she'd known he wouldn't want Alice in the house unsupervised or when he was home, hence their visit together last night while he was at work.

Hanover, having moved upstairs as they spoke, pushed open the door of the guest bedroom.

"As if Malice thought anyone would want to steal her trash bags full of crap," he said, standing in the doorway. Owen edged in behind him and together they looked upon the open bedroom closet.

It was empty and the shelf, rather than leaning against the wall as we had left it, was screwed back in place, completely covering the hole.

While Owen stood there, wearing the same slack jawed expression I'd be sporting later that day as he told me this, Hanover leaned against the doorframe and kept talking, as if the entire earth hadn't shifted on its axis.

"Well, good riddance anyway," he said. "You don't know how much I hated having reminders of her around."

"I know, believe me I know, and Mal...goddammit, *Alice*, knows it too," Karen said.

"I wish you'd stop pretending you like your sister any more than I do," he said. "She was a nightmare to have here, creeping in and out at weird hours, sneaking around with God knows who. Remember we'd be trying to watch TV and she'd start preaching at us about the corporate lies we were drinking in, calling us zombies? This coming from a fucking ghoul."

The faint sound of stifled laughter came through the phone before Karen replied, sounding annoyed at herself for giving in.

"Yeah, well, blood is blood, Bill, and she's my sister so let's just you and me be adults about this, it'll make a nice change," she said, causing Hanover's grin to fade away.

"She back living with you again?" Hanover asked, walking to his own bedroom with Owen following somewhat reluctantly, wanting to hear everything being said but also wanting to stare in wonder at the empty closet. "If she is, more fool you, you'll never get rid of her this time, not without an exorcist anyway."

"No, Bill, she's not living with me. She finally bought her own place, if you must know, over near Steve and Diane's."

"Who the fuck are Steve and Diane?" I interrupted. "And where the fuck do they live?"

Once again, Owen held up a quietening finger but this time I wasn't angry, just hungry for more.

"Pretty amazing that a woman who sleeps hanging upside down can hold down a job, never mind slime her way onto the property ladder," Hanover said, sitting on the edge of his bed, pulling off his work shoes.

"It's called saving, Bill, if you knew how to do that then maybe you wouldn't waste your days playing online poker and your nights at a no-tell, cum-smell motel where half the guests pay by the hour."

"They throw away another five minutes in this charming vein, while I'm practically jumping out of skin I don't have," Owen said to me, a guy practically jumping out of skin he did have. "Then Hanover saves the day."

"Well," Hanover said, "Steve and Diane are such fucking bores I'm glad you got them in the divorce but just the same, hope you've warned them property values in Freeling are about to take one steep fucking drop."

"Freeling," Owen said to himself then.

"Freeling," I said to Owen now.

"I gotta go," Karen said to Bill. "I'm glad they didn't take much and I'm glad you're ok."

"You're still wearing that perfume I got you last year, smelled it as soon as I walked in," Hanover said, matching Karen's softer tone. "You didn't have to give your key back so fast. You never know."

"I know Bill, we both know," she said. "And I'm not throwing out perfectly good perfume, even if it's a cheap knock-off."

The line went dead and Hanover said "bitch" to nobody in particular, the word coming out like a term of endearment.

I let out a breath I didn't know I was holding.

"You think it's her? This Alice?" I couldn't blame him, all signs pointed to yes, but a decent paranormal investigator knows how easy it is to let wishful thinking connect the dots.

"I don't think it's her, Wil, I know."

"We need to go to Freeling, we need to find her, and see if it really is her," I said hurriedly, still not ready to accept his certainty.

"Why do you think I came looking for you this morning?"

"Let's go now," I said. "Freeling isn't too far on the bus, I can get there in an hour and –"

"Wil, you don't get it," he said. "When I couldn't find you this morning, I went by myself."

"Holy shit," I said.

"I happened to be standing on her street when she got home from work a couple hours ago, after a day spent forcing myself in and out of every house in the area because my doorknock-capable partner went AWOL. I followed her inside, stood as close to her as I'm standing to you now. It's her."

"You're sure?" I asked, recovering myself. "Your description was a little patchy, not that I'm blaming you considering the amount of your own blood that was in your eyes, but I mean, you legitimately thought there was a chance it was Hanover in drag. We don't want to go after the wrong woman."

He took a deep, weary breath which could only be for dramatic purposes considering his oxygen-free diet.

"The words that woman said to me as I lay dying are stuck in my ears like dirt I can never clean out. She called her sister while I was there and if I was in any doubt after seeing her, which I wasn't, it went as soon as she opened her mouth."

"Ok, let's say it's her, what's the plan?"

"Turns out she keeps the books for a construction company all the way across town, so when she's gone to work, she's really gone. We go to her place tomorrow while she's working, dig around and find something to nail the bitch."

"What's the address?" I asked, aiming for airy matter-of-factness, nodding along like I believed him when really, I knew he hoped we'd find nothing, that I'd be left with no choice but to kill her, or die trying.

"You get yourself to Freeling and I'll take you to it," he replied.

"I'd like to know beforehand if it's all the same to you," I answered back, feeling sweat break out on my forehead. "No offence but those of us who still have a life to lose would like to take a sneak peek on Google Earth, just to be as prepared as possible."

"Who am I to discourage you taking ownership?" Owen said. "18 Meadow Court, Freeling."

"18 Meadow Court, Freeling," I repeated, for my benefit, not his, making sure it sank in.

"So, tomorrow?" Owen said, and I braced myself against the counter.

I told myself:

This will be easier with him than without him.

I told myself:

You have no idea what he could be capable of if you turn him against you.

I told myself:

Don't let your anger make you shoot yourself in the foot.

Then I looked in Owen's eyes and saw Chris Collins looking back at me out of his murky past.

"In terms of how stupid you think I am..." I began, my body tensing as it realised the trouble my mouth was about to get us in. "Would you say I'm on par with Chris Collins, or in a league all of my own?"

Chapter 27

I felt an all too brief thrill of satisfaction as his usual veneer of self-containment slipped just enough for me to see the panic I'd caused beneath it. He quickly regained his composure but no matter how good the mask, it couldn't hide his eyes which narrowed from surprised circles to watchful slits, giving him the look of a cornered animal, vicious yet shrewd.

"Tell me what you think you know?"

Hands out front in a gesture of placation, his voice slow and measured. Like he was talking me off a ledge or telling me to drop my weapon.

"I know that before you got to me you got to Chris Collins and he ended up dead. I know that you didn't bullshit him about finding evidence or putting the woman in prison and that he agreed to kill her if you found her. And I know that when he wanted to back out, you wouldn't let him. I *don't* know if he killed himself or if you killed him but there's no point asking you because all I'll get is another lie."

"Wil, you need to listen to me."

I came around the kitchen counter and advanced on him before either of us knew what I was doing. He took a step backwards which was good because I had no idea what I would have done if he hadn't.

"I have been listening to you and all you've done is feed me lies and pull my strings. You told me you never got through to anyone else before me..."

"If I'd told you –"

"A lie," I said, jabbing my finger just short of his face, resisting the temptation to put it through. "You told me Doug and Cal were criminals, perverts..."

"I knew they'd ruin everything if –"

"A lie," I said, stabbing at him with my finger again. "You told me you were gone for a year between the night you died and the night you came back..."

"It was months, truly months, before I came back and then –"

"A lie."

"Goddammit," he said, taking another step back. "I couldn't stop Chris. He got scared."

"He was scared of you!"

I closed the distance again, my body shaking with anger and fear.

"How far did you get with him? Had you been to Hanover's house before or is that where you were headed the night you killed him? Because however it happened, you fucking killed him."

He hesitated and despite being a cop with a cop face, it wasn't hard to see him deciding what I did and didn't need to know.

I wanted to shake the truth out of his lifeless lying limbs, but it was useless. I could rage at him for hours and he'd just play it out and bide his time before trying to reattach my strings or failing that, giving me up as a bad job and moving on to the search for his next hitman.

"What happened with Chris isn't important now," he said.

"Chris was important," I yelled, my jabbing finger becoming a fist that I shook in his face. "I'm important."

The first real punch I ever threw connected with no sound and a dull shock that ran up my arm. I threw a few more into his face and body and even though they were connecting rather than going through him, he didn't wince or back away. I kept going until my arms became as tired as the rest of me and then I just stood, staring at the thing before me, so like a person but so inhuman.

The only sound in the room was my laboured breathing until Owen spoke again, slow and cold.

"If we're gonna talk about lies, how about the steaming pile of horseshit you're peddling?"

I was so surprised by this turnaround that I had to replay it in my mind to make sure I'd heard correctly.

"What are you talking about?"

"I'm talking about you acting like some holier than thou hero," he said, and now he was the one getting in my face. "Acting like you give a shit about stopping this woman, about saving lives, when you'd fucking love it if we never found her, if you and I could just spend the rest of your life playing buddy-buddy while you run your stupid little experiments and try to become king of the geeks off my dead back."

I took a moment, let my breathing cycle down, and spoke with what was for me, an uncharacteristic level of self-awareness.

"Would I rather be running tests on you with my Trifield meter instead of breaking into houses? Yes. Would I prefer to be collecting a shelf full of case notes instead of a closet full of firearms and disgusting photographs? Of course. And right this minute, would I choose to have you saying sweet nothings into Doug's ghost box program over telling me lie after lie? You bet. But I could have had all those things, could have played along with you and pretended to know nothing. Instead, I'm going to cut you the fuck out of my life and go after this Alice Taylor by myself."

"Bullshit," he said.

"Bullshit you," I said back, working up a good head of steam now. "I won't let you make me a murderer, so as of now plus five fucking minutes, I'm going to spend the rest of my days pretending you don't exist. Why don't you spare me the effort and move on, go into the light or the flames or wherever you're headed? Meanwhile, I'll find what I need to get her locked up for the rest of her life and I'll do it the right way, the way you should have done all along. You know, if you ever just stopped to think about what you're doing, all the damage you've caused by bulldozing your way through everything and everyone, then Chris Collins would still be alive. Matter of fact, if you had done that in the first place, maybe Esther Peridou's parents would be watching over her instead of her grave and you'd still have a wife, not a widow."

Cruel, yes.

Unnecessarily so?

Go ask Chris Collins.

"Jesus Christ, what I wouldn't give to be able to appear to someone willing to do what needs to be done instead of you...you...freaks." His hands trembled in the air before him, clenched as if strangling an invisible enemy.

"Maybe you should think about how lucky you are that you can appear to us freaks because you sure as shit can't appear to anyone else."

"Lucky, Wil? I'm dead, I've lost everything."

"That's not my fault. I didn't ask for any of this but I'm doing my best to be the kind of person who'll do the right thing. But you? You're not a person, you're a hole in the world, a greedy fucking absence, and I'm not going to let you swallow me up like you did Chris."

He shook his head, opened his mouth to speak but I got there first.

"I'll get into her house, find the evidence I need to find, and get her put away forever. If it's peace you're after, I hope that gives you some," I said. "Goodbye, Owen, and fuck you very much."

"Wil, you don't know what you're doing, we'll only get once chance at this. If you fuck it up, if she gets away, we might never find her again."

I shut my eyes and urged my thoughts away from him.

"For God's sake, Wil."

I thought about the laminated list of questions stuck up in my cubicle at work, provided by Alliance Worldwide in the event of a bomb threat, because they're an insurance company and that happens. Questions based on the notion that if I took such a call, I would calmly remain at my desk rather than make a break for it to save my own skin.

Where did you put the bomb?

Owen shoved me hard. I took a step back, kept my eyes shut.

What does the bomb look like?

Owen shouted out my name again, his voice fainter, as if from a distance.

When will the bomb go off?

Another shove, but it felt like nothing more than a feather falling on my shoulder.

Are you acting alone or with others?

Another shout, but it sounded like nothing more than that same feather falling to the ground.

I opened one eye and then the other.

I was alone, or at least acting it.

I ran around the apartment, gathering my things, keeping myself distracted by loudly singing the MC Hammer classic "Addams Groove" because they do what they wanna do and say what they wanna say and who can't get behind that?

I escaped my apartment without further interference and beelined to the nearest bar, a place named McGinty's by whichever corporate entity owned it and sat at the faux-mahogany counter where I ordered a beer and a whiskey which I drained quickly before ordering the same again. I lost myself in the drinks before me, the bustle of people around me, and the seven different screens mounted behind the bar with a different sport showing on each one. I watched them all intensely and it didn't matter that I didn't know the teams or the rules or the scores, just as long as they kept me from thinking about Owen.

Within an hour I was lightheaded, and I ordered yet another round to make sure I kept it up. The bartender served me but made a little joke about there being no danger of the booze running out. Luckily, I was already too drunk for subtle humour.

I went from lightheaded to toasted to shitfaced.

Sometimes Owen was beside me at the bar, yelling at me, pointing a finger at my chest, but most of the time he wasn't there.

Eventually, everything became slow and disjointed until my awareness of the world around me was just a series of images.

A men's room floor at eye-level.

The bartender shaking his angry head and pointing at the door.

My hand pressed against a telephone pole for support while a couple walk by hand in hand, giving me a wide berth.

My key in my apartment door.

Owen's face, his eyes and mouth open mid-scream wide.

Chapter 28

It was spitting rain as I hustled from my stop to the All Liars building, running a half an hour late, and I could only hope it would rinse away some of the pure alcohol excreting from my every pore because the masking scents of toothpaste, shower gel and deodorant had faded to nothingness before I even left home.

Each incoming call was as tiring as a marathon and every bit of sales jargon I dribbled out was like driving a nail into my own forehead but I was busy and distracted and that was what I needed.

I spent my lunch-hour sleeping in one of the men's room stalls and when I returned to my desk it took me some time to figure out the reason I couldn't find the enter button on my keyboard was because it was hidden by a yellow Post-it which read, '**Wil – Meeting Room 3 – Heather**'.

I stood too quickly and almost fell over.

Steadying myself with my chair, I braced for impact against the look of concern I would no doubt be receiving from Mandy but when I sheepishly raised my eyes to receive it, she wasn't there.

Her desk was empty of everything except computer and phone. No pictures of her little dog, no gel-filled wrist support, no purple sports bottle. I tried to recall if I'd heard her that morning on the other side of our partition and I supposed I hadn't. I felt a pang of loss I didn't have time to question as I made my way across the sea of cubicles to Meeting Room 3.

The blinds were lowered against the wet gloom outside and as I closed the door behind me, the cool dimness of the room was instantly gratifying, a blessed relief from the relentless fluorescent light that hammered down on my desk.

Heather looked up from her laptop long enough to gesture towards the seat next to her at the round table. I ignored this and took one across from her in an effort to keep my fumes to myself.

The swivel chair groaned and squealed beneath me as I cautiously eased into it. Due to the harsh economic climate, it had been some time since we had been given any new office furniture and consequently the chairs in the meeting rooms consisted of the worst specimens traded in by employees from their own desks.

She kept typing and I took turns resting one eye at a time so that I wouldn't look like I was sleeping. She finished and looked up in time to catch me resting my left eye. I rubbed it as if something was stuck in it and mumbled an apology.

"Water?"

"That's ok, it's just some grit, it'll come out."

"I meant to drink," she said unsurely, as if I might have been making a joke, and nodded at the full pitcher surrounded by empty glasses on the table between us.

"No, thanks," I said, not wanting to give the enemy any more ammunition. Even though my throat was dry and my tongue was swollen in my cotton-mouth, and the water looked positively seductive, this had the feeling of a meeting that could end with me being fired if I didn't play it right, and that meant appearing like one of the happy, fully functioning employees I saw beaming at me from the posters on the meeting room wall, rather than a gasping, hungover wreck.

When she started to wheel her chair towards the window it groaned and lurched dangerously, so she stood and walked over instead.

"Little dark in here," she said, reaching for the blinds.

"*No*," I said, somewhat dramatically.

She looked at me wide-eyed, hand frozen in mid-air.

"Sorry, can we leave them how they are? I have a bit of a headache."

I was annoyed that I'd let her outplay me, forcing me into showing weakness, but this was outweighed by my relief as she backed away from the blinds and returned to her chair, carefully rolling back to the table with a prolonged squeal that made us both grimace.

"What's up, Wil?"

As if I had arranged this meeting, as if I hadn't been minding my own business in my cubicle, politely losing my sanity one call at a time.

"Not a whole lot," I replied, angling my head slightly to avoid breathing in her direction.

"Wil, you've had a handful of sick days in all the years you've been here and now this past month you're missing days, showing up late, you sound patchy on the phones and today..."

With a sweep of her hand, she gestured first to me and then the room in general while wrinkling her nose to let me know that despite my best efforts, she was not unaware of the combustible vapours I was pumping out.

"I think I've only missed two and a half days lately and I'm pretty sure this is my first late start in a long time," I said, trying to sound objective, optimistic even, as if defending a mildly wayward colleague.

"I don't mind sick days," she said, waving me away. "I've probably taken more than you and if I'm honest, most of those were unofficial mental health days when I just couldn't face coming in."

Middle Management 101 – Empathise.

Did she expect this to be the masterstroke that got me talking about my problems so she could classify me as broken and discard me accordingly? She was probably prepped for "My girlfriend left me" or "My father's sick, real sick" but I wondered how she'd handle "I had to get drunk last night because I'm ignoring a ghost who wants me to kill someone".

"The missing days aren't the issue," she continued, and I wished she'd just skip to the pointy end of it because if I was getting fired anyway, I'd rather skip sitting with Heather while she practiced her "Handling Problem Employees" training module on me.

She steepled her fingers before her, giving the pocked and stained ceiling tiles a brief, thoughtful glance before proceeding.

"Look...you're always pretty quiet away from the phones, which is fine, I mean that's a lot better than some around here. A customer complained last week because they heard Tommy from Claims in the background of someone else's call yakking about his favourite sexual position."

I was receiving a heavy vibe of "teacher tells wayward student that they get it man, they're cool, they used to skip class too but learning can be tight" but still, I felt one of my periodic pangs of sympathy for Heather, for a life spent dealing with us drones who weren't paid enough to give a shit. Still, Mandy's disappearance and the fact that Heather was using my recent behaviour, admittedly erratic but harmless overall, as an excuse to shitcan me were sure signs of a battle cry from up above demanding cutbacks to which she was responding with typical efficiency. She might even get something extra in her Christmas bonus to invest in her neck scarf collection. Today's item was a filmy swirl of hot pink leopard print.

"What I mean is that you always keep to yourself but lately it's like you've checked out. You drift in and out of here and you don't speak to anyone when you're not on the phone."

I shrugged. It was hard to care, it was hard to sit up.

"Look, Heather, if you're firing me then..."

"Nobody's firing anyone," she said, looking almost hurt.

"Have you had any customer complaints?" I asked, changing tack.

"No, that's not what I mean," she said, once more glancing upward for divine inspiration. "All I'm trying to tell you is that I'm here and happy to help. I know we're not friends and I know you're a private person, but you clearly have something going on. Talking never made anything worse, you know."

I tried to wave her off, to say it was fine, just family stuff, but instead of words I emitted a single, throaty sob that I tried to hide by blurting out the first thing that came to mind.

"Where's Mandy gone?"

"Mandy?" Heather asked, looking nonplussed at the change of topic. "She finished up last Friday. It was meant to be this Friday but she had some things she wanted to get done ahead of starting her new job next week and in typical Mandy fashion, she'd already given us more than the required notice anyway."

"New job?"

"Poached by Fairfield Insurance Brokers, which was a good move on their part because she's a gun." She hesitated, taking in what must have been my obvious look of confusion. "We told everyone she was leaving...there was an email."

I kept staring at her.

"Were you two close?"

"No," I said, because I didn't know how to explain to Heather that Mandy had looked at me every day, smiled at me even though I was mostly too stupid to smile back, that she registered my existence when it so often felt like I could slip out of the world unnoticed. I didn't have the words to express how thinking of Mandy made me think of Tara and Sam and Liam and Jo and all the other people who weren't here to help me now because long before Owen manipulated me into cutting ties with the outside world, I'd been doing a fine job of it myself.

I looked at the floor and tried to compose myself, unsure if I was welling up or if my eyes were stinging from tiredness and dehydration.

There was a squeal of metal and then a hand on my shoulder. I looked up to see Heather standing over me, looking uncertainly from me to her hand and back again as if trying to figure out how it ended up there. She seemed to make a management decision and gave my shoulder a firm squeeze before breaking contact.

"Your job's not the beginning and end of your life, I'm not saying it is," she said. "But if this is how you are at work then I doubt things outside of it are too good right now. You may want to talk about this eventually, a problem shared is a problem halved and all that, and if you do, I'm happy to listen."

The combined shock of nearly launching into a crying fit in front of Heather Bryant and her subsequent display of platonic touching and genuine human warmth brought me around enough to know that I needed to get out of there before I tried to half my problem and ended up fired, arrested, and committed.

"You're right, I do have some stuff going on but I'm sorry, it shouldn't affect my work."

"Can I ask?"

"I lost a friend recently, he died."

I wasn't sure if I was thinking of Owen, who I never really knew, or Chris, who I never actually met, but either way, it felt true.

"I'm very sorry for your loss. If you're interested, the Employee Wellness Program is still running, you get five free therapy sessions."

"I'll be fine," I said. "I'll regroup, get back on the phones and back on script."

"I really hope so, Wil. I just want to help you out you know, you're the one making it about work," she said. "It's not about work. You're a good guy. I don't like to see you falling apart."

I didn't reply, wouldn't have known where to start.

"Maybe you should take a few days off? We all get three mental health days per year ever since that agent in the Stockholm office got…"

"Stabby?"

"Stabby," she echoed, not relishing the word but unable to come up with a more accurate one. "Use them, they'll see you through the rest of this week and hopefully give you the time you need."

A week earlier I would have protested, horrified at the thought of sitting home with nothing to do but wait for Owen. Now, I was sickened at the thought of sitting home trying to ignore him, but I had bigger things to attend to and the extra time could prove useful.

"That sounds good."

"I'm glad to hear it," she said. "Why don't you get an early start and head home now?"

"That's OK," I said. "I'm happy to work the rest of the day."

"No offence, Wil, but I've listened back over some of this morning's calls."

I winced.

"I think it'll be better for you, the company and our loyal customers if we get you out of here until you're back on your A-game," she said, with a grin.

"Fair," I said.

I rose from my seat, causing something, a knob or a wheel, to go rolling away under the desk. We watched its progress together before she gave a weary shrug.

"The modern workplace."

I gave a non-committal humph and the next thing I knew she had her arms wrapped around me.

She held me for a moment then stepped back and even in the dim room I could see her cheeks were glowing the colour of her neck scarf.

"I'm sorry if that was inappropriate," she said quickly. "You really looked like you could use a hug."

I was momentarily lost for words and her sheepish smile faded into a look of concern as she waited for me to scream "Sexual Harassment" and go running to the HR-appointed Workplace Standards Officer, who at all times wore a yellow baseball cap emblazoned with a red 'OK?' so as to be readily identified in the event of a Workplace Standards Emergency.

When I smiled back and mumbled thanks, she relaxed a little and gestured to the door.

We left in opposite directions, two full-grown, extremely embarrassed adults.

I was still processing the meeting on the ride home.

I had thought Owen was some kind of hero, and maybe he was, but I'd also thought he was my friend, and he most definitely wasn't. Chris Collins made the mistake of thinking otherwise and it cost him everything. Conversely, learning that Doug and Cal, rather than wishing me ill, cared enough about my life to want to save it was shocking enough but I really didn't know what to do with the idea that Heather Bryant, who I always considered a walking corporate memo rather than a living person, genuinely cared for my well-being. All this attention would go to my head.

Chapter 29

As soon as I got home, I cranked *Damned Damned Damned* at high volume. I made myself a quick early dinner and a strong coffee and in between mouthfuls, yelled along with Dave Vanian and thought hard about the fact that The Damned's debut LP was the first full length UK punk album and that "New Rose" was the first UK punk single and neither of those things felt very important but I had to think about something so I ate faster and sang louder and tried to remember the track listing of their *Machine Gun Etiquette* album.

When my plate and mug were empty, I changed into a hoody and jeans, grabbed my coat and gloves, killed the music, and ran out the door. If Owen had been there with me, I didn't know about it.

The evening was closing in and thick, dark clouds pressing down overhead threatened that the rain which had been making guest appearances all day was soon about to step up to a starring role. I briefly considered doubling back for my umbrella, but I'd made it out of the apartment once unimpeded and didn't want to press my luck. I zipped up my jacket and hoped for the best.

I walked five blocks to a payphone I remembered seeing on a stroll I'd taken around the neighbourhood back when I'd first moved in, though there was no guarantee it would still be there seeing as public phones were being culled at a rate that made what happened to the plains bison look like a slow, natural decline. As I grew closer to the spot, I pulled hood up and gloves on. The restorative effects of time, food, caffeine, and the evening air had made such significant inroads on my hangover that I even had some saliva in my mouth again.

The phone was still there, mounted on a short metal pole and sheltered by a scratched plastic hood. Better yet, when I picked up the handset, I found it was still actually connected.

The area was a mix of self-storage warehouses and factories which suited my purposes because at this hour of the evening, with most of those places closed or closing, it was all but abandoned, with nothing to encourage foot traffic and only a trickle of passing cars.

I had thought about buying a prepaid burner phone to make this call but then remembered an episode of some cop show where they traced a burner phone back to the store it had been bought from and used CCTV footage to identify the buyer. Sure, it was impossible to use a public phone without looking like a low-level drug dealer but that was the least of my worries.

My finger hovered over the keypad and then I dialled the number, wondering what Owen would say if he were there with me.

"DON'T YOU FUCKING DARE!"

Owen was there with me.

I pretended ignorance but he wasn't fooled.

"Put it down, Wil."

I didn't respond so he pushed me, forcing me to let go of the handset to avoid ripping it off as I fell to the broken-up pavement. My knees rang from hitting the ground but that was good because I closed my eyes and concentrated on the pain.

A tinny voice came from the handset dangling by my head.

"911, what is your emergency?"

"The cops need warrants or at least probable cause, and an anonymous call doesn't give them either," he said, his words quick and firm. "If they go to her house, all they'll do is ask who might have it in for her bad enough to make malicious 911 calls and when they leave, she'll run some place we'll never find her."

"911, are you able to speak?"

I kept my eyes shut and thought of the pain in my knees, listened to a car engine approaching and then moving further away as another one came from the opposite direction, neither stopping to see if the low-level drug dealer on the pavement needed an assist.

"I shouldn't have lied to you. Chris was too weak for all of this, you're not."

He continued along these lines, alternately pleading and bullying but not understanding that every time he said Chris's name, he renewed my resolve, and every time he appealed to a better nature I knew he didn't truly believe I had, he made me more determined to do things my way.

I felt his hand shaking me but only lightly. Eventually, it wasn't there at all.

As very human-sounding steps hurried past, I opened my eyes in time to see an alarmed pedestrian scurrying away, casting an occasional look back to reassure herself I hadn't leapt up and begun pursuit.

"*Is anybody there? We have traced this call and police are enroute to your location.*"

"I'm here, I'm here," I said hurriedly, getting to my feet.

"*Sir, are you OK? What is your emergency?*"

Truthfully, my most immediate emergency was the fact that police were enroute to my location.

"I want to remain anonymous," I rasped, remembering my intention to disguise my voice.

"*Sir, please state your full name.*"

This was not going well.

"Is this call being recorded?"

There was a pause, probably while the operator looked at a colleague, rolled her eyes and mouthed "fuck my life".

"*All emergency calls are recorded. It is a criminal offence to use the emergency services line for your own amusement, it is punishable by –*"

"I have information about murders that happened a few years back and that will help stop some future ones."

"*I can transfer you to a police officer if you have information pertaining to a past or ongoing crime but –*"

"There's a woman named Alice Taylor who lives at 18 Meadow Court,

Freeling. That's Alice Taylor, 18 Meadow Court, Freeling."

"Excuse me, but this is –"

"She was Stephen Hill's accomplice in the Cherry Tree murders," I continued, not wanting to be rude but also not wanting to hang around to find out if a cop car really was about to show up. "The police think Hill acted alone, but they're wrong. They also think he and police detective Owen Hoath killed each other but they're wrong about that too, she killed Hoath after he killed her partner. Lately, she's been watching a child in her neighbourhood and she's going to take him soon if they don't stop her. If they need proof, tell them to dig up her backyard. They'll find the remains of Fenton Meiks buried there. That's Meiks…M-E-I-K-S."

Fenton Meiks was one of the missing children the police suspected Cherry Tree of killing. I didn't feel great about lying but I needed the cops to take action. I hoped the mention of a past victim and a potential future one would impress a sufficient amount of authenticity and urgency on whoever listened back to this. It was unlikely they would find the remains of Fenton Meiks in her backyard, unless she moved her victims' remains around with her the way other people rehome their potted plants, but I was sure in the process of searching her home they'd find other incriminating evidence.

"Sir, where did you get this information? If I could just have your name, we –"

I hung up and walked away, trying to look casual even though no-one was there to see me trying.

Taking an indirect path through back streets that led further still from home, I held my breath as much as I could because when I didn't, I was panting and potentially drowning out the sound of a police chopper overhead.

I made it to the bus stop I was aiming for just in time for the next service. The rain showed up just behind the bus and as I travelled back into the city it ran in fat diagonal streams down the windows and sheeted down the windshield while the oversized wipers smacked at it ineffectually. Inside the rolling tin can, obscured by night and the deluge, I felt safe and hidden and I did my best to enjoy those feelings while I could.

Chapter 30

I stepped onto Meadow Court, walking with my chin tucked into my jacket, which had been soaked through in the few minutes it had taken to dash between buses in the city, and my feet squelching in my sneakers which had unerringly found the deepest puddles as I jogged here from the bus stop out near the expressway.

Unlike my assault on Bill Hanover's house, this time I had my phone with me and on top of helping me figure out which bus to take from the city, it now directed me to Number 18.

Even though I'd suspected there probably wouldn't be a sign driven into Alice Taylor's front lawn warning "Here There Be Monster", a part of me had still expected her house to be some boarded-up, splintering hulk sticking out from the neighbourhood like a dead black fingernail on an otherwise healthy hand. I squinted through the rain at the unremarkable two-storey semi before me and wasn't sure if I was reassured or disappointed.

There were no lights on in the house. There was no car in the driveway but the house had a garage so that didn't mean much one way or another.

I looked around for somewhere to shelter, squinting through the rain and the dark, and saw nothing promising. Meadow Court was a cul-de-sac lined with two-storey boxes similar to Taylor's, all with stubby front yards which meant the party, garden-wise, was at the back. The only trees in sight were slender ones that had been planted along the sidewalk at regular intervals, none of them large or leafy enough to offer me shelter from the rain, neighbourhood curtain twitchers, and incoming cops.

I walked down Alice Taylor's side of the street to where it terminated in a circular turning point and then walked back up the opposite side, returning to the street's entrance without finding anywhere to post myself. I stood there, at a loss, and scanned the street again.

Finally, I spotted my salvation in a front yard across the street from Number 18. I must have missed it the first time thanks to my senses being clouded by rain and sheer panic.

The house which this front yard belonged to had a few lights on downstairs but the curtains were drawn and given the weather and the late hour, I felt pretty safe nobody was about to venture out. I took a last look around to make sure I was alone and unobserved and then made a run for my new digs, slipping and sliding on the wet grass.

The playhouse I crawled into was built to accommodate two little tea-partying girls or one grown man, as long as he was willing to hold himself midway between a squat and the foetal position. The exterior of the glorified plastic box, as much as I'd been able to see of it, was decorated like a hot-pink cottage, with a sloping roof of fake shingles, an opening at one end acting as the doorway and a round hole at the other acting as the window. It wasn't much but it was dry and the window was pointed across the street at Alice Taylor's house.

An hour went by, then another one.

When I wasn't staring at the still, silent house across the street, I was checking the time on my phone, dripping water onto the screen from my sodden hair and clothes.

There was a small chance the police had been and gone in the time it took me to get here but I had been fast, timing my bus connections well, and if my call had been taken seriously enough to send them here so quickly, then surely they'd still be here now and the street would be abuzz with squad cars and yellow tape and people walking around with baggies on their feet.

Maybe Owen was right, and they weren't going to go running around on the orders of some anonymous weirdo, at least not in the middle of the night in this weather. If that was the case, I could stay squashed into my Li'l Dream Home all night and all I'd see is the rain. If I was lucky, I'd still be lucid enough in the morning to watch as the cops finally showed up, purely as a box-ticking exercise, and did nothing except inadvertently alert Alice Taylor that someone was on to her.

The cold and my soaked clothes had set me trembling and it was not particularly comforting that this was now giving way to a numbness that was spreading from my pinned legs to the rest of me, interrupted here and there by painful cramps.

When it got to eleven-thirty, I decided I would give the cops until midnight, at which point I would extricate myself from my box and take the world's most badly needed piss before locating the nearest payphone from which I would make another call, this time yelling that Alice Taylor of 18 Meadow Court had kidnapped me and was determined to murder me in a most horrific fashion. Any requests for further info would be met with inarticulate screams.

Headlights washed over the street, illuminating the thick, shifting sheets of rain, and a police cruiser rolled into view before stopping outside Number 18.

In my excitement, I tried to sit up but neither my body nor its surroundings would allow it, so I just stared harder, pushed my face against the hole, another glassless window in my life, and blinked the rain out of my eyes.

When the car's occupants didn't immediately leap out and start combat rolling toward the front door, I cast a hopeful look to the street entrance, hoping to see the furtive movements of the SWAT team backing up this decoy vehicle, but there was nobody else there.

They just sat there, headlights glowing, and I grew more and more apprehensive as I watched the lone car. Considering their lack of urgency and the fact they'd parked directly outside Alice Taylor's without any attempt at concealment, it seemed they'd taken me seriously enough to come but not seriously enough to think there was good reason to.

Finally, two uniforms climbed out, a male and a female, hurriedly closing their doors and pulling on their hats as they jogged toward the house, shoulders hunched against the rain. They squeezed together under the shelter of the small front porch and the tactical disadvantage of this position if there had been a threat waiting for them on the other side of that door was further proof they didn't expect any.

My only hope now was that their mere presence shocked Alice Taylor into doing something unexpected. I only hoped she didn't end up killing one of them because I didn't want blood on my hands, or more angry ghost cops following me around.

I was too far away to hear anything above the rain pounding down on my plastic roof, but one of them must have knocked or rang the doorbell because a light came on upstairs followed by one downstairs, followed by the porch light. I was relieved to see both cops had bulky frames beneath their shirts which meant vests, ideally bulletproof but at the least, stab proof.

The front door opened a crack, then wider.

Beyond the cop's backs, I could just make out a woman with messy sleep-hair. She was wearing a pink robe or maybe a nightgown. They stayed there for a minute or so before she disappeared inside and they followed, closing the door behind them.

I stared at the door as if I might see through it, strained my ears for screams and gunshots, and cursed the idiot rain. I briefly considered running to their car to radio for back-up on their behalf before slipping away again but I knew my numb legs wouldn't carry me anywhere fast. Hopefully, between the two of them, they'd be able for whatever she threw at them.

Twelve whole interminable minutes after the cops went in, the door opened again.

Both cops emerged as calmly as they had entered.

The guy turned back to the doorway and I caught a glimpse of the woman he was speaking with. His partner stood at the edge of the porch and stuck her hand out, confirming that the rain was still indeed wet.

Once the door closed, the cops beat a hasty retreat for the dry interior of their patrol car.

They executed a neat little U-turn at the end of the street, and then they were gone.

Across the street, the lights went off in reverse order to how they'd come on. First the porch light, next the hall, and finally upstairs until it was if the house had never been woken from its sleep.

More rain blew through my window, but I barely felt it as I rested my forehead on the sill and muttered obscenities like prayers.

I considered myself a dyed-in-the-torn-tee punk, one who knew the system was never on your side, but despite this, my inner child threw a tantrum at the injustice of it all. I had called the grown-up police people whose job it was to fix everything, and they had done nothing. Despite all my doubts about what the cops would or wouldn't do once I involved them, deep down I had not been prepared for this to happen, for the problem that was Alice Taylor to remain mine alone.

When I eventually lifted my head, my saturated hair sending another waterfall down my face, I saw a figure standing across the street, in front of Alice Taylor's house.

The reality of my numb legs and pins-and-needles arms came back to me in a panic, knowing that if Alice Taylor was about to cross the street and gut me with her sharpest kitchen knife, I wouldn't be able to do more than flop around on the wet ground like a landed trout while she did.

But it wasn't her across the street.

Owen stood, facing me, not calling out, not running for shelter from the rain which must have felt like a thousand daggers piercing through him.

I crawled backwards out of the playhouse and collapsed onto the sodden grass, using my almost useless arms to pummel my totally useless legs back to life until I was able to stand.

I skidded and skated across the grass, without the energy or self-righteousness to so much as flip a middle finger at Owen.

As I limped my way out of Meadow Court, my shaking hands shoved into soaking wet pockets, he finally called out to me, his voice rumbling like thunder through the heaving rain.

"You were wrong."

...or maybe...

"She'll be gone."

Either worked.

Hours later, I staggered into my apartment, shivering with cold and exhaustion. I had been too disorientated to attempt catching night buses, but the first two Uber drivers who showed up refused to let a drowned scarecrow into their car and the third only after she'd put a plastic garbage bag over the seat for protection and been firmly promised a glowing 5-star review.

I lurched toward bed peeling off sodden clothes, tearing my underwear away like a second skin. I was still so wet there were beads of moisture on my chest and arms but I didn't have the energy to dry myself so I just crawled under the covers and lay there, half asleep, half awake, entirely out of my mind.

I don't know how long I was lying there before he spoke.

"If you don't do something, nobody will."

"I know that," I replied, through chattering teeth. "Now."

"The cops didn't tell her what the caller...what *you* said. Like I expected, they just asked if she'd upset someone enough for them to make nuisance calls directed at her." His voiced faded in and out, one moment he was in my ear, the next he was at the bottom of a cavern. "I don't think she's going to run but who knows. We need to move quick."

"Tomorrow," I said, using the last of my energy to form the three syllables.

"Tomorrow," he agreed, a hint of surprise in his voice, as if he expected more resistance.

I was fresh out of resistance. He had been right, at least about getting the cops involved, and if I had to be the one to go into that house, I wanted him keeping watch.

Wanted was the wrong word.

I needed him.

"She won't be home, but we can't be too careful," he said. "Bring the gun for protection, I don't want you getting killed and sending me back to square one."

Touched by his concern, I went under, snug in my bed, with visions of impending doom dancing in my head.

Chapter 31

I awoke shivering, my damp pillow smelling of sweat and rain, but felt better after a hot shower and some hotter coffee.

Barefoot, I padded to the bedroom, grabbed last night's jeans from the soaked pile of bedsheets and clothing on the floor, and pulled my phone from a pocket. It was dead and when I plugged it in, a water drip icon flashed up, along with a warning to unplug the charger. I took the damp, dead thing to the kitchen where I discovered I was out of rice, so I dropped it into a box of stale off-brand Ricey Pops instead and hoped for the best.

I sat on the couch with my laptop and opened my manuscript document, finally able to update it with everything Doug and Cal had told me and everything that had happened since then. Owen and I hadn't set a time to meet in Freeling but I knew I didn't need to rush. This was everything he'd ever wanted and he'd be there, waiting for me to finish this.

With the updates made, I hit save and attached the document to an email which I sent to Jo with nothing written in the body and a subject line that read "Open to title suggestions...".

After a moment's hesitation, I clicked "forward" on the same email, changed the subject to "Thank you for being a friend" and sent the manuscript to Liam. It felt right, even *The Golden Girls* reference.

Of course, once they read the manuscript, both Jo and Liam would think I was certifiable but, to paraphrase Owen, I'd burn that bridge when I came to it. If I was still alive and sufficiently un-incarcerated to go around burning bridges.

I used my laptop to place a video call to Jo.

It would be night in Thailand but I couldn't remember a time I called my brother that he didn't answer. I only wished he could say the same in return.

"Wil, what's up?"

His camera was off and he sounded groggy and worried.

"Hey Jo, sorry it's night over there, isn't it? I forgot."

Start with a lie, always the right move.

"If now's not good…"

"No, no, it's good, bro, it's good," he said hurriedly.

Despite the hour, he sounded so genuinely pleased to hear from me that a hot wave of guilt bubbled up into my throat. He always asked so little of his big brother and I could so rarely get out of my own way to meet even that low benchmark.

"Wil, hang on one sec."

Talking, in the background, a mix of Thai and English ending with a woman's voice saying something that sounded very much like "*Tell Wil I said hi*".

Shuffling, the sound of a door closing, and then my brother's face filled the screen, eyes bleary but bright, smiling from ear to ear.

"You look good, Jo."

Even in the low lamplight of his apartment, even as he knuckled sleep out of his eyes, he looked happy and healthy and full of life and the guilt was small change compared to the happiness I felt at seeing him, at hearing his voice. Behind him, a floor to ceiling window showed the dim outline of a Bangkok cityscape, lights of every conceivable colour fizzing it up to nocturnal life.

"Wish I could say the same, but you're looking a little pale and peaky," he said. "You feeling alright? Shouldn't you be at work?"

"There's something going around the office, nothing serious, but I needed the day off for an exclusive all access toilet pass, if you get me."

"You sure? Because if this is you calling to tell me there's something wrong then you should just fast forward to that part."

His tone was jokey but his expression was watchful.

"I promise, everything's fine," I said, which required less explanation than stating that while physically I was fine, I was emotionally not so great, mentally a wreck, and about to walk out my door and enter a house where I might end up killing someone or getting killed myself. "Can't a guy call his little brother?"

"I don't know, can he?"

"Ouch, ouch, you got me." I clutched at my heart. "*Mea culpa, mea maxima culpa.*"

"Hey, no fair," he said. "You know I've been a sucker for Latin ever since you showed me *The Exorcist* back in the day."

"Oh yeah?" I raised an eyebrow, acting like I didn't know this to be true, hadn't pulled out some Latin expressly to defuse the situation. "What age were you again? Eight? Nine?"

"I was seven, Wil," he said abruptly, his face stoney. "A traumatised seven-year-old."

We held this sombre tableau for a second before breaking into laughter.

"*Ego te absolve,*" Jo said, offhandedly making the sign of the cross at me and smiling again, that face-splitting grin he'd always had, almost too wide to be believed, like a cartoon character.

It startled me at times, especially when we hadn't spoken over a long period, how familiar my little brother was to me, as though I had seen him mere hours ago. I looked at the man's face before me on the screen and saw in it a child's face, a teenager's face, a face I knew almost as well as my own. The tuft of hair atop his head that never quite sat down was present and correct and I bet when he was bored or nervous, he still squeezed his right forearm with his left hand. When he was tired, as he was now, his left eye still drifted off centre a little, a hangover from an astigmatism our parents had corrected when he was a toddler. I could remember him running around with an eye patch and my own jealousy over this swashbuckling fashion accessory.

I wished concentrating on Jo worked the same way as concentrating on Owen, could make him appear by my side. As good as it was to hear him, to be able to see him thanks to the wonders of technology, nothing could beat his presence, his solid warmth, the way he always seemed to know what I was thinking. Not for the first time, I wondered if this ability of his to see right through me was the reason I pushed him away so much over the years. Surely nobody could look at me so intently, could know me so well, without realising there was little there to see, nobody much there to know.

"You still there, Wil? I think the screen's frozen."

I came back to life.

"All good, must be my stupid Wi-Fi," I covered, losing track of how many lies I was up to already. "How's things? How's Law?"

"Law's good. Her section finally finished up a huge project so she's going to spend the next couple of weeks doing the bare minimum, catching up on sleep, and watching dog videos online to recover."

"Sounds like she needs the rest," I said, not without awkwardness. I'm sure I'd barely mentioned their relationship in the years they'd been together, I couldn't even have said how many. "I'm glad you two are doing so good together."

"Thanks, when she's not annoying me, I love the shit out of her."

"You always were the romantic."

"Hopeless," he agreed.

"Work still busy?"

"Oh brother, busy and about to get busier. The project Law's area finished was the last part of a Beta test for a whole-of-system overhaul. Now that's done, we have to roll it out across Asia Pacific and guess which idiot they've got looking after implementation?"

"You idiot?"

"Me idiot."

"You sound like you're complaining but I can see your nerd boner from here," I said. "That sounds like a big deal, they must think you're pretty hot shit."

"Probably picked my name out of a hat, no big thing."

Growing up together, I had held my few small victories up for everyone to see while Jo, naturally humble, stubbornly so, hid his behind a wide smile and an eyeroll.

"You know, Jo, I'm not saying you'd ever downplay your wins because of how you think it will make me feel or look or whatever, but don't, OK? I'm just proud of you. I'm always proud of you."

It wasn't a lie.

The day I watched him drive out of our neighbourhood, doing on his first attempt what I to this day had never managed, I was jealous, sure, angry, yes but only at myself. More than anything, I was proud. I remembered school friends kicking the shit out of their little brothers for trying to tag along with us, or who stood by when someone else was kicking the shit out of them, as if they were strangers. Not me. Sure, I was no boy genius but I was smart enough to know my little brother was worth more than a gang full of friends.

"Jesus, thanks Wil," he said, his brow furrowing. "And we're sure you're not dying?"

"Not today."

I hope.

"What about you, what are you up to, aside from being a sicko?"

"Well, I sent you an email with a kinda manuscript attached, maybe you can give it a read some time. All notes are welcome as long as they're glowing and positive."

"Oh, did you finish it?"

This took me a second.

Then I cringed.

That last time Jo visited, when we'd spent a few days together before he went on to see the folks, I confided in him that I was working on a book. We were eight beers deep at that point which matched how many months I'd been working on the project but outnumbered the pages I'd completed. Given this lacklustre progress, it was safe to say *How To Kill It Nightly – Tools and Tips for Paranormal Investigators* had been a doomed enterprise. In the months following Jo's visit, my input, along with my interest, had dwindled away.

That manuscript now sat gathering virtual dust in an obscure subfolder on my laptop, unfinished and unloved, but I hoped what I had been working on these past weeks, what I had sent to Jo and Liam, would become a much better contribution to the paranormal community than just another thrown together "*How To...*" and that its almost total lack of tools and tips would be compensated for by firsthand documented experience of the paranormal.

"I kind of pivoted from what I was working on before, this is a little different, you'll have to read it to see what I mean," I said. "Need your help with a title though, that's not my strong suit."

"Colour me intrigued," he replied. "Hope it's got a good ending, I'm a sucker for a big finish."

"I'm working on the ending today actually," I said, thinking of where I needed to go in a while. "But you should have enough to keep you going for now."

I marshalled my features into a smile before they could break ranks and signal for help that I knew Jo, or anyone on this side of breathing, was unable to offer.

"So, any more thoughts about coming over here?"

He said it in a perfunctory manner, unable to stop himself from asking but bracing himself for my usual crap. I owed him better.

"Where would you take me, what would we do? Sell me on Thailand."

He laid out a detailed itinerary that included temples, tuk tuk tours, floating markets, Muay Thai fights, and specific street food vendors. He wanted to take me to a deserted gated community on the outskirts of Bangkok which was said to be haunted. He wanted all three of us to go north to Chiang Mai where Law was from and south to Nai Harn Beach because apparently since I had never swum in the waters there, I had yet to live.

Just then, there was no place I'd rather be than sitting on a mountain top in Thailand with Jo and his fiancé, looking down at the Indian Ocean as it disappeared over the edge of the world.

I told him this.

"Do it then," he said, waving his hands emphatically. "I've been here years, and you still haven't visited. Once you get used to the constant humidity and intermittent rioting, you'll never want to leave."

Why hadn't I visited?

Telling myself I had more immediate, supernaturally inclined travel priorities like Stonehenge or the Stanley Hotel or Australia's Monte Cristo

Homestead didn't add up when I had never gone to any of them. And even if I had travelled to those places, poking around for signs of afterlife, I would not have found anything better than what awaited me in Thailand. My brother, with open arms and a spare room.

"Well, if you're not going to shut up about it…"

"I'm not."

"Then let me check with work to see what leave dates are free in the next few months and we'll work something out."

Another lie maybe, depending on what happened in the coming hours, but if events allowed, I would make sure it came true.

Eventually, it was time for me to say goodbye. I would have happily kept speaking with Jo for hours, days even, but I had someplace I needed to be.

I said I loved him and he returned the sentiment. I knew if things went wrong, if this was the last time we spoke, then it had been enough to talk like we used to, and to know that whatever happened to me, Jo had Law and his life and he would be alright.

I sent a final email, this time to edwardandlorrainetagg1967@aol.com, and told my parents simply that I loved them, missed them, and hoped they were doing well. It was not lack of love that stopped me from calling them but the knowledge that however much I could hold myself together before my little brother, I could not expect to stay so strong under parental scrutiny. Greatest of all their flaws was their love for me and now was not the time to come undone by it and start crying down the virtual phoneline to them.

I got dressed, tugged on my jacket and went to the kitchen where the trademark-goading sounds of *"Crack, Popple, and Zap!"* left me with little hope of finding a moisture-free environment within the box of Ricey Pops. I retrieved my phone, blew rice dust from its crevices, but sure enough when I tried turning it on, I was greeted with the same blue drip of doom.

Maybe it was for the best.

If my phone worked, I might call Doug or Cal who would tell me to find a deep body of water and throw the gun into it before I did something I'd regret and take the laptop and Polaroids to the police and give them a chance to redeem themselves for their weak showing last night. They would tell me it wasn't my burden to carry, and that would be a lie, and that I had done everything I could, and that would be a bigger one.

I dropped my useless phone back into the cereal and went to my bedroom closet where I took out the Polaroids and laptop. I grabbed a mostly unused notebook, ripped off a page and wrapped it around the stack of photos, securing it with tape before writing **'Do Not Look!!'** on it in my most strident penmanship.

With the closed laptop balanced on my knees, I sat on the bed and wrote a longer note.

"Doug and Cal, these are the photos and laptop I found in the home of Bill Hanover, 13 West Street, Elmsview, but I think Hanover is innocent and clueless. The photos belonged to his cousin Stephen Hill and/or Hanover's ex-sister-in-law Alice Taylor, who is the woman I told you about. Her address is 18 Meadow Court, Freeling. Sorry to dump these on you but please hold them for a couple of days and I'll come and take them back. If I don't, then mail them anonymously to the police and use her place as the return address. Thank you for your help, no matter what happens it was appreciated, Wil."

I bundled the laptop, Polaroids, and note together in an unruly but functional package constructed of tape and notebook pages and scribbled Doug's address on it before leaving it by the apartment door to take with me when I left.

Finally, I stood before my open closet, eyeing the gun and the clip.

I was not someone who had ever expected to pick up a gun, let alone do so with the knowledge I might use it on another person. Owen and I could say it was for my protection but only one of us wanted that to be true. Owen wanted me to act as his instrument of vengeance or justice or whatever-the-fuck and the gun would simply make me a more efficient tool. For my part, if I chose to bring it, it would be purely due to fear for myself, my safety, and my life. Despite my best intentions, I knew full well that same fear would make me use it.

I met my own gaze in the cheap strip of mirror glued to the inside of the closet door.

Who was this person staring back at me?

Maybe not as much of a coward as I'd always feared, but no hero either, not unless heroes usually felt scared shitless.

I thought of dead children, the ones that were and the ones that might be, and of parents who would never tuck their child into their bed again, of Owen's widow who would never again sleep next to her husband in theirs.

Was I doing this for all of them?

And if so, why didn't I feel better about it?

The man in the mirror looked at me, his eyes asking the same questions.

With no answers between the two of us, our collective gaze slid back to the gun.

Chapter 32

Standing at the entrance to Meadow Court, less than twenty-four hours after my last visit, the setting couldn't have looked more different.

Instead of submerged shapes and shadows, offset by the glare of street-lights and thronged with cascading rain, now there was stillness and sunshine, with only a few puddles left to testify to last night's downpour and a single wisp of white cloud allowed for set dressing in an otherwise pristine blue sky. Traffic from the nearby expressway hummed in the background, sounding to all the world like bees, out enjoying the unseasonably warm weather. Somewhere reassuringly far away, a dog barked.

Owen appeared down Meadow Court, near Taylor's house, walking toward me.

"She gone?" I asked.

"Wil, little late," he said, by way of hello. "Went to work this morning as expected."

"We didn't make a time."

"True."

"Plenty of time for me to get in and out before she gets back from work, I'm sure."

"Also true."

We stared each other out for a long moment before he spoke again.

"Number four on the next street over backs on to her house," he said, pointing the way.

I turned and started walking but he stepped forward to block my path.

"Wil."

I almost went through him out of spite.

"Don't we have somewhere we need to be?"

"Just listen to me for a minute, before we go any further."

A nod was the politest response I could muster.

"I've lost or forgotten a lot of myself since coming back, manners included," he said, reaching out his hand. "I'm sorry I haven't done this before."

It took me a couple of seconds to realise what he was doing. I put out my own hand, holding it open. He placed his around mine, the concentration clear on his face, and once more I had that alien sensation, so unlike skin on skin. We shook three times, slowly, and released.

"I tell myself all these things are falling away because of how focused I've been on getting to this woman but if I'm honest, there are parts of me that died that never came back, and parts of me still dying that I can't get back." He paused, gave me a look that seemed to ask if there was any point continuing and I gave him another nod. "I can feel myself fading, becoming a photocopy of a photocopy, and I've been worried...no...afraid, very afraid, that if I lose myself before I get to her, before what needs to happen happens, then I'll be left here, wandering like some kind of zombie, forever. Maybe that's what ghosts are, the ones who just float around saying "boo" anyway, people who got left behind with unfinished business but ran out of time and lost themselves before they made whatever connection they needed to make. They can't move on, can't go back, they're just stuck without any idea of how to come unstuck."

"Photocopies of photocopies," I said, turning over the thought.

A tiny elderly lady walking a tiny elderly Cavoodle approached on the sidewalk. I placed one hand against my ear and said a few "yeahs" and "uh huhs" while giving her the brief, distracted smile of a man on a hands-free call. She smiled back, the dog gave a half-hearted yap, and they continued on their way.

This was not the first time I pretended to be on a call, or crossed the street, simply to avoid exchanging pleasantries. So much time spent avoiding the living, so much time spent seeking out the dead, believing they'd be easier, uncomplicated. It was almost funny.

"I know I haven't done everything the right way, if that even exists under the circumstances, but I'm sorry for asking so much of you and even if it doesn't seem like it, I am truly grateful for your help."

"Were you ever really Chris's friend?" I blurted out the question, which was easier than asking if he'd ever really been mine. "Did you even give a shit about him?"

"Chris needed a friend, so he got one," he said, with disarming bluntness. "He didn't deserve what happened to him. I pushed him too hard, expected too much of him, and it ended how it ended. I couldn't risk that happening again. That's why, with you, I –"

"Lied, manipulated..."

"I went slower. I told Chris up front that when we found her, we needed to kill her. He agreed that would be the safest thing for everyone. Then he lost his nerve."

"So, you killed him?"

"We argued, things got out of hand, he hopped a train to get away from me and then he jumped off a bridge. You want me to say it was my fault. Sure, it was, but I didn't kill Chris. For all I knew, he was my one and only chance at ever making contact, I wouldn't have thrown that away."

"I wish I could believe you," I said, and meant it. "But I don't know if I do."

"Wil, I –"

"I'm here, I'm doing this. The more we talk, the more risk of me losing my nerve and making a run for it. Just do this much for me, if you really are sorry and grateful and all that other good shit then, when we get inside that house, watch out for me. Please."

I held his gaze, pleading for him to see me not as a pawn or a weapon but as Wil Tagg, son of Edward and Lorraine, brother of Jo, a man who had done no great good in his life but no great harm either and who neither deserved nor wanted to die today.

"Wil, I promise, whatever happens next, we're in this together."

I stared into his eyes a moment longer, still wishing I could believe him.

He sounded sincere, he looked genuine, but all of that was for nothing if one those parts of him he'd said was dead or dying was his capacity to give a shit about anything apart from getting the woman.

"Come on then," I said, sighing deeply. "Lead the way."

He walked ahead of me, both our heads on swivels, keeping a close look out, knowing I might only get one clean shot at breaking into Alice Taylor's house, not wanting a nosey neighbour or bored delivery driver to trip us up at the finish line. Sure, my finish line was a clean getaway with plenty of damning evidence in hand and Owen's looked more like the bullet-riddled corpse of Alice Taylor but for now at least, they were both in the same direction.

I was wearing a hoody under my jacket, a double-layering move I already regretted given the day's warmth. Out of habit, I slid my hands into the pockets. I felt something unexpected in there and pulled out a Polaroid. My immediate revulsion, so strong that the word "swoon" would not have been much of an overstatement, faded when I saw that it was not one from the godforsaken stack I'd mailed off in the city to Doug and Cal. Showing only an empty doorway in Bill Hanover's house, it was the one I'd taken of Owen that night, which must have been the last time I'd worn this sweater.

I studied the photo while I followed Owen, not because there was anything to see, but because something was sticking in my mind, a question taking shape.

"This would have been a lot easier for you if I'd been some lovelorn accountant who needed you to tell his secretary he always loved her," Owen said, not turning around as he spoke. "Nice and safe, some enlightening conversations, a whole lot of EMFs and EVPs and then up, up and away, into the light."

I couldn't see the sardonic grin on his face as he spoke but I could hear it and, despite myself, one jerked at the corners of my mouth.

"You're not fucking wrong there," I said, slipping the photo back into my pocket. "But maybe lovelorn accountants don't get to come back, maybe you need a better reason."

"You don't think love is reason enough for the Big Guy to let you play out some overtime?"

Despite what I thought of Owen, despite the temptation of hitting him where it hurt, I stayed silent. It would have felt too cruel to discuss my devout atheism, my near certainty there was no Big Guy or Gal looking out for any of us, with a man whose entire being was in the most precarious position possible.

We turned the corner onto the next street. Owen came to a stop and I did the same, just short of walking into him.

"That path next to their garage leads to their backyard," he said, pointing out the house. "No gate, thankfully. Their back fence isn't too high and once you're over it, you'll be in her yard. Her backdoor doesn't look like it will be a problem."

"Alright," I said, having acquired quite the ability to provide positive single word responses to dishearteningly complicated statements.

"The couple who live there are home but they're ancient and not exactly *compos mentis* so just move quick and they'll never know you were here."

I felt a twinge at the use of Latin and thought of Jo, seven years old, petrified with terror while watching *The Exorcist* with his equally petrified ten-year-old brother who had lied about already seeing it "a ton of times".

I shook the recollection away, this was no time to go tripping down memory lane.

"I'll go in and make sure they're not standing right at their window," he said. "When I call out, you haul ass."

"Alright," I repeated.

He disappeared inside the house, and I stood a respectful distance from their front yard, trying not to look like I was about to launch an assault on the place. When I shoved my hands back into my pockets, my fingers once again found the Polaroid of Owen and I slowly regained the mental ground I'd been working up to before.

There was no guarantee the Polaroids I found in the hidey-hole in Hanover's house were taken with the camera I found in his bedroom, the one I used to take this photo, but it seemed too coincidental not to be the case. But why was the camera in Hanover's room and not bundled in with Alice Taylor's belongings?

Maybe he'd gone through her stuff and claimed it in lieu of the back rent he never expected to see. If that was the case, surely she would have grabbed it when she and her sister were collecting their things but Owen hadn't mentioned an argument about the camera's disappearance being part of Bill and Karen's phone conversation and if he had noticed it missing himself, which his cop eyes couldn't have failed to do in light of learning about the sisters' visit, there's no way he wouldn't have mentioned it since it only served to strengthen his case against Alice Taylor.

I'd ask him about it once we were safely inside. For reasons I couldn't put my finger on, the possibility of the Polaroid camera's ongoing presence in Bill Hanover's bedroom bothered me.

"GO NOW!"

With no time left for quiet contemplation, I bolted from my spot on the street.

I hit the old folks' backyard and made a beeline for the wooden fence at the rear only to be caught off-guard by a gang of gnomes hanging out around a mossy water feature. I jumped in time to clear them but before I could congratulate myself on my catlike reflexes, I careened into the fence with a thud that shook both me and it.

With no time to catch my breath, I pulled myself up but my ankle clipped the top of the fence as I went over so instead of springing to a ready position in Alice Taylor's garden, I landed face first in a flowerbed.

I rolled on to my back, crushing some flowers in the process, and spat out a mouthful of dirt. Wheezing air that tasted like damp earth, I took a quick self-assessment. I'd bent my left pinkie back beneath me in the fall. Not great but not broken. The ankle I'd caught on the fence also seemed as if it wasn't broken but a sprain was a distinct possibility because I could already feel it swelling and throbbing, gearing up to explode inside my sock.

"You did great just now," Owen said, stepping through the fence and moving on to the back door before I could read his expression for sarcasm. "They didn't see a thing."

I got to my feet and limped after him through overgrown grass, brushing dirt from myself.

"Along with the lock on the handle, it's bolted from the inside here," he said, pointing at a shoulder high spot on the door.

"I thought you said the door wasn't a problem?" I said, pulling on my thick woollen gloves and wishing I'd thought to buy a more suitable pair since my last B&E.

"It's not," he said. "Look closer at the frame."

The paint was flaking from the doorframe and when I pressed a finger against it, the wood sank under my touch. I came away with flecks of paint and wood stuck to my glove.

"It's eaten through with woodworm. All the locks in the world aren't going to help you if you don't look after your house,' he said, priggish about this residential negligence. "Hit it with your shoulder a couple times, the frame won't hold."

I stepped back, readying myself.

"There's an alarm panel at the other end of the house. Once you're in, go straight up the hall to the front door, keypad is on your left. Press 7-6-2-1 then the green button. I watched her disarm it when she got home yesterday."

"How long have I got to turn it off?" I asked, conscious of my ankle slowing me down.

"Just hurry."

In my head, Joey Ramone sang about doors that should never be opened and Owen Hoath told me that one guy should never try to take a door by himself. I wasn't sure what Joey would say if he were here, but I doubted Owen would advise much in the way of caution if I bothered to ask right now.

"Owen?"

I didn't look at him, kept my eyes locked on the door.

"Uh huh?"

"Remember what I said. Look out for me in there, no matter what you think of me."

"What I think is that you're trying your best," he answered, with a tenderness as touching as it was worrying.

I rushed the door and felt it give against my shoulder, heard wood cracking, but the door stayed put. I hit it again and this time it flew open, screws and other parts of the now useless locks tinkling across the tiled floor with me stumbling in after them.

Regaining my footing, I sprinted up the hall, my ankle screaming at me to slow down or at least have the decency to hop. The keypad was where Owen said it would be and when I punched in the code the flashing red light changed to a steady green.

I breathed a sigh of relief and backhanded the sweat from my brow.

I turned and found him standing right there, closer than he usually liked to get, staring at me with an expression I hadn't seen before, a little like the frown of concentration he had when he was levelling himself with the floor, or when he shook my hand, but there was an intensity to it now that was almost unseemly.

"Alarm's off," I said, eager to break whatever strange spell had been cast over Owen, who had never seemed so ghostlike. He neither responded nor looked away.

What he did was take a single step back, looking very much like a man about to break down a door.

Then he rushed me.

I was thrown back against the front door, the impact emptying my lungs as I slid to the floor, cracking my tailbone on hard tile.

Dazed and winded, with my poor ankle and throbbing pinkie yelling in agreement that things were really getting ridiculous around here, I found myself alone, staring up at the ceiling.

I opened my mouth to call out for Owen, ask what the hell he thought he was doing, but before I could make a sound, I was overtaken by convulsions so severe it was as if everything inside me, every bone, every vein, every straining tendon, was being wrenched apart, while my skin stretched and pulled as though fit to burst.

I shuddered and spasmed on the floor, wracked by seizures that coalesced into one endless wave and turned me into a single, clenched muscle.

My body was a prison with me trapped inside it.

Then something changed.

I was no longer trapped.
I was going away.
I was gone.

Chapter 33

I sat in a kitchen I didn't recognise, my legs kicking rhythmically against my chair, while a woman I didn't know placed a crustless sandwich on the chequered tablecloth before me.

"There you go, bub," the stranger said, tousling my hair. "Plain cheese, your favourite."

She moved to the counter, her back to me while she chopped vegetables.

My favourite sandwich was ham and cheese and mustard with the crust and I was a full-grown man who was able to sit with his feet firmly planted on the ground and I wanted to stand up and shout all of this except...

Except, I was home, warm sunshine was pouring through the window, and I was sitting at my always-place at the kitchen table, my mother was getting dinner ready, and plain cheese sandwiches without the crust were the best. I wondered what the hell was going on but also what I should do after I ate, maybe get my homework out of the way or go climb trees while the sun was still high in the sky.

Sometimes, I would scoot down in this chair and stretch, my toes just brushing the linoleum, practising for when sitting on a chair and touching the floor wouldn't be mutually exclusive states of being. It would be too hard to do this and enjoy my sandwich, so I contented myself with kicking my heels against the chair legs. This may have looked like childish fidgeting to an observer but was secretly part of an intense exercise regime designed to make sure that when adulthood came calling, it would find a well-conditioned body deserving of growth and maturity.

Adults often commented that I was a serious child, in too much of a hurry to grow up, but I didn't think there was anything wrong with taking serious things seriously, in becoming the person I already knew I wanted to be as soon as I could. Besides, even if I was only nine, when I looked around at the world, I saw too many people acting like children. It seemed to me that one more grown up couldn't hurt.

One of the adults who accused me of over-seriousness was my mother which was why, as I ate my sandwich, I made my disciplined routine look like innocent distraction while I kicked my legs an exact number of times together, then an exact number separately, before repeating the pattern. It was also why, when my mother turned from her chopping to smile at me, I made sure to return an even wider smile of my own, through a mouthful of bread and cheese.

My mother the stranger gave a soft little laugh and looked at me the way mothers do when their children are being accidentally cute.

Leaving her vegetables, she stood over me once more, reaching out to wipe away food from my chin.

"Are you remembering to chew, Owen?"

I looked up at her with another wide and smeary grin as she raised the chopping knife in her other hand, a wet sliver of potato still stuck to its blade, and thrust it into my throat.

"Ouch, Jo, it hurts there, you dick!"

I swallowed red liquorice instead of cheese sandwich and massaged my throat where Jo had poked it with the trick-knife's retractable plastic blade.

The packaging promised "Real Metal Effect!" and "Realistic Stabbing Action!" and unlike many of our afterschool purchases from Gag City, it was completely as advertised.

I had spent my own pocket money on a bag of red liquorice and the latest *Hellblazer* and despite my subsequent jealousy-fuelled remorse, Jo had refused to trade the knife for the candy, the comic, or even both, something I would be relieved about by that evening as I lay on my bed inhaling raspberry liquorice along with John Constantine's latest hellblazing adventures. Anyway, Jo was more than happy to share, and we had been taking turns killing each other since arriving home an hour ago.

Except this house wasn't my home anymore and hadn't been for years and an hour ago I was still on a bus travelling to Alice Taylor's neighbourhood. I remembered speaking to my brother Jo before *leaving* home but also being with him at Gag City before *coming* home to this house. It was hard enough reconciling these conflicting memories without contending with the nagging voice in my head telling me that neither made any sense because I didn't have a brother, I only had a sister whose name was Jen, and I'd never even heard of John Constantine.

But that was ridiculous because my brother was right here, and his name was Jo, and John Constantine was the motherfucking *Hellblazer*.

We heard a car pull up and without word or plan, looked at each other with wide, excited eyes before scrambling to positions by the front door. I threw myself on the carpet, Jo stood over me, and we grinned maniacally at each other, chests heaving in excitement.

As the door opened, Jo clutched the knife above his head in both hands and I raised my own defensively, both of us struggling to look serious.

"You're such an asshole!" Jo spat with convincing disgust, a true thespian though he had yet to reach a double-digit birthday.

"I'm so sick of you!" I yelled back, louder but less convincing.

"Wilhelm! Johan!"

Our mother stood, framed in the doorway, a jumbo pack of toilet paper in one hand, keys in the other. Her use of our full names, heavy on each syllable, was the first sign this stunt was going to cost us. The second was our father crowding into the doorway behind her, a paper grocery bag cradled in each arm. His presence at the scene of any crime automatically meant a harsher sentence.

"What the hell?"

This was the nearest my father came to swearing.

"Go on, you don't have the balls," I yelled at Jo, deciding the show must go on.

There was a split-second of hesitation in which I could see Jo weighing up the trouble he was about to bring upon himself but then, to his eternal credit, he unleashed a ferocious roar and brought the knife down into my stomach.

Our mother screamed, our father yelled, groceries went tumbling, and we broke into hysterics so overpowering that Jo ended up beside me on the floor.

Our parents were too distraught to notice the lack of blood pouring forth from a wound I didn't have and must have taken our uncontrollable laughter for something like insanity because suddenly our father had Jo by the wrist, wrenching the knife from his hand, and our mother was all over me, turning me this way and that, saying my name over and over, only one syllable now.

Jo and I caught each other's eye, bringing on new waves of laughter.

Kids.

Then my father was standing up, pushing the blade into his palm with "Realistic Stabbing Action!" and the look on his face only made me laugh harder again until I thought I'd strain something. My mother looked up at him and he repeated the trick for her.

We would spend the next two weeks of summer confined to the house without TV or computer privileges but in that moment, which was years ago and also now, I was happy because somewhere in my uncaring kid's subconscious, I had been given tangible evidence of parental love. It was in the way my father disarmed my assailant, so brilliantly portrayed by Johan Tagg. It was in the way my mother cried and repeated "Oh, thank god, thank god" while stroking my hair because she did not yet have the presence of mind to start yelling.

I writhed in my mother's embrace, still laughing despite myself, with my brother next to me doing the same and our father standing over us taking in the scene, his eyes glinting with "Real Metal Effect!" and I felt very happy.

My mother's hair fell into my eyes and when I brushed it away, everyone was gone.

I was back in Alice Taylor's hallway.

I was standing but couldn't remember getting to my feet.

Owen had possessed me, had tried to possess me. I knew in my sore veins, bones, and skin that this was so.

It was ridiculous, he was being ridiculous.

I took an experimental step forward and found that walking was possible. Thinking of the open back door, I took another one, and a nuclear bomb went off in my head.

I was in the passenger seat of a car. I looked over and saw Owen driving and I knew he was taking us somewhere I did not want to go.

On the radio, Elvis sang "here we go again" like a man in the know.

I knew what was going to happen next and though there was no way out for Owen, I thought my presence here was entirely unnecessary.

I warned this Owen from years ago, one who just wanted to get home and eat dinner in front of the TV with his wife, what was about to happen, but it was like yelling at a movie screen. I screamed at him to stop the car, to let me out, and tried to pull his hands from the wheel but he didn't so much as twitch.

I pleaded with the Owen he was now, a hungry ghost who just wanted to eat me, but he was distracted because he was remembering his own death and there was a him who had gone through it and a him who had to go through it, over and over.

And then there was only one of us in the car, driving slowly through the suburban streets.

Mingled feelings of elation and panic at the miraculous act of driving only lasted a second or two before vanishing entirely. I drove every day, nothing special. I begged to be let out, of the car, of Owen's memory, but this ran parallel to thinking back on the long shift I'd just worked, the endless paperwork and futile court appearances, the lowlifes and the perverts, and looking forward to getting home to Anna, to the clean quiet and the peaceful warmth.

We saw the hand at the basement window and brought the car to a stop and then I was carried to his fate, couldn't even shut our eyes.

We heard the scream, made the snap decision, entered the house, looked at the ruined child discarded in the sitting room, a sight sadder and stranger than Owen had been able to express.

His breath shuddered but he never turned back. His fear and my own were the same and I couldn't comprehend how someone could be so terrified and keep going forward but that's what he did so that's what I did and our passage through the house went just as he had described.

I heard the breaking glass, came crashing out of the bathroom, choking on bleach and blood and water and our thoughts were a mishmash of determination and disgust, of terror and anger.

Anger above anything.

Anger so overpowering that it solidified us in purpose and for a while there was no misalignment of self, no wrestle for control. I was him, he was me, and together we burst through that bedroom door with gun raised.

There was time to take in the empty room before me, the window nailed shut, a sheet of torn black plastic hanging to one side. There was time to see the smashed panes and splintered wood that showed someone had been trying to force their way out, a heavily dented metal lamp still rocking on the floor the likeliest tool.

But there was no time to turn and face the corner behind the open door, the only place a person could be, before a blue-gloved hand flashed before me, something glinting in its grip.

I spun around unsteadily, but with eyes and gun trained on the man standing back against the wall. He gazed at me with a sort of nervous fascination, his attention divided between my gun and me, or rather what he had done to me.

His blue gloves and shoe coverings were unstained, his white shirt immaculate. On the floor between us lay a scalpel, a fine line of red on its edge, as if it had nothing to do with him.

A wave of sickly heat filled my chest and I knew this was connected to the spreading pool of blood that was about to reach the discarded scalpel just as I knew the sirens I could hear in the distance were coming this way.

I lived the second in which Owen entertained shooting him in the leg, to incapacitate rather than kill. I lived the half a second after that in which Owen thought of the broken boy downstairs and of Cherry Tree's future as an inmate-celebrity and in which he decided no such future should be written.

"I'm not armed," Cherry Tree said, more a dare than a plea. His eyes, rather than sparkling with innocence, had all the emotion of a shark's, a dull reflection of light serving as an imitation of emotion.

I shot him in the chest.

He stumbled back, hit the wall and fell forward onto his knees.

I put a hand to my neck but the hole was so large that I couldn't cover it and when it started to sink in I jerked it away, hot and dripping.

I fell to my knees, the world grey and spinning, as if I and the man kneeling with me were trapped together on an out-of-control amusement park ride.

Tiltawhirl or no, I kept my gun trained on his head.

The sirens were louder, help would be here soon, but I knew, as much as I could in that moment, not soon enough to help me. I could only hope they were fast enough to help the child in the basement, could only hope the scream I heard from outside hadn't signalled that it was too late, had always been too late.

He was clutching his chest where I'd shot him but past the obvious pain, a hint of a smirk soured his unremarkable features. He opened his mouth to speak but I had neither the time nor inclination for famous last words.

Another shot, followed by the wet smack of blood and meat hitting the wall behind Cherry.

I had been aiming for his head but the gun had dropped, sending the bullet into his throat which was poetic really. We could choke away our lives together.

His wet shrieking turned to gagging as he swatted at the hole in his throat as if it was a stubborn wasp he could chase off. Then his hands dropped from his wounds, fresh blood gushed onto the floor, and he collapsed face first before me.

Cherry Tree, the monster, the myth, now just a short, scrawny corpse, his once immaculate shirt sodden with blood, his pressed khaki pants stained and stinking with evacuated shit and piss.

I fell onto my back, felt the muscles in my neck tearing at my wound as my weight shifted. I knew I couldn't stay conscious for much longer and I knew, as much as I could in that moment, that by conscious I meant alive.

All my body wanted was sleep but I fought it, tried to lift my head but it was weighed down with the blood in my mouth and nose and eyes and I was drowning.

I kicked and wretched and thought desperately of Jo, my brother, who I would never see again and of my parents, who I had abandoned long before now, and at the same time I thought of Anna, of our children that would never be, of making love to her, of an empty hospital bed she would never sit beside.

I desperately tried to summon her image but she was eyes and teeth, shoulders and ankles, all floating on a stinking, crimson scum. I tried to say her name but couldn't speak, tried to hold on to her but I was falling out of reach.

Chapter 34

A phone was ringing.

Anna was before him and he was filled with desire; to talk to her, touch her, kiss her. Hopeless desires he told himself, harmful desires.

She was dressed in a shapeless, stained t-shirt, hair greasy and wild, eyes red-rimmed and pouched and still, she was beautiful.

She sat on the couch, staring ahead at a TV that wasn't turned on. An empty wine bottle lay on the carpet near her feet and an empty glass dangled loosely from her hand as if forgotten.

The phone rang for what felt like a very long time before she noticed it.

When she held it to her ear, she didn't even say hello.

He leaned in as close as he could, began to reach out but stopped because he had tried to touch her too many times to want to repeat the failure.

Filled with anticipation, he strained to hear the caller.

"Hi, is this Anna?"

"Who's this?"

She said this automatically rather than with any curiosity. In the months since they had been taken from each other, he had seen her every day and every day she was more lost, less there.

He had told the truth about waking up in an ambulance, but it had been minutes rather than months later and it was his own body he saw as he fell out of the vehicle, not some stranger's. Cutting out a year had left less to lie about, less chance of Wil –

ME, I AM WIL

– finding out about Chris.

He had watched his coffin lower into the ground, desperately yelling at the people gathered around to stop what they were doing, that they were making a mistake. As if they could just open the lid and let him jump back in to take up where he left off. He looked at his wife for help but her blank stare was directed at a box that was both full and empty as it disappeared into the earth.

He visited with his parents, watching them weep in separate rooms, his mother over her newspaper clippings, his father into his drink. He really did find out about Veronica Hill through his nephew's school project but while he had spent plenty of time with her in the home, it had only been to scream at her, challenging her to see him and what her son had done to him.

"My name's Chris, I'm a friend of Owen…of your husband."

A kaleidoscope of their lives together; happy, sad, fighting, laughing.

Then a more straightforward vision of an Anna who was older than the one sitting before him now with the phone to her ear, eyes still locked on the dead television screen, and an Owen who was older than he ever got to become. They sat together on a couch, flanked by adults and kids, most of whom looked a little or a lot like them. All smiling, trying not to fidget, waiting for the photographer to take the shot.

The camera snapped and the family froze but before Owen had time to admire the picture, it became a home movie.

Rewinding.

Their family scattered backwards from the couch and their grandchildren became babies and then became nothing and their son's graduation ceremony began with square hats falling into everyone's hands and ended with never happening and their daughter fell back on to a bicycle that was bought because she was never born and however desperately Owen tried to stop the life he meant to live undoing itself, he couldn't. His and Anna's lips came apart countless times, she became younger, and the tape slowed to a stop with her alone in the house that had been theirs, on the phone to a stranger.

"Are you there?"

"Do you work for a newspaper or a TV show, Chris?"

Now, she just sounded tired.

I struggled to concentrate on their conversation because Owen's need for Anna was a buzzing wall of white noise around us. I was beginning to see her just as he did, to feel her loss just as he did and my heart, wherever or whoever's it was right now, was breaking. I wanted just as badly as him to be able to caress her and tell her I was here, that nothing was broken that couldn't be fixed.

I saw now that my own feelings for the opposite sex only ever occupied my mind, my eyes, my crotch. All the women I had ever been with, all the women I told myself I should be with, had never really touched me and I had never touched them, not where it mattered. I had made sure of that, keeping my distance no matter how close.

But Owen's heart, his lungs, his fingertips, every square inch of him was for Anna and it hurt, and it was as exquisite as it was terrible.

"No, I'm just a friend with a message."

She said nothing.

"About three weeks after you and Owen started dating, he...um...lost control of himself while you were fooling around on your couch. He was so embarrassed he tried to leave but you told him it was the highest compliment he could give a girl. You slept together for the first time that night."

I could feel her in my arms, beneath me, on top of me, her smell, her taste. I could feel his sense of loss as this memory shot through him and my own pain as I pushed back, trying to reject his emotions and intentions which crowded against mine like a mob trying to break through the last row of riot shields.

"Your first place together was Apartment 10B, 4 Thomas Reilly Close in Maitland. The heating didn't work and the bottom kitchen drawer smelled like gone-off cabbage no matter how many times you cleaned it so you didn't keep anything in there except air freshener. The shower ran cold when the toilet flushed and –"

"Chris, you have my attention, please just tell me what you want."

Still tired, still distant, but there was some curiosity now.

"Sorry, Owen asked me to remind you of those things to prove that I'm speaking on his behalf, that I'm not just some crazy person."

"When and why did he tell you all of this? Did you work together?"

There was a pause, and I could practically here the deep breath Chris was taking, and then he launched into it. He told her that the "when" was yesterday and the "why" was because Owen was still here, was in fact standing by her side right now.

As Chris spoke, I felt Owen gathering himself, putting everything into reaching her.

"Anna, I'm here, I'm right here."

But she didn't react.

Chris kept talking and Anna became dismissive and then furious and Chris started to stutter and repeat himself and then she hung up.

The phone rang almost immediately but she didn't answer, instead letting it drop from her hand to land next to the empty bottle, just more trash. It rang, fell silent, and rang again until eventually Chris gave up.

When there had been silence for a few minutes, Anna spoke.

"Owen, are you really here?"

"I'm here, Anna, right in front of you."

"Owen, if you're here, talk to me. Please, I need you."

Tears were running down her cheeks, but it was no use, no matter how hard they tried. I could feel how different this was to him and me. This was all push and no pull, a faulty connection.

"Anna, I'm here." Yelling now. "I'm here and I love you."

He tried to run his hand along her arm like he always did when she was upset but it sank into her and he recoiled, feeling disgusted and disgusting.

Eventually, she stopped calling out to him.

Following her to the bathroom, he watched her take more of the pills she had been given in lieu of the help nobody was able to give her. The label instructed not to mix with alcohol but she had given up on such formalities.

He stood, watching her face in the mirror, alone with her reflection, alone with him.

He opened his mouth to speak, and I knew this was important, that what he was about to say would affect many lives, even the one he had left behind.

Suddenly, I felt him closing down this memory, ripping me away from it.

I fought back, surprised to find I even could, but he was stronger and though I felt the words forming on his tongue, could almost make out the shape of them, they escaped my grasp.

I came back to myself again.

Myself was halfway up the stairs and climbing.

My legs blazed with pain as I forced them to a stop and I gritted my teeth against the protests of a body caught in the midst of civil war.

"Goddamn it, Owen, stop this, now."

My voice came out hoarse and hushed but when I spoke again, it sounded even harsher, the words jagged and angular, more a collection of sounds than words.

"You-ca-can't-do-this-forever-Wil-let-happen-I-will-go-when-done."

I wanted to scream but my mouth shut before I could make another sound. I wanted to have never heard my own voice speak to me with such coldness. I wanted to never ever feel as afraid and alone as I did which was almost funny because you could never be less alone than when sharing your very being with someone else.

I was filled with rage and that was good because it was all my own. He was stealing my body, my words, the breath from my lungs, and I was furious.

You're not a ghost Owen, you're a monster.

You can't do this forever, Wil. I'll go when I'm done. Just let it happen. You can't win this. I'm too strong, I've been practicing.

No sooner had the question formed in my mind than it took us away.

Wil lay on the floor of his laundry room, a thin line of drool pooling on the tiles. I felt pity for him but not enough to leave him be. I was getting through to him, even if he would not yet admit it to himself. Our meet-cute in the city library was only a day away, a fact I couldn't know then but remembered now.

He would do what I would ask of him because I would make it seem like the only thing to do and I would push him more gently than I had pushed Chris, who had taught me that men like this could not be trusted to do the right thing for its own sake, too many opinions and reservations getting in the way of the required certainty. Maybe a cop or doctor or soldier would take less pushing but none of them had ever so much as blinked at me.

Something about the paranormally inclined, something about Chris, about Wil, worked.

I had tried other ghost hunting groups after Chris because it meant less chance of Doug and Cal interfering but there had been no blinks, no hitched breaths, no luck.

First Chris, now Wil.

Lonely people reaching out.

Maybe I was like them now.

Maybe that helped.

I had a second chance with Wil, maybe a last chance. I would practice and I would be ready. This thing I was now, that only looked like me, was responding to my will less and less, as though its memory of itself was fading. I'd try to move forwards but would remain still, try to step sideways only to fall backwards. Whatever time I had to do what needed to be done, it was almost surely running out and then...

Carefully, I lay down next to Wil.

I took a moment and then shoved sideways into him.

Searing.

Tearing.

Roaring.

I was gripping tightly to the safety bar of a rollercoaster as it sped from a curve and launched itself up a steep slope. I looked beside me and Anna was there, laughing and crying at the same time, her hair whipping every which way. A greater shock ran through me, almost unbearable, but she just threw her arms in the air, screamed louder, and we went into the fall together.

Darkness became light as my eyes found Wil's, like a kid adjusting his Halloween mask. I blinked, once, twice, and then looked from side to side.

I bore down and one of Wil's hands began to twitch and flex, soon the other did the same.

I settled into Wil's skin and our minds drifted together.

An office party.

I eyed a woman across the room and then, coming to some decision, shambled my way over.

"Mandy?"

She broke off mid-conversation with some guy from Risk Assessment. They both looked at me doubtfully.

"Mandy, come 'ere," I said conspiratorially, gesturing to a quieter part of the room. She looked an apology at Risk and came with me.

"Look, I know we don't know each other very well but..." I trailed off, first trying to remember what I wanted to say and then, once I remembered, plucking up the courage to say it.

"Mandy McSherry, I just thought that if you ever...that if you'd like to go somewhere with me, to dinner or something, then that would be good."

"Wil, I..."

Her tone signalled a '*no*' on the way and I was glad to be too drunk to feel the hardest part of the fall.

"You don't have to, Mandy...Mandy McSherry. Don't even worry about it, it was a stupid idea. I have to go anyway, it's late and I'm almost drunk so..."

She placed a hand on my arm to stop my gibbering.

"Wil, you seem nice but right now you're hammered and I'm pretty sure you have throw-up on your sleeve," she said, her eyes remaining kind and focused on me even as she withdrew her soiled hand and held it away from her. "How about we get you a ride home and you ask me again sometime when you're sober? Then we'll know if you're really interested."

I forced myself out of this scene, not for the first time finding myself frightened by how quickly I could lose myself in Wil's head. His memory acted like a counterweight that pulled him up to the surface as it pushed me down.

I had managed to raise us to a sitting position but Wil started convulsing and as he fell back to the floor, I was thrown out of his body and into his downstairs neighbour's living room. Still, the practice was paying off and as one of Anna's lifestyle vloggers was fond of saying, it was about progress, not perfection.

Chapter 35

When I returned, I was climbing the stairs on all fours, like a good dog. While I had been lost in Owen's past, in the present he had found it easier to manoeuvre me upstairs crawling instead of walking.

I visualised throwing myself down the steps but before this thought could even reach full bloom, my right hand shot out and grabbed the stair rail, the sweat sodden glove squeaking against the wood. I had not asked my hand to grip the rail and when I tried to remove it, it didn't respond.

I looked up and saw we were nearly at the top of the stairs. Sweat stung my eyes and blurred my vision but when I blinked it away –

"Come on Billy, just say the words, say you did it."

I was in a tiny room with three other men. Fluorescent light bounced off every scratched and stained surface.

Two were dressed like office workers but I knew they were detectives because Owen had known they were detectives. I didn't need his help to recognise the casually dressed man on the opposite side of the metal table because I had been in his house, in his bedroom, had seen photographs of him.

Owen spent a lot of time in police stations looking for someone with the right qualifications and in Bill Hanover, he had found him. A man with the right type of violent and inhumane sexual predilections to fit into a narrative suited to Owen's requirements and my coercion. What interested him just as much, what made Bill the perfect candidate, was the smattering of firearms charges sprinkled over the list of his dirty deeds. He wanted me to have a gun because he wanted it to be fast. Too fast for her to get away from me or if it came to it, too fast for me to let her get away from him. Something like guilt twinged his unknowable insides when he considered the story he was weaving, the players he was moving around, but he swallowed it down. There was an eternity for guilt but right now, time was precious.

Bill Hanover shrugged and threw his hands up, offering a confused "who me?" smile. Reading Hanover's file over the detectives' shoulders, full of near misses, reluctant witnesses, and nearly but never enough evidence, Owen guessed this lamblike grin got quite a workout.

Hanover was still wearing it when he strolled out of the station an hour later but as Owen followed him to his car, it curdled into something more canine. By the time Owen caught up with him at the address listed on his file, to find him pushing aside bags of his ex-wife's clothing in the closet of his spare room, all trace of humour had vanished, leaving only the bared teeth of a ravenous predator. Hanover removed the trick shelf and it was only after he spent some time handling and checking his weapon with a reverence bordering on fetishism, shuffling through his deck of Polaroids with the loving intent of a baseball card collector, that this look of hunger abated.

Once Wil did what needed to be done, I'd have him put those Polaroids in the mail. As horrible a delivery as they would make, there were two detectives who'd greet them like an early Christmas present. Then, Wil and I could —

ME, I AM WIL

Then, Wil and I —

FUCK YOU OWEN, I AM WIL, WIL IS I

Then, Wil was lying in bed, studying Tara's sleeping face. She had been stroking his hip absent-mindedly as she nodded off and her hand rested there still.

He told himself she might be the one, or at least *some* one worth hanging in there for, and also told himself he needed to break up with her as soon as possible. He needed her, he didn't need her, he wanted her, he wanted to get away from her. She slept peacefully, breathing softly, while he lay still and silent, his thoughts the loudest thing in the room.

He wanted to turn over, get comfortable, but if he did then her hand would move and while it was there, he felt cared for and worth caring for and this was strange and wonderful and frightening. I felt him let the frightening part of the equation consume everything else until he turned over and shut his eyes, pretending to himself that her hand slipping away didn't feel like a loss.

When he opened them...

When I opened them, I was at the top of the stairs, still climbing on my knees and elbows, and with all the authority and will I had left in me, I ordered my body to a halt.

Owen, stop this.

Please.

There was no answer, but I knew I wasn't alone. I could feel him prodding and poking beneath my skin. This was betrayed by the fact that while I was able to struggle to my feet and stand, my right hand once again shot out to grip the stair rail, under no orders from me. We were on the last step, where the stairs ended and the landing began.

I was so tired and it was becoming impossible to separate myself from the morass of memory we had become. If I could just gather my thoughts, if I just had five fucking minutes alone in my own head to put everything together, if I –

"If you can't do this, something that actually means anything, then what's your fucking point? You should be dead, not me."

"Maybe I should be," Chris said.

He paced up and down the platform while a wind I couldn't feel swept over us. Across the tracks, the bush Doug and Cal were hiding behind rustled but Chris was too keyed up for this to draw his attention and I willed for it to stay that way.

He hugged himself against the cold, against me.

What was I supposed to do? There was a job to be done and he was the only one who could do it. Was that my fault? He needed a friend, I gave him a friend. He needed purpose, I gave him that too. Still, he dithered and whined and a violent impulse to wring his neck startled me.

That wasn't me.

I was the good guy.

"I'm so scared, I don't think – "

"You don't need to think," I growled, losing my patience. "What's right is right."

I liked Chris, maybe in a way I loved him, but right now he was Cherry Tree and he was my death and he was being apart from Anna and he was my fear and my uncertainty and I hated him.

I heard a train coming, still some distance off, and we both knew if he took it to get away from me, I couldn't follow.

He stopped pacing and faced me.

"But what if it's *not* right, just because you think it is doesn't make it so. Being dead doesn't make you all-knowing."

I told him for the hundredth time that it would be ok, that all he had to do was take the train to the Freeling stop and wait for me there. We'd go to Meadow Court together, like we had planned and discussed again and again. I didn't add that I'd already be there waiting if I could have trusted him to get on the train without me here to hold his hand.

He started to cry and I stopped myself from caring while making sure to sound like I did because I needed him to calm down before he became so hysterical that I couldn't get through to him, before the two snooping fucks hiding across the tracks felt compelled to intervene.

"I'm sorry, I *can't*. I need to go home. I need more time to – "

"THERE IS NO FUCKING TIME!"

My patience failed completely, and I hit him so hard his head flew back.

It was a mistake, a moment of madness, but as much as I apologised and told him I only wanted to snap him out of it, there was no denying the visceral thrill I felt when my fist made contact.

"It doesn't matter, hit me all you want," he said. "Doesn't make you less dead or more right."

"I don't want to hit you."

That was a half-truth. I *did* want to hit something, but I didn't want to hurt Chris. Whatever had been lies, the truth was he had tried to be a friend to me. I glanced again across the tracks but our watchers made no move to come to his defence.

"I shouldn't have hit you but if you don't do this, I'll find someone else. It'll take more time but I'll find someone and we'll get to her."

Jesus, I sounded like the bad guy.

"No, you won't. I'm going to talk to the rest of the guys in DAPI like I should have all along. I'm going to tell the cops. I don't care what they think about me."

He was shouting now, eyes blazing at me, but the incoming train still nearly drowned him out. I didn't dare turn around to see how close it was in case I broke whatever hold I had left over him. Every day, I felt less me, less here, and no matter what I told Chris about finding someone else to help me, even if that could work, there was no guarantee I had enough time left to try.

The train roared in, doors hissing open, but no passengers emerged from the sparsely populated cars. He looked at the train then back to me.

"Chris. Don't."

He took a step back, away from me, closer to the nearest door of the train.

"Chris, what are you thinking?"

When he replied, I read the words on his lips as much as heard them above the clamour of the wind and the idling train.

"What *was* I thinking, Owen? And what the fuck are you thinking?"

Then he was stepping off the platform and the train's doors were closing at the same moment, as if conspiring to take him from me.

I lunged, powered by nothing but desperation, and everything changed.

Suddenly, I remembered people I never knew and places I never was. I was dead but no longer dead, me but not only me, a man without a body who was somehow stumbling through a moving train.

Get out get out get out

Chris's voice but in my head.

In MY head, Owen, MY head. Get the fuck out

Our momentum and the gathering speed of the train sent us sprawling into a seat and we landed in some approximation of a sitting position, limbs splayed haphazardly.

He tried to understand what was happening to him while I tried to understand what I was doing to him, our thoughts tangling around each other's until they made no sense.

Chris told me again to get out of his head and in another place and another time Wil told me to get out of his and I could feel their hatred and their scorn. I pushed them away, stamped them down. When you were doing the right thing, the ends could justify the means.

You'll see Chris, I'm right, I know what's best...

He won't see anything Owen because you he's dead, because you...

I bore down, regained my focus, and it felt simultaneously like flexing a muscle and raising my voice and I was stronger and louder than either of them, than both of them together.

A middle-aged couple stared at us.

Chris reached out a hand, trying to ask for help but on instinct I slammed his mouth shut and he could only moan at them. They stood and hurried to the next car, the man pushing the woman along protectively.

We were alone.

I was in pain, but I'd felt worse.

It was like I was roughly plugged into Chris's nerves, almost able to feel the seat beneath us, almost able to smell the fetid train car air surrounding us, almost like a normal, living human instead of whatever I was.

The feedback of Chris's senses, however dulled, diluted my pain and made it bearable, gave it shape and purpose.

With an effort, I raised his hand and flexed his fingers. I tried blinking and after a few seconds his eyes slowly closed and opened. Gaining confidence, I shot out his arm and grabbed a nearby handrail and squeezed it hard and it felt so fucking good to hold and feel something even if it wasn't Anna and even if it felt like I was wearing an oven mitt instead of skin and —

— then I *was* Chris and a man who I hated, a man who was my father, was towering above me and thumping my ear over and over and telling me I don't listen good enough and then I was me again and I was bleeding out on the floor and Chris was screaming at me to let him out of these memories and —

— then I lost concentration and Chris came flooding back just as the train came to a stop and before I could regain control we leapt to our feet and ran through the open door, nearly knocking over a woman laden with shopping bags in the process, and then we were on the platform and in the confusion of fighting for control we teetered on the platform's edge, almost falling back against the departing train, until finally one or both of us regained balance.

"I'm not going to kill anyone," Chris yelled into the night.

In the corner of our vision, the few late-night commuters who had exited the other cars favoured us with weary, wary glances and rushed toward the elevators and stairs that led down to street level, not comforted by the shouted promise, not realising he was defying me rather than reassuring them.

I felt myself being pushed down, becoming smaller. An image came to me of two pairs of hands grappling for a steering wheel.

I was so busy trying to quieten Chris's thoughts, to take charge again, that it took me too long to understand what he was thinking, to see where he was going.

By the time I understood, it was too late.

He walked into the guardrail with such force that I felt the pain in his midsection. The city lights blinked at us over the shadow strewn underpass below.

Chris tried to talk to me but I didn't want him to gain more ground, so I clambered and clawed inside him even harder.

Maybe he begged for me to stop, to leave, to save his life but –

HE DID OWEN AND YOU HEARD HIM YOU HEARD EVERY FUCKING WORD

– but somewhere in his mind or mine I thought that if he was so willing to kill himself then he didn't deserve this life or this body and maybe with enough time and practice I could put him away completely and stay here and live out the rest of the life I was owed in the skin of a man who didn't want it.

His understanding of my thoughts hit me at the same time as my own awareness of them and I felt his horror and my shame. I hadn't meant it, not really.

Just do what needs to be done Chris, then all of this will be over.

"Please, Owen, I won't...I don't want to hurt any...anyone."

He fought to speak and I fought to stop him because if he was speaking then he was in control. He grunted in frustration and gripped the upper rail.

Despite me trying to keep him in place, he lifted one foot and then the other onto the lower rail and then he was standing, swaying in the wind, leaning forward to stop me from throwing us back onto the safety of the platform.

Inside, I swore once again that if it wasn't him, it would be someone else and he replied quietly but firmly that it wasn't him. With that, as if forming these words cast aside any last trace of indecision, I felt his inner thoughts swell and rush around me and it was all I could do to keep from being washed away.

He thought about his father and couldn't think of anything good and of his mother and wished she had done better for herself and for him. He thought about the few people in his life he considered friends and I saw a pretty girl called Emily kiss him on the lips and she tasted of beer and chewing gum. I knew it was his first kiss and that it was one of precious few memories that time and context hadn't turned from good to bad for Chris.

I felt his sadness and regret, his final conviction that I couldn't stop myself so he would have to.

I tried once more to jerk him away from the guardrail, to finish what we had started, what he had promised me. He leaned further forward, the whipping wind sending the tears in his eyes streaming back, his arms held out to either side, Christ on a cross, keeping his traitorous hands well away from snatching distance of the rail where I might make use of them.

He cast a last inward glance directly at me but this time, I felt neither anger nor fear from Chris, only pity.

Seeing this as a moment of weakness, I made another bid for control, but I was mistaken.

He had never been stronger.

"For God's sake, Owen, she's your wife."

These words were still leaving his lips as he leaned toward the city skyline, past the point of no return. His feet left the rail and then the ground was hurtling toward us and there was no-one left to fight with because there was nobody left to fight for.

Chapter 36

I jerked back to consciousness, my arms held out before me, but I was not falling toward broken blacktop, I was standing before a closed door.

One outstretched hand was reaching for the handle. The other held Hanover's gun, which was just as it should be. I had already flicked off the safety and racked back the slide to chamber a round. The weapon felt alive and ready in my grip, as solid as a promise fulfilled.

I was worried that Wil wouldn't bring it today but when he showed up out front, the shape had been so obvious in his pocket, I didn't even have to ask. Any fear that it might be unloaded, that he brought it only to bark rather than bite in case of an emergency, was dismissed by its telling weight.

On the other side of the door, my wife slept, doped out on pills and alcohol, just like I left her when I went outside to meet...

To meet who?

Hadn't I just been thinking about...?

Never mind.

I couldn't remember why I'd been struggling so much, or how I got myself so confused.

Anna was my wife and Jo was my brother and I was dead and I was alive and everything was so easy, I had no idea why I'd made it hard.

Sure, there was that voice in the back of my mind, but it was so small and stupid that whatever it was trying to say couldn't possibly be important.

I remembered the words I first spoke to Anna the day Chris called her. When I watched her in the bathroom mirror, looking as lost and hopeless as me.

At first, they felt cruel, profane, but the more I said them, the more sense they made, the more their true meaning overrode their violence.

"Kill yourself."

Anna, looking at herself in the mirror, looking at me.

"Kill yourself to be with me."

Anna, sitting in the driveway in her car, barely able to summon the energy to turn the key in the ignition, never mind go anywhere.

"Kill yourself, then we can be together."

Anna, on our couch, head in her hands.

"I'm right here, waiting for you. You don't have to be sad or scared. Just let go."

Anna, getting through a bottle of wine a day which became a bottle of vodka, going through pills quicker than her helpless, sympathetic doctor could prescribe them. Anna, who never had more than two champagnes at a party because she got light-headed and didn't approve of taking more than the recommended two aspirin per four hours even if she had a killer migraine.

I couldn't be sure if my words were part of the reason the booze and the pills disappeared into her faster and faster, I only knew they weren't working fast enough. I had wanted to give her a lifetime of happiness but now I could give her an eternity of it, as long as I could bring her to me before I went away somewhere she could never reach.

Eventually, with time dragging on and the outcome too uncertain, I decided Chris needed to do for Anna what neither she nor I could do for her. Even then, I kept up those poisoned whispers because if what she was taking didn't kill her, it would at least make it easier for him to do it without her ever having to know, ever having to feel as afraid as I had.

Chris was gone but I was here and now, finally, there would be an end to our suffering.

They taught us to put our finger on the trigger only when ready to fire but there was no chance of an accidental shooting here and I curled my finger around it, ready to squeeze.

The gloves made me a little clumsy, but I had plenty of training.

It was instinctual.

I took hold of the door handle, and I was somewhere else, in a house where bleach and blood filled my senses and horror filled my mind.

Chapter 37

I screamed at Owen, but it was no use.

He wasn't listening.

He was in Cherry Tree's house and he was in his own home.

In both, there was a door.

If she dies, we will be together.

The thought that had taken root on the day Anna hung up on Chris and grew until it wrapped around Owen like a vine.

If she dies, we will be together.

In two houses, in two different lives, I opened the door.

The curtains were closed but I could make out the motionless figure on the bed.

I stepped into the room and squeezed the trigger.

Chapter 38

And shot myself in the foot.
It was instinctual.

Chapter 39

The pain resulting from my act of sabotage was immediate and overwhelming.

I felt Owen's surprise, his outrage, and his panic.

Whether my elation made me over-confident or my agony distracted me, I don't know, but before I could follow up my Pyrrhic victory by dropping the gun, Owen raised it again.

I commanded my arm to lower, my hand to open, my finger to release the trigger, but my moment of strength had been just that, a moment, and could not compete with the deathless force that was Owen Hoath.

I felt the pressure of the trigger give under my finger and this time the bullet went into the sleeping figure on the bed.

I had lost and Anna Hoath was lost and all was lost, to be broken and never to be fixed.

Owen, determined to the last, took a step forward, readying to take one final shot to make sure it was over.

Before he could take it, an arm clamped around my neck, pulling me backward and a strong hand clutched my wrist, thrusting my arm in the air. Somehow, Owen kept a grip on the gun, managed to force my squeezed nerves to pull the trigger, but it only resulted in bringing down a shower of plaster on my head.

The acrid smoke of gunfire doused my senses and behind me whoever was restraining us was yelling but the gunshots had turned my head into an amplifier giving squealing feedback and it was all white noise to go with the white light dancing in my eyes and none of this was as disorientating, for me or for Owen, as the bedroom closet bursting open.

Between the weak light and a strong conviction that only monsters burst out of closets, it took us a second to recognise Douglas J. Allan.

While Owen tried to break free of our captor, I no longer had the presence of mind to do anything but watch Doug's fist as it flew into my face.

My amplified head turned into a bell, ringing like it might shatter, but Owen was so keyed up he didn't even feel it. My legs tried to buckle but he wouldn't let them give way and the fingers on my wrist bit in harder but still he wouldn't drop the gun.

He used my free hand to punch Doug in the stomach and sent the returning elbow into a soft part of the person behind us but all the bucking and raging the disembodied supernatural being attempted couldn't overcome the fact that he was driving a standard issue human. As the hold around my neck tightened and Doug hit me again, knuckles crunching into my temple, I sank into oblivion.

Before I went completely under, I heard the gun hit the floor followed by a heavy thud that could only be me doing the same thing, and then Owen was screaming in my ears, yelling at me to get up, even as my body shut down around him.

Chapter 40

"Owen?"

When I tried to open my eyes, only one obeyed. When I attempted raising a hand to inspect the other one, I found they were both tied behind my back.

I was fine with this.

I tried once more to open the offending eye but the painful pressure it caused in the hard, swollen-over ball of flesh that had once been my eyelids convinced me to give it up.

"Owen?" Anna Hoath repeated more forcefully.

I had never met this woman yet I could still remember a whole other lifetime, one we had spent together, though it was already beginning to unravel like a dream upon waking.

I couldn't open my mouth, couldn't even shake my head to tell her I was just me now.

"I'm here, Anna."

I slid my one good eye past her to where her husband was standing.

She glanced over her shoulder but seeing nothing, looked back to me.

Her eyes, a shade of brown so deep they were almost black, stared into the red haze of mine, while white and black spots fought it out for my field of vision.

Doug and Cal were in the room too, both staring at me, not at Owen or Anna, and that made sense because Anna was dead – because Owen – because *I* had killed her. And now here she was, still within inches of her husband and both of them still alone because Owen's scheming and dreaming had done nothing but send her even further from him and make me a murderer in the process.

Helpless to answer the question in her gaze, to apologise for what I had done and had failed to do, it was all I could do to return it for a moment before I went under again.

"Wil?"

Time had passed, though I couldn't say how much.

Again, I tried to open my eyes and again only one did as I asked. The white and black spots had quit the field and the red haze had softened to a pinkish glow that gave Doug's pale, harried face some colour.

"Wil?"

This time, I managed a nod.

Once again, I let my eye travel around the room.

Anna stood, watching me, while her husband stood by her side, watching her.

Doug and Cal sat side by side at the foot of the bed, directly opposite me. I was propped up in a sitting position against the wall between the room's two windows, both now open, letting in sunlight and letting out some of the cordite stench of gunfire.

"Is that you?" Doug asked. "Just you?"

"Just me," I croaked.

"Prove it," Cal said, not unkindly.

I sat quietly for what might have been one minute or five before clearing my throat. Doug flinched but held his ground.

"*The Frighteners* is Peter Jackson's true fantasy masterpiece, Refused are the shape of punk to come, and Benjamin Radford's *Investigating Ghosts* is a masterwork."

Doug and Cal looked at each other and nodded.

Having imparted this wisdom, I fell into a coughing fit.

The pain this caused my tender throat and throbbing head was quickly forgotten when I jarred my foot. Having lain in wait for my attention, it screamed at me now from amidst a woozily large puddle of drying blood. I did my best to hold it still as my coughing descended into wet, undignified moaning.

Someone had removed my shoe and sock and replaced them with a tidily constructed but already soaked through mix of pads and bandages. Cautiously, I wiggled my toes and the pain caused by their half-hearted little dance saw me off for another round of blackout.

When I came to again, it was to the sound of footsteps on the stairs, muffled through the closed bedroom door.

I opened my eye and found it was finally free of its red haze.

Anna and Owen were gone but Doug and Cal were still in their same positions at the foot of the bed. When I parted my lips to speak, each of them hurriedly held a finger to my split, swollen lips to quieten me. This alone almost made me yelp in pain, but I swallowed it.

Then Anna was in the room again, closing the bedroom door behind her.

Owen was not with her.

"They're gone. They didn't like it, but I told them I didn't know anything about any gunshots. Being a war widow means people, especially cops, play nice with you," she said. "Lucky they didn't go into the living room though, there's blood dripping down from the ceiling onto my couch."

She looked down at my semi-exploded foot, in which the raucous alarm bells of pain had given way to a numbness that would have been cause for me to worry if I had sense enough to do so.

"We're just lucky it wasn't the officers who were here the other night," Doug said, with an edge to his tone that seemed aimed at her. "I'm sure *they* would have wanted to investigate further."

She ignored him, stared at me.

"Owen?"

I shook my head very gently while Doug responded on my behalf.

"We think he's just Wil again."

Hot tears flowed down my cheeks, from my open eye and closed one alike.

She had opened and closed the bedroom door with her own hands.

She was speaking with Doug.

She was alive.

Everything that had happened, everything that had almost happened, and Anna Hoath was alive.

She was not murdered.

I was not a murderer.

If I could have moved, I would have stood and lifted her in my arms to feel her weight and her warmth and revel in who she was, who she *still* was, and in what I had not done to her.

But I couldn't, so instead I just looked at her and if there was fear and mistrust in the look she returned, it didn't matter because Anna Hoath was alive.

She sat on the side of the bed, perched on the edge though it seemed to me that this was more to do with a general sense of unease than to any objections against sharing her bed with Doug and Cal. It was some time before I could take my eye off her but when I finally did, blinking away tears, I cast my monocular glare upon them.

"What. The. Fuck?"

Chapter 41

"When I got home after dropping you off the other evening, Cal and I spoke _"

"Argued."

"OK Calvin, we *argued* into the early hours of the morning about what to do." He rolled his eyes in Cal's direction, a comforting bit of normality in an abnormal situation. "Cal wanted to try one last time to convince you to stay with us and then, if you still refused, take you by force again and this time hold you captive. I thought the likeliest result of this would be you reporting us to the police to get us out of the way while you went ahead with what you were doing. I also agreed with your point that taking you out of the picture wouldn't stop Owen."

Once Doug and Cal stopped lobbing logic bombs at each other, they agreed that they had not yet done enough and that even if it had to be without my support or knowledge, they needed to do something more. They also agreed that they had no idea what this something more might be.

"That's when I thought about Chris's notebook," Doug said. "We needed to know more about Owen, find something we'd missed that might make a difference. There was certainly nothing left to gain from our recordings or any of the online articles about Owen and Cherry Tree and everything that happened..." he trailed off, casting an uncomfortable glance at Anna but she was gazing at the floor and didn't catch his look. "But maybe there was something in Chris's notes that would help us to help you."

Reading between Doug's flat lines, I could guess that when he broached the subject of the notebook, the one thing Cal had forbidden him, he fully expected his motives to be questioned. Instead, Cal readily if unhappily agreed that it was the only avenue left to them.

Later that morning, when Doug showed up at the home of Jack and Wendy Collins, he did his best to look as respectable as possible despite his face being coloured a mottled purple of sleep deprivation and bruising.

Wendy Collins answered the door but neither she nor Doug had a chance to say hello before Jack Collins crowded in behind her to ask who it was and what they wanted. The questions were ostensibly addressed to Wendy but the scowl was directed at the stranger from whom she could not possibly yet have learned these things.

Doug answered honestly by telling them who he was, how he had known their son, and what he was after – a certain notebook belonging to Chris that might be in their possession.

From there on, he was less than honest.

"I didn't tell them that I knew where they lived because Chris had once visited them back when Cal and I were following him. I also didn't tell them why I really wanted the notebook."

Instead, he said he had been working on a book with Chris and while he had tried to struggle on without their son's notes, not wanting to bother them in their grief, he had finally reached an impasse.

When Jack Collins asked what kind of "book", he flavoured the word with the kind of distaste usually saved for "turd" or "verruca". When Doug told him it was supernatural fiction, Jack fired back that all that "supernatural shit" was fiction, no matter what some weirdoes wanted to believe. Doug offered only a tight smile in response, the best he could do without giving offence to a man who seemed as eager to take it as give it.

He went on to explain that a publisher was in place and with the help of Chris's notes, there could soon be a book sold for real money with their son's name on it as co-author which would result in some of that real money going to them. Wendy started to look at Doug more warmly when he mentioned her son's name on a book jacket. Jack never looked at him warmly, but the mention of money changed his belligerence to a shrewd watchfulness.

I flashed back to a third-hand memory in which I was a young Chris, too young to cross the street alone, with Jack Collins looming over me like a giant, pummelling me with fists the size of my head.

Jack's avarice quickly gave way to disappointment as he gathered the thoughts scattered by Doug's mention of money and informed him that they had thrown away their son's belongings, including any "useless crap like that".

Even this brief encounter with Chris's father left Doug with a bad taste in his mouth and seeing no reason to prolong it, he thanked them for their time and made to leave.

"Wait, please."

The first words Doug heard from Chris's mother were so quiet he wasn't sure he'd really heard them until he turned back to find her holding up a trembling finger, its nail chewed to the quick, gesturing for him to hold on.

She squeezed past her husband and disappeared into the house. Jack Collins watched her go, his meaty forehead contorted into furrows of puzzlement, as if a piece of his furniture had started moving of its own accord, and then settled his glare back on Doug.

They stood in a silence neither bothered breaking until Wendy reappeared, squeezing her way forward past Jack's bulky frame, and thrust a box into Doug's hands. The two men shared an uneasy glance, both aware she had done this quickly to prevent Jack from intercepting the box. It was plain cardboard, distinguished only by the words "Good Cutlery" written in cramped, backward sloping handwriting across the top.

"All of Chris's writing I could find is in there," she said. "I gathered it all together when we emptied his apartment."

The look Jack gave Wendy, one she pretended not to see, said there'd be a price to pay for this small mutiny. The look Jack gave the box said Wendy had been right to get it out of his reach before he could ransom its contents to Doug for an upfront payment or finder's fee. Doug held the box close to his body and took a half step back from their doorway.

"He used to write me stories when he was little, he was very talented," Wendy said. "If there's anything that will help with finishing our son's book, please take it." Her hushed tones faded to a whisper as she wilted under her husband's disapproving stare.

Doug almost promised to return her son's belongings when he was finished with them but stopped himself. He had a strong impression they were safer in his house than this one. Instead, he thanked Wendy Collins and walked away without another word to her husband.

He drove the box home to Cal where they opened it together and amongst the jumbled scraps of bad teenage poetry, DAPI case reports, and other odds and ends, found the notebook they wanted.

"I don't know if Wendy Collins has ever read it, but it's all there in black and white, plain for anyone to see, at least anyone with a frame of reference who knows it isn't fiction," Doug said. "Chris's notebook was the key to everything."

Chris's words told them that contrary to what any of us believed, rather than being asked to bring someone to justice, he had instead been asked to stage a reunion. Now that they knew what was really happening, and who it would happen to, the same all-powerful *couple-kwan-do* that enabled them to break into Chris's apartment and snatch me from a busy city street kicked into overdrive.

Less than twenty-four hours since he had last parked outside my office building, Cal returned, in his mother's car this time to avoid being spotted by Owen or me. When I left work, he captured and analysed some footage, once again cursing his luck that the only way he had of detecting Owen was so slow.

"And unbelievably fucking annoying to use as a real-time tool," he added. Finding no sign of Owen, he used his phone to send Doug a simple message. WAIT.

A word he and Doug would send each other dozens of times over the following days as they traded shifts, following me from home to work and back again, checking for Owen and never finding him.

After days of stakeout duty, of barely seeing one another, of avoiding Cal's mother's phone calls asking when exactly she could expect her car back, I finally shook things up by calling in sick for work. Cal, who happened to be on stalking duty that day, followed me to the movies, to my solitary dinner, and then home.

Just as he was resigning himself to another night in the car, lowering his seatback as near to horizontal as he could achieve in a Mirage, I rushed out of my apartment building.

After hurriedly righting his seat and swiping the remnants of his takeout dinner from the dashboard, he swore at the oncoming cars delaying him from executing an urgent, illegal U-turn. When he finally caught up to me, he was just in time to see me walk into McGinty's.

Hours later, when I fell out onto the street, he was ready, all thoughts of sleep pushed aside, and he was filming. While I lurched away into the night, he played his snippet of footage back with his filter applied and saw Owen with me, just the white ball of trouble they'd been waiting for.

He grabbed his phone and even though this time he called Doug instead of messaging him, it was still just a single word statement.

NOW.

In their home, Doug hung up on Cal and hurriedly dialled another number, finally safe in the knowledge that since Owen was with me, he could not be listening in on either side of the call he was about to make.

In Meadow Court, in the middle of another endless night, Anna Hoath picked up her ringing phone.

Chapter 42

The three of us looked to Anna to take up the story but instead she took a deep breath, stood from the bed, and walked into the bathroom.

When she returned, she was holding a green first aid box smeared with red fingerprints that I guessed were a recent addition.

"Need to put more dressing on your foot, the blood's soaked right through now."

She knelt by my foot and opened the box.

"Shouldn't we change out the wet stuff first?" Cal asked.

She looked over her shoulder at him.

"First Aid 101, removing bandages takes away any good clotting work. Best to keep layering for now," she said, and turned her attention to me. "You'll need a hospital sooner rather than later though."

I nodded weakly, tensing myself for the imminent pain as she began to wrap a fresh roll of dressing around my foot, but her touch was gentle, if not exactly affectionate.

"We could take you right now," Doug said. "Now you're back with us, so to speak."

"Not on your life," I said. "I need to hear the rest of this."

That was part of it, to be sure, but I didn't have the energy or the right words to explain the even greater reason I would willingly refuse being taken away from here to a hospital where they'd do wonderful things like properly care for my wound and fill me full of painkillers. I had the sense we were finally, all of us, coming to an ending, as long as I stayed here, stayed open to how such a thing might be brought about.

"Pretty badass move," Cal said, pointing at my foot.

"It wasn't enough to stop him though," I said, raising my eyes to the ceiling because looking at the bloody foam squeezing out from between the layers of bandages was making me woozy. The only disadvantage of this was that I could see the ragged bullet hole in the plaster and found it impossible not to imagine the matching one in my foot.

"Everybody here is still alive. If you hadn't done what you did, there's no guarantee that would be the case," Doug chimed in and once again, I sensed this was aimed at Anna.

"Get him a glass of water," she said to Doug, though it sounded very much like a "fuck you too".

He left the bedroom without comment.

"Bullet went clean through, and you've still got five toes," Cal said, sounding uncharacteristically upbeat.

"We could fist bump but..." I dipped my head behind me to indicate my bound wrists.

"Want me to cut you loose?" Anna held up a small pair of scissors from the first aid box.

"No," I said, despite the throbbing in my arms and shoulders. "Best not."

"Is he here now?" However matter of fact she tried to sound, or how she busied herself with my foot, she couldn't hide the need in her voice.

"He was when I came to the first time but I don't see him now," I said. "I doubt he's gone too far but if he doesn't want me to see him then I can't."

From the corner of my eye, I saw Doug return and then he was holding a glass of blessedly cold water to my sore lips. After a few sips, I nodded to indicate I was done, and he retook his seat next to Cal.

"Can you call him or summon him or whatever you do?" Anna asked, again casually, and though her fingers never hesitated as they tucked and tugged at my bandages, I still felt the weight hanging on every word.

Wondering if perhaps she expected me to produce a Ouija board or crystal ball, I considered her request. Her husband had frightened the life out of me, but just now I was tied up, unarmed, with only one good eye and one functioning foot, and if Owen wanted to repossess this mess, then good luck to him.

"Owen?"

I said it louder than intended, my pummelled throat an uncertain instrument. Everyone jumped and Anna's fingers slipped, pressing down on my foot which made me jump too, so at least we were square.

"No sign of him," I said, after a moment.

Her only response was to snap the first aid box shut.

"It's safe to look now," she said, getting to her feet.

Though pink blooms were already spreading through the new material, it was less obscenely wet and red down there than it had been. I offered my thanks which she accepted with a perfunctory nod.

After returning to the bathroom to wash her hands, she took her seat on the bed again.

"I don't get many calls at two in the morning, certainly never any good ones," she said, her gaze fixed on the floor, at nothing in particular. "I almost didn't answer Doug's call. To be honest, I'm normally so fucked up by that hour of the night, it's a miracle I was able to."

When a tired, spaced-out, and in her own words, fucked up, Anna Hoath answered her phone, the stranger on the other end had scarcely finished introducing himself as Doug Allan before he was moving swiftly on to tell her that contrary to her belief and everyone else's, Stephen Hill was not her husband's murderer. He did not allow her time to think over or respond to this before going on to inform her that her husband was now a ghost who was roaming the earth searching for his actual killer, Hill's secret female accomplice.

However disoriented she was before answering the phone, Doug's opening salvo had left her doubly or triply so but, while the calls from creeps and perverts in the immediate wake of her husband's tabloid-worthy death had slowed to a trickle over time, before stopping entirely, this kind of lunacy wasn't entirely new to her.

She wanted to hang up, common sense demanded it, but she was remembering a call from long ago. Months, she thought, maybe longer but she couldn't be sure because the timeline of her life had broken into two distinct periods, Before Owen's Death and After Owen, and while Before Owen's Death was orderly, seasonable, and measurable, After Owen was a tumbling mess of days and nights that collapsed back on themselves at times and stretched endlessly, emptily forward at others.

"It was like he read my mind because then he asked if I remembered getting a call from someone named Chris," she said. "I told him that I did and that I thought maybe I was talking to him again now, except he was calling himself Doug instead of Chris. I didn't really think that though, he sounded different to how I remembered the other guy, but it gave me some time to think. Or at least, I thought it would, but Doug just kept on going."

"Desperate times," the man in question said from his seat on the bed, offering an unapologetic shrug.

"He told me Chris had been helping Owen get to this woman but had been killed in the process, before they could find her. He knew this because of a journal Chris had left behind that explained everything. He said that his friend Wil was helping Owen now and that if we didn't help them get to the woman, what happened to Chris might happen to Wil."

She paused and drew a steadying breath.

"Still, all I wanted to do was hang up on him, but..."

Her composure faltered and she let loose a throaty sob, fighting back tears with obvious effort.

"Anna, you don't have to, if –"

She waved away Doug's concern and continued.

"Before I lost Owen, when everything was normal, I never felt crazy or stupid. But since then?" She shook her head and gave a humourless laugh. "Since then, feeling crazy and stupid is an everyday thing. After that call from Chris, there were times I swore I felt something with me here in the house, a presence or just a feeling of being watched, and for just a second I'd allow myself to hope that maybe Owen really was still with me...and then I'd come to my senses and accept that these moments were further proof I was losing my mind. Believe me, when you're on three different anti-depressants and none of them do anything but make it easier to get drunk, a trip to the loony bin never feels too far off. So, I don't know that I really believed what Doug was telling me but I sure as hell *wanted* to believe that Owen might be here, watching over me."

She offered a sad, sweet smile and looked up at the bullet hole in her ceiling.

Doug asked Anna to meet with him right away but whatever she was willing to entertain over the phone, whatever she wanted to believe, the man on the phone was a stranger and it was dark out.

Instead, she agreed to meet the following day and Doug, sensing he needed to build some trust, asked her to pick the place. She figured if he was up to something, if he was a card-carrying member of the Cherry Tree Fan Club who wanted to meet her to settle some club business, the location she named would be enough to scare him off. When he agreed, she was disappointed to find it didn't dispel as many of her doubts as she'd hoped.

Chapter 43

When Cal received a message on his phone from Doug that simply said "Done", he was once again parked outside my apartment.

In the time since I staggered into my building, my apartment lights had come on and stayed on but with no other signs of activity, no sighting of me near the window or the tell-tale flicker of a screen, he assumed I had passed out. He was probably right.

With me tucked in, and secure in the knowledge that Doug had made contact with Anna, even if he couldn't yet find out what had come of it, Cal began to nod off.

"Which is when you appeared at your apartment window acting like an absolute creep."

"Elaborate, please," I said.

"You had your palms pressed against the glass," Cal said, miming the action. "At first, I thought you were going to open the window, but you just stayed like that. I wasn't sure if you were speaking with Owen or too drunk to figure out how to open your own window. I started filming and it was all fun and games until I zoomed in and got a good look at your face."

He shivered involuntarily at the memory.

"Your mouth was wide open like you were screaming but the street was quiet so I would have heard you if you were. Your eyes were rolled back so far in your head I could barely see your pupils and you kept opening and closing them but not like blinking, more like some mechanical fault. Deeply freaky shit."

Eventually, much to Cal's relief, my eyes settled back into a more normal position, and if my pupils were strangely dilated, at least they were visible. I took one palm from the window, then the other, leaving sweaty prints on the glass. Then I held my hands before me, staring at them as if I'd just discovered their existence.

"You balled them into fists, slowly, opened them, closed them again. Then you turned and walked away like a fucking zombie and I couldn't see you anymore," Cal said. "Given how you were acting, I was ok with that."

After taking a few minutes to gather his thoughts, he remembered to stop recording.

He played back the footage, looking for the white orb.

Considering my behaviour, he was not entirely surprised to find it lodged in my chest, or to see that the pale glow which normally enveloped the orb was now surrounding me.

Shaken but not deterred, he followed me to work that morning.

"You looked like shit, but at least you looked like yourself," he said.

Once he felt sure I wasn't going to walk straight back out of the office, he drove home. Doug was at the front door before he'd brought the car to a complete stop and Cal didn't bother to kill the engine, just waited for Doug to climb in before taking off again. If Owen knew they were interfering, their home was the least safe space for them to openly discuss what they were up to.

Cal pulled into the empty lot of a long-closed Borders that had yet to become a newly opened anything despite years of successive "Coming Soon" signs from various optimistic but doomed commercial ventures. After parking, he picked up his camera and filmed a full three-hundred-and-sixty degrees, capturing the car's interior and the potholed, litter strewn lot around them.

Once they played back the footage and felt sure they were alone, Doug told Cal about his call with Anna and its successful outcome. Cal then told Doug about what he'd seen through my apartment window and showed him what he'd caught on camera.

As two men who once tried and failed to induce possession on others, purely for scientific purposes, they had to admit that what they assumed to be the real thing looked extremely unappealing. What this new tangle meant they could only guess at, but it certainly wouldn't be anything good.

After catching each other up, there was not much time left before Doug was due to meet with Anna. Cal drove to a quiet little side street he knew near the meeting place and when Doug left, he once again made as much room in the little car as he could and passed out.

The bruised, baggy-eyed and otherwise unremarkable looking man who approached Anna outside the police station where her husband had worked did not reach out a hand to shake hers, nor did he pull out a blade or throw acid in her face.

He handed her a scuffed notebook and explained this was the journal belonging to Chris which he had mentioned over the phone. Before they discussed anything further, he thought it would be a good idea for her to read it. There was a bench directly across the street and he suggested she might like to sit there. He told her he would go for a walk and give her some time. Without further comment, he left and after some deliberation, Anna crossed the street, took a seat, and read.

By the time he was making his way back to her, Doug wondered if he would find the bench empty or if he would be pounced on by colleagues of Anna's husband with a lot to say about a man playing sick mind games with a grieving widow.

Instead, he found her there, alone, with her head down, studying the open notebook on her lap. When she looked up at him, he saw she had been crying and he braced himself for rage or disbelief.

When she simply asked him for more time, he walked on without a word.

The next time he returned, Anna was no longer alone. She was standing by the bench, Chris's notebook held in one hand, deep in conversation with a woman in police uniform.

He spun around, hurrying back towards Cal and the car. He hadn't made it far before his phone rang. After seeing the number, he hesitated, then took the call.

"I saw him making a run for it but the woman I was speaking with was just someone who worked with Owen," Ann said. "We knew each other from some social things back then. She was only saying hello. She didn't even ask why I was hanging around there, probably didn't think any answer I'd give her would result in a comfortable conversation. I told him it was safe to come back."

Despite suspecting he was about to be arrested, Doug turned around and walked back to Anna, deciding to return the trust she had placed in him by meeting.

Finding her alone once again, he sat down beside her on the bench. When he asked if she had finished reading Chris's journal, she told him that she had. When he apologised for lying about the nature of her husband's death, for using the story Owen had fed me about a mystery woman to convince her to meet with him, she said that without condemning or condoning, she understood his reasoning.

"I didn't like to lie but I didn't think Anna would believe that her husband was trying to kill her," Doug said, looking to me as if for some kind of absolution. "Or *want* to believe it."

"Right on all counts," Anna replied, saving me from having to do so. "If you led with that on the phone, I'd never have agreed to meet. You did what you had to do, Doug."

They sat on the bench for a while and spoke, or rather Doug spoke and Anna listened.

He explained who I was and what I was doing, about the lies I knew Owen was telling me and the ones I still believed to be truth, chief amongst them my belief that I was being sent after Owen's murderer, not his widow. He explained about Karen Taylor, a paper target Owen had pointed me at in his efforts to get to her.

He had just told her about the latest development, the fact that her husband seemed to be able to possess me, most likely without my knowledge, when she stood abruptly.

At first he thought she was about to walk away, that this last tidbit, the news that her husband was engaging in an activity more commonly associated with the devil and his demons, had overwhelmed her. Instead, she looked down at him and said that if the three of them were going to figure out what to do about all of this, they had better go wake his partner, Cal, who he had told her was parked, and most likely passed out, a few blocks over.

Doug had to knock loudly on the car's misted windows to rouse Cal, who emerged from the Mirage with black hair sticking in every direction and, Anna noted, even more undereye baggage than his partner. In fact, they both looked exhausted to the point of collapse.

With introductions made, they stood by the car and spoke.

All three knew I had no idea who Owen was sending me after. They knew I was armed and that if I got near Anna, any choice or restraint on my part might no longer be a factor if Owen took control. They could not risk telling me any of this or having me arrested for stalking Anna because the best-case scenario would be to destroy my life and the worst would be to simply send Owen on to his next recruit.

A chill wind sent them into the shelter of the Mirage and Anna was so deep in conversation with these two strange, strung-out men that it was some time before she realised that she'd broken the golden rule regarding getting into cars with strangers. But she did not feel afraid, not of them anyway. In fact, it took her a while longer to figure out what she was feeling.

Not alone.

She had been in crowded rooms, at family functions, in doctor's offices, in restaurants with the few friends unflagging enough to continue casting themselves against her numb indifference, and she was alone.

She had been in her home, thoughts of Owen on her mind, the sense that he might be close enough to touch if such a thing was possible, but still, she was alone.

Here, in this cramped car, with tufts of white cat hair stuck to the seats, speaking with these so-called paranormal investigators about things ridiculous yet undeniable, for the first time After Owen, she felt like she was not stupid, she was not crazy, and she was not alone.

Together, they sat in the parked car and kept talking until it got them somewhere.

Chapter 44

"But why in the name of holy fuck did you wait for me to show up here? Why take that risk?"

I was glaring at Doug and Cal but instead of defending themselves, both looked at Anna.

"They said it was up to me how I wanted to handle it," she said, returning their stares defiantly. "As much as I could believe a lot of what they told me, what Chris had written down, I didn't believe Owen would ever really hurt me. I felt that if things reached a certain point, he'd see that what he was doing was wrong. I needed him to get to that point so that it would wake him up and maybe send him on, so he could finally have peace."

"You shouldn't have let her," I said to the two sheepish-looking men before me. "You should have talked her out of it. What if...?"

Anna raised a hand to cut me off.

"Trust me, they didn't want this, said it was much too dangerous. I told them if they didn't let me do it, I'd start calling Owen's old work-friends and dropping their names in very bad ways," she said. "Desperate times," she added, with an unapologetic shrug of her own, and I caught Doug stifling a smile.

"We barely convinced her to let us put pillows in the bed instead of her," Cal said. "She's stubborn."

Owen Hoath had broken through the afterlife and bent the will of the living to get his way. Anna Hoath had blackmailed Doug and Cal and placed them all in mortal danger to get hers. Stubborn was a kind word for either Hoath coming from Cal.

"You could have told me what you were doing," I insisted. "I could have helped."

"We didn't think we could get to you without Owen knowing," Doug said. "Even if we did, we had to consider the possibility that he might have access to your memories, to anything you knew, as soon as he possessed you again."

"Plus, we didn't know what you'd do."

"What do you mean?" I asked, looking at Cal who was pointedly not looking at me.

"Chris knew the whole time who he was being asked to kill and still came close to doing it. You knew Owen was lying to you, that Chris was dead because of him, but you stayed on the track he put you on. We couldn't be sure that if you found out what he was really up to you, you wouldn't agree to kill Anna for him."

"I wouldn't have," I protested. "No fucking way."

"We couldn't be sure," Cal said, still not looking at me, and now Doug averted his gaze too.

I wanted to argue the point, to make them take it all back.

But here we were.

I *had* stayed on the track Owen had pushed me on, had gone back to him though I knew what happened to Chris. I believed deep inside that I never would have agreed to kill Anna for Owen, but lately I had learned many of the things I believed about myself weren't necessarily true. I looked at Anna and tried to offer some apology, some explanation, but the sentence wouldn't form and when Doug started speaking again, it was a mercy.

After their meeting with Anna, Doug took over shadowing duties from Cal.

Last night, he followed me in his car as I went to an out of the way payphone to call the cops and then stayed on my tail as I made my way to the bus stop and on to the city.

While I changed buses, he called Cal, who was home resting, and warned him that it looked like I was on my way to Anna's neighbourhood, that the flimsy plan she had coerced them into might be called into action sooner than any of them had expected. After replying with a few choice swearwords regarding said plan, Cal told him he'd make his way over there now.

When I arrived in Meadow Court, Doug parked near the entrance to the street and watched as I wandered up and down in the pouring rain before squeezing myself into a child's playhouse across from Anna's house. Meanwhile, as per Anna's plan, Cal parked a couple of blocks away, out of sight but within sprinting distance of the house.

Later, Anna spent some time in her living room with two polite and deferential young police officers who explained the crank call they received and asked if she knew who might want to play such a prank on her, malicious or otherwise. When they asked if the name Karen Taylor meant anything to her, she pretended ignorance. She explained that due to her second-hand celebrity status amongst people interested in serial killers and dead cops, this was not the first bit of nonsense thrown at her. Thanking them for their concern, she dismissed it and them at the same time.

When I limped away from Meadow Court, drenched and dejected, Doug called Cal and told him they could head home for the night. As agreed with Anna, they could not call or message her to let her know what was going on outside her house in case Owen was with her.

"When the cops left, all I could do was trust my genius plan and my new friends," she said, with only a trace of cynicism. "If you were about to come bursting into my house, I had to believe Doug and Cal would be there to stop you."

Doug followed me home and during the night, he and Cal swapped places, Doug driving off in his car as Cal pulled up in the Mirage, which his mother was now threatening to report as stolen.

He was still there late this morning when I appeared outside my building. As I walked away, he noted the grim look on my face and the obvious bulge in my jacket pocket, which apparently, I did a "shit-poor job of hiding". He called Doug without even waiting to see what direction I was headed. He had a feeling this time wasn't a drill.

In a reversal of their previous positions, this time it was Cal who parked near the entrance to Meadow Court, keeping an eye on me, and Doug who parked a couple of streets over, staring at his phone, his window cracked in case he heard any screaming.

When Cal called him to say I was making my way around the back of the house, clearly being guided by Owen, Doug knew he needed to get himself through the front door of 18 Meadow Court as quickly and quietly as possible.

As Doug raced toward the house, calling Anna and whisper-shouting at her to open the front door for him right away, and as Cal got out of the car to trail me and Owen from what he hoped was a safe distance, both men had the separate but same feeling that these hectic moments represented the last in a series of increasingly poor decisions that would result in catastrophe.

Owen thought he had left Anna passed out from last night's bottle and last night's pills but the truth was that in a shorter space of time than most rehab programs could dream of, Anna Hoath had become, at least for now, a recovering alcoholic and opioid addict, as well as a light sleeper. The vodka bottle she brought home yesterday had been filled with water and the pills she put in her mouth were washed down the sink rather than down her mouth when she pretended to swallow them under the faucet.

She was at her front door within seconds of Doug's call and after letting him in, made him wait impatiently while she reset the alarm, despite his protests that there was no time. While punching the keys, she patiently explained that she had never slept without it activated since she was widowed. Her husband was a good cop, and good cops noticed things like that.

Then they were in her bedroom, having a whispered argument about pillows but this time, Doug refused to back down.

"Lucky for me," she said, picking out some stuffing from the hole I had put in her mattress.

Having finally relented, she and Doug hurriedly made a reasonable likeness of her sleeping form with her pillows and after throwing the covers over them, she removed herself to the relative safety of her ensuite's bathtub while Doug hid in her closet.

After what felt like a lifetime, Doug heard the backdoor slam open, the sound of locks and screws hitting the floor.

In her ensuite bathroom, even with the door closed, Anna heard a faint but familiar series of beeps as I disarmed the security system.

"What I didn't tell Doug was that the alarm was a final test," she said, offering him an apologetic grin. "Call me silly or sceptical or whatever, but some part of me still thought there was a chance that there was nothing supernatural about all of this and that maybe you were just some crazy asshole. If that was the case, then you'd break in and two minutes later the alarm would be screaming the house down. When I heard you punching in the code, I knew it was all real, that Owen was down there with you."

While Doug stood in the bedroom closet, calming himself with a Wing Chun circular breathing exercise Cal had taught him, and Anna held herself in her bathtub, facing the reality that her dead husband was coming to kill her, Cal cautiously approached the open back door.

"You guys are like ninjas," I said, laughter wheezing out of me. "Like ninja guardian angels."

"Would have killed you if we had to," Cal said, but I pretended he said, "you're welcome".

When he felt he could wait no longer, Cal entered the house and crept up the hall, filled with the certainty that he had left it too late and that any second now he would hear gunshots overhead telling him that they should never have let themselves be led by Anna's naïve certainty that allowing her husband to come close to killing her would snap him out of it.

He was about to mount the stairs when he saw me halfway up them. He froze, sure he had given himself away, but as I fought against each upward step, growling recriminations back and forth in a conversation whose shifting meanings he couldn't quite grasp, he realised that both Owen and I were too preoccupied to notice him.

"I was tempted to stop you there and then, figured if Anna's insane undead husband hadn't seen the error of his ways by now, he probably wasn't going to," Cal said. "No offence, Anna."

What stopped him, as much as he didn't like it, was the promise they had made to play it Anna's way. If he did the wrong thing now, they might never get a chance to end this and after what happened to Chris, he couldn't face the prospect of another irretrievable wrong.

So, he followed my torturous progress up the stairs and once I opened the bedroom door, he moved fast, if not quite fast enough to stop me from shooting up Anna's bedroom, or my own foot.

"Can't win them all," Cal said.

Chapter 45

We sat in near silence for some time, my wheezing breath and the flutter of the curtains in the afternoon breeze the only sounds.

Eventually, Anna spoke.

"Any sign of him?"

"Still no," I said, and swallowed the "sorry" I had almost added.

A long beat.

"How is he?"

I chewed on this for a while before giving her an answer as honest and impartial as I could considering the less than charitable feelings I harboured for her dearly departed.

"Scared, lonely, furious, missing you," I recited, channelling the churn of emotions I'd experienced while Owen tried to claim squatter's rights in my head. "He lost you and now he's losing himself and believe me, he is not coping well with either."

"Clearly, look at the fucking mess he..." Cal said, but a look from Doug quietened him again.

"Tell her I never wanted to hurt her. I've been trying to protect her."

"He's back," I said, trying my best not to make it sound ominous.

Owen stood by the bed once more, looking down at Anna.

I was surprised to find that rather than causing the levels of anger and disgust I was feeling for him to shoot off the scale, the sight of Owen did quite the opposite. Sure, I was pissed off and felt more than a little betrayed all things considered, but the single most powerful emotion I felt upon seeing him now was sadness.

A simple sadness best described as grief, as wide as it was deep.

Grief for the victims of men like Stephen Hill and Bill Hanover, girls and boys who would never become grownups like those they had trusted to protect them.

Grief for Chris Collins, who lived a life harder than his gentle soul deserved, whose last friend had proven to be his worst, and whose death had been a sacrifice, not a suicide.

Grief for the living people here with me now, for Doug and Cal who had spent so much time blaming themselves for things beyond the control or understanding of any of us, and for Anna Hoath, who had lost so much, who once had a life with her best friend, her lover, until she didn't.

And finally, for Owen Hoath, an asshole of the highest degree, but one who lived his life protecting others and died for someone else's sins, who had seen things and been things nobody should ever have to, who had been a best friend, a lover, until he could be neither.

"Tell her what I said, Wil."

I looked around me at the widow who had lost more than her heart had been able to take, who had gone on living in only the strictest biological sense of the word, at the two exhausted men at the foot of the bed, leaning against one another for support, all of whom had risked death in an effort to pull some meaning from the chaos they found themselves in, and last of all at the murdered man standing nearby, who finally returned my gaze with his own; weary, wretched but resolute.

I had got so much wrong, had been too weak to even lay claim to the space between my two ears, but somebody needed to end this mess and that was something I could do.

I hoped.

"Owen wants to speak to Anna, alone. I can't take myself out of the equation but..."

I looked at Doug and Cal and then to the door.

Unsurprisingly, they didn't move.

Owen watched me, measuring my motives.

"Take the gun with you, wherever it is," I said. "Anna will yell if she needs help. Even if he takes me over again, I'm on the ground, my hands are tied and I'm not exactly going to get far on foot."

They looked to Anna for guidance.

"It's alright," she said. "I'll be ok."

They stood and Doug picked up the gun from the bed. As they left, Cal inadvertently walked through Owen and even if I was now looking at things from up on the high road I was trying to take, I couldn't help enjoying a less than honourable sense of satisfaction as I watched Owen swear and jerk away.

Cal shut the door behind them and then it was just me, Anna, and Owen.

"You know, despite everything, up until a couple hours ago, I still suspected this might all be some crazy plot and I'd end up being murdered by those two and whatever cult they're part of."

"I've been there," I assured her.

"Tell her what I said, Wil," Owen demanded, with more entitlement than I felt was reasonable given recent events. "I only ever wanted to protect her from all this pain. If she –"

"Anna, listen," I said quickly, not wanting to listen to him tell me how great it would be for everyone if the woman sitting before me died. "I know you probably don't want to hear this but when Chris Collins agreed to do what Owen was asking, he thought it was the right thing. He didn't have a bad bone in his body, he was just..."

Just what?

I summoned up the second-hand memories I had of Owen's possession of Chris, revisited what it had been like to feel that man's feelings from a distance.

"He wanted to do something great in his life, something right, and he believed in Owen. He wanted to be a hero like him and he thought doing what Owen wanted was the way to do it. But he would never have killed you, no matter how hard he tried to convince himself he could, and when Owen tried to force him, he killed himself instead. He wanted to be a good guy."

I had been talking fast, shutting out Owen but also Anna, desperately wanting to be an advocate for the one person in all of this, living or dead, who wasn't here to defend himself.

"He *was* a good guy," Anna said. "You don't need to defend Chris to me, Wil. I read his notebook, I know who he was, at least a little, and I know what he did to save me before I ever knew I needed saving. I mean, I wasn't thrilled he agreed to kill me in the first place, but I know Owen could be…"

"Stubborn?" I said, echoing Cal's sentiment.

"At the very least," she said, with a wan smile that soured quickly into a pained grimace. "I read what Chris wrote about Owen wanting him to kill me and I listened to Doug and Cal tell me that he was trying to fool you into doing the same thing and still, I never really believed he would let it happen. The Owen I knew would never do this."

For the first time since I had known her, in this lifetime at least, tears spilled down her cheeks. She clasped her hands so tightly in her lap that they were a rigid white ball of bone and sinew and I reminded myself that she was not just a widow who lost her husband, but a woman in shock who had just survived a murder attempt orchestrated by that same man. The urge to rise and comfort her was half mine, half Owen's, and completely impossible.

"Does he hate me now? Is that it?"

Owen started to speak, to tell me what to say, but I beat him to it.

"He never hated you," I said, speaking firmly with the truth on my side. "As fucked up as all this is, he loved you and he still loves you. It was about getting you two back together so he could look after you and, even if he wouldn't admit it to himself, so you could look after him."

"Why didn't he just talk to me? Instead of total strangers," she said, waving one hand at me. "Doesn't he know how badly I miss him? How much I've needed him all this time?"

"I tried," he said. "Tell her I tried, every minute of every day for months I tried, but she never heard me."

This, I was willing to repeat.

"But why? Nobody wants to see him or hear him as badly as me. But I can't, even now. Why can't I?"

There was an ache in her voice that once again made me wish I could hold her and I didn't need Owen in my head to know he felt the same.

Johnny Thunders sang that you can't put your arms around a memory, that it doesn't pay to try, but the truth of this never really struck me until I watched these two souls, one living, one dead, both lost, reaching out to each other with such hopeless desperation. No future was permitted to them now, only past, and no matter how much they wished it could be otherwise, they could be nothing more than a memory to one another. If this was what love did to people, there were at least some advantages to going without.

"I don't know, but I think people like Chris and I are just more susceptible."

"Ghost nerds, you mean?"

I took the insult with a grain of salt under the circumstances.

"That's part of it. But also, we..."

What was it Owen had thought?

"We were lonely people reaching out," I said, once again feeling the firmness of truth in the words. "Between that and the ghost-nerding, I think we were sort of hardwired to receive Owen's signal."

She laughed but there was no humour in it. She jammed the heels of her palms into her eyes and when she took them away, there were no more tears, only a shining brightness left in her red-rimmed eyes.

"Did he think he could kill me and I'd be ok with it?" Anna said. "That we'd skip straight to happily ever after?"

"He thought that once you were together, you'd understand why he did it, that you would think it was the right thing to do."

"And what do you think, Wil?"

"I think there's no guarantee that if you die, the two of you will be together. He thought the same deep down but having had a VIP backstage pass to Owen's mind, I can say that for as much lying as he did to me and Chris, he did plenty to himself too."

Anna nodded at this.

"He was always a means justify the end kind of guy," she said, casting her eyes about the room. I gestured with my head as best I could in Owen's general vicinity. She looked up and if I hadn't known better, I would have sworn she was looking into his eyes. "I'm sorry Owen, but you are, you know you are."

"She's miserable," he said. "I can look after her if she lets me, if she comes to me."

"He says he knows how miserable you are."

While Owen glared at me for censoring him, Anna glared at me since she couldn't glare at him with any guaranteed accuracy.

"My best friend went out one morning and never came back to me," she said. "Of course, I'm fucking miserable but that doesn't mean I want to die. Jesus Christ, should I feel guilty for wanting to live? Because that must mean I don't love him, right?"

"Ask her if crying herself to sleep every night is living? If pulling razor blades out of the bathroom cabinet and staring at them is living? It's going to happen eventually. I wanted it to be while I'm still here to look after her."

I had been him and I knew he kept any doubts about his plan submerged in the depths of his conviction. I also knew that the living Owen, the one who had not yet lost himself in the silence of no-heart-beating and no-lungs-breathing, would never have entertained this bullshit. He was still Owen, not an imposter, but he was becoming the worst of him, not all of him, and certainly not the best of him. I knew this to be the truth because deep within those same depths, he knew it too.

He couldn't help himself.

But I could.

"He understands, or he's trying to anyway," I said. "He says that it's getting harder and harder to be himself. He said that because his love for you was always the strongest part of him it's becoming the only thing left of him. The rest of him feels like a photocopy of a photocopy."

"Shut up," Owen said sharply.

I ignored him.

If he wouldn't speak the right words, I would. I looked at him and nodded for Anna's benefit, as if listening, as if he wasn't yelling at me to stop.

"He says he kept all of his love, but a lot of his common sense didn't make it back intact."

I smiled as if he had and that made her smile, which was good.

"Chris was an accident. He never meant anything to happen to him, to push him into doing what he did. This is me talking now, not Owen. I can promise you that. A bad series of events that never should have gone the way they did. I –"

I looked at Owen again, as if he had interrupted me.

He was in fact speaking but I had heard every swearword he was using before. I nodded and told him that I understood.

"He's asking, if it won't scare you, to pretend I'm not here. He says I'm not quoting correctly, too much artistic licence. He's probably right, I like to editorialise." I allowed myself a self-deprecating shrug and hoped I wasn't over-egging the pudding. "If it's ok with you, I'll just be his voice. Does that make sense?"

"As much sense as anything just now," Anna replied.

I turned my gaze back to Owen, doing my best to speak softly while he yelled obscenities over me.

"Ok, Owen, I'll do it, word for word. What do you want to say?"

Chapter 46

"Hi, Anna."

"Owen, is that you?"

Despite everything he'd done, she looked at me with nothing but naked hope in her eyes.

A pause while I pretended to listen to him.

"No, I don't think Wil or I could go through that again. I'm still here," I said, gesturing with my head to where Owen was standing, yelling abuse at me. "But I'm not *here.*" I nodded down at my chest as best I could.

"Are you in pain, Owen, does it hurt?"

"Only when I try to do things a dead man shouldn't."

She took an uneven breath, sat up straighter, looked like she was turning something over in her mind. She had been looking at me but now returned her gaze to where he stood and once again, with uncanny synchronicity, met his eyes with hers.

Owen fell silent, giving up his tirade of abuse for now.

"The minute they told me what happened to you, that you were gone, all I could think was how much pain you must have felt, how scared you must have been."

"Scared? A tough guy like me?" I said, aiming for Owen's laconic wit. "It was all over before I knew what happened." I tried not to let the memory of the pain and terror I felt inside Cherry Tree's house show on my face.

"When you died, I lost the best person I've ever known, everything that was important to me. I don't want to die but if you really think we can be together then..."

Owen screamed yes, tell her yes, and I waited before speaking.

"No, Anna," I said, gently but firmly, not willing to let her wander down that alley. "The only thing I can guarantee is that I'll always love you and my only promise is that when the time comes, if it's meant to be, we'll find each other. But that time isn't now, and I should never have tried to make it be."

I gave the kind of weighty pause I felt appropriate of a man amid a scathing self-assessment.

"I'm so sorry, Anna. I was scared and confused, and I forgot who I was."

"I miss you so fucking much," she said fiercely, not missing a beat, staring so hard at the empty space her husband occupied that she might have summoned him through effort alone.

"You should, I was pretty great."

She laughed at that, some of the intensity going out of her.

"I want to be happy, Owen," she said, and it was clear she meant it as an apology. "I might never be again but I could try...I want to try."

"Don't be sorry for living and don't ever be sorry for being happy. You..."

I widened my eyes and let my jaw drop, staring in confusion at Owen who stared back at me in almost equal confusion.

"Owen?" I exclaimed. "What's happening?"

"Wil, what's wrong?" Anna asked.

Sensing where I was going with this, Owen exercised a typical lack of hesitation by rushing me.

First, he tried to possess me again and it had such little effect on me that I managed to not so much as flinch, just continued staring wide-eyed at the space near Anna where he had stood, as if he was still there. I was not drunk or asleep and I was no longer ignorant, wilfully or otherwise. My words and thoughts were my own and I would never give them away again.

The woman on the bed looked to me for answers, the hole in my foot throbbed and ached, the lilac-scented breeze brushed against the curtains and I was I and I was here, in this place, conscious and connected. I felt in control for the first time since I'd met him, maybe for the first time full-stop.

I might have been hardwired to receive but now, finally, it felt like I commanded the mechanism.

He roared in pain and frustration as he passed through me and then had to extricate himself from the bedroom wall.

"Owen, where are you?" I asked, feeling a calmness so alien to me it was practically jarring.

Giving up on possession, he punched and kicked me, but while he cried out in pain with each useless blow, I felt nothing at all.

"Wil, tell me what's happening?"

"I don't know Anna, it's like he's flickering, he's back again but..."

Owen finally gave up his efforts and took a step back.

Even while doing my best not to look at him, pretending I was watching him fade in and out across the room, I could see the panic writ large on his face.

"Wil, don't do this."

"Owen, can you still hear me?"

"Seriously, Wil, stop it."

"Please tell me what's going on?" Anna said.

I could tell I was scaring her and didn't want to drag it out.

"Yeah, I can still hear you, just." I raised my voice, as if shouting over some psychic storm.

"He's fading," I said, turning to Anna. "I don't know what's going on, but he wants me to tell you, he wants me to say..."

I looked once more to where Owen wasn't standing, listened carefully to words he wasn't saying. Anna echoed the movement, trusting me that she was once more looking into her husband's eyes. The man in question stood near the bedroom door, as if he wanted to run away from this scene but had nowhere to run to.

"I think I'm going away, Anna. It feels...I feel light," I spoke the words slowly. "It feels like I can breathe again."

"Stay Owen, please, just a little while more."

"I can't, I was never meant to stay. I think I was only ever here to say goodbye, I just didn't realise."

"Where are you going, Owen, what do you see?" I asked desperately, playing the part of the ghost nerd experiencing the sight of a spirit crossing over.

"*OWEN?*" She called his name with a desperation that hit me like a slap.

The door burst open but when Doug and Cal saw me still on the floor and Anna on the bed, they stayed where they were, uncertain.

"Anna, everything is alright," I said. "I'm not afraid anymore."

I spent so much of my life in an abstract state of discomfort I couldn't correct, like an itch I couldn't scratch, but in this moment, I felt such a sense of purposefulness, of *rightness*, that it was almost overpowering.

"I'm glad Owen, I'm glad you're not afraid," she said. "I love you, don't ever forget it. Wherever you go, you deserve to be safe and warm and happy, remember that too."

"We'll see each other again, sweetheart, I know that now," I said, ready to finish this.

She looked at me and through her tears I saw something new in her eyes. Doubt.

"I never called her sweetheart in my life," said the real and stubbornly present Owen.

"I'm sorry Wil, but I need to know it's really him talking," Anna said. "I need –"

"Anna, I'm sorry, he's nearly gone, I can barely –"

"*I NEED TO KNOW!*"

She screamed so loudly that both Doug and Cal took a step back into the corridor.

"Owen, please, what are the three P's?"

"I can't hear him Anna, he's –"

"Please Wil, I need to know."

"Anna, I –"

Owen crossed the room, returning to the spot I had been pretending he never left. He knelt down on one knee, hissing as he adjusted its placement on the floor, and then he was before her, like a suitor with marriage on his mind.

"Pain, punishment, paternity suit," he said, but I didn't repeat the words. If he was lying to catch me out, he'd undo everything, bring us all back to the brink.

"Go on, Wil." As he spoke, he placed a hand over hers, neither of them reacting to the contact. No comfort for her but no pain for him either. "It's the punchline to a bad joke her dad always told."

With no choice, I repeated his answer. When she sighed with relief, I did my best not to do the same.

I told her that he was kneeling before her now, and she lowered her chin. For an instant, with their lips close enough to kiss, I saw the young couple they would have been on their first date and all the ones after it, a whole future ahead of them that must have looked like an eternity.

"I'm sorry," she said. "I just had to be sure."

"Once a cop's wife, always a cop's wife," he said affectionately, and I passed this on.

"Wil, if you're really doing this, if I'm never going to speak to her again, I want her last words from me to be my own."

Again, I hesitated, worried he would make a last-ditch attempt to pull his plans back together, but then I saw the way he was looking at his wife. I knew that even if he could not truly move on, a white lie for which I felt no guilt in telling, he was finally letting go.

"I can do that."

Anna asked for no explanation to this statement, and I offered none. In the doorway, Doug and Cal existed only on the periphery of my awareness, and probably nowhere at all in that of Owen and Anna Hoath.

"I'm sorry we never got to say goodbye, but I'm saying it now," I said, echoing him word for word. "I love you, Anna. I always have and I always will."

"I love you too, always have and always will," she said, holding herself together with nothing but grit. "Goodbye, Owen."

"Goodbye, Anna," he said, with a tender gravity I did my best to convey in the repetition.

I stared at him for a moment, readying myself for what was to come.

"There's a light," I said with awe. "It's like it's coming from inside him... it's so bright."

I squinted against this imaginary blaze of ethereal light, pretending to watch Owen Hoath cross over.

Instead, I watched him smile at Anna, only for Anna. I watched a man who had fought the darkness inside himself and finally won, albeit with a little help.

"He's smiling," I said. "The light, it's all around him, he's…"

I drew a breath.

"Wil?" Anna asked.

"He's gone."

Owen slowly took his hand away from Anna and stood. The single step he took back, away from her, looked like it cost him the world.

Doug moved to the bed and sat next to Anna. When he put his arm around her, she collapsed into him. Cal leaned against the doorframe, looking like it was the only thing holding him up.

"Wil?"

Owen was the only one speaking but I couldn't respond.

"Wil, can you see this?"

I did my best not to react as he turned in a circle in the middle of the room, looking around him at something I couldn't see. Then he came to a standstill, gazing past me with a hundred-yard-stare that slowly seemed to come into focus, as if whatever he could see was coming closer.

Casually, carefully, I turned my head to follow his gaze but there was only the windows and the wall and nothing remarkable about any of it.

"What in the name of…?"

He did not sound afraid, only curious.

"You cannot be serious," he said, shaking his head in apparent wonder.

As if waking from a dream, he looked down at me.

"Wil, I better say sorry to you while I still can because…"

His lips were moving but I could no longer hear him.

Seeing that none of the others were watching me, I shook my head gently. Picking up on my meaning, his lips stopped moving and he looked at me a little awkwardly, like a struggling charades player.

Then, finding a solution to his predicament, he bowed, slowly and deliberately. Whether this meant "thank you, well done" or "fuck you, well played" I would never know but it didn't matter. What mattered was that the last look he ever gave me was not one of anger or fear or hurt.

On the face of Owen Hoath, there was only peace.

He turned once more, to look at his wife, a smile tugging at his lips, and then he was gone.

I didn't see any white light and I didn't see him float away.

He was there and then he wasn't.

Epilogue

When I pushed back against my publisher's requests for me to change the ending to something less ambiguous than "he was there and then he wasn't" my newfound literary agent warned me I might be about to blow a once in a lifetime opportunity, by which she meant her fifteen percent of a once in a lifetime opportunity. One besuited guy whose job title at the publishing house is so convoluted I can never remember it, and who always calls me Willy, warned that my "artsy-fartsy did-he didn't-he" ending might just about fly with the reading public but would be a "serious fucking downer" for the ten-part streaming adaptation he was trying to line up.

It's not that I don't sympathise with their desire for a more cathartic "Unchained Melody" type ending but they're thinking of fiction rather than fact and as such, feel no responsibility toward the latter.

I would love to say for certain that when he finally saw how wrong he was, Owen moved on to a better place, that in saying goodbye to Anna, in taking that step back, he found the peace that had eluded him.

But I can't.

I don't know where he went, if anywhere. I only know I have never seen him since the day he disappeared. What I have written in these pages is what happened, not what any of us wish happened, and the only lies present are those I took to be truths.

Because my publishers, editor, and agent consider this a work of imagination – genre: paranormal thriller – they dismiss my refusal to refer to it as such as artistic devotion or a writer's joke for which they praise my commitment while eyeing each other nervously. Even showing them a certain video on my phone hasn't swayed them, though they have applauded my use of mixed media.

I eventually got the chance to read Chris's notebook. I didn't learn anything new but it gave me a chance to meet Chris all over again, this time without Owen in the way. I never knew Chris and I have never understood anyone better. Doug and Cal have struck a deal, via my agent, to have Chris's notes and their own story published as a prequel to this book which, according to sales projections I don't understand, will be prequel worthy. Unlike me, they do have noble intentions. Half their profits will go to Chris's parents as promised and half to various paranormal research institutions. They're not even putting their names on the cover.

After the events in Anna's house, I warned Doug and Cal to keep a close eye on their mail and once I reclaimed Hanover's photos, I took them in-shaking-person to the police. I went through more interrogations and signed more documents than I can count before they believed I was not an accomplice and while I'm not allowed to go into particulars, you would be safe to assume that as far as the police and courts are concerned there was no ghost involved. I might have a whole new respect for the truth but like Anna, I'm not crazy and I'm not stupid.

Bill Hanover is currently going through a trial process that will inevitably end with him spending the rest of his life in prison. They are still trying to identify some of the children from the Polaroids but those they have are alive and if they're not particularly well right now, some are finally getting better. Many had never spoken about what happened to them until Hanover was locked up. Some still haven't. I hope they do. I hope if any of the children yet to be named didn't survive him, that they are at peace, are feeling the warm embrace their parents never got to give them. His ex-wife, the real Karen Taylor, had no knowledge of what he was, and no charges have been brought against her.

I can't say everyone lived happily ever after but some of us are at least living happier.

After the ex-members of DAPI learned the truth about Doug and Cal and about what happened to Chris and to me, we reformed with a strict no-more-secrets proviso. I don't know if I learned some crucial life lesson or if through Owen's feelings for Anna, I experienced the difference between infatuation and love, but I can now be in the same room as Sam and retain much of my higher-brain function.

That's not to say I don't steal an occasional glance.

Sorry Sam.

Sorry Sam's husband.

I don't know if Liam will ever forgive me for leaving him in the lurch but if I say sorry for long enough maybe he will.

Sorry Liam.

Anna and I have spoken on the phone a couple of times, exchanged emails, but have not met in person since that day in her bedroom.

For my part, I have problematic feelings for her that can only be left over from Owen, and for hers, I'm sure I am a reminder of the person she most needs to get past if she stands any chance of finding some peace of her own. She has returned to full time employment for the first time in years and is attending meetings that help keep her away from the substances she needs to keep away from. For a war widow, she's doing ok, I only hope she knows it, keeps doing ok until it becomes normal.

When I came clean about Owen's departure, she didn't exactly heap me with praise, but she didn't yell at me either. I almost said nothing but I needed to tell her the same truth with which I ended this book. Owen's last actions truly were good and right, and his last look really had been a smile meant only for her.

I occasionally whip out my phone and record video of my surroundings and I know Doug and Cal do the same, all of us checking our footage using Cal's Special Ghost Viewer specifications. There has been no sign of Owen or any other paranormal activity which we agree is as reassuring as it is disappointing.

I often wonder where Owen is now, and whether his final disappearance was genuine or just one last lie, an act of selflessness performed because he knew he had to stop, for everyone's sakes.

Owen, if you ever read this over someone's shoulder or eavesdrop on their audiobook or stand by their couch making fun of the prestige limited streaming series version of events, to quote Anna, I hope you are safe and warm and happy. You were an absolute prick, but you were also the best and bravest man a lot of people ever knew.

I still sit in old buildings, taking the temperature of abandoned rooms and photos of empty chairs. Cal still uses his Special Ghost Viewer on footage of Liam emerging from crawlspaces, Stuart sleeping on floors, and the Davis sisters staring at inanimate objects. Sam still happily drowns herself in white noise and Doug still monitors us all from Central Control. I thought that confirming the existence of ghosts would be the answer but to quote Henry Sidgwick, first president of the Society for Psychical Research, "the mystery of death is not solved by dying just as the mystery of life is not solved by living". Besides, how could we ever give up on gadgets, ghostbusting, and promises of high yield?

It seems as though this story was never really my own.

I'm not the hero cop who died trying to save innocent lives. I'm not the grieving widow who lost everything and was brave enough to struggle on with nothing. I'm not the man who sacrificed himself rather than hurt someone else. I'm not part of the couple who risked everything to fix the mistakes of their past.

I'm the idiot who blundered through these people's stories.

I'm a failed murderer and a failed saviour.

I'm the guy whose bullet-scarred left foot aches when it's about to rain.

I'm the hopeful romantic who emailed mandy.mcsherry@fairfieldinsurance.com over a week ago asking if it was too late to ask again and who is still nervously waiting on a reply.

I'm the tourist sitting with the air-conditioning cranked in a Thai hotel room, sweating from the humidity, looking forward to seeing his brother and future sister-in-law later for our third dinner in a row, and I'm the son who paid for the newly arrived middle-aged couple currently watching a Thai soap opera in the next room to fly from their beach-adjacent home to here.

I'm also the aspiring moped rider who spent today's lesson ricocheting around the streets of Bangkok.

Not a car, but it's a start.

Since this story was never really mine, it's hard to say where it started.

On the floor of an old prison or in the men's room of a city library? The evening Owen Hoath and Stephen Hill killed each other, or the night Chris Collins killed himself? Maybe it all started the day Owen and Anna first met. And did it end in 18 Meadow Court when Owen vanished, or does it end when he and Anna are finally reunited?

It was my story to tell at least, so that's something, and if not being the hero of it is hard for me to take, so be it.

Eventually, you have to move on.

Acknowledgements

It takes a village to raise a book and How To Contact The Living has been no exception.

Sincere thanks to those who have given their time, encouragement, feedback, and support throughout the process of writing this book. Any faults in this book are on me so if you're going to send threatening emails, please refer to the following pages for my contact details, and leave these poor souls alone...they've suffered enough during this process.

Thank you...

To Mam and my sister Emma, for supporting me in all my endeavours and for encouraging my writing at times when it was probably unwise to do so! To my brother Andrew for reading an early draft and being a tireless champion of me pursuing my dreams. Special thanks to my brother Alan - my official First Reader for all my writing - who read the first ever draft of this book and somehow survived to tell the tale. Al, our inspiring conversations and your feedback, ideas, and relentless typo termination have made this book and anything else I've written better than I ever could have made it.

To my early readers, in particular Chris Daly and K. Thoroughgood, who shared their eyeballs and their insights when I needed them most. KT - your invaluable suggestions, notes, advice, and willingness to listen to me go on and on (and on) about this book over Phở were a greater help than you'll ever know.

Finally, to Ellen, I say a huge thank you. Not just for multi-tasking by being my wife, my soul mate, and my best friend - all of which must be exhausting - but for living with this book as much as you've lived with me for so many years. Elle, I appreciate you helping me to form this story, one I've always wanted to tell, for holding me up when it was threatening to knock me on my ass, for sacrificing time together so I could go have arguments with the laptop, for reading and listening to endless drafts, re-drafts, and re-re-drafts, and for being the reason I know how to write about what it feels like to love someone so much you feel it not just in your heart, but in your lungs, your fingertips, every square inch of you.

About the Author

Thanks for reading How To Contact The Living!

If you'd like to learn more about me, please visit my website: **www.bryanfarrellauthor.com** where you can access lots of fun content including my author bio, free stories, and extras including **How To Contact The Living – Special Features** and **Official Spotify Playlist**.

Sign up to my e-mailing list to get a free short story and be first in the know about upcoming releases!! Go to **www.bryanfarrellauthor.com/contact** and Subscribe.

You'll also find me on **Goodreads** where I spend much too much time adding to my teetering To Be Read pile instead of actually reading anything. I also post random things on my Instagram profile **@paranormal_punk**.

YOUR OPINION MATTERS!

If you enjoyed this book, please sing it from the rooftops by telling your friends (or even your enemies), posting about it on your social media, or best of all, posting a review or rating on Amazon, Goodreads, or your preferred bookshop's website.

As an indie author, positive reviews and word of mouth from readers like you make the world of difference to me, not just for advertising (though that sure helps) but also because authors write to connect with readers and this author loves to hear when he's made contact with a reader in a meaningful way.

Also by Bryan Farrell

13 Stories

Nightmarish creatures send humanity into hiding within the earth's depths. A lonely soldier on a WWII battlefield dreams of going home. The past returns to haunt a suburban couple.

Thirteen short stories bubbling over with punks, ghosts, rogue yoga balls, half-price séances, Taylor Swift-inspired mayhem, and a meditation app that is most definitely not user-friendly. You'll laugh, you'll cry, you'll wish there were thirteen more.

If you'd like to get a free sneak peak and read a story from this collection, sign up to my emailing list and it will arrive hot and fresh into your inbox! Just visit www.bryanfarrellauthor.com/contact **and Subscribe.**